Literature in Heisei Japan,
平 成 文 学 に お け る 様 々 な 声
1989-2019

Editor: Angela Yiu

上智大学出版
Sophia University Press

Literature in Heisei Japan, 1989-2019

平成文学における様々な声

Editor:

Angela Yiu

Sophia University Press

One of the fundamental ideals of Sophia University is “to embody the university’s special characteristics by offering opportunities to study Christianity and Christian culture. At the same time, recognizing the diversity of thought, the university encourages academic research on a wide variety of world views.”

The Sophia University Press was established to provide an independent base for the publication of scholarly research. The publications of our press are a guide to the level of research at Sophia, and one of the factors in the public evaluation of our activities.

Sophia University Press publishes books that (1) meet high academic standards; (2) are related to our university’s founding spirit of Christian humanism; (3) are on important issues of interest to a broad general public; and (4) textbooks and introductions to the various academic disciplines. We publish works by individual scholars as well as the results of collaborative research projects that contribute to general cultural development and the advancement of the university.

Literature in Heisei Japan, 1989-2019

Published by Sophia University Press

Printed and distributed by GYOSEI Corporation, Tokyo
ISBN 978-4-324-11374-5
Inquiries: https://gyosei.jp

Contents

Preface

On April 30, 2019, Japan's former emperor Akihito retired and his son, Naruhito, ascended to the throne, bringing an end to Heisei and ushering in the new era of Reiwa. Even though the arts are not restricted by the imperial demarcation of a period, the thirty years of Heisei Japan provide a valuable framework in which to reflect on the evolution of contemporary literature. Two fundamental questions came to mind when I thought about putting together a volume of critical essays on the literature of this time: Is "Japanese literature" an adequate and appropriate label for literary creations during the past three decades? Is it possible to provide an overall definition for a body of work called "Heisei literature"?

The answer to both questions is a resounding "No." The first No is straightforward, because the landscape of literature in Heisei Japan was transformed by many non-Japanese, Zainichi, and plurilingual writers such as Yi Yangji, Hideo Levy, Mizumura Minae, Tawada Yōko, Yang Yi, and On Yūjū, some of whom are featured in this volume. The conventional understanding of Japanese literature as works written mainly in Japanese by Japanese authors does not begin to capture the scope of literature in Heisei Japan.

The second No requires more elaboration. It was possible to label Meiji (1868-1912) literature as such because it signaled a clear departure in form, language, and modes of circulation from Edo literature. Representative writers such as Natsume Sōseki and Mori Ōgai played the dual role of artist and intellectual with first-hand overseas experience, creating works that captured the birth of a modern nation state and the lives of people negotiating the surging waves of Westernization and modernization. Taishō (1912-1926), although short-lived, was marked by an openness summed up in the expression "Taishō democracy"; the leading writers of that age—Akutagawa Ryūnosuke, Tanizaki Jun'ichirō, and

Satō Haruo—inherited the legacy of modernization from Meiji writers and took experimentation in modernist art and literature to new heights, creating Japanese *modanizumu* with a lasting influence that rivals modernist movements in the U.S., Europe, and other parts of Asia. The first twenty years of Shōwa (1926-1989) were marked by the rise of ultra-militarism and ultra-nationalism, leading to the "dark valley" of the war years and Japan's catastrophic losses from the atomic bombings of Hiroshima and Nagasaki. Postwar Shōwa—the era retained the same name, but Shōwa 20 (1945) marked a watershed often referred to as the "First Year of Postwar" (*Sengō gannen*)—was allowed a "second act" and went through a complete make-over as Japan transformed into a democratic state under the Allied Occupation Forces and eventually experienced the "economic miracle" of the 1970s and an economic bubble in the 1980s. Writers who came of age in postwar Shōwa—Ōe Kenzaburo, Inoue Hisashi, and Abe Kōbō—continued to critique wartime Japan, questioned the abrupt switch of allegiance after the war, and focused on the search for an identity for postwar Japan on an individual and collective level.

Another factor that made it possible to identify distinct periods of Meiji, Taishō, and Shōwa literature was the existence of the *bundan* (literary establishment), which was sustained in each era by a constellation of major writers, influential critics, key journals, and prestigious awards that upheld literary standards and qualities deemed appropriate and reflective of the time. For better or for worse, the formidable and hierarchical *bundan* began to wane by the end of Shōwa, giving rise to a more democratic literary landscape. In the mid-1980s, scholars and critics such as Karatani Kōjin and Nakasawa Shin'ichi brought about a new wave of intellectual interest in New Academism, a neologism that refers to interdisciplinary discourse on Western-oriented semiotics, structuralism, deconstructionism, post-modernism, etc. Karatani, later joined by the scholar Asada Akira, founded the journal *Hihyō kūkan* (*Critical Space*) in 1991 and, for a decade or so, attempted to corral literary criticism into an elevated debate akin to European and Ivy League theoretical discourse.

In his book *Kindai bungaku no owari* (*The End of Modern Literature*), Karatani argues that modern literature since the Meiji era was elevated as a channel to discuss intellectual, political, and moral concerns, but that mission now seems to be over. "Once literature is liberated from carrying the burden of those issues, literature will exist only as entertainment" (2005, 47). "The end of modern literature" is a concept that many authors, readers, and scholars continue to contest, but there is some validity to the assertion that the erudite, soul-searching, philosophically probing, politically relevant, and profoundly aesthetic writing characteristic of Meiji, Taishō, and Shōwa ended with Ōe Kenzaburō's late works. By 2002, *Hihyō kūkan* ceased publication, and with it the last attempt at highbrow literary criticism came to an end.

With the breakdown of hierarchy in both the *bundan* and in literary criticism, we witness a leveling of the creative terrain. Literary production now must compete with movies, manga, anime, multimedia, and a multitude of Web-based platforms to engage readers in the age of the Internet, compounded by decreased attention spans and demands for instant gratification. In a round-table talk with the scholars Kurihara Yūichirō and Osawa Hidemi, Sasaki Atsushi points out that the term *J-bungaku* (J-lit) became trendy around 1998 as a derivative of J-league in sports and J-pop in popular culture (*Bungei* 173). The Akutagawa Prize and Naoki Prize continue to present on average two awards per year to writers—arguably, largely to boost sales in bookstores—but it has become difficult to separate "pure literature" from "popular literature" (although the Akutagawa Prize seems to give more weight to thought-provoking issues while the Naoki Prize seems to favor entertainment and storytelling). However, in addition to these prominent prizes, a profusion of "new writer" awards have come into being. In particular, the *Hon'ya taishō* (Bookstore Grand Prize), introduced in 2004, further democratizes the selection process by eliminating panels of judges who are scholars and established writers and instead basing the outcome on votes from bookstore staff. Many award-winning titles have been made into movies, such as Ogawa Yōko's 2003 novel *Hakase no aishita sūshiki* (*The Professor and the Housekeeper*, 2009) and Onda Riku's *Hachimitsu to enrai* (*Honey and Distant Thunder*, 2017), making the Bookstore Grand Prize a much-coveted award.

The flattening of the literary landscape in Heisei Japan does not mean that literature per se came to an end. It only means that "modern Japanese literature"—from Higuchi Ichiyō to Ōe Kenzaburō—had run its full course by the late 1980s. Rather, literary expressions in Heisei Japan became diffused among a multitude of forms, media, and voices, making it impossible to circumscribe and define a body of work under the label of "Heisei literature."

Nonetheless, there have been attempts to do so. After the Diet passed the special bill for Akihito's retirement in June 2017, some journals began putting together retrospectives of literary development in the Heisei years. Among them, the Autumn 2017 issue of the journal *Bungei* published two "maps," one called "Gendai bungaku shiin 2017" ("Contemporary Literary Scene 2017"), and a prospective one called "Contemporary Literary Scene 2020," a prediction of what the future will look like.[1] The 2017 map features over 90 writers scattered across two intersecting axes, creating quadrants labeled "Society" at the top, "Individual" at the bottom, "Narrative" on the left, and "Language" on the right. Situated in the middle of the intersection is Murakami Haruki, surrounded by islands labeled "plurilingualism," "experimental," "I-novel," and "crossover," each populated by a variety of writers. The 2020 version of the map has the same intersecting axes, but with different islands labeled "fiction as pop culture," "between mother tongue and foreign languages," "new reckoning of the female sex," "linguistic avant garde," and more. This time, sitting at the nexus is Murata Sayaka, whose Akutagawa Prize-winning novel *Konbini ningen* (*Convenience Store Woman*, 2016) and its subsequent English translation garnered much attention at home and abroad. Neither of the maps provides a clear delineation of Heisei's rather chaotic literary scene, however, and it is noteworthy that the *kanji* for "map" (*chizu* 地図) is glossed as *shiin* ("scene"), a telling sign of the lack of commitment to definitive mapping.

Another inconclusive attempt to define literature in Heisei Japan is a discussion entitled "Heisei no shōsetsu wo furikaeru" ("Looking Back at the Fiction in Heisei") in a collection of essays called "Heisei to bungaku" ("Heisei and Literature") that appeared in the May 2019 issue of the literary journal *Subaru*. The writers Saitō Minako and Takahashi Gen'ichirō each selected their ten favorite works and suggested themes to categorize literature in Heisei, such as "the estranged self," "the resurgence of regional and translated languages," "Heisei in comparison or in relation to Shōwa," and "war in daily life." Yet a third example is a 2019 monograph called *Heisei no bungaku to wa nan datta no ka* (*What on Earth was the Literature of Heisei?*), which the scholars Shigesato Tetsuya and Sukegawa Kōichirō organized under chapter headings such as "Murakami Haruki in Heisei," "From Love to Comradery," "After the Big Earthquake," and "Cross-Genre Writers." All of the above efforts at categorization are idiosyncratic and personal. None provides a comprehensive analysis of what constitutes or differentiates literature in Heisei, evidence of the futility of such attempts.

Given the impossible task of defining "Japanese literature" and "Heisei literature," I decided to decouple "literature" from "Heisei" and "Japan" and reconfigure the three words into a simple title for this volume—*Literature in Heisei Japan*—to affirm that, first, literary production has not come to an end despite its new and amorphous form, and second, its multitudinous expressions go beyond the conventional categorization of literature based on the nation (Japan) and time frame (Heisei). Pairing Heisei with Japan but dislodging it as a modifier for literature simply marks three decades in the recent past that provide an opportunity for retrospection and taking stock, even though the imperial demarcation of time is not particularly relevant on a historical, political, and quotidian level.

While periodization based on imperial reign is no longer significant to the collective psyche of the Japanese public, Heisei is not without its defining cataclysmic moments. The economic bubble burst in the early Heisei years, leading to a slow and painful recession lasting two decades. The neologism *kakusa shakai* ("social/economic discrepancy") came to define a society where the income gap and opportunities between the haves and the have-nots continue to widen. Heisei also experienced some of the worst natural and human-made disasters in a century, such as the Hanshin Earthquake in 1995 and the Great Eastern Japan Earthquake and its concurrent tsunami and nuclear plant explosion and meltdown in 2011. One event that shook Japanese society to the core occurred in 1995, when the religious cult Aum Shinrikyō indiscriminately released Sarin nerve gas in the heart of Tokyo, a terrorist act that revealed the extent to which a religious cult could control the minds of so many followers, many highly educated yet in search of identity, spiritual shelter, and a sense of belonging.

The economic downturn, the widening social, economic, and gender gaps, and the disasters and traumas of Heisei Japan certainly find their way into quite a few artistic works produced between 1989 and 2019, but those literary expressions are often private and individual, never solely defined or prescribed by upheavals in the social, political, and natural world. As such, the critical essays here examine artistic expressions in an amorphous age that has outgrown the conventional identification with nation and the definable literary genres and standards of previous eras. Exigent circumstances compel these writers to examine their identity and society, leading to the creation of captivating stories of self-discovery, social and historical reflections, and wild imaginings of an alternative reality.

Furthermore, the dissolution of established notions of modern Japanese literature and conventional modes of literary criticism lead to experiments with new approaches to creative expression. Some writers play with Japanese and foreign languages to connect with the past, define the present, and fashion a new future; some explore spaces seen and unseen that define contemporary Japan; and some gaze steadily at the self to craft a new language to define the individual, explore the body and sexuality, question gender dynamics, and foster new configurations of the family.

Aware of the impossible task of comprehensively covering and mapping literature in Heisei Japan, this volume focuses on just a selection of creative voices from those thirty years. Selected writers and artists include Abe Kazushige, Asabuki Mariko, Fukazawa Ushio, Ishimure Michiko, Kawakami Hiromi, Kiki Kirin, Kimura Saeko, Kore'eda Hirokazu, Mizumura Minae, Murakami Haruki, Murakami Ryū, Oyamada Hiroko, Shiraishi Kazufumi, Tagame Gengorō, Takagi Nobuko, Tawada Yōko, Tsushima Yūko, and Yū Miri. Contributors include scholars from Germany, Hong Kong, Italy, Japan, Jordan, Poland, and the United States who trained in Europe, Japan, and North America, bringing a diverse and international perspective to this study. Their critical essays are organized under three categories.

Language. One of the most important dimensions of examining new developments in literature is to analyze the use of language in conveying the cultural, social, intellectual, and aesthetic phenomena of an age. This section explores the language of translation, linguistic experiments, plurilingual writing, cross-border writing, the blurring of fiction and non-fiction, narrative experiments in storytelling, and the development of post-colonial *Nihongo bungaku* (Japanese language literature) and Zainichi/post-Zainichi literature. Thompson and Kurita, in their respective analyses of Takagi Nobuko's *Narihira* and Asabuki Mariko's *Tracing the Flow*, examine how contemporary language looks to the past for new inspiration and creativity. Kono probes the art of plurilingual literature and translation in the reading of Mizumura Minae's *I-Novel: From Left to Right* as world and global literature. Strecher and Washburn explore new forms of narrative by Murakami Haruki and Tsushima Yūko that challenge and reinterpret traditional forms of storytelling and create, paradoxically, both a resonance with and a break between the past and the present.

Spaces Seen and Unseen. To locate traces and footprints of the past thirty years, we turn our focus to an exploration of physical and imaginary places, spaces, and environments. Essays on space examine urban space, the hidden space of the underclass, the space of memory, spaces of peripheral realisms, and the ambivalent space in between social and political existences. Iwata-Weickgenannt and Kasza look at the space of memory in the works of Yū Miri and Shiraishi Kazufumi; Giammaria digs into the hidden spaces of the underclass and underworld of the Kabukichō in the works of Murakami Ryū to illuminate a world seldom seen in daylight; and Haag takes us to the marginal world of Zainichi and post-Zainichi literature where individuals constantly struggle with the legacy of a colonial past and finding space to exist in Japanese society. Essays on the environment incorporate eco-criticism, political and environmental issues in post-trauma Japan, and post-disaster literary theory. Hweidi examines environmental devastation in Ishimure Michiko's *Lake of Heaven* and explores the possibility of atonement and healing. O'Neill and Slaymaker, in their respective examinations of the works of Tawada Yōko, Kawakami Hiromi, and Kimura Saeko, focus on the more-than-human world as well as post-3.11 literature to ask questions about what we have learned in the aftermath of disasters in a precarious age.

Family, Identity, Gender, Body. What is closest to our daily life and individual experience is the constantly changing sense of family and individual existence that typifies the Heisei years. This group of essays explores new configurations of family through the discovery and redefinition of individual identity, gender, and body; examines subjection; and offers literary critiques of violence, gender, queer literature, aging, and other concerns. Thornbury looks at gender and aging in Kore'eda Hirokazu's film featuring Kiki Kirin—one of the most memorable actresses in the Heisei period—to reflect on the changing family. Yiu analyzes the fantastical imagery and use of space in Oyamada Hiroko's stories about young women negotiating work, marriage, pregnancy, and child-rearing in the context of contemporary Japan's extreme gender gap. In their essays on Tagame Gengorō's manga and Abe Kazushige's work, Maude and Roemer explore queer literature and homosocial narratives and open a new discourse to explore LGBTQ literature in Japan.

In compiling this anthology of critical essays, I came to more fully appreciate the challenge of labeling or mapping a huge and sprawling body of work across the three remarkable Heisei decades. At the same time, I was delighted to discover the multiple perspectives and voices as well as the social, political, and personal issues jostling to be seen and heard through stories of great immediacy and intensity. I hope this study will throw light on the literary landscape of this thirty-year period and provide a glimpse into what is new and exciting in contemporary literature in Japan.

Acknowledgements
I would like to thank the contributors who pledged their faith and time to this book project even at its budding stage in 2019, continued to engage in our online workshops and discussions throughout the pandemic years, and endured the stringent deadlines of publication. The Covid requirement of sheltering in place and the ubiquitous Zoom meetings that resulted provided me with the impetus and technology to re-establish contact with my old friend Beth Ward from our graduate school days at Yale, and our monthly conversations (which she called "rendezooms") resulted in a happy collaboration with Beth offering her expertise as copy editor for this volume. Munia Hweidi, who received her doctoral degree in Japanese Studies in 2022 after studying with me at Sophia University, assumed the role of managing editor and proved to be a most dependable and trusted colleague. I am proud and grateful that my son, Hitoshi Takei, volunteered to design the book cover. I feel truly blessed and humbled that all these individuals came together to make this publication possible. They deserve the credit for this work, and I am responsible for its inadequacies and imperfections.

This book project received generous advice and support from Sophia University, especially the Institute of Comparative Culture, the Special Research Grant Program in the Faculty of Liberal Arts, and the Center for Research Promotion and Support. Finally, I would like to express my heartfelt gratitude to Sophia University Press for selecting this work for publication and promotion.

Angela Yiu
Tokyo, 2024

---

1 For a view of the maps,
see https://prtimes.jp/main/html/rd/p/000000090.000012754.html (accessed August 1, 2023).

References

Bungei. 2017. "Gendai bungaku shiin 2000-2020" ["Contemporary Literary Scenes 2000-2020)"] (Autumn 2017): 169-280.

Karatani Kōjin. 2005. *Kindai bungaku no owari* [*The End of Modern Literature*]. Tokyo: Inscript.

Saitō Minako and Takahashi Gen'ichirō. 2019. "Heisei to bungaku" ["Heisei and Literature"]. *Subaru* (May 2019): 133-156.

Shigesato Tetsuya and Sukegawa Kōichirō. 2019. *Heisei no bungaku to wa nan datta no ka: gekiryū to mujō o koete* [*What on Earth was the Literature of Heisei: Beyond Turbulence and Unaffectedness*]. Tokyo: Harukaze shobō.

PART 1:

LANGUAGE

I. The Past in the Present

Kyoko Kurita, Pomona College

Dissolution of the Novel: Asabuki Mariko's *Ryūseki* (Tracing the Flow)

There is no denying that globalization has changed literature worldwide, especially with the pervasive influence of the internet and other technological innovations of the last few decades. While we are now more aware of diversity in the world than before, we have also seen progressive standardization and simplification. The advent of internet culture has brought about the worldwide dominance of the English language, threatening the existence of less prominent cultures and languages. Globalization often prioritizes the convenience of those who can manipulate English. The value of literary works is gauged by the existence of English translation. What is difficult to translate into English is what needs to be discovered, and yet, ironically, it is often left behind, lost and forgotten. This phenomenon naturally skews the visible topography of world literature.

With the information technology (IT) revolution, literature has declined in popularity while science, technology, engineering, and mathematics fields have grown worldwide. In 2004, in *Kindai bungaku no owari* (*The Apocalypse of Modern Literature*), Karatani Kōjin (b. 1941) declared the end of the era when literature carried special importance. Concomitantly, the popularity of literary theory has also declined. What, then, do we talk about when we talk about contemporary Japanese literature?

What is now considered contemporary Japanese literature mostly overlaps with the Heisei Period (1989-2019). What stands out in the history of this period are the effects of the "Lehman Shock" (the 2008 global financial crisis) on the Japanese economy and several large-scale natural disasters that shook the core of

Japanese sensibilities. In *Heisei bungaku towa nandatta no ka?* (*What was Heisei Literature?*), Shigesato Tetsuya (b. 1957) and Sukegawa Kōichirō (b. 1967) argue that those unprecedented difficulties in fact constituted fertile ground for innovation and creativity in literature, and that a number of talented writers—those established and new alike—produced a wealth of notable literary work that dealt with a wide range of topics (2019, 14-17).[1] The burst of energy in literary expression attests to the necessity of literature despite the significant changes in the world we live in and in the way we consume literature.

Kawamura Minato (b. 1951) is one of the few scholars who considered the definition of Heisei literature well before the Heisei Period actually ended. In his essay, "Heisei bungaku towa nani ka?" ("What is Heisei Literature?," 2009), he attributes the major characteristics of Heisei literature to writers' efforts to overcome boundaries and borders in every sense of those words. Globalization that had begun in the nineteenth century along with colonization magnified its force and diversified its ramifications with the advent of the World Wide Web. We must acknowledge, however, that at the same time there has been a converse trend to identify regional and national characters and to strengthen them. Contemporary writers are expected to serve two masters—global themes and regional specificity.

It was Tsubouchi Shōyō's (1859-1935) epoch-making *Shōsetsu shinzui* (*The Essence of the Novel*, 1885-1886) that introduced the Western idea of the "novel," or *shōsetsu*, to Japan in the late 1880s, and henceforth the term gained wide currency. Shōyō's essay publicized the notion that shōsetsu was a modern genre devoid of any moralistic or ideological stance. (It is generally believed that the novel as a modern literary genre was established in nineteenth-century Europe, replacing the long-standing prestige of poetry.) Like many other words that were coined or reframed in the Meiji Era, the definition of shōsetsu was quite loose; now, as a result of the IT revolution, the word and its use seem to be facing another phase of transformation. Today, shōsetsu seems to fit the concept of "fiction" better than "novel." A perusal of bookstores and advertisements in print or online shows that the word *noberu*, a transliteration of "novel," has come to surpass the use of shōsetsu in popularity. This may signify a paradigm shift in what *bungaku* (literature) and shōsetsu represent in the popular media. Along with technological change, multimedia presentation as well as the re-interpretation of works in other art forms have become commonplace.

The use of multimedia has also influenced the way temporality is perceived in art. Sasaki Toshinao (b. 1961) argues in *Jikan to tekunorojii* (*Time and Technology,* 2019) that there is no longer any past or present in the reception of art. He introduces Brian Eno's comment by saying:

> I think that in music there is no history any longer: everything is present. This is one of the results of digitization, where everybody owns everything: you don't have just your little record collection of things you saved up for and guard so carefully. (29-30)[2]

The same thing can be said for any category of art. Nowadays, multiple works from different time periods can be referents or components in a single work. Furthermore, the use of multimedia presentations has made the genre distinctions of art much less relevant than before. Thus, we cannot simply accept the notion that literature is dead. It may be just that the categories and rubrics of literature are configured differently today. It is within this context that I would like to introduce Asabuki Mariko.

Asabuki Mariko

Asabuki Mariko's name is not much known outside Japan because her works have not yet been translated into English or any other language, as far as I know. However, she is one of the most innovative and imaginative writers today, sharing global themes and interests common among all readers and writers of the world while being deeply grounded in traditional Japanese literature. Her works are examples of how two masters can be served without committing treason against either one.

Asabuki was born in Tokyo in 1984. Her birth year falls within the range of those who are called the Millennials, born between 1981 and 1996. The internet has been a part of their lives ever since they became aware of their environment; as a result, Millennials are generally comfortable and versatile in the use of word-processing and digital tools. It goes without saying that the IT revolution brought about significant changes in the way people think about what is real. Existing norms and taboos lost their validity, and the perception of self and gender has gone through significant transformation. Asabuki owes a great deal to the internet for her broad range of knowledge and global viewpoint. The internet must have also helped to liberate her from limitations and restrictions traditionally placed on novel writing.

Public figures nowadays communicate with their followers not only through publications and public appearances but also through their websites and a variety of social media. Asabuki is no exception. A quick web search alone picks up numerous comments from and to her, and images of her, uploaded by different organizations. *VOGUE JAPAN* selected her as one of the most influential women of 2011.[3] Asabuki is not simply a writer: she is a multifaceted entity who is constantly evolving. Her writing shows her abilities to approach topics through multiple media and disciplines, sometimes crossing the boundaries of time and space. She has a wide vocabulary, which creates a sense of freedom and playfulness. Her often mysterious storylines lure the reader more deeply into her imaginative world.

It seems unfair to attribute an artist's talents to her family background; at the same time, one would be remiss if one failed to acknowledge it. Asabuki has an impressive list of notable relatives. The most famous among them are two great-aunts, both Francophiles. Asabuki Tomiko (1917-2005) was a renowned translator-essayist who is widely recognized for her translations of works by Françoise Sagan and Simone Beauvoir. Ishii Yoshiko (1922-2010) was a dynamic *chanson* singer and essayist who popularized *chanson* in postwar Japan. Asabuki Mariko's father is the scholar of French literature and poet Asabuki Ryōji. Although her mother does not seem to have had a career per se, her influence on Asabuki's intellectual and creative development appears to have been essential. Asabuki's essays attest to her mother's dedication to musical and literary composition, as well as her attention and care, which enabled Asabuki to have a happy and fulfilling childhood.[4]

At Keio University, Asabuki majored in classical Japanese literature with a focus on the Edo Period. Her master's thesis was on the famous Kabuki and Kyōgen writer, Tsuruya Nanboku (1755-1829), and his representative piece, *Tōkaidō Yotsuya kaidan* (*A Ghost Story of Yotsuya on Tōkaidō Road,* 1825). Although she does not work on Edo literature any longer, Asabuki still loves reading *Kadokawa kogo dai-jiten* (*Kadokawa's Comprehensive Dictionary of Classical Japanese*) and *Kokka taikan* (*A Compendium of National Poetry*),[5] which are hardly entertaining for the typical reader. In those classical Japanese words that functioned once upon a time, Asabuki acknowledges feeling "the vestige of the lips" (*kuchibiru no konseki*) of the people who used to utter them. Moreover, she has the desire to resurrect some words, to bring them to the lips of today's readers in the hope that they will function in some altered form, again evoking the vestige of the lips (Horie and Asabuki 2016, 128-9).

Asabuki enjoys not only seeing words in books, but also physically moving her lips to read the words out loud. Through the appearance and the sound of the words she tries to have a better understanding of the lives of the people who are no longer here. Since her childhood she has enjoyed listening (via YouTube) to writers such as Haniya Yutaka[6] and James Joyce read their own works (Horie and Asabuki, 115). This dialogic relationship that she builds between past writers, their works, and readers resurrects the past in the present and creates a strong sense of a past reality that is almost physical. Just as Brian Eno postulated for music, readers today become acquainted with literature from different areas and times on even terrain, as if we were all contemporaries.

Asabuki made her writing debut in 2009 with *Ryūseki* (*Tracing the Flow*), which was originally serialized in *Shinchō* before being published in book form by Shinchōsha. The following year it received the 20th Bunkamura Deux Magots Prize, the Japanese version of the French literary prize, Prix des Deux Magots. Horie Toshiyuki, the 124th Akutagawa Prize-winning author and professor of French literature at Waseda University, was responsible for the selection. Despite its literary merit, *Ryūseki* was not a commercial success. It consists of a series of mysterious, often disjointed scenes without an overarching plot. Horie in fact frankly confessed that it is so original that he had trouble explaining its literary merit in a conventional way (Horie and Asabuki, 109). The following year, in April 2010, *Gunzō* carried Asabuki's short story "Ieji" ("The Way Home"), which was later included in the same volume when *Ryūseki* was published in *bunko-bon* (small paperback) form. "Ieji" is also an unconventional, fantastical piece with an elastic sense of time and space.

It was Asabuki's second novel, *Kikotowa* (*Two Women*, 2011), which won the 144th Akutagawa Prize and made her famous. It tells the story of two girls, Kiko and Towako, growing up together, and their reunion twenty-five years later. Although Asabuki already had an idea for her third book when she received the Akutagawa Prize, it was not until 2016 that *TIMELESS* (titled in English in capital letters), started appearing in *Shinchō* (also subsequently published as a book by Shinchōsha, in 2018). It did not win any prizes, perhaps because it depicts a woman devoid of romantic desire. Without any emotional or physical bond, Umi marries her friend, Ami, a man whose grandmother is an atomic bomb survivor.

They have a child, Ao, but Ami disappears, in a way rather similar to what might happen in a Murakami Haruki story.

Asabuki has also published two collections of essays: *Hikidashi no naka no umi* (*The Ocean in My Drawer*, 2019) and *Daichō kotoba meguri* (*A Playbook: Journey Through the Words,* 2021). They present, in short bursts, memorable vignettes from her childhood and recent encounters, impressions, and emotions she holds dear to her heart. Moreover, due to her broad interests, Asabuki has been active in a variety of venues, ranging from the Japanese game of chess to modern music, movies, and modern art, as well as literature. Although she was only twenty-five years old when *Ryūseki* was published, it would be a massive task for a reader to trace all the influences from the fields of art, culture, and history that went into its creation.

***Ryūseki*: An Anti-Novel Novel**

The best way to introduce Asabuki to someone who has not yet read her works, I believe, is to delve into her debut novel *Ryūseki.* As is often the case with a debut work, one finds here the kernel of elements Asabuki develops in later works. Identifying the key topics of her literary beginning will help the reader grasp the quality of Asabuki's innovation and contributions to contemporary Japanese literature.

It may be useful to remember here that the advent of the novel in the nineteenth century coincided with scientific innovation and industrialization in many parts of the world. Realism and logic gained importance in fiction writing, and the novel was considered the genre best fit for the modern era. Even today, audiences assume that the narrator will guide them through an autonomous world of fiction, a supposed microcosm of the real world, from the beginning to the end of a plot following a logical progression. In other words, the reader enjoys being controlled by the storyteller with the expectation of arriving at a certain goal.

Ryūseki, in contrast, appears to prevent the reader from getting into the story right from the start. Asabuki gives no indication of who the narrator is. The *mise-en-scène* opening that begins with ellipses gives the reader a sense of being a temporary voyeur of an ongoing narrative, which no one is able to access in its entirety. The only information the reader has is that the narrator is trying to read a book on board a train. Rather than telling the reader what is in the book, the narrator describes the difficulty of understanding its content:

> ...Without being able to read a single page, day after day, my eyes have been tracing the lines of a page. Somehow or other the lines flow from one to the next, bit by bit, and the gaze arrives at the last line of the last paragraph of the page. Perhaps because the gaze acknowledges that there is no more unread text left on the page, the finger flips over the page...and it was...and to become a.... While the eyes follow each and every character that forms a vertical line under the waves of light, the words the book puts forth merely form dappled patterns on the cornea and are not linked to meaning.[7] (Asabuki 2016, 9)[8]

The detachment the narrator feels toward the printed text in the book naturally parallels the disconnection that the reader of *Ryūseki* experiences. Why would an author wish to begin a narrative by suggesting the impossibility of understanding the text?

Asabuki reveals that her skepticism about understanding any written text was the starting point of her creative experiment:

> We do not doubt that we share a common mother tongue to communicate with others, whether that be Japanese or English. Based on that notion we choose words to express our thoughts, carry on conversations, and read books. However, a strong suspicion arose as to whether I was truly catching the meaning of the words or the work of fiction some total stranger wrote. That led me to acknowledge how much distance there is between myself and words. (Horie and Asabuki, 110-111)

Asabuki recollects the astonishment she felt when she first encountered a poem by Yoshimasu Gōzō and found that the words printed on the paper made no sense to her.[9] That puzzlement, in fact, was what drew her to his poems. She seems to consider that the gap between the author's intent and the reader's interpretation exists naturally and also changes over time. She comes to the realization that there is no reason to prioritize one over the other:

> When one reads a novel silently, there has to be a voice that is sounding in each reader's mind. That voice, however, is probably different from what the author had originally intended.... (Horie and Asabuki, 114-115)

Asabuki's encounter with Takemitsu Tōru (1930-1996) solidified her conviction that the gap between the author and the reader is to be cherished. In the essay "Dokusho no yōtai" ("Different Modes of Reading," 1996), Takemitsu writes:

> …I was reading, savoring each line, each phrase of Italo Calvino's short stories and the collected *haiku* poems by Buson.
>
> The words in those texts did not offer any definitive message. In other words, they were not the kind of writing that tried to explain some causal relationship. They were products of subtle and deep observation; and yet, or because of it, they gave the reader the freedom and the opportunity to develop new ideas. They were composed of poetic language. (85)

In addition to the gap between the author's intention and the reader's interpretation, Asabuki introduces the awareness of a gap between the author and the author as the reader of his or her own text:

> "Writing" also necessitates "reading" what one just wrote. For example, if I write three lines and read them, those three lines themselves generate a new form of "writing" that leads me rewrite those three lines. A line that has been written generates momentum not only to read the next line, but also to rewrite the same line again and again. (Horie and Asabuki, 117)

Asabuki's comment seems to highlight the fact that polyphony exists even within a single line written by a single author. The author who becomes the reader engages in the act of reading, which leads to further writing and rewriting. Thus, reading and writing become thoroughly integrated into each other, creating a Möbius strip. Publication of a text fixes it to a certain version, but that is merely accidental. The author's act of reading and writing does not stop evolving.

This perspective on the unity of reading and writing suggests that the reader is also a writer of his or her own version even if it may never be printed. What matters most is not that a certain version becomes published, but that the polyphony that is born out of reading and writing constantly generates energy for rewriting and rereading. The reading public until recently believed in the supremacy of the text. However, the new, electronic form of text production has led us to question it. Some say that theoretically speaking, repeated typing by a monkey might eventually produce a Shakespeare sonnet. A text is often a cluster of words that happened to come together by accident, even if the author had a certain goal in mind. There is no single text that is more authentic than others. Different versions constantly get produced by the author or the reader, feeding back into the ocean of text production and reception. Reading is not limited to a simple act of following the plot from the beginning to the end. The reader, like the narrator at the start of *Ryūseki*, is bound to experience nagging puzzlement.

The Narrative Viewpoint, the Narrating Subject

There are a number of ways in which *Ryūseki* challenges novelistic norms, and the lack of the narrator's clear identity is one of them. Asabuki carefully avoids mentioning any personal pronoun in the text. Gender, age, and other defining features are mostly left ambiguous. Gender oscillates between male and female occasionally, for no obvious reason.[10] The historical context appears to extend from the Edo Period to modern times, as if the story were carried along by multiple narrators who are flaneurs in time and space. It is different from stream-of-consciousness writing since there is no sustained subject that exhibits transformations of mood or focus. All of this makes it a major challenge to determine how best to refer to the ever-shifting narrator, and which personal pronoun to choose when describing the text in English. Asabuki skillfully takes advantage of the syntactic characteristic of Japanese that a sentence does not require mention of the subject. The ambiguity of the narrator's identity consequently poses a significant challenge to translators.

Asabuki's use of an amorphous narrator and also a series of narrators whose identities change seems to derive from her attitude toward writing. She confesses that her writing is not motivated by something she wants to express or a message she wants to deliver (Horie and Asabuki, 118). In fact, she is skeptical about the validity of a single, sustained narrative subject in fiction-writing. She believes that human thought, which is ambiguous and exists beyond a given time and space, is generated and confirmed mainly through the senses. Though language and thought are foreign to each other, she tries to transfer the content of the thought to words as best she can.

Asabuki reveals that she originally had intended to publish *Ryūseki* without her name or a title (Horie and Asabuki, 121). Although her wish was not granted, this episode reveals her concept of what writing is all about. It is as if she catches a fish in the current of words and releases it back into the stream to be caught by someone else in some other context. The words surely belong to the flow, and they are entirely free of limitations. Given this approach, Horie's reaction to this narrative without a clear narrator is quite apt: he felt "as if someone was whispering, as if voices of different quality and speech speed were descending from outside the letters or the text" (115).

In addition to a certain narrative perspective, the idea of a single subject is also absent in this work; in fact, the idea of the individual itself is questioned. At one point in the story the narrator, who at this juncture appears as a middle-aged man, explains that his consciousness as *jibun*, or he himself, exists not only at present, but multitudinously: "Myself as a young boy, myself after I have become smoke…I am here and there, and everywhere…" (Asabuki 2016, 61).[11]

Sometimes the self does not even have a human shape. This middle-aged male narrator in *Ryūseki* keeps thinking about how he as a corpse would burn:

> All the organic matter that comprises this body disintegrates finely and the particles that are too small for the eye to behold disperse in all directions. They stroke someone's lips and cheeks, or get inhaled into someone's lungs. They travel through many living bodies this way. (68)

The focus of the narrative resides in the cohesion and the dissolution of countless microscopic particles, sometimes forming life, sometimes breaking down and dispersing to all corners of the world. This vicissitude, the gathering and scattering of elemental matter, marks the movement of time in the history of life-forms on earth. The individual is insignificant in such an environment. Everything is divisible and alterable and participates in the flow. The narrator is a calm observer of time flowing without any religious overtone.

The distinction between what is real and what is imaginary also carries little significance in *Ryūseki*:

> As if to impale the heaven—is a cliché, but it fits the sight of this chimney at a crematorium. Its long white shape that is drawing a slight, gentle curve stretches upward with the air of an entasis. It stands tall to exercise its maximum efficiency. The white smoke is trailing from the top, exhibiting its industriousness. A streak appears in the sky, but quickly diffuses in all directions and dissolves into thin air.
>
> I know this is not an actual scene. (46)

The image of a white chimney, reminiscent of pillars in Roman ruins, appears repeatedly throughout the work as if to keep reminding the reader of the eventual death of all sentient beings.

Ryūseki introduces other phantoms beside chimneys that blur the distinction between the surrounding environment and the internal world:

> On the surface of many puddles that formed after the rain, I confirmed the images of what could not have been reflected on puddles….I first thought that this was one of those optical illusions caused by the refraction of light. I started seeing those suddenly. At different places and times, images of things

that cannot be reflected on the surface of water emerged nonchalantly. (46-47)

What the eyes behold now and the memory of what they beheld in the past coexist in these scenes. Yoshida Ken'ichi (1912-1977), a novelist and literary critic whom Asabuki holds in high esteem, wrote in his book-length essay *Jikan* (*Time*, 1976):

> ...The present is the time when one is together with time and being aware of time passing. Time on a clock does not assist us in distinguishing the past and the present. When one's thought returns to the past, that *is* indeed the present. Time is ticking even in that time of recollection, and one can affirm one's existence while recollecting. That is what I consider valid memory, valid recollection. (1998, 22)

A description may combine the perspectives of different times and multiple viewers. However, the narrator can bring them together to build the sense of here and now. What is real and what is not, what is happening now and what has happened in the past, are all on the same platform. In fact, the text has the possibility of presenting a kind of hyperreality, like a metaverse, by suggesting related information, images, sounds, etc., to create a multi-dimensional reality for the reader.

In Flux

Asabuki mentions in her essay, "Chigurisu to Yūfuratesu" ("The Tigris and the Euphrates"), that her favorite poet is Nishiwaki Jun'zaburō (1894-1982). She describes Nishiwaki's *Ushinawareta toki* (*Time Lost*, 1960) as a collection of poems in which the meanings of words become undone in the end and flow away like water (Asabuki 2019, 127). It seems that Asabuki's ambition in writing *Ryūseki* was to imitate in prose what Nishiwaki does in poetry. In fact, the prose in *Ryūseki* often reads like poetry. Unlike ordinary prose fiction, the narrative often lacks a descriptive, expository quality, leaving the reader to come up with her own interpretation. The meandering, exploratory monologue gives the reader a sense of being led by a flaneur, or even a time traveler. This is related to the perception of the narrator's own stance: the subject, the center of the described environment, does not play an important role in *Ryūseki.* Instead, the text conveys a recurring image of something in flux—drifting of particles, smoke, water, or flow of consciousness and time. Asabuki reminisces:

> Since my childhood, I have felt that I am no more than a mere living organ-

> ism that will eventually drift away. Up to this moment numerous organisms have died, and many are dying and also are being born as we speak. I may give birth to a child at some point. Even if I know that the child will also die at some point, I still bear a child. Looking at a river is a relief to me because I can come to terms with the fact that I will eventually die and so will everyone else. I am no more than a single life in a large current of many lives. (Horie and Asabuki, 119-120)

The concept of flow for Asabuki refers not only to the physical and mental changes that occur around an individual but to the transformation of all life forms, from birth to death to rebirth, for generations. As in the Buddhist belief in the reincarnation of lives from one creature to another, Asabuki attempts to present her world view as one in which all things are interrelated at the most fundamental level of their existence.

The word *ryūseki*, a term in hydrodynamics that implies the imprint, trail, or mark of the movement a fluid makes, exemplifies the author's affinity for the fluidity and mortality of all life forms and the inconstancy of the environment surrounding them. The overall image of the world in *Ryūseki* emerges as a large river of all living entities streaming across time and space endlessly. "There is no beginning; it has already begun," Asabuki writes, as if to countermand the biblical declaration. "In the beginning there was logos" (2016, 13). The recurring images of decay and death in this work remind the reader of the unity of life and death, a part and a whole.[12]

The nameless narrator in *Ryūseki* treats even a printed text as if it were alive and part of the general flow. The narrator ruminates:

> The molecules of the ink adhering to the paper, the physical substance of the letters on the page, begin to quiver, bending every which way. They melt, dislodge from the page, and flow away in all directions. Intracellular fluid, blood, and even rivers all continue to flow ceaselessly as long as there is life in them. Would letters, in a similar way, try to liberate themselves from stability and run away? Breaching the binding and slipping out of the book, trying to flow away, beyond the confines. But where are they headed? (12)

The narrator watches what becomes of the escaping ink molecules:

> Would it become a monster? An ogre? Out of the amorphous maelstrom appeared a set of eyes, legs....The soft, flexible body formed the firm shape of a face, and it started walking. It didn't grow horns. It became a human. (12)[13]

A printed text appears fixed and unalterable, and yet what the reader makes of it is up to each reader. Just like the entanglement of life and death, reading and writing are inseparable, and they are always in a state of flux.

The Flow as a Modern Ruin

The following memorable passage from *Ryūseki* describes a surprisingly dark and dreary scene. The narrator is a ferryman who travels up and down a river, carrying "humans and nonhumans"[14] as passengers:

> The smell of things, the smell of burning human corpses.
>
> Even though the smells are familiar, on a warm evening the stench assaults the nostrils. With the breeze the surrounding sounds and odors linger along the river. The smell of the ocean and the smell of the sludge wafts in. Perhaps because the crematorium is nearby, the smell of burning corpses is always around. Or could it be the smell of grilled fish, like river herring?[15] Either way, it stinks. The stench of fish and birds. The smell of women's face powder mixed with the sound of *samisen* strings. The smell of black tooth dye.[16] A roofed dinghy is squeaking. Appears to be the sound of a tryst. (24)[17]

The ferryman, *samisen*, and black tooth dye are suggestive of a scene in a story written in the Edo Period. However, there appear a number of artifacts that indicate otherwise:

> To carry a customer on a boat and take them to where they request. This is how I[18] earn my daily wage. The passengers aren't limited to humans. It really depends. Some rare reptiles, taxidermized animals, a USB memory stick, a letter case for confidential documents, a suitcase, a piece of wood carefully wrapped, a lukewarm parcel wrapped in cloth, a cardboard box.... Since they are objects necessarily transported late at night, they cannot possibly be anything decent. Whether they are humans or not doesn't matter much to me. I just have the customers on board and transport them to the designated locations. I said "just," but in fact it is tough to "just" deliver. (25)

The river not only encompasses the shadow of death and decay but also attracts a variety of elusive tokens of memories of the past. What is transported along the river seems to be insignificant memorabilia, mostly outer casings of what used to contain life or records of human activities.[19]

This river in fact constitutes a form of modern ruin. As Julia Hell and

Andreas Schönle state in their introduction to *Ruins of Modernity*, "The ruin is a ruin precisely because it seems to have lost its function or meaning in the present, while retaining a suggestive, unstable semantic potential" (2010, 6). Although the study of archeology examines ancient ruins, there has been a trend in appreciating the sites of modern ruins in the past few decades for the very reason Hell and Schönle suggest.[20] Abandoned theme parks, non-functioning factories, dilapidated schools and other remains of what used to be symbols of progress and success: some find nostalgic beauty in them as if their decrepit state proves in hindsight that they were once the sites of many activities. They are attractive to the modern audience because "[r]uins emancipate our senses and desires and enable introspection," to borrow Hell and Schönle's words (8). Asabuki appears to appreciate the freedom the ruin provides, whether the ruin is concrete or metaphorical.

Asabuki also treats classical literature as a kind of ruin in *Ryūseki*. The ferryman-narrator suddenly remembers what he may have done in the past: he was fired, so he stole money from the workplace; killed his father-in-law, his wife, and a colleague; and in desperation killed another young woman (31-32). He then questions if he really committed those crimes:

> What was my work before? Was I making umbrellas? Was I selling medicine? Oh, that's right. I was fired, so I stole some money from the workplace.... No, I stole some money so I was fired.... Wait, was that the case? Anyway, I killed my wife and a co-worker, and fled here. Was that it? Did I kill my father-in-law? (43-44)

A reader well-versed in Edo literature realizes that the narrator is referring to a character named Tamiya Iemon in the most famous tragic Kabuki play of the Edo Period, *Tōkaidō Yotsuya kaidan*.[21] The narrator wonders, "Is this my own predicament? It feels like I am patching together some pieces from a story. And yet it gradually starts to feel like my own" (32). Asabuki is alluding to the reader's experience of being immersed in the world of fiction from long ago, so much so that the events in the story feel like her own. The empathic reading makes ambiguous the temporal and spatial gap between the story and the reader, between the ruin and the modern observer. The classical text, written in a style and with a vocabulary no one would use today, is a kind of literary ruin. However, Asabuki resurrects those forgotten words by pronouncing them. By shaping her mouth to pronounce them she connects with the people of bygone era. This is the vestige of the lips.

Asabuki's interest in ruins does not remain in the abstract. Toward the end of the work, Asabuki depicts a gory scene of human ruins. The orgy of humans and nonhumans concludes in the dissolution of their physical bodies that melt into one flowing form:

> Fluid oozes out of their bodies and drips down. Those who are in their prime and those who are not, men and women, all alike dissolve and flow away. Warmth drips from the gaps between the bones. As humans and nonhumans suck each other's lips they reverberate synchronically, and their body heat radiates outward. When the outlines of their bodies become indistinct, cracks appear throughout their bodies. All the fluid stored inside wells up, and it flows out through numerous pores of the human skin. (80-81)

While the ruins of a Roman city would reveal broken pieces of inorganic materials that were used to form some structure many centuries ago, the ruin Asabuki depicts comprises living beings dissolving and flowing together, creating a kind of primordial soup. These living beings come to disintegrate and lose their individual form, joining the flow of time and the flow of all that had life and may return to life in the future.

What is Asabuki's intent in creating such a bizarre scene? This large, flowing assemblage of life forms and their elements seems to symbolize the notion that we all share the collective knowledge and memory of history, as well as physical substance on earth. New life appears and tries to tell a new story. No matter how different it may be, it is born out of what existed before; and after the new narrative is consumed and decays, it gets integrated back into the pool of collective memory. As if to demonstrate this concept, the narrator in *Ryūseki* transforms from one character into another: at one point the narrator assumes the identity of a married man with a son, at another point a young boy, or a woman, even the ashes of a burnt corpse. Those different manifestations of the narrator, including the self that observes the narrator's own death, are not bound to one particular time frame; in fact, they may all exist simultaneously without any end point (61-62). The narrating self also repeats the process of coming to life with a physical shape, disappearing, and being reincarnated as a different person (82).[22]

The idea that a self is merely an accidental formation may go against the Western notion of the self as a unique, independent and irreplaceable being that combines the body and the mind. However, as Robert Ginsberg (1937-2022), a scholar and professor of aesthetics and philosophy, writes in his *The Aesthetics of*

Ruins:

> The ruin liberates matter from its subservience to form. As the chains of form are smashed, matter emerges in our presence, reformulating itself for our refreshed experience. Matter, which once had been conquered in the original, returns in the ruin to conquer form. (2004, 34)

The idea that the vicissitudes of existence on earth follow a similar cycle of coming into shape and disintegrating seems to lie at the center of Asabuki's motivation for this work.

Coda: A Calm Gaze Over the Flow of Life

Although some of what Asabuki depicts is specific to Japanese culture, the theme of the eternal cycle of life and matter is universal. *Ryūseki* gives the reader a sense that the narrator is zooming out, away from the particularities of the world, creating a maximum distance between the narrator and the subject, until the history of all life forms is within the observer's scope. The work's uniqueness derives from Asabuki's aspiration to obtain a perspective—which may be called ultra-objectivity—that captures the entirety of human activities. The narrator is one who can be anyone anywhere, any time. It is questionable if there has been any narrator who has been as self-effacing as the one in *Ryūseki*. In a way, Asabuki's originality derives from her effort to minimize individuality and maximize universality.

Yomota Inuhiko (b. 1953) summons Marcel Duchamp's idea of "*inframince*" in his commentary on *Ryūseki*. Inframince is a word Duchamp coined, and Yomota defines it as "something slight, extremely thin; something that exists between presence and absence, and is just about to disappear" (2016, 133). He finds in *Ryūseki* the most beautiful and bold execution of this idea. Yomota's reaction is a testimony to the exceptionally unassuming quality of the narrator in this work.

The significance of what appears insignificant, elusive, ineffable, or fragile has captured artists' attention for centuries. Today, when there is much skepticism about grand narratives, the sensitivity to detect seemingly insignificant elements of life seems particularly meaningful for grounding oneself to stand firm amidst paradigm shifts. Asabuki is one of the most recent advocates for such an approach to literature. Her ability to perceive such faint signs seems to derive from her humility—her conception of herself as a miniscule existence in the universe;

and from her empathy—her navigation of history and all corners of the world in her mind. The images *Ryūseki* creates within the reader will disintegrate and disappear, and yet the elements of her vision and sentiment will always be present in this world, as they always have been.

---

1 We see a similar outburst of artistic creativity after Japan's defeat in WWII.

2 Brian Eno's full interview, first published in *Time Out Sydney* (May 15, 2009), can be accessed at https://andrewpstreet.com/2009/05/15/brian-eno-interview/

3 Along with Asabuki, eight other women were selected.
See https://www.vogue.co.jp/fashion/news/2011-11/25/woty

4 For details, see Asabuki's family history in *Hikidashi no naka no umi* (2019).

5 *Kokka taikan* contains a comprehensive list and index of all the important classical Japanese poems. The most recent edition was published in twenty volumes, 1983-1992.

6 Haniya Yutaka (1909-1997) was a writer and critic influenced by Marxism and Sternerism.

7 Asabuki inserted meaningless fragments of a sentence in classical Japanese.

8 Quotations of Asabuki's works in this chapter are translated by the author.

9 Asabuki does not mention which poem by Yoshimasu she read.

10 The narrator, who is at one point a punter, is described as a pale-faced man with the hairstyle of a lower-ranking samurai (42). A few pages later, the narrator is in the modern era, and he goes home to his wife and a small child (48). Later the narrator suddenly declares that he has become a woman (74). And again the narrator suddenly declares that the gender has shifted back to female, without any explanation (80).

11 In a somewhat similar vein, Hirano Keiichirō advocates for *Bunjin shugi,* the idea that the self is not composed of a singular and unchanging identity, but formed in response to the interactions one has with other people or the environment (See Hirano 2012).

12 This is a theme Asabuki continues to pursue in other fictional works and in her essays.

13 The original Japanese text does not give any particular identity.

14 The Japanese for "humans and nonhumans" is *hito ya hito de nai mono.*

15 *Konoshiro* is a kind of small herring about ten inches long and shaped like a leaf. Although it is not very common today, it used to be abundant, and was a part of the regular Japanese diet since ancient times. It was known to smell like a human corpse when grilled. Asabuki mentions *konoshiro* here because there is a legend in which the parents of a beautiful young woman burned this fish in a coffin to trick a regional governor, who wanted to marry her, into thinking that she was dead, so that she could escape his clutches to marry her lover.

16 The mention of the *samisen* and tooth dye suggests thc tryst of a courtesan and a customer on board the boat.

17 This, in fact, is Asabuki's and Horie's favorite passage. (See Horie and Asabuki 2016, 124).

18 Although it is necessary to use "I" in the English translation, Asabuki carefully avoids the mention of the subject in the original.

19 Asabuki may intend to use the act of transporting passengers on a boat as an allusion to the role of metaphor in literature.

20 One notable example is *Beautiful Japanese Ruins*. (Yōsuke, Keiichiro Matsumoto, and Funiku Ōkami 2016).

21 See "Part II. The Beginning of the End of Edo Kabuki: Yotsuya kaidan in 1825" in Satoko 2016, 97-227.

22 The narrator says, "Yet again, I take a physical shape..." implying that the narrator repeats the process of being born and dying.

References

Asabuki Mariko. 2016. *Ryūseki*. Tokyo: Shinchōsha. Reprinted from *Shinchō* (2011), No. 1.

———. 2019. "Chigurisu to Yūfurates." In *Hikidashi no naka no umi*. Tokyo: Chūō kōronsha.

Ginsberg, Robert. 2004. *The Aesthetics of Ruins*. Amsterdam and New York: Rodopi.

Hell, Julia and Andreas Schönle, eds. 2010. *Ruins of Modernity*. Durham and London: Duke University Press.

Horie Toshiyuki and Asabuki Mariko. 2016. "Nagare saru inochi to kotoba" ["Words and Lives that Flow Away"]. Transcribed conversation between the two authors. In *Ryūseki,* by Asabuki Mariko. Tokyo: Shinchōsha.

Hirano Kei'ichirō. 2012. *Watashi towa nanika?* [*What is I?*] Tokyo: Kōdansha.

Karatani Kōjin. 2005. "Kindai bungaku no owari." In *Kindai bungaku no owari*, 35-80. Tokyo: Inscript. Originally published in *Waseda Bungaku* (May 2004).

Kawamura Minato. 2009. "Heisei bungaku towa nanika?"
imidas: https://imidas.jp/jijikaitai/l-40-067-09-01-g148

Sasaki Toshinao. 2019. *Jikan to tekunorojii* [*Time and Technology*]. Tokyo: Kobunsha.

Shigesato Tetsuya and Kōichirō Sukegawa. 2019. *Heisei bungaku towa nandatta no ka*. Kamakura: Harukaze Shobō.

Shimazaki Satoko. 2016. *Edo Kabuki in Transition: From the Worlds of the Samurai to the Vengeful Female Ghost*. New York: Columbia University Press.

Takemitsu Tōru. 1996. "Dokusho no yōtai." In *Jikan no entei.* Tokyo: Shinchōsha.

Yomota Inuhiko. 2016. "Kaisetsu, Anfuramansu no kioku." In *Ryūseki*, by Asabuki Mariko. Tokyo: Shinchōsha.

Yoshida Ken'ichi. 1998. *Jikan*. Tokyo: Kōdansha.

Yōsuke, Matsumoto Keiichiro, and Ōkami Funiku. 2016. *Utsukushii Nihon no haikyo* [*Beautiful Japanese Ruins*]. Tokyo: MdN Corp.

Mathew W. Thompson, Sophia University

Making Love to the Past in Takagi Nobuko's *Narihira*

> The lover's mind vacillates between three ideas:
> 1. She is perfect.
> 2. She loves me.
> 3. How can I get the strongest possible proofs of her love?
> (Stendhal [1822] 2004, 47)

The focus of this chapter is Takagi Nobuko's *Shōsetsu Ise monogatari: Narihira* (*Narihira: A 'Tales of Ise' Novel*), which was serialized in the evening edition of *Nihon Keizai Shinbun* between January 4 and December 28, 2019, before appearing as a single volume in May of the following year. True to its title, *Narihira* is a novelistic adaptation of the Heian period classic *Ise monogatari* (*The Tales of Ise*), a collection of short, anecdotal stories about the life, liaisons, and poetic exchanges of an unnamed "man" who has been (and continues to be) associated exclusively with the famed ninth century poet Ariwara no Narihira (825-880). In Takagi's hands, the laconic prose and narrative lacunae that are so characteristic of the classical text are fleshed out and elaborated upon; the end result can perhaps be best described as an unabashed tribute to a very idealized Narihira, a man who, in spite of the pain it brings him, chooses to devote himself wholeheartedly to the ways of love and poetry. But despite any changes made to the original plot or any narrative cosplay imposed upon the character Narihira, there is nothing new about how Takagi's *Narihira* relates to and reveres its source material. It is, in other words, only the most recent in a long series of commentaries, translations, and reinterpretations that have attempted to breathe new life into *Ise monogatari*, helping contemporary readers make sense of its poetry and its protagonist and thereby securing the text's privileged position within Japan's literary canon for the last millennium.

As a novelistic adaptation, however, *Narihira* translates more than just the classical text it is based on; it also translates the Heian period and imperial court culture as a literary space for modern consumption, and thus is part of the process by which the past is continually made subject to the present in Japan today. I suggest that *Narihira* is a love story in two overlapping ways: it is as much about love in the past—the various encounters that structure the cultural memory of Ariwara no Narihira's life—as it is a novel that makes love to the past. In *Narihira*, the Heian past, ultimately unknowable and untranslatable, is crystallized as an idealized expression of courtly elegance (*miyabi*), a figurative lover for the modern reader.

Takagi Nobuko

The task of introducing Takagi Nobuko 髙樹のぶ子 (1946-) is not an easy one. At a glance, the list of awards and accolades she has received since she began writing at the end of the 1970s would suggest an author who has been a central figure within literary circles. She established herself early in her career, receiving the illustrious Akutagawa Prize in 1984 for the novella *Hikari idaku tomo yo* (*To a Friend Embracing the Light*, 1983). She has since gone on to receive the Tanizaki Prize in 1999 for *Tōkō no ki* (*Translucent Tree*, 1999), the Kawabata Yasunari Prize in 2010 for *Tomosui* (*Inhale*, 2010), and the Japan Art Academy Prize in 2017 for her distinguished contribution to the literary arts, among numerous others. And yet, for such a well-credentialed and productive writer (she has published over 60 novels or collections of short stories), Takagi and her works have received little critical attention. Aside from several novels that have been adapted for television or film, her name has been conspicuously absent from scholarly discussions of contemporary Japanese literature, both inside and outside of Japan,[1] and only one novel and two short stories have been translated into English.[2]

Certainly, one reason for this ambivalent treatment is that, as a writer, Tagaki does not slip neatly into any of the categories or genres that are so often brought to bear on the field of contemporary Japanese writers in order to serve them up in a manner that is readily digestible by the public. This is not to say that her writing tends toward obscure or avant-garde challenges to the stylistic boundaries of postwar fiction, for it does not—she prefers to call herself a down-to-earth *shōsetsuka*, a novelist, as opposed to the more intellectually elevated *bungakusha*, or literary writer (Gotō 2000). Nor is it to suggest that her oeuvre is so diverse or eclectic that she does not have a fixed reputation: she has experimented in a variety of styles, but is first and foremost known as a writer of love stories. Rather, Takagi does not fit any conventional categories because her works are characterized best by the liminal space they occupy. In the 1980s, when Takagi began writing in earnest, there was a reaction against the structurally fragmented and often intellectually challenging narratives that predominated in the 1960s and 1970s, and a consequent movement in literature toward novels that incorporated elements of myth and folktales or otherwise placed a strong emphasis on storytelling. Takagi rode the wave of this trend in her works, and one result was that she found herself caught between the Scylla of novels that entertained on one side and the Charybdis of pure literature on the other. Neither extreme suited her, but she found it difficult to navigate her own path. In 1999, after winning the Tanizaki Prize, Takagi reflected on her twenty-year career, which by that point included successful publications in literary magazines (*shōsetsu zasshi*), women's magazines (*fujin zasshi*), and newspaper serializations, each representing a different target audience in the world of Japanese publishing. "I could make my home in any one of them," she wrote, "and yet it seemed that none of them wanted to take me in" (1999a, 319).

If Takagi was, and continues to be, a literary exile of sorts—too intellectual for mass consumption but too story-driven for more critical tastes—then one factor that has contributed to this displacement, and also is one of the defining characteristics of her writing, is her association with love stories. Although love is a near-universal element of contemporary fiction, the love story as a genre, the principal intention of which is to portray love not as romance but as a disruptive, often violent transformation, is less commonly seen. Given its ubiquity in other narrative media, its liability to be mistaken for mere emotional gratification, and the nebulous boundary it shares with the topics of sex and sexuality, few writers with literary aspirations seem willing to try their hand at love stories.

But it is precisely within this milieu that Takagi has established her reputation. She is known primarily as a writer of contemporary love stories that explore the dynamics of human passion, both erotic and Platonic, conventional and taboo (see, for example, Yonaha 2006). Her approach to the subject matter is distinctive. On the one hand, Takagi does not use love to argue a point; there are no lessons to be learned, nor does it contain the promise of growth or a coming-of-age. Instead, she depicts love as a series of aesthetic moments that enable lovers to sublimate the anxiety and ecstasy of their metamorphosis. There is nothing romantic or spiritual about Takagi's love stories; love is an unrelenting force of nature, a tide that ebbs and flows with the bodies and lives it inhabits. This emphasis on the body and sensuality is, on the other hand, another characteristic of Takagi's style. Indeed, her writing often leaves little to the imagination. One critic noted, with tongue in cheek, that Takagi's detailed sex scenes cast very few shadows, an ironic twist given that she won a prize named after Tanizaki Jun'ichirō, author of the well-known aesthetic treatise *In'ei raisan* (*In Praise of Shadows*, 1933).[3] Much of the attention that Takagi has garnered as a writer of love stories stems from her willingness to explore topics that are unconventional or taboo, and her interest is in characters who remain loyal to their desires no matter the social or moral cost to themselves.

This reputation for passion and subversion of conventional morality has, in turn, been heightened by the narrative of her own life that Takagi has shared with readers. Early in her thirties, she chose to leave her husband of eight years to sustain an affair with a married man. Takagi's own love story, however, came with a heavy cost: she was forced to sever all bonds with her three-year-old son. It is perhaps not surprising that critics have tended to locate traces of these traumatic events in the themes of passion and betrayal that populate Takagi's stories (Gotō 2000, 60-61; Yonaha 2006, 11). Much like Murakami Haruki's well-documented love of music or Murata Sayaka's experience working at a convenience store, the personal life of the author becomes an integral part of the marketing and reception of her works, veiling them in the likeness of truth and credibility.

Putting aside for the moment the ethical and aesthetic questions surrounding the postmodern fetish for authenticity, we might note that Takagi is not the first writer in Japanese history who has been shrouded in the persona of a passionate woman willing to do anything for love. Ono no Komachi (ninth century) and Izumi Shikibu (978-?) were two of the most celebrated poets of the Heian period, and the reception of their poetry is inextricably bound up with their notoriety as women who, it was imagined, were involved in numerous affairs. Structured by the moral landscape of premodern Buddhism, female sexuality tended to be viewed as a pernicious force capable of hindering the pursuit of salvation in both men and women. As a result, while the poems of Komachi and Shikibu were recognized as masterpieces, the poets themselves came to be remembered as little more than stereotypes of female attachment, women who inevitably suffered the karmic consequences of indulging their desires when they were young and beautiful.

The epistemic changes that redefined the concepts of art and beauty in the nineteenth and twentieth centuries released writers like Komachi and Shikibu from the moral condemnation of their sexuality, but that sexuality continued to define them: the historical legacy of their cultural memory, reified by the performance of gender in modern Japan, ensured that their reputations and works would remain bound up with the concept of love. Although they may be respected for it now, Komachi and Shikibu will always be associated with a particularly elegant expression of passion and longing, not because that is all they wrote about, but because that is all we are conditioned to remember. There is nothing in the career of Takagi that invites us to make a direct connection with Heian writers like Komachi and Shikibu, yet we can say that their reputations are intertwined with the same gender values, and the same metaphors, that have shaped the conceptualization of women's literature since the Meiji period. Takagi, in other words, co-opts and is co-opted by a discourse that has associated modern women writers with the concept of miyabi: with the body, with passion, and with a psychological interiority focused on emotion, all qualities that are invariably traced to classical prose and poetry.

Viewed from this perspective, Takagi's creation of love stories grounded in novelistic adaptations of classical works does not seem unexpected, but her foray into this subgenre, one that has a well-established tradition in postwar publishing, took place only very recently in her career. She described this turn towards the past and Japan's classical legacy as a long-anticipated goal, a change of course that she felt was appropriate once she had approached her seventies (2021b, 246). With this shift, Takagi joined a small circle of well-established writers, such as Tanabe Seiko (1928-2019) and Hayashi Mariko (1954-), who have worked extensively with the adaptation or translation of classical literature. Takagi's first adaptation was *Shōjo ryōiki* (*A Girl's Record of Miraculous Events*, 2014), a series of semi-episodic stories that follow the adventures of a young woman, Asuka, whose life becomes interwoven with the karmic cycles of cause and effect, sin and punishment—building upon the Buddhist anecdotes narrated in the early ninth century *Nihon ryōiki* (*Record of Miraculous Events in Japan*).[4] The second was *Shōsetsu Ise monogatari: Narihira*. And it is with this re-telling of *Ise monogatari* that Takagi joined a thousand-year-old tradition of interpretation and commentary that can be likened to a discursive love affair with the concept of miyabi and the legacy of waka poetry, the dominant poetic form throughout much of Japanese history.

The Making of a Modern Narihira

Takagi deserves considerable praise for what she accomplished with *Narihira* because *Ise monogatari* is not a text that lends itself easily to a novelistic adaptation. Few classical texts present as many challenges to the reader, the commentator, or the translator. This was as true eight hundred years ago as it is today. In part this is due to the history of the text's development: conventional wisdom has it that *Ise monogatari* was not authored as such; it was instead written, compiled, edited, and played with over centuries by many minds and many hands before its status as a classic—a text that must be codified and preserved intact—preempted any further alterations. The entire process likely began in the late ninth century and arguably only ended with Fujiwara Teika (1162-1241), who collated and compiled several manuscripts that became the definitive version in the following centuries.[5]

A more significant challenge that *Ise monogatari* presents as a text is the form it takes, and the interpretive conventions that particular form has encouraged. In structure it is a collection of 125 short passages—the shortest being only a few lines, the longest no more than several pages—each an individual "tale" that consists of one or more waka poems embedded in a lattice of simple, colorless prose. While the relationship between the poems and the prose in *Ise monogatari* is interdependent, it is also decidedly unequal: if the former are the undisputed stars of *Ise monogatari*, shaping the reader's emotional response to each tale, then the latter plays a supporting role, situating the poems within a narrative context. This interpretive interplay, in turn, was founded on the characteristics of poetic practice in the Heian period. Although waka poetry had many purposes in court society, from the practical to the romantic to the ceremonial, it was strongly associated with emotion, a means of taking "the human heart as its seed and bringing it forth as myriad leaves of words" (Ozawa and Matsuda 1994, 17). Constrained to only 31 syllables in length, however, waka poetry is not a form that is suited to telling an involved story or providing the background that explains the emotions in question. Even the pronouns are left unspoken, leaving many waka with no outward indication of who wrote them, who they were intended for, or why they were written in the first place. One consequence of this ambiguity was the pragmatic need to record waka in a manner that enables interpretation. Waka anthologies, for example, typically arrange poems by season or topic within individual chapters, allowing readers to situate them within a thematic structure. Likewise, they might list the names of the poet and the recipient, or even include a brief anecdote that outlines the circumstances of their composition. Another consequence, it must be presumed, was the encouragement of a certain curiosity, a tendency to think about waka as the lingering traces of an untold story. After all, something intriguing must have taken place to prompt the need to compose poetry. It is precisely the desire to tell stories like these that led to a text like *Ise monogatari*.

Viewed collectively, the episodes that make up *Ise monogatari* give an account of one man's life from his coming-of-age to his death, with a particular focus on his various romantic encounters, which range in tone from the acutely passionate to the gracefully elegant to the absurdly ironic. With one exception,[6] this man is never named, but there has never been any question of who he is: Ariwara no Narihira, the son of an imperial prince who achieved a modest career at court and earned a name for himself as a poet. For centuries the text's reception was—and continues to be—premised on the conceit that the poems can be associated with the historical Narihira, and thus function as traces of the decadent life he was rumored to have lived, the tantalizing circumstances of which are revealed by their inclusion within a tale told by waka. (In reality, only one quarter of the poems in *Ise monogatari* can be positively identified as Narihira's compositions; the rest are of unknown authorship or can be attributed to other poets.)

This association between poem and person—a metonymy that remains imaginary regardless of who the author of a given poem actually was—was the interpretive structure upon which *Ise monogatari* was composed and transmitted over time. As a result, there has always been the temptation to read *Ise monogatari* as a biography of Narihira's life. If we make the attempt, something approximating the following narrative emerges: The man, who has just come of age (*uikōburi*) politically, experiences a romantic coming-of-age as well when he encounters two beautiful sisters while out hunting (episode 1).[7] Later, he forms an illicit attachment with Fujiwara no Takaiko,[8] a woman who is destined to become a consort of Emperor Seiwa. Takaiko's family learns of the affair and takes steps to ensure that the man is no longer able to see her (episodes 3 and 4). After attempting (and failing) to run away with Takaiko, the man becomes disgusted with life in the capital and decides to journey to the east with several close companions (episode 9). Later in his life, the man is appointed an imperial huntsman and sent as a messenger to the Ise Shrine, where he spends a bewildering night with the Ise Priestess, Princess Yasuko,[9] (episodes 69-72), for whom sexual liaisons of any kind were strictly forbidden. Back in the capital, the man comes to serve Prince Koretaka,[10] who takes religious vows after losing the imperial succession to Emperor Seiwa (episodes 82-83). The story ends after the man falls ill and he composes a poem that suggests his death is imminent (episode 125).

The portrait of the man—let us bow to tradition and call him "Narihira"—that emerges from these details is that of a tragic lover and down-on-his-luck courtier, an old-fashioned, elegant dandy with a gift for poetry who cares more about following the dictates of his heart than he does for pursuing a career. He is an impetuous lover, willing to violate even the strongest moral and political taboos in the name of passion. He is also a friend and loyal companion, willing to honor Prince Koretaka even after he becomes the victim of political machinations and loses his influence over affairs at court. The problem with this narrative, and the pleasant image of Narihira it conveys, however, is how loosely most of the remaining episodes contribute to it. They feature a parade of different liaisons, each with no apparent connection to what comes before or after. In some episodes he is an earnest, innocent lover; in others he is an old hand playing a familiar game; and in still others he is a glib, shallow caricature of a gallant. There is, in short, little consistency to be found. It is precisely this lack of uniformity and the questions it raises that has shaped *Ise monogatari*'s reception since it first appeared.

As we would expect of any text that has occupied the position of a respected, canonical work for over 1,000 years, each successive era of Japanese history favored a different interpretation of *Ise monogatari* as part of the process of keeping the text relevant and translating it into more contemporaneous social values. And needless to say, the real Narihira, whatever his romantic attachments, political alliances, or poetic intentions, had little bearing on this textual development. From its outset, when the first poem was framed within a lattice of prose, the man of *Ise monogatari* has always been a product of the imagination, a consequence of both the lingering traces of its historical era in cultural memory and the various hermeneutics that have structured the reception of waka poetry. For example, one particularly persistent feature of commentaries on *Ise monogatari* has been a tendency to read Narihira's performance of miyabi throughout the text as a critique of the rapacious ambitions of the Fujiwara, who dominated court politics in the ninth century. Narihira, in other words, became a figure of resistance through which later generations of disaffected courtiers voiced their discontent with the status quo—an elegant lover who embodied a form of elegant protest (Okada 1991, chaps. 3-5). Likewise, his affair with Fujiwara no Takaiko became not just a violation of imperial prerogatives but a satirical transgression that undermined one of the pillars of Fujiwara hegemony (Marra 1991, chap. 2).

Similarly, the reception of Heian court literature like *Ise monogatari* has been entangled in moral and intellectual polemics that have been mobilized to justify, or apologize for, their focus on passion and sexuality. Throughout the Kamakura and Muromachi periods, for example, the practice of waka, which had previously been questioned by moralists for its sins of "wild, frivolous speech" (*kyōgen kigo*) and sensual content, came to be widely reevaluated as an "expedient means" (*hōben*), a type of allegory that could aid in the transmission and understanding of Buddhist doctrine. As one of the foremost poets of the past, and as the titular hero of one of the most respected poetic texts, Narihira was unavoidably elevated by this discourse. It was not uncommon for commentaries to describe Narihira as a Buddhist deity who chose to dwell in this world to reveal the meaning of the dharma through *Ise monogatari*, or to blithely suggest that all of the over three thousand women with whom Narihira purportedly formed attachments were able to achieve Buddhahood due to his affections (Klein 2003, 133; Bowring 1992, 462-463).[11] Later, in the seventeenth and eighteenth centuries, the literary reputation of Narihira as a lover extraordinaire became a convenient source material for new genres of prose that sought to capitalize on the urban demand for literature that playfully and candidly explored themes of sexuality and love (*kōshoku*). These decidedly more earthy portrayals of Narihira stood in stark, ironic contrast to the concomitant attempts made by nativist *kokugaku* scholars who sought to reaffirm the cultural and intellectual importance of the "national tradition" of classical texts like *Man'yōshū* (*Collection of Myriad Leaves*, c. 875), *Ise monogatari*, and *Genji monogatari* (*The Tale of Genji*, c.

1008). Writers and philologists like Kamo no Mabuchi (1697-1769) and Motoori Norinaga (1730-1801) weaponized Narihira, Genji, and other protagonists in a bid to shift Japan's intellectual focus away from Chinese texts and toward native ones.

As definitions of literature shifted in response to the introduction of Western ideas in the Meiji period, and as the politics of national identity spurred a series of subsequent reinterpretations of the Heian period's position within the cultural legacy of Japanese history throughout the twentieth century, the association between court literature and love took on a new urgency. The topic of love, rich with its links to realism, became one of the central concerns of the modern novel and one of the most potent means by which the self could give expression to the modern experience. As such, no longer were court tales stigmatized for morally questionable content, nor were they venerated solely for the role they played in the foundation of the waka poetic tradition. Instead, elevated by their new position as part of an established canon of national literature, Heian works like *Ise monogatari* were rediscovered as expressions of a national ethos. Within this brave new world, the memory of Narihira was shackled by *Ise monogatari*'s status as a classic, creating an expectation for it to transmit the cultural legacy of the imperial court to modern readers both inside and outside of Japan. For centuries prior Narihira had been associated with poetic wit, old-fashioned manners, and a stylish ennui, all characteristics interlaced with historical conceptions of miyabi—but such elegance stemmed more from his links with the tradition of waka poetry (an elegant pursuit *par excellence*) than from his character. By the late twentieth century, however, the identity of Narihira became all but inseparable from the concept of miyabi, which in turn became deeply entangled with both the memory of the imperial court and the discourse on Japanese aesthetics in the postwar period.

There is perhaps no better illustration of this trend than Takagi's *Shōsetsu Ise monogatari: Narihira*. The novel tells a story of Narihira's life that draws extensively from the poetry in *Ise monogatari*, but its tone and structure could not be more different from the original. *Narihira* begins with Narihira as a young man of fifteen years with a gift for poetry and a penchant for playing the lover. After "coming-of-age" through an experience that evokes the original—a hunt near the old capital and an unexpected but tantalizing glimpse of two young sisters—he spends the remainder of his youth pursuing a variety of different relationships, some tragically whimsical, others deeply sensual. In all of these encounters, Narihira is a man drawn unapologetically to the dark, shadow-filled chambers that provide the setting for his nocturnal visits, and to those fleeting moments when desire and need are sublimated into love.

The first major turning point of Narihira's life coincides with a period of court infighting that history remembers as the Jōwa incident,[12] which cements Fujiwara dominance at court and eventually results in the declining political fortunes of Narihira's friends and allies. Rather than struggle against the (historically inevitable) wave of Fujiwara hegemony, Narihira chooses to accept the bitter cup of his own political impotence and navigates the crisis by embracing his reputation as a harmless but talented poet and lover. This decision ultimately shapes the course of Narihira's life and leads him to form two attachments of particular intensity that define his character and his views on poetry: the first is with Fujiwara no Takaiko, the second with Princess Yasuko. Although Narihira cannot hide the fact that part of the allure he feels for Takaiko and Yasuko stems from their ties to power and the imperial family—legitimate access to which he was denied early in life due to the exile of his father, Prince Abo—he is nonetheless desperately, painfully in love with both women and willing to risk any worldly consequence for a chance to give form to his passion.

Takagi's *Narihira* ends much as *Ise monogatari* does: when faced with the prospect of his own mortality, Narihira uses poetry to reflect on the meaning of his life. Alone except for the presence of a single gentlewoman, a student of poetry and thus a vehicle for Narihira to pass along his art, his decline is far from celebratory, but neither is it tragic. Much like Edmond Rostand's Cyrano de Bergerac, though of very different temperament, Narihira is a man who lives his life on his own terms, a man who forsakes the lure of worldly success in favor of the pursuit of beauty, whether it takes the form of love, of loyal friendship, or of poetic composition. The quaint, tongue-in-cheek nostalgia for the lost refinement of miyabi from an older, simpler time in the original is transformed here into the essence of Narihira's character. In Takagi's own words: "The way Narihira lived his life was *miyabi* itself" (2021a, 240). Combined with the aesthetic elegance of Narihira's behavior is the soft and romantic refinement of his surroundings, a vision of space, of nature, and of the city in the Heian period that smooths the hard edges of court society into an idyllic still-life. There is, in short, a reduction that takes place within the novel: Narihira is a beautifully rendered caricature, a distillation of everything a Heian lover is imagined to be in postwar Japan. And by conforming so closely to this fetish for miyabi, he becomes a kind of surrogate, or *katami*, to borrow a concept from *Genji monogatari*—a means for the modern reader to make love to a past that no longer speaks for itself, and proof the past makes love to us in return by answering our every expectation.

Love in the Past, Love for the Past

Shōsetsu Ise monogatari: Narihira lives up to its title in that it is, in many ways, a faithful adaptation of *Ise monogatari*. Although it takes numerous liberties with the structure and content of the original text—necessary changes given the challenge of replacing an episodic poem-tale with a character-focused novel—*Narihira* also expresses an unabashed reverence for its source material, particularly the poetry. Although the order of their appearance differs markedly, Takagi's novel contains roughly two thirds of the poetry found in the original, each of which is reproduced in its original classic Japanese. In every instance, these poems are followed by a short explanation, a modern language commentary delivered as part of the narration that translates the intent of the waka for contemporary readers. Takagi's preoccupation with the original text is also visible in how she situates the poetry within the larger story. While not episodic in nature, the contents of nearly every chapter of *Narihira* are nonetheless structured around the circumstances behind the composition of individual poems even as they serve to advance the plot. If *Ise monogatari* can be understood as a series of short, prose scaffolds that frame and contextualize a selection of waka, *Narihira* can be understood as an extended narrative that provides more embellished chronological and psychological context—precisely the kind required in a novel—for the episodes outlined in *Ise monogatari*. The net effect is that of multiple, intertextual layers of commentary.

The use of the word "commentary" here should not be understood as an inadvertent byproduct of *Ise monogatari*'s transformation into the novel *Narihira*. The latter may take the form of a fictional biography of Ariwara no Narihira, but far more intriguing is the manner in which it participates in and adapts the theories, conjectures, and patterns of reading that have surrounded *Ise monogatari* for over one thousand years. Narihira's romantic encounter with the Priestess of the Ise Shrine stands out as an episode that has garnered considerable attention from commentators over the years, and Takagi's version of the event in *Narihira* suggests that she translates elements of that tradition from commentary as much from as the original text.

In *Ise monogatari*, episode 69 plays out as an ambiguously worded story of frustrated desire. Narihira, serving as imperial huntsman, journeys to the Ise Shrine where he is entertained by the Priestess, Princess Yasuko. Late that night she visits him, and although he leads her to his chambers, we are told that she leaves several hours later without exchanging a single word with him. The following day they exchange poems that reflect upon the dream-like quality of their encounter, as though neither is sure of what, if anything, really happened. The suggestive ambiguity of the passage is further heightened by the taboo that such a liaison would necessarily entail. For the Priestess of the Ise Shrine, maintaining a state of physical and spiritual purity was a sacred duty, and any relations with a man risked undermining divine support for the emperor's reign. Later medieval commentaries on episode 69 were predictably preoccupied with the question of what happened while Narihira and the Priestess were alone together. At stake was not simply Narihira's reputation as amorous poet and lovable rascal but also the reputation of the *Ise monogatari* and the privileged position the text had come to occupy within the tradition of waka poetry. The opinion of Heian readers, however, seems to have fallen on the side of scandal: by the mid-Heian period it was a well-established rumor that Narihira not only had an affair with Princess Yasuko, but also that she gave birth to a son as a result.[13]

In *Narihira*, the encounter with the Priestess of the Ise Shrine, which occupies a significant portion of the final third of the novel, expands greatly on the general outline of events as they are found in *Ise monogatari*, and at the same time, seems to draw inspiration from the various forms of commentary and rumor that circulated widely. Although the nebulous, ethereal quality of the original meeting is preserved in *Narihira*, thus conforming to the outline of episode 69, it offers narrative clarity to the reader by giving its protagonist another chance: 10 days later, Narihira manages another liaison with the Priestess by sneaking into the inner precincts of the Ise Shrine by boat.[14] Throughout both encounters Princess Yasuko is depicted as a forlorn victim of court politics. She and her brother, Prince Koretaka, have lost their influence at court due the stranglehold the Fujiwara have on court politics. Her appointment as Priestess is only further proof of the impotence of her maternal relatives, the backing of whom was essential for the careers of imperial offspring. Not only does this suggest a form of political exile, but her duties require that she sacrifice any real possibility of love for the reign of an emperor who has shown her nothing but contempt. As the son of a prince who likewise found himself on the wrong side of court machinations, it is only Narihira who understands and appreciates Princess Yasuko as the young woman she is. Although the burden of guilt and sin ensures that their affair lasts but a single night and that they will never be able to see each other again, Narihira later receives word that their union resulted in a child. He is allowed to see and hold the child one time—a final piece of himself that he is forced to cede in the face of political necessity—before the boy is given to the care of the Takashina family.

Typical of Takagi's writing, there are no villains or antagonists in *Narihira*; nonetheless, these scenes function as a soft-spoken condemnation of the Fujiwara and their usurpation of power from the imperial family. As two figures who are marginalized for their family connections, Narihira and Princess Yasuko's affair is suggestive of an aesthetic insurrection, a means to restore dignity and autonomy to the imperial family, accomplished not with power or ambition but rather with love and the ideal of miyabi. Similar to the qualities attributed to waka poetry in the preface of *Kokin wakashū*, Takagi's Narihira is a man whose way of life can inspire pity in gods and demons, bring peace to the relations between men and women, and quell the fierce hearts of warriors (Ozawa and Matsuda 1994, 17).

Narihira is meticulously researched and there is beauty and an artistry in the way that Takagi stitches together the disparate narrative nodes of *Ise monogatari* with various traditions of commentary. It clings faithfully to the centuries-old view that Narihira's love affairs and poetry embodied an implicit critique of court intrigue and the rise of the Fujiwara. It lays bare all the major relationships and infidelities that Narihira has been suspected of over the years and gives them an air of historicity and credibility by yoking them to the poetry of *Ise monogatari* and to historical events such as the Jōwa and Ōtenmon incidents.[15] The novel juxtaposes what it describes as the emotional sincerity of Narihira's waka poetry, written in Japanese, with the artifice and formality of the Chinese poetry (*kanshi*) that was more prestigious in the early Heian period, a stance that echoes the *kokugaku* rhetoric in the eighteenth and nineteenth centuries.

In its final chapters, *Narihira* pays creative homage to one of the oldest theories of *Ise monogatari*'s origins: that it was compiled by—and took its name from—the well-known poet Lady Ise (c. 875-c. 938), who was thought to have been Narihira's lover despite being born only a few years before his death in 880. Takagi's novel, in short, renders *Ise monogatari* and Narihira in a way that is functionally little different from the centuries of commentary it borrows so much from. Even as it is premised on a reverence for the classic it adapts, *Narihira* structures and regulates our understanding of *Ise monogatari* much as that text binds and contextualizes our reading of the poetry that is contained within its prose. One unavoidable effect is that much of the ambiguity and uncertainty of the original text is sacrificed to conform to Takagi's aesthetic vision of Narihira's character.

One of the features of *Ise monogatari* that has long troubled scholars and commentators is the erratic portrayal of "the man." In certain episodes he exhibits the miyabi he is so often remembered for, but in others he is just as likely to come across as a buffoon, an incorrigible rake, or a cruel, vindictive lover. Despite the sometimes contradictory messages of the source material it adapts, *Narihira*, compelled by the formal constraints of the novelist's genre, planes over the rough spots of Narihira's character. Every chance encounter he stumbles upon, every poem he sends or receives, every darkened room where sound and smell and touch come alive, every romantic setback and political disappointment—all contribute to the portrait of Narihira as a man of passionate desires, heightened sensitivity to beauty, and an artless grace and refinement. The aesthetic uniformity of this portrayal is in turn inseparable from the depiction of love in the novel. Narihira loves as he lives. Although his many affairs end in bitterness or misery of one kind or another, *Narihira* nonetheless presents each romantic encounter as a shared moment of unadulterated beauty and sincerity. And the waka poetry that so often flows out of such scenes—a natural manifestation of insuppressible emotion—seems to anticipate the ideal articulated by the renowned waka poet Ki no Tsurayuki several decades after Narihira's death: waka is the means to give voice to the feelings in our hearts (Ozawa and Matsuda 1994, 17).

In this regard, Takagi's characterization of Narihira, in particular the aesthetic ideal he embodies as a lover, is all but indistinguishable from the cultural legacy of waka poetry as it has come to be imagined in postwar Japan. In the final chapters of the story, as his health begins to fade, Narihira spends his time reflecting on the life he has lived and the poetry he has written with a young, precocious gentlewoman known only as Ise. He faces his own death with the hope that he has helped to usher in a new age for waka poetry, and through it a more transparent, sincere form of literary expression. Concerning love, he has suffered many disappointments in life, but he regrets none of them. He has come to recognize that within the bitter inevitability of endings there is not just pain but also beauty. The implication behind his conversations with Ise—whose hand, the reader is invited to assume, is ultimately responsible for preserving Narihira's poems and thus beginning the long process of *Ise monogatari*'s compilation—is that Narihira's poetic ideals anticipate with uncanny precision the rise of waka's popularity towards the end of the ninth century. As such, his sensibilities lay the foundation for the *mono no aware* aesthetic—i.e., the inclination to see beauty and feel pity in response to the sadness invoked by ephemerality—that plays a central role in how the classics of Heian literature such as *Genji monogatari* are remembered today.

There is, in other words, a pronounced preoccupation with the past that runs throughout the novel *Narihira* and the character of Narihira. It is a vision of Heian court culture and poetic practice drawn from the popular imagination, a tapestry woven with lofty reverence directed at classical literature for its warp and the soft elegance of miyabi for its weft. It is a collective reverie in which the past is idealized by and at the same time made subject to the present, becoming both the intimate lover and the ineffable other. In this way, Takagi and *Narihira* participate in the creation of what Naoki Sakai calls a "structure of visibility": together with other presentations of Heian period culture that appear in mass media, film, manga, etc., it makes visible a wholly invisible past as though in confirmation of what had previously been only imagined (1999, chap. 3). And, as Stendhal coyly remarks in his treatise on the nature of love: "Only through imagination can you be sure that your beloved is perfect in any given way" ([1822] 2004, 51). *Narihira* is, thus, a love story twice over: a novel in which Narihira makes love to the Heian court, and an adaptation of a classic that allows the modern reader to make love to the past.

---

1 Aside from a handful of short pieces in literary magazines, the most noteworthy critical work is *Takagi Nobuko: Gendai josei sakka yomihon,* vol. 6 (2006), edited by Yonaha Keiko, who, to my knowledge, is the only scholar to write about Takagi repeatedly.

2 *Translucent Tree*, translated by Deborah Iwabuchi (2008), "The Shadow of the Orchid" ("Ran no kage"), translated by Avery Fischer Udagawa (2006), and "Melk's Golden Acres" ("Meruku no ōgonbatake"), translated by Dink Tanaka (2011).

3 The critic, Ikezawa Natsuki, was in fact one of the members of the Tanizaki Prize committee (Ikezawa et al. 1999).

4 *Shōjo Ryōiki* has since been republished under the title *Asuka-san no Ryōiki* (*A Record of Asuka's Miraculous Events*), 2020.

5 For a clear, concise account of the various theories that attempt to trace the origins of *Ise monogatari*, see Mostow and Tyler (2010, 3-5).

6 Episode 63 of *Ise monogatari* stands alone in giving a name to the protagonist. There is general agreement that this episode is a very late addition to the text, made perhaps by an overzealous commentator.

7 All references to episodes within *Ise monogatari* are based on the *Tenpuku-bon* printed in the *Shinpen Nihon koten bungaku zenshū* series. See Katagiri et al. (1994).

8 Also known as the Nijo Empress, Fujiwara no Takaiko (842-910) played an instrumental role in the Fujiwara's rise to power in the ninth century. Before she became an imperial consort at the age of 25, it was rumored that she had taken Narihira as a lover.

9 Princess Yasuko (848?-913) was the daughter of Emperor Montoku and Ki no Shizuko. Her appointment as Ise Priestess was precipitated by the declining fortunes of her maternal family, which lost their power struggle with the Fujiwara.

10 Prince Koretaka (844-897), the brother of Princess Yasuko, had expected to follow emperor Montoku to the throne, only to be replaced as imperial heir by a much younger Fujiwara prince.

11 For example, Fujiwara no Tameaki's *Gyokuden jinpi no maki* (*Jeweled Transmission of Deep Secrets*, c. 1273-1278) and *Aro monogatari* (*A Tale of Crows and Herons*, late fifteenth century).

12 The Jōwa incident, which took place in 842, was a series of political machinations orchestrated by Fujiwara no Yoshifusa (804-872) and his allies, which resulted in the future Emperor Montoku becoming crown prince.

13 By the early eleventh century, Narihira's illegitimate son was thought to be Takashina Moronao (d. 917?), who had been adopted by Takashina Shigenori, a high-ranking official at the Ise Shrine. See, for example, Suzuki (2013, 225-230) and Mostow and Tyler (2010, 150-151).

14 This chapter in *Narihira* features the poem found in episode 70 of *Ise monogatari*, in which the man recites a waka to one of the Ise Priestess' attendants, seemingly asking how he can visit the woman he longs for. Although this episode was treated as a chronological continuation of the events founds in episode 69 by centuries of commentators and scholars, it does little to clarify the details of Narihira's relationship with Princess Yasuko.

15 The Ōtenmon incident refers to a fire that destroyed the main gate of the imperial palace in 866. After various accusations were raised, the fire was ultimately blamed on Tomo no Yoshio (811-868), a rival of Fujiwara.

References

Gotō Masaharu. 2000. "Gengai no shōzō: Takagi Nobuko (shōsetsuka)—ren'ai wa kanarazu jikan ni yabureru mono desu." *Aera* 13, no. 10 (March): 60-64.

Ikezawa Natsuki, Marutani Saiichi, Kōno Taeko, Inoue Hisashi, Hino Keizō, and Tsutsui Tasutaka. 1999. "Heisei 11 nendo Tanizaki Jun'ichirō shō happyō—Jushōsaku 'Tōkō no ki' Takagi Nobuko." In *Chūō kōron* 114, no. 11 (November): 314-318.

Katagiri Yōichi, Fukui Teisuke, Takahashi Shōji, and Shimizu Yoshiko, eds. 1994. *Taketori monogatari, Ise monogatari, Yamato monogatari, Heichū monogatari: Shinpen Nihon koten bungaku zenshū.*, vol. 12. Tokyo: Shōgakukan.

Klein, Susan Blakely. 2003. *Allegories of Desire: Esoteric Literary Commentaries of Medieval Japan*. Cambridge: Harvard University Asia Center.

Marra, Michele. 1991. *Aesthetics of Discontent: Politics and Reclusion in Medieval Japanese Literature*. Honolulu: University of Hawai'i Press.

Mostow, Joshua and Royall Tyler. 2010. *The Ise Stories: Ise monogatari*. Honolulu: University of Hawai'i Press.

Okada, Richard. 1991. *Figures of Resistance: Language, Poetry, and Narrating in "The Tale of Genji" and Other Mid-Heian Texts*. Durham and London: Duke University Press.

Ozawa Masao and Matsuda Shigeho, eds. 1994. *Kokin wakashū: Shinpen Nihon koten bungaku zenshū*, vol. 11. Tokyo: Shōgakkan.

Sakai Naoki. 1999. *Translation and Subjectivity: On Japan and Cultural Nationalism*. Minneapolis: University of Minnesota Press.

Stendhal. (1822) 2004. *Love* [*De l'Amour*]. Translated by Gilbert Sale and Suzanne Sale. London: Penguin Books.

Suzuki Hideo. 2013. *Ise monogatari hyōkai*. Tokyo: Chikuma shobō.

Takagi Nobuko. 1999a. "'Awai' kara no dasshutsu." *Chūō kōron* 114, no. 11: 319-322.

———. 1999b. *Tōkō no ki*. Tokyo: Bungei shunjū.

———. 2006. "The Shadow of the Orchid." Translated by Avery Fischer Udagawa. In *Inside and Other Short Fiction*, edited by Ruth Ozeki, 203-233. Tokyo: Kodansha International.

———. 2008. *Translucent Tree*. Translated by Deborah Iwabuchi. New York: Vertical.

———. 2011. "Melk's Golden Acres." Translated by Dink Tanaka. In *Speculative Japan 2: "The Man Who Watched the Sea" and Other Tales*, 145-162. Yunomae Machi: Kurodahan Press.

———. 2020a. *Asuka-san no Ryōiki*. Tokyo: Ushio shuppansha.

———. 2020b. *Shōsetsu Ise monogatari: Narihira*. Tokyo: Nihon keizai shinbun shuppan honbu.

———. 2021a. "Narihira wa kotoba ni kokoro wo gyōshuku shita." *Voice* 517, no. 1 (January): 238-241.

———. 2021b. "Omoi wo koto no ha ni nosete." *Sekai* 940, no. 1 (January): 246-250.

Yonaha Keiko. 2006. "Takagi Nobuko no sakuhin sekai." In *Takagi Nobuko: Gendai josei sakka yomihon*, vol. 6, edited by Yonaha Keiko, 8-15. Tokyo: Kanae shobō.

Ⅱ. Plurilingual Literature and Storytelling

Shion Kono, Sophia University

Toward a Hybrid "Literature in Japanese": Japanese Literature in Plurilingual Contexts and the Case of Mizumura Minae's *An I-Novel*

In the contemporary literature scene in Japanese since the 1990s, there have been increasingly prominent writers working with multiple languages, and plurilingualism has emerged as a defining issue (Yiu 2000). For example, Levy Hideo (b. 1950) is a scholar of classical Japanese literature and a native speaker of English but has published several novels in Japanese. Tawada Yōko (b. 1960) writes fiction, poetry, and essays in Japanese and German and has won multiple prestigious literary prizes in both languages. On Yūjū (b. 1980; Chinese name: Wen Yourou) was born in Taiwan but grew up in a Japanese-language environment beginning at the age of three, and writes fiction and nonfiction exploring the space between languages. These authors, writing in more than one language and often not in their native tongue, challenge the notion that only a native speaker can write Japanese literature, or that Japanese literature is necessarily bound up with the idea of Japan, Japanese people, or Japanese culture.[1]

In recent scholarship, these authors are often referred to as "cross-border" (*ekkyō*) writers, or writers of "literature in Japanese" (*Nihongo bungaku*). But I wish to highlight the fact that they choose the language in which they write out of multiple linguistic options. Until recently, the issue of language choice has not been a significant theme in studies of modern Japanese literature, as there have been very few non-native Japanese-speaking authors who are proficient enough to create literature in Japanese, or native speakers with the ability to write in multiple languages beyond Japanese. However, language choice should not be treated as an exceptional issue, as Tawada emphasizes in *Exophony*, because "all the languages of creative writing have been chosen." Tawada adds: "The exophonic phenomenon compels one to ask the question about why a certain language has been chosen, as opposed to 'normal' literature that remains in the mother tongue—the question that has not been asked before" (2012, 8).[2]

In this essay, I will consider the issue of language choice in Mizumura Minae's (b. 1951) *An I-Novel* (*Shishōsetsu from Left to Right*, 1995), one of the most significant novels from the 1990s to the 2010s in terms of plurilingualism and literature in Japanese. Mizumura made her debut as a novelist with *Light and Dark Continued* (*Zoku meian*, 1990), a novel intended as a sequel to Natsume Sōseki's *Light and Dark* (1916). She has published several novels, including *A True Novel* (*Honkaku shōsetsu,* 2002) and *Inheritance from Mother* (*Shinbun shōsetsu: Haha no isan,* 2012). But she is perhaps best known to the wider reading public for *The Fall of Language in the Age of English* (*Nihongo ga horobiru toki*, 2009), in which she argues for the survival of national languages in a world where English has become dominant. Mizumura positions herself in juxtaposition to a writer like Haruki Murakami, who has adapted more to the current global literary market for translated literature. Yet Mizumura is one of the contemporary Japanese authors whose work is widely read in translation—and who perhaps, as Stephen Snyder points out, even benefits from the growing global interest in Japanese literature cultivated by Murakami (Snyder 2016).

Mizumura's *An I-Novel* revolves around the character "Minae," who, like the author herself, moved from Japan to the United States when she was twelve years old and was encouraged to write in English—but who, as a graduate student in French literature at an elite university on the East Coast, ultimately decided to write fiction in Japanese. Minae recounts many reminiscences and past conversations, capturing many episodes in her life vividly. Several photos are inserted throughout the novel and add realism. The novel touches upon several themes: her family history back in Japan, her stories of two Japanese girls growing up in the United States, and the prejudices and racial tensions around her Japanese expatriate communities.

In this chapter, I will read *An I-Novel* as a drama of language choice for a Japanese-born person growing up in the United States (and in the globalized world) in the late twentieth century. On this point, Mizumura, in an essay describing writing the novel, asserts: "My story is not just a how-I-became-a-writer story. It is a how-I-became-a-Japanese-writer story, and that story necessarily runs parallel to the story of how I failed to become a writer in the English language" (2004). Mizumura emphasizes that it is not just a novel about becoming a writer; it is a story about how she chose the language to write in. In particular, I will describe the intellectual and social contexts in which this choice was made, in order to highlight the historical significance of her decision.

I must clarify that it is the language choice of Minae, the protagonist and narrator of *An I-Novel*, that I wish to discuss here, through her thoughts and the events in her life that are depicted in the novel, and not that of the author Mizumura.[3] One issue that complicates the matter is the autobiographical nature of the novel, as the experience of Minae the character evidently echoes that of Mizumura the author. The literary structures of autofiction, the I-novel, and self-referentiality are all central in assessing the significance of this novel, which I will address below. Another issue for discussion is the question of what exactly it means for Minae to become a *Japanese* writer, when Mizumura says that the novel is "a how-I-became-a-Japanese-writer story." I contend that, ultimately, Minae's choice in this novel should be characterized as a move toward hybrid Japanese literature that Minae herself could not envision at the time she makes the decision.

Mizumura's *An I-Novel*, a bilingual work written in Japanese and English, was originally serialized from the October 1992 issue to the October 1994 issue of *Critical Space* [*Hihyō kūkan*], a critical theory journal co-edited by Karatani Kōjin and Asada Akira. The novel was then published in book form by Shinchōsha in October 1995 and later in the bunko paperback editions. The English edition of the novel, translated by Juliet Winters Carpenter, was published in 2021. Mizumura famously stated that "the only language into which it would be impossible to translate the work would be English," as the author tries to convey the "linguistic asymmetry" between English and any other language of the world (2004). This statement by Mizumura and the original bilingual form of the novel raise important questions about the issues of (un)translatability and linguistic hybridity, not only in terms of the novel itself, but in terms of the act of writing described in this novel. It is also important to note here that the novel has been significantly revised in each of these versions. As Carpenter, the translator for the English edition, notes, "In the course of translating *An I-Novel*, as often happens in literary translation, a variety of changes to the text were made as, working closely with Mizumura, I tried to keep, paradoxically, to the truth of the original novel" (2021, x). The present discussion is based on the English edition published in 2021 by Columbia University Press, unless otherwise noted; my reference for the bilingual edition is the 2009 Chikuma bunko edition.

The I-Novel, Autofiction, and Self-Referentiality

Let us closely consider the relationship between the protagonist and the author. In her aforementioned essay, Mizumura writes that this novel is "basically an autobiographical novel" (2004). Given the use of the same name, and the overlap between Minae the character's profile and Mizumura the author's publicly known profile, there seems to be consensus that the construction of the protagonist's life trajectory in this novel is intertwined with the author's own experience.

Mizumura's writing practice engages with existing genres both in modern Japanese literature and contemporary literature as a whole. The title of the novel refers to the genre of the "I-novel," or "*shishōsetsu*"—the autobiographical subgenre of *shōsetsu*, or narrative fiction—in modern Japanese literature. Is *An I-Novel* a shishōsetsu? The question is complicated because of the fluidity and ambiguity of the term. When narrowly defined, the I-novel refers to a style of fiction in the early twentieth century that, emerging from Japanese naturalist literature, aimed at representing the author's life truthfully. There have been attempts to define shishōsetsu as a genre (see Hijiya-Kirschnereit 1981) or to explain it as an effect of literary-critical discourse (see Suzuki 1996). The novel's title in English rather directly ties this work to the genre: in the original Japanese title as serialized in *Critical Space*, the words "Modern Japanese Literature" (*Nihon kindai bungaku*) precede what later becomes the novel's standard title in Japanese (*Shishōsetsu from Left to Right.*) However, the use of the term "I-novel" in this novel is quite ambivalent. Minae the character is aware of the connotation of the traditional sense of the term and tries to steer away from it in her own writing. She states: "If I were to build my own life in Japan, family would only be a guilt-inflicting, energy-depleting burden. I had no desire to start my new life in the style of the 'I-novel,' that confessional exposition of, often, too-binding family ties" (Mizumura 2021, 311). At the same time, the novel is full of trivial details, presumably from her personal life, which makes the novel "I-novel-like" in a broad sense.

Is *An I-Novel* a work of autofiction, then? Some early reviewers of the English translation mention the term "autofiction" in the discussion of the novel (see, e.g., Barekat 2021, Sacks 2021). One even associates the two concepts by stating, in the title of his review no less, that "Autofiction's First Boom Was in Turn-of-the-Century Japan" (Barekat). Coined by Serge Doubrovsky in the 1970s, the term has attracted much attention in contemporary literary circles. Scholars have debated over the precise definition of the term, and while there is no clear consensus, there are some characteristics that are frequently mentioned: "a combination of real and invented elements; onomastic correspondence between author and character or narrator; and stylistic and linguistic experimentation" (Effe and Lawlor 2022, 1). But is the genre of the I-novel a kind of autofiction, or vice versa? The scholar Justyna Kasza asks this very question and argues that the research model of approaching shishōsetsu as a form of autofictional writing would help expand the Eurocentric focus on the term "autofiction," and discusses *An I-Novel* in this context (2022). As these concepts continue to be critically re-evaluated,[4] Mizumura's novel is at the forefront of this examination, and is frequently mentioned in scholarship on autofiction.[5]

Regardless of this ambiguity, though, it is important to keep in mind that this is a novel about writing. *An I-Novel* depicts Minae's struggles, questioning, and search for understanding as she becomes a writer, seen through her monologic narration as well as the depiction of her own life. The autobiographical features of the novel suggest that it is a mirror of the author's own writing experience of the novel itself. I will come back to this issue of self-referentiality at the end of this chapter.

The Significance of a Language Choice

Now let us examine the nature of Minae's choice in language and in career. The novel unfolds within a day in the life of Minae, the fictional stand-in for the author Mizumura. It is dated in a diary entry on her computer as "Friday, December 13, 198X."[6] According to Minae, it was the twentieth anniversary of her family's "Exodus," i.e., their arrival in the United States from Japan. Minae was by then a graduate student preparing to take an oral exam. On this day, Minae and her sister Nanae have a long phone conversation in which Minae reveals to Nanae that she will try to become a novelist writing in Japanese. The fact that the entire novel is structured around this day implies the momentousness of the decision Minae conveys to her sister. In this section I will connect the details of Minae's life as described in the novel to illuminate the sociocultural contexts in which she finds herself and the concrete choices she has in front of her.

Minae's decision is a turning point in her life's trajectory, in that she will quit graduate school and pursue a career in writing. As a multilingual writer, she also has a choice of languages in which to write. Why does Minae decide on Japanese, a language she has very little experience writing in for much of her adult life? Why does she not opt to write in English, which she seems to do well after spending twenty years in the U.S.? Minae's choice of Japanese as a language for writing seems to be a big gamble given her lack of experience; writing in English would have been much more reasonable. When Minae explains her decision, she emphasizes her yearning for the language that has been fueled by her long-time reading of Japanese literature. Minae (the narrator) explains:

> In the final analysis, did not literature arise out of the deep desire to do something wondrous with a language? In my case, it was a desire to be born once again into my language so as to appreciate and explore it anew. As I spent ungodly amounts of time assembling futile strings of words in languages that remained foreign to me, this desire had grown inexorably, year by year, until my craving to write in Japanese now seemed intense enough to move mountains. (84)[7]

There are episodes in the novel about this desire and nostalgia for her native language, such as reading volumes of modern Japanese literature at home after immigrating, and writing her former address in Tokyo repeatedly in vertical script (237). However, having a strong and profound desire to write in Japanese is not a sufficient reason to pursue this path as a writer. As Nanae questions her, we learn that Minae had never written anything in Japanese prior to this decision (83). The novel lacks concrete episodes that document her ability to write in Japanese. Her decision to choose a career writing in Japanese just for the sake of attachment to the language is mysterious.

Since the novel does not provide a direct reason for Minae's decision to write in Japanese, I suggest we take an indirect approach: her decision can be better understood through the paths she does not choose. Until this point, Minae has had a solid career writing in English, and the novel includes episodes recounting her formative experiences as a student of English. If we analyze these episodes, we can identify several possibilities where her career options in English would be more realistic given her education and her training; and in some cases, they would have more securely situated her in mainstream literary trends. These options illuminate what she did *not* end up choosing, and in what circumstances she made that choice.

Learning English, Making a Career as a Writer

Each of these potential paths require further examination. First, as a graduate student in French literature, Minae could have become a researcher or a teacher in Western language and literature. Despite the instability of an academic career in humanities, if she were to receive a doctoral degree from an elite university, there is at least a realistic possibility of long-term employment in research or teaching. There is no such career path to becoming a creative writer and the employment prospects are far less stable. Although Minae seems to struggle in graduate school—signs of procrastination abound—at least she can make concrete progress as long as she follows an academic path.

Despite its relative practicality, though, the novel suggests that an academic career in Western literature poses a more fundamental question about her relationship with the English language, and, significantly, that question is linked to her memories about her teachers. Most prominently, the image of studying Western literature is tied to her graduate school mentor, whom Minae calls "Herr Professor." The professor is modeled after Paul de Man, the eminent scholar and critic under whom Mizumura (the author) studied while she was a graduate student at Yale University.[8] Herr Professor was born in a "small European country" and in his scholarly work he used English, French, and German superbly, although none of these was his native language. Minae writes: "His colleagues were in awe of his keen mind and the depth and breadth of his knowledge. He was European intellectualism incarnate" (256).

As a faculty member at one of the most prominent academic institutions in the United States, Herr Professor represents "European intellectualism," but Minae notes that she felt deprived of the opportunity to be the same kind of scholar. Minae recalls an episode when, as a high school student, she was engaged in watercolor painting, and her English teacher told her: "You know, you should be working on your English." Minae felt he was imposing English on her because she was an Asian immigrant. Minae's reminiscence of the moment reveals the line of her thinking:

> I somehow was certain that he would not have spoken in the same way if I were a French or German girl. Something told me that, for him, my language from faraway Asia was utterly unimportant—so inconsequential, in fact, that I would have been better off just forgetting it and devoting myself to learning English, the key to a better world. But my indignation must have gone deeper. What was the point of my learning the language if as an Asian girl I could have no legitimate claim to it? The children of Italian immigrants eventually became heirs not of **Dante** but of **Shakespeare**, but someone like myself could not be heir to English in the same way—so I must have believed somewhere deep down, however nebulously. I didn't so much believe it as sense it. (259)[9]

Minae reacted strongly to the English teacher's words, as "indignation" suggests. She sensed discrimination and condescension from the teacher. Significantly, the question of studying English was for her a matter of "becoming heir to English." The children of all European immigrants can inherit English, becoming "heir of Shakespeare," rather than heir to an author of their own national literature (e.g., Dante for an Italian girl). The teacher's comment was infuriating because this opportunity was closed for an Asian girl; it was her race, not her language ability, that mattered in inheriting English.

However, in graduate school, watching as Herr Professor suffers from cancer, Minae sees signs of a change:

> So it was in a way symbolic of the fall of the West that the flesh housing his spirit should be attacked by cancer cells. People with prewar classical educations were rapidly disappearing from academia. Western literature was being taught by people with no knowledge of Latin and Greek, and the spread of multiculturalism meant that introductory courses in literature now included as compulsory reading whole sections of *The Tale of Genji*. (258)

Minae sees in Herr Professor's decaying health some significant historic shifts that can be generally described as "the fall of the West" in American academia around the 1980s: the reduced emphasis on Western classical education, the spread of multiculturalism, and the broadening of the literary canon to include non-Western works such as *The Tale of Genji*. In this episode, Minae connects these changes to the issue of inheriting English, which for her is central to an existential question. English is no longer the main language of Western civilization, inheritable exclusively by children of European immigrants; it has now become a universal language. In *The Fall of Language in the Age of English*, Mizumura explains through the notion of "universal language" that English has become a language for knowledge and wisdom for all civilizations, not limited to a particular culture or civilization. In the context of Minae's personal question of linguistic inheritance, English had become a "language that even a non-native [speaker] could choose to inherit" (2021, 260). Perhaps there is a leap in Minae's logic here, as the fact that English has become available as a language she *could* inherit does not mean that she will actually do so. Perhaps Minae's view has been so skewed by the fact that she does not choose this path that, as we will see below, she looks back with some remorse.

A second career path for Minae—assuming she did claim an inheritance of English language—would be to become a novelist in English. Minae's friend from high school days, Sarah Bloom, who is herself an aspiring novelist, gives Minae a concrete suggestion for how to become an Asian female novelist in a multicultural age. Sarah says that "the more marginal you [are], the better." "You're a woman. You're Japanese. You're perfect. You have all the necessary attributes" (264). Sarah elaborates on this vision even further:

> "Oh, come on," Sarah replied instantly. "You can write about your grandmother."... "And about your mother," Sarah went on. "And about yourself." She elaborated, saying I could write about how my grandmother had died a prisoner of Oriental ignorance and superstition; how my mother, having grown up resenting that environment, was liberated by the American Occupation forces; and finally how I, the third generation, had become even more liberated thanks to my having landed in America. "The Americans would love that, especially the feminists! Maybe you can strike a movie deal. Oh, Minae, you'd be rich and famous!" (264-265)

Sarah Bloom's description of a female Asian novelist, half in jest, points to a starkly different situation for Minae after the rise of multiculturalism: being an Asian immigrant would now be an advantage, not a liability, and even offer the possibility of success. Even her family history about her grandmother and her mother would be something "[t]he Americans would love." What Sarah recommends for Minae is a strategic use of Orientalism, in which the author constructs an autobiographical story of liberation, utilizing the image of Asian society as an inferior mirror of the United States. Minae herself is quite reticent about Sarah's suggestion; her use of hyperbolic phrases such as "Oriental ignorance and superstition" and "liberation" in her summary of Sarah's imagined plot elements suggests Minae would not opt for such a strategy as a novelist.

While Minae will not use her past experience in Japan in this way in her novel, the writerly strategy of drawing on one's past is one with which Minae is familiar. In *An I-Novel*, there is a memorable episode about Mr. Keith, her middle school English teacher. Minae arrived in the United States without much English-language education and describes how she was placed in a remedial class. It was Mr. Keith who encouraged her and gave her the confidence to write compositions in English. Mr. Keith particularly appreciated her essay entitled "My Favorite Moment in Autumn," with details from her experience in Japan. Looking back, Minae realizes that the essay was full of "commonplace emotion and unoriginal expression" in Japanese, but when translated into English, it transformed into something new and remarkable (246). What Minae remembers most from Mr. Keith is his message: "Don't forget your Japanese" (249). This is contrary to her high school teacher's advice to prioritize the study of English. Minae is aware of Mr. Keith's prescience that, in the age of multiculturalism, the knowledge of Japanese would give her an advantage in writing English with a special touch.

However, Minae ultimately does not choose this path. In a poignant reminiscence, she explains why:

> Naturally, I did not forget my Japanese. But could he have imagined that the girl he said that to would go further and spend the next twenty years doing everything she could to escape English? Mr. Keith's advice was based on the assumption that English would eventually become my first language, and over the course of that year he tried to speed me toward that goal, assigning me a special tutor and handing me extra grammar books. I liked him very much. I think I even loved him—with the deepest gratitude for him as a teacher and respect for him as a human being. But, unable to respond to his warm solicitude, I never did more than temporize, and guilt over my inability to respond distanced me yet further from English—and, alas, from him. (249)

Minae does not choose the path that Mr. Keith has laid out for her—to become a writer of English without forgetting Japanese—because, ultimately, she is unable to abandon her first language, despite her gratitude toward and respect for Mr. Keith. It is the language that she already claims as her own. This fact separates Minae's choice from writers who are truly between languages, without a language to call their own.

Another factor influencing her decision was remorse. Minae writes: "By the time I realized what an incomparable privilege I had passed up, I had gone too far down a road from which there could be no turning back" (260). In short, Minae (at the time of decision) recognizes the "chances" and "privilege" of writing in English using her position in a multicultural environment; but realizes that it is too late for her to seize the opportunity.

There is yet a third, somewhat understated, career possibility. Although Minae's field in graduate school is French literature, she also participates in a seminar on modern Japanese literature taught by a professor nicknamed "Big Mac"—apparently modeled after Edwin McClellan, professor of modern Japanese literature, whose seminar Mizumura also attended as a student at Yale. Minae describes the class on Akutagawa's short story "The Ball" ("Butōkai," 1921); the discussion among the professor and graduate students as reproduced in the novel is lively, serious, and critical.

Does Minae's strong interest in Big Mac's seminar suggest that she could also make an academic career reading and writing about Japanese literature in English? There are hints throughout *An I-Novel* that Minae had a sustained interest in Japanese literature, from back in the days when she avidly read "musty volumes of modern Japanese literature" (92). Minae was fascinated by the works of the female Meiji writer Higuchi Ichiyō (1868-1912). Given her immersive reading experience and her training as a literary scholar, Minae may well have been able to make a living as an English-language scholar of Japanese literature.

Thus, at another level, the novel is a document of the changing reception of Japanese literature in the United States in the late twentieth century. In the 1960s, when Mizumura was in junior high school, most American bookstores did not carry translations of Japanese literature. By the time she was in graduate school in the 1980s, *The Tale of Genji* was already part of the canon at American universities, and her awareness of the expansion of the readership in Japanese literature was evident. But again, an academic career is not what Minae will choose. In a conversation with Big Mac, Minae reveals that she would like to pursue creative writing in Japanese. Big Mac approves, saying, "Well, I supposed you can give it a try," and adds, curiously, "well, whatever you do, try not to mix up your Japanese with English" (270-271).

All three career paths Mizumura might have chosen as a writer in English—to be a scholar of Western literature, an Asian female novelist, or a scholar of Japanese literature—were credible options reflecting her education, experience, and training. In a changing cultural environment in the U.S. in the latter half of the twentieth century, the significance of each of these options changed, and Minae's story of her personal cultivation and development involves quite a drama. Ultimately, though, the novel depicts how she did not choose any of these options. There were disadvantages to each, but there is no strong reason to choose what she did instead—to become a novelist in Japanese. Minae's decision to not pursue those three alternatives is not simply borne out of her attachment to Japanese language; rather, the choice was constrained by her personal history as well as changing social environments for reading and writing. If anything, these possibilities suggest that she picked perhaps the most difficult and unintuitive career option available to her at the time.

Conclusion: Toward a Hybrid "Literature in Japanese"

In conclusion, I wish to return to the question of the autobiographical and self-referential dimension of fiction writing. The construct of the I-novel highlights another significant point regarding what I believe to be the central question of Mizumura's novel: how Minae came to choose a career path as a novelist in Japanese. If the novel is indeed autobiographical, then Minae (the character) is modeled after Mizumura (the author)—but then the converse must also be true, that Minae (the character) is the author of this novel. Following this logic, Minae Mizumura's *An I-Novel* is a novel that Minae (the character) would write after she became an author. In other words, the text of *An I-Novel* in the reader's hands itself embodies the novel "in Japanese" that Minae would write *in the future*. Considering the hybrid form of *An I-Novel*, it is not the "Japanese" novel that one is likely to imagine; but the book itself is located at a future point in the career path she would choose in the context of the novel. It is also the kind of novel that "mix[es] up [her] Japanese with English," about which Big Mac had warned.

In light of this "future" novel, we might consider once again what Minae's choice entails. The most obvious formal feature of the novel (in the original) is that it is written in a hybrid style moving between Japanese and English. In particular, the original, bilingual version forces the reader to confront this hybrid form. Minae the narrator writes mainly in Japanese, but substantial portions are in English, making it difficult to follow the plot without being able to read both languages. In fact, the direct, vivid voices of Minae and Nanae (both of whom use a linguistic mixture of Japanese and English) are the most authentic representations of their plurilingual, composite identities.

Mizumura has in the past argued that this novel represents the tension between English and other languages—and because of this formal structure, the work is translatable into most languages but untranslatable into English. It is interesting, then, that the novel *Shishōsetsu from Left to Right* was rendered in English as *An I-Novel*, with the English words in the original represented by bold type in the English translation. The formal tension created by the plurilingual prose is thus displaced by text using differentiated typefaces. The plurilingual experience of the original is translated, albeit in a limited way.

If this is the work that Minae ended up creating after choosing to become an author writing in Japanese, then it is not a reactionary return to Japanese identity, but rather a new iteration of Japanese literature, one that is hybrid by design. More important, despite Mizumura's insistence to the contrary, the novel is translatable insofar as plurilingual existence is a common condition. When the novel was originally published in the 1990s, it was lauded as a work that shattered the commonly held notion that Japanese literature must be written only in the Japanese language, in Japan, and in accordance with Japanese culture. Now that the novel has been translated into English, it joins a growing body of texts such as Christine Brooke-Rose's *Between* (1968), Lee Yangji's *Yuhi* (1989), and the works of Tawada Yōko—writings that convey the plurilingual experience as a human experience.

---

1 Levy Hideo has discussed this issue extensively, for example in *Ware teki nihongo* (2010); it has also been famously formulated by Komori Yōichi (1998).

2 The translation into English is my own.

3 Henceforth I will refer to the character/narrator as "Minae" and the author as "Mizumura," although both bear the same name.

4 See, for example, recent edited volumes, one in English on the "autofictional" (Effe and Lawlor, 2022) and one in Japanese on *shishōsetsu* (Ihara et al., 2018).

5 Umezawa's comprehensive, critical re-evaluation of *shishōsetsu* in the 2017 expanded and revised edition of *Shishōsetsu no gihō* includes a chapter on Mizumura's *An I-Novel.*

6 The 2009 bilingual Chikuma edition has "Friday, December 13, 19XX" but the 2021 Columbia University edition specifies the decade—the 1980s—in which this dialogue took place, adding more historical context.

7 All quotations from *An I-Novel* are drawn from the 2021 English translation of Mizumura's work.

8 Mizumura wrote about her memories of Paul de Man as a great intellectual influence (2013).

9 As we have noted, Mizumura's novel was written in both Japanese and English. In Carpenter's English translation of the novel, bold type is used to represent text that was in English in the original bilingual edition.

References

Barekat, Houman. 2021. "Autofiction's First Boom was in Turn-of-the-Century Japan." *Boston Review* (May 14). https://www.bostonreview.net/articles/autofictions-first-boom-was-in-turn-of-the-century-japan/

Effe, Alexandra and Hannie Lawlor, eds. 2022. *The Autofictional: Approaches, Affordances, Forms*. Cham: Palgrave Macmillan.

Hijiya-Kirschnereit, Irmela. 1981. *Selbstentblössungsrituale: zur Theorie und Geschichte der autobiographischen Gattung "shishōsetsu" in der modernen japanischen Literatur.* Wiesbaden: Steiner. [Published in 1996 as *Rituals of Self-Revelation: Shishōsetsu as Literary Genre and Socio-Cultural Phenomenon.* Cambridge: Harvard University Asia Center.]

Ihara, Aya, Ayumi Umezawa, Shimon Ōki, Yūji Ōhara, Dai Ogata, Jun Ozawa, Tatsuya Kōno, and Yōsuke Kobayashi, eds. 2018. *"Watakushi" kara kangaeru bungakushi: shishōsetsu to iu shiza* [*Literary History Considered from "I": The I-Novel as a Perspective*]. Tokyo: Bensei shuppan.

Kasza, Justyna Weronika. 2022. "Autofiction and Shishōsetsu: Women Writers and Reinventing the Self." In *The Autofictional: Approaches, Affordances, Forms*, edited by Alexandra Effe and Hannie Lawlor, 247–266. Cham: Palgrave Macmillan.

Komori Yōichi. 1998. *Yuragi no nihon Bungaku* [*Fluctuating Japanese Literature*]. Tokyo: NHK Books.

Levy, Hideo. 2010. *Ware teki nihongo* [*Japanese according to "me"*]. Tokyo: Chikuma shobō.

Mizumura Minae. 2004. "Authoring *Shishosetsu from Left to Right.*" *91st Meridian* 3.2 (Winter). https://iwp.uiowa.edu/91st/vol3-num2/authoring-shishosetsu-from-left-to-right/

———. 2009 (1995). *Shishōsetsu from Left to Right* [*An I-Novel*]. Tokyo: Chikuma bunko.

———. 2013. "Itsushika mishiranu fūkei no nakani" ["Somehow in the Unknown Scenery"]. *Shisō* [*Thought*] 1071 (July): 95-100.

———. 2015 (2009). *The Fall of Language in the Age of English.* Translated by Mari Yoshihara and Juliet Winters Carpenter. New York: Columbia University Press.

———. 2018. "Sakka intabyū: shishōsetsu to iu 'fikushon'" ["The I-novel as 'Fiction'"]. Interview with the author in Ihara, Aya et al., eds., *"Watakushi" kara kangaeru bungakushi: shishōsetsu to iu shiza* [*Literary History Considered from "I": The I-novel as a Perspective*]. Tokyo: Bensei shuppan.

———. 2021. *An I-Novel.* Translated by Juliet Winters Carpenter. New York: Columbia University Press.

Sacks, Sam. 2021. "Fiction: 'An I-Novel' Review." *Wall Street Journal,* March 12, 2021.

Snyder, Stephen. 2016. "Insistence and Resistance: Murakami and Mizumura in Translation." *New England Review* 37 no. 4: 133-142.

Suzuki Tomi. 1996. *Narrating the Self: Fictions of Japanese Modernity.* Stanford: Stanford University Press.

Tawada Yōko. 2012. *Ekusofonii: bogo no soto e deru tabi* [*Exophony: A Journey out of the Mother Tongue*]. Tokyo: Iwanami gendai bunko.

Umezawa Ayumi. 2017. *Shishōsetsu no gihō* [*An Art of the I-Novel*]. Expanded and revised edition. Tokyo: Bensei shuppan.

Yiu, Angela. 2020. "Literature in Japanese (Nihongo Bungaku): An Examination of the New Literary Topography By Plurilingual Writers From the 1990s." *Japanese Language and Literature* 54, no. 1: 37-66.

Matthew C. Strecher, Sophia University

Murakami Haruki: The Power of the Story

Murakami Haruki (b. 1949) has been a key figure in Japanese literary circles for more than four decades. Born in Kyoto and raised in a suburb of Kobe, Murakami attended Waseda University during the turbulent final years of the 1960s, eventually graduating after seven years with a degree in theater arts. A lifelong aficionado of jazz music and an avid reader of American fiction, he began his adult life as a jazz café owner in Tokyo, and only started writing at the age of twenty-eight. Strongly influenced by American culture, his work was tinged from the very start with what has come to be termed a *mukokuseki* "nationality-less" and *hon'yakuchō* "translationese" style by numerous critics in and out of Japan.[1] Murakami is not the progenitor of what we are calling "literature in Japanese," a term meant to encompass what is sometimes called "exophonic" Japanese literature, produced either by non-Japanese writers or written by Japanese authors in other languages. He is, however, a key figure in the gradual but inexorable shift away from the traditional (i.e., twentieth century) conception of Japanese *junbungaku*, or "pure literature," a mode of writing that is generally understood to be written by, for, and about Japanese people, and in the Japanese language. Such literature was by its nature exclusive and exclusionary, "setting up linguistic, cultural, and national boundaries for a distinct national Japanese literature" (Shan 2013, 198; see also Strecher 2017, 2022). Murakami's *mukokuseki* style and his tendency to avoid Japanese cultural markers in his work have consistently confounded those boundaries and placed him, always, outside mainstream Japanese writing.

Murakami's rejection of the strictures of junbungaku is plainly visible in his début work, the Gunzō Prize-winning novella *Hear the Wind Sing* (1979).

Murakami writes that, after a failed attempt to produce "something like a Japanese modern novel (so-called 'pure literature')", he tried again, this time writing in English and translating himself back into Japanese. "I say 'translated,'" he continues, "but it wasn't a precise translation, rather something more like a free 'transplanting.' The inevitable result was the emergence of a new Japanese style. It was also entirely my own individual style" (Murakami 2015, 44, 47).[2] Murakami's new mode of writing found approval among some critics and launched his career as a novelist, but it was not enough to earn him the coveted Akutagawa Prize, by which new writers in Japan are identified as "serious."[3]

Yet this is precisely what many of us find refreshing about Murakami's writing: its determined simplicity, its rejection of the decorative, and, above all, its disavowal of the ambiguous. Gone are the long sentences with unstated subjects, painstakingly constructed syntaxes in which a single particle makes such a difference in meaning. The complexity of Japanese grammar has long acted as a kind of shibboleth that prevents all but native speakers, and the most adept non-native speakers, from unraveling its lines with any certainty. In defiance of this code, Murakami states his subjects clearly, leaving his readers (and translators) with little doubt of what he means to convey.

If we take away traditional literary style, then what is left in Murakami's writing that makes it significant? The answer is the *story*. Perhaps more than any writer since Tanizaki Jun'ichirō, Murakami is a storyteller *par excellence*. The distinction between "literature" and "story" here is both simple and critically important: a writer of literature is a creator, concerned with producing something artistically innovative, new, and fresh; the storyteller's craft, dating back to the earliest human cultures, is to be a keeper of the collective memory of the tribe. The storyteller's work is akin to that of the shaman, the medicine man, the priestess—one whose task is to awaken something basic and primordial in the listener. As a novelist, Murakami sees his role as the latter: a spinner of yarns around a vast campfire who not only entertains but also guides listeners and readers to something within themselves that has always been present, yet is hidden in the shadows of memory, of the unconscious. These, paradoxically, are new stories that we already know. They are retellings of ancient tales, borne in the trappings of the contemporary. This is why Murakami's popularity and readability extend beyond his native Japan, reaching and moving a diverse international audience. His is literature for a global age—a time driven by high-speed, borderless communications and typified by the challenging and breaking down of national and cultural boundaries. It is also a rejection of junbungaku—whose apologists have reacted by dismissing Murakami and reinforcing and redefining those same national and cultural boundaries.

The Role of the Prophet

Here we assign to Murakami the quasi-religious role of spiritual guide, and the point is not made lightly. Murakami tells stories of great sages, of seers and heroes, yet he tells them through protagonists who are nondescript, silent, passive, and virtually invisible. The Murakami "hero" is very nearly an anti-hero, with nothing obvious to recommend him (or, occasionally, her). Neurotic and introverted, with a puzzling obsession for women's breasts that rightfully irritates feminist readers and critics alike, his sole virtue appears to be that he *listens*. "I have always been inordinately fond of listening to stories from strange lands," the narrator of *Pinball, 1973* says in the first line of that novel, setting the tone for a narrator who does a good deal more listening than he does talking.

The point of this is not merely to construct a narrator who is a good listener, but to create one who is marked by his passivity. From the seemingly endless stream of silent Bokus who narrate Murakami's early fiction to Okada Tōru in *The Wind-Up Bird Chronicle* (1994-95), Mr. Nakata of *Kafka On the Shore* (2002), Kawana Tengo of *1Q84* (2009-10), and Tazaki Tsukuru in *Colorless Tsukuru Tazaki and His Years of Pilgrimage* (2013), Murakami protagonists act as conduits, mediums, empty vessels who absorb and then discharge messages from the "other world" that lies beyond the physical realm. Their task is to hear those on the other side and pass along their stories to others. They are what Joseph Campbell calls people of "personal experience" with the divine, the shaman figure who maintains an individual relationship with his own personal deities (1988, 37). In simple terms, Murakami's protagonists serve, almost without exception, as living links to the supernatural world.

Those links are of vital importance, both for characters within the fictional world and for readers of Murakami's fiction, because they restore, one story at a time, the broken lines of communication between modern humanity and its rapidly fading, almost completely ignored past. This is not merely the documented past, but a deeper, primordial antiquity that predates writing, civilization, and history—but not storytelling. These are the stories preserved in the collective unconscious of all humanity, from the first humans to the present. It is an eroding link whose loss is grounded, according to Carl Jung, in modern humanity's over-privileging of the rational, in the arrogance of scientific achievement. "Rationalism and doctrinairism are the disease of our time; they pretend to have all the answers," writes Jung. "But a great deal will yet be discovered which our present limited view would have ruled out as impossible" (1961, 300). Campbell advances a similar concern, stating that "[t]he psychological dangers through which earlier generations were guided by the symbols and spiritual exercises of their mythological and religious inheritance, we today . . . must face alone. . . . This is our problem as modern, 'enlightened' individuals, for whom all gods and devils have been rationalized out of existence" (1949, 96).

Murakami's stories address this problem through powerful elements of the mythic, the world underground, and, in the Jungian and Campbellian sense, the primordial, archetypal narrative. The concerns of which Jung and Campbell write are fundamental to the human condition: Why are we here? How did we get to be as we are? And in a somewhat deeper sense: What is the mind? Is it the same as the soul? What happens to us after we die? Basic and timeless philosophical conundrums like these underpin Murakami's writing from the start, and not surprisingly, they outweigh the style in which his story is presented. This is not "Art," but a return to our primal origins.

Paradoxically, those origins appear in forms that are demonstrably contemporary, while also touching on the primordial past: an electronically constructed artificial subconscious that takes the form of a medieval-style town filled with unicorns (*Hard-Boiled Wonderland and the End of the World*, 1985); a deep, metaphysical forest guarded by two soldiers who deserted from the Japanese Imperial Army more than six decades earlier, and at whose heart rests a sleepy village complete with electricity and television reruns of *The Sound of Music* (*Kafka On the Shore*, 2002); journeys through hospital floors that lead into the very depths of the earth, where a faceless Boatman ferries people across a subterranean river (*Killing Commendatore*, 2017). What each protagonist seeks in these diverse settings is the same: a clearer sense of who they are, and where they fit into the wider world. What they discover, in many cases, is what every intrepid explorer of ancient myth and legend has found—namely, the collective weight of all human history and all human memory, bound up in the archetypal sensations (hatred and fear, lust and desire, war and chaos) that bear those memories and remind protagonist and reader alike that these archetypes from our primordial past remain constitutive aspects of our present lives. Murakami's fiction, perhaps more than any other of the age, restores our connection to these ancient narratives, linking long forgotten (or repressed) primordial memories to contemporary, everyday experience. His heroes are Campbell's people of "personal experience" with the divine, adventurers going where most of us no longer dare.

Hearing the Voices

Murakami's protagonists are well-known for listening to stories, as noted above. But the stories to which they lend their ears are not always ordinary. In some cases, they suggest mental illness. In his first novel, *Hear the Wind Sing*, the protagonist spends his time with a girl who is missing one of her fingers and who, in moments of repose, hears the unwelcome voices of her past calling out to her. "When I'm all on my own and it's quiet," she tells Boku, "I can hear people talking to me … people I know, and people I don't.… It's usually horrible stuff—like that I ought to get on with it and die—and then they say dirty things, too" (Murakami 1990c, 106). Something similar occurs with the character Naoko in *Norwegian Wood* (1987), though in her case the voice comes from her boyfriend Kizuki, who has preceded her in death. "I'd swear I can feel Kizuki reaching his hand out of the darkness to me. 'Hey, Naoko, we can't be apart,' he says. I never know what to do when I'm told such things" (Murakami 1991a, 206). In the end, Naoko has little choice but to listen to the voices emerging from the darkness.

These voices take on a new and slightly less neurotic, more magical tint in later Murakami fiction. *Dance Dance Dance* (1988), for instance, begins with the protagonist hearing the voice of his lost girlfriend calling to him for help. Here it is a hotel that serves as a proxy for the Underworld, focusing the magical power of the voices of the dead: "She was calling to me through the circumstance of the Dolphin Hotel. Yes, she was seeking me once more. Enveloped by the Dolphin Hotel, I could encounter her once more. It was likely she who was shedding tears for me" (Murakami 1991b, 12). Unlike the voices heard by Naoko and the nine-fingered girlfriend, this voice appeals directly to the narrator in his dreams, calling him not to death, however, but to adventure.

Such other-worldly calls to adventure strike two chords simultaneously: first, they mark the narrative as one in which the hero must pursue some quest; and second, they suggest a quasi-sacred aspect to that quest, for every adventure is also a reenactment of the great deeds of mythic heroes of antiquity. Whether Murakami is himself aware of this is quite beside the point; his narratives undeniably contain heroes whose task is to hear the voices from the "other world" and respond in some significant manner. In *The Wind-Up Bird Chronicle*, the unemployed and thoroughly ordinary protagonist Okada Tōru receives several telephone calls from a woman whose voice he cannot identify, though she clearly knows him. Rather than overtly calling him to adventure, she merely says that, if he will give her ten minutes of his time, they can fully understand one another. Dim-witted as he is, Tōru fails to grasp that this *is* his quest, and that the unidentifiable caller is none other than his own wife, who he is about to lose. Hence, what might have taken him ten minutes in the end requires months of his time and 1,200 pages of text. By the end of the story, Tōru will have traveled underground (quite literally, passing through a magical portal at the bottom of a dry well), navigated a labyrinth, discovered his wife's prison at its center, and fatally injured the evil entity that holds her.

How does such a tale relate to the everyday reader? All quests, we might say, are fundamentally similar. There is an object lost, stolen, missing, or threatened; the protagonist undergoes trials and training to become stronger and wiser, ultimately transforming into a hero; obstacles are raised and overcome; a showdown between the hero and the thing that blocks her or him leads to resolution. But is this not also part of our everyday life? Our quests are less dramatic but no less real: an education, a happy and stable family life, prosperity and good health, success in our work, a home of our own, and a sense of belonging are all part of real-life quests enacted daily. Conflicts, struggles, and resolutions occur not in the underworld of Hades or in the Minoan labyrinth, but at work and home. Yet they are no less significant for this. Murakami's stories, like other mythic tales, are fanciful representations of the most common and ordinary of conflicts, even if they progress along the unlikeliest of paths. This layering of the ordinary and the extraordinary is, in fact, a large part of what makes these tales so accessible to such a widespread readership.

As occurs both in myth and in real, everyday life, Murakami's heroes benefit from the help of wiser individuals. Naoko from *Pinball, 1973* shares stories with Boku that awaken him to the existence of other worlds, and the crying voice of *Dance Dance Dance* is that of a clairvoyant girlfriend who disappeared at the end of the novel's forerunner, *A Wild Sheep Chase* (1982). That girlfriend, whose ears possess miraculous powers, is responsible for keeping Boku on the right path to his quest object. Okada Tōru is likewise assisted by a Second World War veteran, and by two sisters, Kanō Malta and Kanō Creta, all of whom are able to read hidden messages in the flow of water, and an equally enigmatic woman calling herself "Nutmeg" who, along with her spicy son "Cinnamon," provides Tōru with the practical means to fulfill his quest.

Such figures have the power to communicate with a world beyond the everyday, and thus in Campbell's terms serve as a form of "divine assistance." They are, however, secondary characters within the narratives they inhabit, their powers unexplained and inexplicable. In the novel *1Q84*, on the other hand, Murakami focuses significant attention on the "hearer of voices" (*koe o kiku mono*) as a central role. In that work, which centers on Kawana Tengo, a young man with a gift for writing, and Aomame Masami, a young woman with a talent for assassinating violent, abusive men, we are introduced to a powerful spiritual figure known in the story as "the Leader." While bearing some superficial resemblance to the notorious leader of the Aum Shinrikyō cult, Asahara Shōkō, the Leader in Murakami's novel is nonetheless a relatively benign, even sympathetic character. Possessed of the power to hear the voices of otherworldly earth spirits known as "the Little People," the Leader is also tasked with a fertility rite in which he is immobilized and then mounted by prepubescent girls, an act that makes him a target for assassination by Aomame. Prior to his death, the Leader explains his principal function as the hearer of voices to Aomame as being "'like a circuit that connects 'them' [spirits] and 'us'" (2009-10, 2:201). Like any prophet, his task is to capture messages from the "other world" and convey them, rendered intelligible through interpretation, to the masses. It is a fitting metaphor for what Murakami himself does: capture narratives from his inner mind and render them intelligible to his readers. In fact, Kawana Tengo in some ways represents this function as well; a brilliant stylist, he spends the early part of the novel rewriting a narrative written by the Leader's daughter, which starts out virtually indecipherable, ostensibly due to her severe dyslexia, but more likely because it is an unfiltered series of images drawn from the "other world." Tengo's reconstruction of the narrative becomes a brilliant work of literature that vies for the coveted Akutagawa Prize. It is interesting that this prize is the goal of the narrative's reconstruction, for it suggests the possibility, albeit unlikely, that a narrative of true significance—one that connects humankind to its primordial, spiritual past—

can meet the exacting demands of the Japanese literary community, with all the restrictions on what constitutes literary merit that prevented Murakami himself from attaining the prize.

The "hearer of voices" returns in Murakami's second-latest novel to date, *Killing Commendatore* (*Kishidanchō-goroshi*). In this work, the "voices" initially take the form of ritual bells rung in an underground chamber, and later appear as Japanized characters (wearing 583-710 CE Asuka period clothing) in a painting depicting the scene in Mozart's opera *Don Giovanni* in which the title character murders il Commendatore, the father of Donna Anna. Most prominent among the characters in the painting is the eponymous Kishidanchō himself. But what is his function in the novel? In simple terms, it is to open the doors to histories lost through deliberate repression.

In this instance, Kishidanchō breaks through the barrier of silence surrounding a man who witnessed the 1938 Nazi takeover of Austria, the Anschluss, and whose brother participated in the 1937 Rape of Nanjing and later committed suicide. Readers may wonder, why Mozart? Why *Don Giovanni*? Apart from the obvious fact that the opera premiered in Vienna a century-and-a-half earlier, *Don Giovanni* is the timeless story of a man seeking in vain to escape the judgment of his own past misdeeds. Thus, just as the painter shares the pain of his traumatic experiences in 1938 Vienna, perhaps he also warns later generations that they will one day be called upon to confront these events that are, in his own time, being suppressed.

These forbidden topics, buried by decades first of official suppression, later by habit, have festered inside the mind of the old man, now stricken with severe dementia. Through the actions of Kishidanchō, the narrator—for once a hearer of voices himself—is able to journey into the Underworld and retell from an individual perspective these (nearly) erased moments in history. For these are not the conventional histories found in books and official accounts—coherently organized narratives of events that make sense—but the individual, lived experiences of those for whom those same events could not make sense.[4]

As will be clear from the above, Murakami's self-appointed task here is not merely to reconnect his readers with a primordial past, murky and vague, but also to connect them with more recent events that have been homogenized and sterilized into more conventional histories. At the same time, by depicting these events in the highly abstracted form of a painting—at its most archetypal level, one that depicts the displacement of the older generation by the younger, a "changing of the guard," but also conveys inherited responsibility—Murakami permits, even requires, that his readers overlay these events with relevant narratives from within their own cultural sphere of experience.

One takeaway from this admixture of East and West (*Don Giovanni* in Asuka dress, for instance) is that memories of war, violence, trauma, pain, and death are neither culturally nor linguistically bound; rather, they form an archetypal foundation to the collective human experience, endlessly repeating themselves throughout history, however well they are concealed by successive generations. We cannot escape; the harder we try to ignore our past, the more vigorously it reasserts itself into our present. The painter's cautionary message, detected and deciphered by a modern-day hearer of voices, is directed not just to later generations of Japanese, but to later generations of humanity writ large.

In each of the stories outlined above, and countless shorter ones, we find that Murakami's texts demonstrate both the unwanted and the essential role of the "hearer of voices" in the modern world. Dismissed as mad, as occult, such spiritually connected persons have the potential to keep modern society, comfortably hiding from its unflattering past, a little more honest. This is not literature; it is a forcible remembrance. These texts, with varying degrees of symbolism and metaphor, hold a mirror before our eyes, daring us to look. This is one of the fundamental ironies of Murakami fiction: awash in the trappings of the contemporary bourgeois lifestyle, it nevertheless upholds the power of the story, of narrative, not as bourgeois entertainment, still less as a form of literary art, but as an invitation—a *challenge*, in fact—to become more aware of our primordial past. This is why, in one Murakami story after another, the hero must ultimately jettison his worldly goods before he can attain his true quest.[5]

Touching the Primordial Narrative

Elsewhere (Strecher 2014, 87) I have described Murakami's form of narrative as "primordial memory," by which I mean those grounding, archetypal narratives that seem to predate culture and are common to virtually all human experience. Archetypal narratives are fundamentally similar across linguistic and geographical boundaries: stories that invoke the process by which we confront the world, our place in it, and our limitations. These are the myths and legends of gods and heroes who face adversity, mystery, fear, evil, and death; but they are also stories of ordinary people who confront the same issues—and they are familiar to us because the truly important conflicts and challenges faced by modern humanity are not really all that different from those faced by our distant ancestors. The archetypal narrative is related to the archetypes posited by C.G. Jung as contents of the collective unconscious, with the shared function of giving greater meaning to the situations, people, and events—all "narratives"—that we face in our daily lives.[6]

If this is so, then it might logically be argued that our specific, individual experiences in the material (everyday) world are grounded in more universal, archetypal experiences. We suffer the passing of our parents individually, but as an archetypal event the death of parents takes on greater significance as an ordeal and a rite of passage. Few would deny this, yet the point of Murakami's fiction is that modern humanity is increasingly unaware of that deeper significance. Perhaps this is what the author meant when he told an interviewer in 2005 that his work is "to write deep stories" (Murakami et al. 2010, 330). His fiction, magical and non-magical alike, connects with deeper, universal memories shared by all humanity, of all times, with the archetypal narrative itself.

The universality of such archetypal memories, shared by all, may be why Murakami Haruki has failed to impress the keepers of the sacred flame of jun-bungaku, yet has somehow touched practically everyone else, regardless of age, nationality, linguistic group, cultural origins, social class, or religious affiliation. As Jay Rubin has noted, Murakami "grasps the mental phenomena experienced by people everywhere—we could call them universal phenomena—and expresses them through simple, refreshing images that pay no heed to nationality, race, or religion" (2016, 30). These "universal phenomena" of which Rubin writes are precisely those elements of the archetypal or primordial narrative and include our most fundamental psychic experiences: fear, love, joy, hatred, hope, despair, desire, and so forth. To some extent all writers rely on these aspects of the human psyche, yet Murakami, in his use of setting and motif, more explicitly links them to the various myths and legends that ground the cultures of the world. In this sense he is even rarer than the various writers of "world literature" whose works have achieved widespread acclaim outside their home countries (e.g., Umberto Eco, Salman Rushdie, Jorge Luis Borges); he is a *global* writer in the truest sense: one whose works do not merely cross international borders, but *obliterate* those borders. Unlike Eco or Rushdie, whose stories offer readers a telling and sensitive window into their own cultural memories (wartime and postwar Italy and post-independence India, respectively), Murakami's narratives ignore most cultural trappings and show little interest in exposing the specific challenges of his own (postwar Japan) milieu, fixating instead on the overarching narrative of human struggle, of our quest for answers to universal questions that have been asked since the dawning of human history: Why are we here? What do our lives mean? How did we come to be as we are? These are not Japanese questions, but *human* questions, and this is why Murakami is so widely read and accepted on a global level. His reliance on what are essentially mythic tropes and structures—again, on the *story*—thus makes sense, for myth is common to all and remarkably similar even across cultures separated by vast reaches of time and space.

The Rise of Global Literature

The movement toward the global in literature was both predictable and necessary in the context of developments in technology in the late 1980s. As personal computers became increasingly prevalent beginning in the mid-1980s, and as use of the Internet virtually (pun intended) exploded from the end of the 1980s into the early 1990s, the world changed irrevocably from one of distinct physical locations, separated by oceans and continents, mysterious and unseen, to one of common space shared by all. "Japan" was still "Japan," but it was also suddenly accessible to all with the click of a mouse; and the reverse was equally true. Many younger Japanese in this era no doubt gained their first real glimpse of the world at large through the Internet. With the rise of social media later in the 1990s, direct contact with strangers in faraway lands, operating with different cultural codes, became not only possible but commonplace. Almost overnight, a vast world was shrunk to the size of a computer screen, and as we learned about one another, we recognized what Campbell had been saying for almost half a century: that all cultures are grounded in roughly the same narratives. "Why is mythology everywhere the same, beneath its varieties of costume? And what does it teach?" Campbell asks in the opening pages of his seminal work *The Hero With A Thousand Faces* (1949, 3); the answer, as he shows in his analyses of hundreds of myths and legends from around the world, is that our stories emerge from the common space of shared human memory, a collective space that is now almost perfectly metaphorized by the ubiquitous cyberspace of the Internet. My point is that global literature has always existed in the sense that our stories, whatever their cultural origins, have been fundamentally similar, but the Internet has made us more directly aware of this fact. Moreover, the Internet forms an equally effective metaphor for the archetypal narrative, grounded in the collective unconscious championed by Jung; for cyberspace gradually absorbs, upload by upload, posting by posting, tweet by tweet, the entirety of human knowledge and experience. Like global literature itself, the Internet knows no borders and has no limits.

While Murakami's début predates the widespread use of the Internet by nearly a decade, he is unquestionably a writer who speaks for the Internet generation, exposing and exploring their common narratives and showing his global readership just how alike they really are. His rise did not occur because of the Internet, but it did ride a perfect wave of unprecedented access to cultures throughout the globe. Superficially, his works are culturally specific, being (mostly) set in Japan, written in Japanese, and topically playing on events featured in Japan's recent historical past, particularly the Second World War and the student unrest of the late 1960s. But these cultural specificities are not his point; the much more vital aspect of Murakami's work is the universality of the underlying narrative, inviting readers to superimpose—to layer—their own cultural specificities atop each story and respond appropriately. A certain irony attends the fact that the twentieth (and now, twenty-first) century events depicted in these texts awaken a narrative that is timeless, predates writing and history, and extends back into the earliest recesses of collective human memory and imagination. Murakami's heroes and antiheroes literally enter the Underworld, delving deeply into primordial caves, the better to understand both things that have happened to them directly and, more broadly, those that have befallen humankind in the last hundred years. This was the revolution in Japanese literature that began, in part, with his simple experiments with language in 1979.

Murakami Haruki's writing has always been marked by paradoxes: serious messages hidden in often silly (though often not silly) stories; complex ideas expressed in simple language. We identify yet another of these paradoxes here: the use and metaphorical expression of the most elaborate and sophisticated communication apparatus ever devised by humankind—the Internet—with a grounding narrative that almost certainly predates the first writing ever chiseled into a stone. In a sense we have come full circle: from agrarianism to the industrial revolution, from hand tools to electronics, and with each successive advancement in our technology, we left our spiritual origins a little further behind, until we could no longer see those origins, nor even remember that we had them. Using the very technology that seemed destined to complete that separation of humankind from its origins, Murakami's stories break open the barrier and reestablish contact.

Joseph Campbell would no doubt have been pleased.

Conclusion: Implications of the Murakami Revolution

Even as the word "revolution" takes shape on the page here, we must reject it. Whereas the "Meiji Restoration" (*Meiji ishin*) was much more a revolution than a reversion to ways of the past, the Murakami phenomenon is a true restoration, for this author has succeeded, perhaps more than any other in modern Japanese history, in restoring the original function of the storyteller. The true revolution in Japanese literature occurred, arguably, when writers first sought to produce the modern "novel" (*shōsetsu*) in the late nineteenth century, and further attempted to codify its structure, style, and content in the early twentieth (see Hirano 1961, 1972; Strecher 1996). Indeed, "literature" itself began when writers stepped beyond mere storytelling and sought to create art. In the West this has been traced back to the early eighteenth century, to Daniel Defoe and Samuel Richardson (as discussed in Watt 1957; Davis 1983). In fact, literature as we understand it today is a relatively recent thing, a mere three centuries old in the Anglophone world, and barely one century old in Japan. Prior to this we had stories, tales whose purpose was not to be evaluated as art, but to remind us of our past and guide us through our present and future. This is also one of the most basic functions of myth and legend (see, e.g., Eliade 1958, 1963). As opposed to literature, which bears the specific cultural and linguistic markings of the social context that produces it, storytelling is ubiquitous throughout human history and prehistory, and throughout the world. It is practiced in both advanced and developing societies and cultures. It is an important tool in the socialization process in cultures with strict religious codes, as well as in those with less-defined sacred traditions, or those with none at all. And it has at last found a global welcome in mainstream reading circles, in counterpoint to the overly ritualized and codified world of formally judged and heavily critiqued literary art.

These are bedtime stories, and they still thrive in what we teach our children: sacred tales that relate to our origins; fables that teach us about ethics and show us right from wrong; fairy tales that remind us to be cautious, not to stray into the woods, to look both ways before crossing the street, to respect sleeping bears, and to beware of strangers bearing gifts. These are what we had before "literature," before narratives were separated into "art" and "all the rest." Storytelling is what Murakami has brought back to center stage. Whether he intended to or not, he has restored the respectability of simply telling stories, something largely relegated to the newly constructed category of *taishūbungaku* "mass literature" by Japan's literary establishment in the early twentieth century (see Tsurumi 1985; Strecher 1996). When Murakami opened that forbidden door—a Pandora's box—in 1979, gradually gaining approval from established writers around the world (and a very few in Japan as well), he created an opportunity for a veritable swarm of fellow storytellers, from Ogawa Yōko to Kawakami Hiromi who, unlike Murakami, were quickly recognized as worthy and significant writers of literature. What changed? We might surmise that their acceptance by the literary establishment in the 1990s was, in part, enabled by Murakami's success as a storyteller more than a decade earlier. One does not wish to overplay this scenario, however; it is equally possible that the literary establishment, not quite ready for the challenge to its autonomy represented by Murakami in pre-Internet 1979, had come around to a more open-minded view of the possibilities of storytelling by the time of Kawakami's début in 1994. Today the gap between junbungaku and taishūbungaku—between pure literature and storytelling (mass literature)—appears to have narrowed. Murakami's writing may not be the "literature in Japanese" that forms the theme of this volume, nor perhaps literature at all. It may be more useful to think of it as a disruption that compelled the literary establishment to reconsider, as it had done at various points in the past, what is and what is not literature.[7] If, as I have argued above, junbungaku is synonymous with Japan's national literature—writing in Japanese, by, for, and about Japanese people—then surely Murakami Haruki posed a threat to that ideal; his language, thematics, style, and setting were too alien to be junbungaku. Yet it was also not easily dismissed. Murakami's writing was clearly "other"; but what was it? In 1979 this was a most vexing question; today, in a world fully acclimated to globally accessible cultures, it is less so. Now Murakami's work is simply a revival of storytelling at its best.

There is no question that Murakami has a chip on his shoulder about the literary establishment in Japan. Nor can we deny that he has deliberately disrupted many of the traditions of Japanese literature. "I don't believe in this 'duty toward tradition,'" Murakami told a French interviewer in 2003, and two years later he noted—with some evident pleasure!—that the Japanese literary world had accused him of wrecking their institution. "They said I was destroying the traditions of Japanese literature. Well, to judge from the results, maybe they were right (laughs)" (Murakami et al. 2010, 149, 333-334). While stopping short of crediting Murakami with destroying Japanese literary tradition all by himself—even he could not achieve that, much as he might like to believe otherwise—we may reasonably say that he re-drew some of the boundaries that used to demarcate literary art in Japan, and through his success as a storyteller, encouraged others to challenge those boundaries even more. Insofar as those traditions were politically motivated constructs to begin with (Hirano 1961, 1972), designed to exclusify and protect Japanese literature from dangerous foreign influences (Strecher 1996), one is disinclined to lament this return to the basics of storytelling, or this broadening of the parameters of Japanese literature to include more than merely literature by, for, and about Japanese people.

My purpose in this chapter has been to argue, first and last, that Murakami Haruki's writing has always represented a return to—or at least a re-emphasis on—simple storytelling of the pre-literary type. This is why it was so confusing: critics responded to it, yet could not quite articulate why. At the same time, within the context of this volume, I have sought to show Murakami as one important step in the process of challenging both the primacy and the definition of Japanese literature as junbungaku. To repeat: Murakami does not represent exophonic literature in Japan, but he does represent a steppingstone on the path to reconsidering exophonic literature, so-called "literature-in-Japanese," to be an important component of Japanese literature. His contribution was to attack—we must use this forceful word—the strictures governing the Japanese literary tradition at the time of his début, while placing at the forefront a narrative structure that proved itself to be global both in appeal and accessibility. Murakami did not erase what was Japanese in his fiction; he made it irrelevant to the reception of his stories, which were, and still are, about *all* of us.

---

1 The term *mukokuseki* is liberally used in Fujii's collection of essays (2009). For more on *hon'yakuchō*, see especially Kazamaru (2006) and Strecher (2014).

2 All translations in this chapter are the author's own, unless otherwise stated.

3 Nearly all of the Gunzō Prize judges used the word *karui* (light) in describing Murakami's style. Shimao Toshio added that he could not recall what had been written, but that it seemed like something that might have occurred in America. Maruya Saiichi similarly noted a strong American influence (Maruya et al. 1979). For a useful discussion of the role of literary prizes in determining writers' positionings in the literary sphere, see Mack 2010.

4 For a detailed discussion of recovered personal histories in the works of Murakami Haruki, see Strecher 2021.

5 The most dramatic instance of this, arguably, occurs in *Kafka on the Shore*, when the titular character deliberately drops bits and pieces of his survival kit as he presses deeper into a massive forest, surrendering himself completely to its dangers and rewards. Yet as early as *Hear the Wind Sing*, Murakami's début work, the narrator notes in the opening pages that he spent much of his youth letting go of things from his past. If we pay attention, we note that the comforts of bourgeois modernity are more often thrust upon the Murakami narrator (as is spectacularly demonstrated in *Dance Dance Dance*) than celebrated or sought by him.

6 Jung's theory of the archetypes is well known, but an accessible introduction is available in *Analytical Psychology* (1989), a collection of his foundational lectures from 1925. My concept of the archetypal narrative, like Jung's archetypal figures, motifs, and events, has its origins in Plato's *Politeia*, in which he argues that all things in the material world (*kósmos aisthētos*) are emanations from an original form (*archē*) in the realm of forms (*kósmos noētós*). Jung argues throughout his published works that the myriad archetypal forms populating the collective unconscious serve to help us identify and make sense of all we see in the material world. My point is similar to Jung's, except that I extend the archetypal function to narrative forms such as we commonly see in myth and legend. It is an idea, incidentally, wholly in agreement with Campbell's (1949) contention that all myths and legends are fundamentally alike.

7 As I have discussed elsewhere (Strecher 1996), the definition of *junbungaku* was fiercely debated between 1923 and 1935, and again in the early 1960s. Both of these periods coincided with strong influxes of Western culture into Japan, thus prompting a renewed sense of urgency in determining what was and was not purely "Japanese" literature. It was out of these debates that *junbungaku* was defined, along with various types of writing that were deliberately excluded from that category.

References

Campbell, Joseph. 1949. *The Hero With A Thousand Faces.* Princeton: Princeton University Press.

———. 1988. *An Open Life: Joseph Campbell in Conversation with Michael Toms.* Edited by John Maher and Dennie Briggs. New York: Larson Publications.

Davis, Lennard. 1983. *Factual Fictions: The Rise of the English Novel.* New York: Columbia University Press.

Eliade, Mircea. 1958. *Rites and Symbols of Initiation: The Mysteries of Birth and Rebirth.* Translated by Willard Trask. New York: Harper and Row.

———. 1963. *Myth and Reality*. Translated by Willard Trask. New York: Harper and Row.

Fujii, Shōzō. 2009. *Higashi Ajia ga yomu Murakami Haruki* [*Murakami Haruki as Read in East Asia*]. Tokyo: Wakakusa shobō.

Hirano, Ken. 1961. "Junbungaku to Taishūbungaku" ["Pure Literature and Mass Literature"]. In *Gunzō* 16 No. 12 (December): 154-172.

———. 1972. *Bungaku: Shōwa jūnen zengo* [*Literature: Around 1935*]. Tokyo: Bungei shunjūsha.

Jung, Carl G. 1961. *Memories, Dreams, Reflections*. Translated by Richard and Clara Winston. New York: Pantheon Books.

———. 1989. *Analytical Psychology: Notes of the Seminar Given in 1925 by C.G. Jung*. Edited by William McGuire. Princeton, NJ: Bollingen Series XCIX, Princeton University Press.

Kazamaru, Yoshihiko. 2006. *Ekkyō suru "Boku"—Murakami Haruki, hon'yaku buntai to katarite* [*"Boku" Crosses the Border—Murakami Haruki, Translation Style, and the Narrator*]. Tokyo: Shironsha.

Mack, Edward. 2010. *Manufacturing Modern Japanese Literature: Publishing, Prizes, and the Ascription of Literary Value.* (Series: *Asia-Pacific: Culture, Politics, and Society.*) Durham, North Carolina: Duke University Press.

Maruya, Saiichi, Sasaki Kiichi, Sata Ineko, Shimao Toshio, and Yoshiyuki Junnosuke. 1979. "Dai 22 kai Gunzō shinjin bungakushō happyō" ["Presentation of the 22nd Gunzō Literature Prize for New Writers"]. *Gunzō* 34 no. 6 (June): 6-73.

Murakami, Haruki. 1985. *Sekai no owari to hādo-boirudo wandārando* [*Hard-Boiled Wonderland and the End of the World*]. In Volume 4 of *Murakami Haruki Zensakuhin 1979-1989* [*Complete works of Murakami Haruki 1979-1989*]. 8 vols. Tokyo: Kōdansha.

———. 1990a. *1973-nen no pinbōru* [*Pinball, 1973*]. In Volume 1 of *Murakami Haruki Zensakuhin 1979-1989* [*Complete works of Murakami Haruki 1979-1989*]. 8 vols. Tokyo: Kōdansha.

———. 1990b. *Hitsuji o meguru bōken* [*A wild sheep chase*]. In Volume 2 of *Murakami Haruki Zensakuhin 1979-1989* [*Complete works of Murakami Haruki 1979-1989*]. 8 vols. Tokyo: Kōdansha.

———. 1990c. *Kaze no uta o kike* [*Hear the Wind Sing*]. In Volume 1 of *Murakami Haruki Zensakuhin 1979-1989* [*Complete works of Murakami Haruki 1979-1989*]. 8 vols. Tokyo: Kōdansha.

———. 1991a. *Noruwei no mori* [*Norwegian Wood*]. In Volume 6 of *Murakami Haruki Zensakuhin 1979-1989* [*Complete works of Murakami Haruki 1979-1989*]. 8 vols. Tokyo: Kōdansha.

———. 1991b. *Dansu dansu dansu* [*Dance Dance Dance*]. In Volume 7 of *Murakami Haruki Zensakuhin 1979-1989* [*Complete works of Murakami Haruki 1979-1989*]. 8 vols. Tokyo: Kōdansha.

———. 1994-96. *Nejimakidori kuronikuru* [*The Wind-Up Bird Chronicle*]. Tokyo: Shinchōsha.

———. 2002. *Umibe no Kafuka* [*Kafka on the shore*]. 3 vols. Tokyo: Shinchōsha.

———. 2009-10. *1Q84*. 3 vols. Tokyo: Shinchōsha.

———. 2013. *Shikisai o motanai Tazaki Tsukuru to, kare no junrei no toshi*. [*Colorless Tazaki Tsukuru and His Years of Pilgrimage*]. Tokyo: Bungei shunjū.

———. 2015. *Shokugyō to shite no shōsetsuka* [*The Professional Novelist*]. Tokyo: Switch Library.

———. 2017. *Kishidanchō-goroshi* [*Killing Commendatore*]. 2 vols. Tokyo: Shinchōsha.

Murakami Haruki, Jonathan Ellis, and Mitoko Hirabayashi. 2010. "Yume no naka kara sekinin wa hajimaru" ["In Dreams Begins Responsibility"]. In *Yume o miru tame ni mai'asa boku wa mezameru no desu* [*I Awaken Every Morning in Order to Dream*], 327-359. Tokyo: Bungei Shunjū. Originally published in *The Georgia Review* LIX, no. 3 (Autumn 2005).

Rubin, Jay. 2016. *Murakami Haruki to watashi* [*Murakami Haruki and Me*]. Tokyo: Tōyō Keizai Shinpōsha.

Shan, Lianying. 2013. "New Chinese Immigrants in Japan: Cultural Translation and Linguistic Hybridity in Yang Yi's and Mao Danqing's Japanese-Language Writing." *Japanese Language and Literature* 47, no. 2 (October): 193-234.

Strecher, Matthew. 1996. "Purely Mass or Massively Pure? The Division Between 'Pure' and 'Mass' Literature." *Monumenta Nipponica* 51, no. 3 (Autumn): 357-374.

———. 2014. *The Forbidden Worlds of Haruki Murakami*. Minneapolis: University of Minnesota Press.

———. 2017. "East Meets West, and Then Gives it Back: Reinventing Japanese Literature in the Contemporary Age." *Perspektywy Kultury* [*Perspectives in Culture*] 19: 53-80.

———. 2021. "History and metaphysical narrative space." In Gitte Hansen and Michael Tseng, eds., *Murakami Haruki and Our Years of Pilgrimage*. London: Routledge, pp. 23-50.

———. 2022. "A False Peace: Literature in the Age of Heisei." In *Japan in the Heisei Era (1989-2019): Multidisciplinary Perspectives*, edited by Noriko Murai, Jeff Kingston, and Tina Burrett, 261-271. London: Routledge.

Tsurumi, Shunsuke. 1985. *Taishūbungakuron* [*Theory of Mass Literature*]. Tokyo: Rokkyō.

Watt, Ian. 1957. *The Rise of the Novel: Studies in Defoe, Richardson and Fielding*. London: Chatto and Windus.

Dennis Washburn, Dartmouth College

Tsushima Yūko's *Laughing Wolf* as Confabulatory History

During her lifetime, Tsushima Yūko was recognized as one of the most distinguished voices in contemporary Japanese literature. Though perhaps not quite as well-known internationally as some of her near contemporaries, such as Murakami Haruki or Tawada Yōko, she was the recipient of almost all major literary awards in Japan, which honored her compelling style and ethically powerful storytelling. As Karatani Kōjin noted in a memorial letter following Tsushima's death on February 18, 2016, her achievements made her a serious candidate for a Nobel Prize.

Born on March 30, 1947, Tsushima was the third child of Ishihara Michiko and the novelist Dazai Osamu. Her given name was Satoko. Her father was at the height of his fame in the immediate postwar years, having published two short novels, *The Setting Sun* (*Shayō*, 1947) and *No Longer Human* (*Ningen shikkaku*, 1948), that secured his reputation as a leading figure of the *Burai-ha* (the Decadents). He was, however, an unstable personality who suffered from alcoholism. In 1947 he left Michiko for Yamazaki Tomie, a beautician and war widow with whom he committed suicide the following year. Though Tsushima had no direct memory of her father, his suicide was widely reported, and the aftermath profoundly affected her childhood. When she was twelve years old, her family's trauma was compounded by the death of her older brother, Masaki. Because Masaki was mentally disabled, he had of necessity been the center of Michiko's attention, and his death was keenly felt.

At the time of Masaki's death, Tsushima was enrolled at Shirayuri Gakuen Junior and Senior High School, a Catholic institution for women founded in 1881. Shirayuri University was chartered in 1965 and Tsushima entered the following year, majoring in English literature and studying French. During her college years her ambition to become a writer was kindled by a prize she received for an essay, "A Dream and the Modern Times," in which she argued for the importance of the imagination as a universal human trait.[1] In 1969 she entered graduate school at Meiji University but was apparently an indifferent student.

Tsushima married in 1970 and the following year published her first collection of short stories, *Carnival* (*Shanikusai*). In 1972 her short story "Pregnant with a Fox" (*Kitsune o haramu*) was a runner-up for the Akutagawa Prize. The irony of this near miss was not lost on her, since her father had held an obsessive grudge over his failure to win the prize when it was inaugurated in the 1930s. That same year Tsushima gave birth to her daughter Kai (the playwright Ishihara Nen). A few months later she divorced her husband and began life as a single mother. In 1976 she had a second child, a son born out of wedlock, who tragically drowned at their home in 1985 when he suffered a seizure while bathing.

It was during the decade between her son's birth and death that Tsushima penned the works that established her critical reputation in Japan: "A Bed of Grass" (*Kusa no fushido*), for which she received the 1977 Izumi Kyōka Prize; *Child of Fortune* (*Chōji*, 1978); *Territory of Light* (*Hikari no ryōbun*), which won the inaugural Noma Prize for New Writers in 1979; *The Shooting Gallery* (*Shateki hoka tanpenshū, 1973-1984*), a collection of stories that included "The Silent Traders" (*Danmari'ichi*), which was recognized with the 1983 Kawabata Prize; and *Woman Running in the Mountains* (*Yama o hashiru onna*, 1980). In 1986 she received the Yomiuri Prize for "Overtaken by Evening Light" (*Yoru no hikari ni owarete*), a first-person tale based on the death of her son.

In one form or another, these publications were all deeply grounded in Tsushima's personal experiences. The protagonists are women whose families have experienced the abandonment of a father or the early death of someone close, or who are themselves divorced and have faced the challenges of being a single mother in a culture that often looks askance at women in such circumstances. Her fiction thus came to be viewed as an example of the I-novel (*shishōsetsu*), a genre of autofiction that has occupied a central position in modern Japanese literature and is frequently (although not exclusively) associated with female authors. At the same time, because she focused so much on the struggles of women and other marginalized individuals in contemporary society, treating them not didactically as victims but as fully realized characters with understandable desires and human agency, Tsushima came to be viewed as an important feminist author.[2] While she never overtly rejected these characterizations of her literary practices, her reflections on these critical terms (discussed below) suggest that she did not believe they fully captured the essence of her art.

An important turn in Tsushima's career took place in the late 1980s and early 1990s. Always preoccupied by the liberatory power latent in the voices of marginalized people, she was increasingly engaged in the study of *yukar*, the oral literature of the Ainu, including it in the lectures on Japanese literature she gave at the University of Paris in 1991. Although she had long been engaged with social and political issues, due in part to her connection with Nakagami Kenji through the coterie journal *Literary Capital* (*Bungei shuto*), she became more publicly active. In 1991 she co-authored, with Nakagami, Karatani Kōjin, Tanaka Yasuo, and others, a statement protesting the participation of Japan's Self-Defense Forces in the Persian Gulf War. She was also involved in protests over nuclear power, taking a more activist stance on the environmental issues that would become increasingly important elements in her fiction.

While it is true that Tsushima consistently drew on her own lived experiences for her fiction, her later works exhibit greater formal experimentation. These include *Fire Mountain: Chronicle of a Wild Monkey* (*Hi no yama-yamazaruki*, 1998), winner of both the Tanizaki and Noma Prizes; *Laughing Wolf* (*Warai ookami*, 2000), winner of the Osaragi Jirō prize; *Golden Dream Song* (*Ōgon no yume no uta*, 2010), which combines fiction, travelogue, and oral epics from several Asian languages; and *The Culling Times* (*Kari no jidai*, published posthumously in 2016). All are striking for the ways in which they play with multiple voices, with abrupt temporal and spatial shifts, and with representations of social inequalities.

These developments in Tsushima's literary practices did not represent a break with her earlier works but grew directly out of them. The act of writing was itself a lived experience for her, a struggle and a sacrifice that cultivated a vulnerable imagination.[3] Her emphasis on the importance of vulnerability emerged out of her engagement with social issues and with the terms used to characterize her fiction—a self-assessment that provides insight into her aesthetic aims.

Tsushima's Autofiction

The I-novel may employ a range of narrative strategies: confessional literature, which deals explicitly with events in the author's life; the *roman à clef*, which adopts the pretense of protecting privacy through a thin veneer of fictionalization; and autofiction, which transforms real-life events by situating the author-persona in an imaginative fictional setting. At first glance the delineation of these strategies may seem like a distinction without a difference, but in Tsushima's case the high degree of fictionalization of her life experiences is a crucial aspect of her art. It is thus perhaps more precise to describe her works as autofiction rather than as I-novels.

This distinction matters because one of the criticisms that has been made of the I-novel as a genre is that it requires little in the way of literary talent to depict the subjectivity (or inner life) of characters.[4] This criticism has often been aimed at women authors, a view exemplified in Usui Yoshimi's essay "The Young Woman Novelist of Today." Usui attempts to explain the extraordinary popularity of emerging female authors such as Harada Yasuko, Sono Ayako, and Ariyoshi Sawako in the 1950s. Citing Hirabayashi Taiko's comment that most established, older women authors drew almost exclusively on revelations of their personal experiences for their fiction, Usui claims that their lack of creativity explains both the decline of interest in the I-novel and the rise of young female writers who show greater imagination in their fiction. In his view, these younger novelists make up in talent what they lack in personal experience of victimization, poverty, illness, or heartbreak. The sources of this generational shift, Usui argues, are changes in the social status of women in postwar Japan and in the nature of the Japanese novel itself. He notes that the works of male writers also reflect these changes—but then his brief state-of-the-field report takes on a more overtly misogynistic tone. Male writers, he believes, are more than just spinners of tales, relying instead on their intellectual powers to construct their novels. Modern (postwar) female authors, in contrast, rely solely on their imagination. He concludes with the following claim: "Literature requires something more than talent, and it is in meeting these other requirements that the difficulties lie for Japan's young women writers in the future" (1957, 522).

The underlying biases in Usui's analysis render his critique tone-deaf, reminding us of the cultural milieu in which Tsushima developed as an artist who was compelled to respond critically to the expectations imposed on female authors. She gives a clear account of her resistance to such expectations in a first-person essay published in the *Chicago Tribune* in 1989 that provides personal details of her background and explains her aesthetic and ethical motivations for writing. Tsushima begins by noting that she never liked her birth name, Satoko (里子) in part because it was chosen by her mother, who she describes as a methodical woman fond of symmetries. She took the pen name Yūko (佑子) because it suggests the spirit of giving, a possibility of happiness, and a kind of freedom achieved by moving outward toward others. The source of her desire for movement was her experience of reading Western literature. She tells us that she is fond of characters like Scarlett O'Hara and the heroines of Tennessee Williams' plays, all of whom struggle against the constraints they face in everyday life. Tsushima notes that these characters may be self-destructive but empathizes with their efforts to break free: "Women figures I created in my novels also don't compromise with reality. They may appear stoic but are strong enough to search for their own happiness in their own way."

Tsushima explains that her constant themes are love and solitude, and that she writes about only those things familiar to her. She then implicitly addresses Usui's critique by claiming that she never writes about happy women because she believes that misfortune is not always a bad thing. As a storyteller, she acknowledges that tragedy is more dramatic than success, but her preference for writing about unhappy women is not just an aesthetic choice but an ethical one. For Tsushima, happy people can lose sensitivity and, consequently, their human qualities. In contrast, unhappy people have a chance to grow through hardships and discover true humanity. The value she places on empathy and vulnerability, nourished through personal struggle, stands as a rebuttal to critics who viewed women writers of autofiction as not fully formed artists and, by extension, as an indictment of the broader societal constraints women face. "I write fiction, but I experience the fiction I write," she claims; and in this way her own life is transformed into literary art that seeks an answer to the question, "What is of value to an ordinary human being?" As her pen name suggests, the transfiguration of her life into fiction makes it an offering, a gift to others.

Tsushima's Feminism and Vulnerable Imagination

Although there is a long history of criticism in Japan that connects female authors to literature of a highly personal, introspective nature, Tsushima was motivated by larger considerations that are reflected in her focus on the value of vulnerable imagination. Tsushima no doubt saw herself as a feminist writer, but she was also aware that the term 'feminist' had taken on ambiguous shades of meaning that emerge more clearly for her when viewed from the perspectives of different cultures. She explored these matters in two short essays published in 1994: "The Word 'Feminism'" and "The Possibility of Imagination in these Islands."

Tsushima begins the essay on feminism with the following quotation from Hasegawa Shigure, which she likens to a poem, a *tanka*: "What would become of women without the support of other women?" (*Onna ga onna no kata o motanakute dō shimasu ka*) She tells us that she came across this statement in Iwabashi Kunie's *Critical Biography of Hasegawa Shigure*, where it is cited as Hasegawa's curt response to critics who argued that she had relied far too heavily on women for the contents of her book, *Accounts of Beautiful Women*. Tsushima was startled by the bluntness of Hasegawa's retort and stirred by a sense of nostalgia since she felt it was no longer possible to make such a statement in Heisei Japan. In her essay, Tsushima examines the fundamental sense of feminism as expressed in Hasegawa's words. She notes that feminism was introduced to Japan in 1911 by Hiratsuka Raichō in the literary magazine *Blue Stocking* (*Seitō*). It subsequently appeared in other literary venues, such as the inaugural issue of Hasegawa's own journal *Women's Arts* (*Nyonin geijutsu*) in 1928. Feminism is also referenced in the proceedings of the Conference of Women Writers in 1940, by which time, according to Tsushima, it had become entangled with other political ideologies: socialism, anarchism, and nationalism. Co-option of the meaning of feminism, as well as opposition to its aims, arose largely due to wartime nationalism. Hasegawa's formulation of feminism as a movement that stressed the need for women to support women was not entirely effaced, but the force of her fundamental conception was weakened by continued political suppression.

Moving outside the Japanese context, Tsushima notes that whenever she travels abroad, she is invariably confronted, as a Japanese woman author, with questions about both the I-novel and feminism. She believes that both words serve as "code" to interpret types of fiction among inner circles of academics or cognoscenti; as such, their meanings become more difficult to define with precision. She reports that she was once asked directly about the meaning of the term I-novel but found herself unable to answer, given what she calls the "obscure" nature of the genre.

Tsushima tells us that she experienced a similar challenge coming up with a precise definition of feminism. She recalls a conversation with an American scholar of Japanese literature who asked her why an older, distinguished Japanese woman author who once supported Japanese feminism now claimed that the movement was no longer of concern to her. Although their mutual puzzlement is treated lightheartedly, Tsushima assumes that the American scholar is unaware of the fact that the resistance to feminism in Japan is rooted in the belief that it represents the extreme dogmatism of radicalized women. She reassures the American scholar that this misunderstanding will fade with the younger generation of writers. However, she is later mystified by a trend at that time (the 1990s) of younger women writers denying any connection between their literary works and feminism. Upon encountering these disavowals, Tsushima realizes the confidence she had displayed earlier to the American scholar was misplaced and expresses concern that careless usage of feminism as a critical term will end up doing a disservice to all women. She concludes the essay by noting that the ironic reality for female authors in Japan is that they spend untold hours writing novels and criticism yet remain at the "starting line" of their profession. Thus, because a generally accepted sense of the meaning of feminism has yet to be captured in the Japanese language, she believes Hasegawa's *tanka* remains salient.

Tsushima's view of feminism may seem transactional, but it highlights the vulnerable status of women. Within the context of her aims as a literary artist, the need to cultivate empathetic imagination to represent the vulnerability of the marginalized and powerless takes on greater urgency. This is the central concern of her essay on the possibility of imagination in contemporary Japan, in which she returns to the question posed a few years earlier in her 1989 essay: What is of value to an ordinary human being?

To answer this, she begins by observing festivals and ceremonies that reenact some of the religious beliefs of the original inhabitants of Japan, seeing in the power of faith among the common people a hope for imaginative revival. This hope is based on a reading of Japan's past that challenges official historiography. Tsushima's history of Japan is presented as a systematic subjugation of the indigenous populations of the archipelago—peoples referred to in the earliest imperial chronicles as barbarians (*emishi*). Even though their existence has been largely erased, their presence remains deeply embedded in the consciousness of the Japanese people. In support of this point, Tsushima argues that, during the Tokugawa period, when the population was under strict authoritarian control, many peasants longed for what they perceived as the freedom of the indigenous peoples to move about and to go beyond set social and territorial boundaries. She cites the example of women with illegitimate children in the Edo period for whom escape to *emishi* culture was the only way to escape reprobation.

Despite the repression the indigenous population suffered, its marginal position paradoxically allowed a freedom of movement outside the boundaries of official culture that is reflected in what Tsushima identifies as the open-hearted imagination apparent in the oral tradition of *yukar*. These mytho-poetic narratives give voice, often in the first person, to the spirits and creatures of the natural world, allowing listeners to enter that world and gain a deeper understanding of its value and their place in it. These works act as vestiges of the memory of ordinary people, though Tsushima remains concerned that the modernization of Japan, with its emulation of Western norms and its violent drive for so-called progress and civilization, may result in the complete erasure of shared memory and cut off the "very life of Japanese culture itself." She recognizes the impossibility of a return to ancient cultures but believes that it is possible to revive "the imagination of the *emishi*." This belief was deeply rooted in her literary practice, for she saw in the cultivation of vulnerable imagination a potential power "that all human beings on this planet have in common. And that imaginative power is no less than a love of the Earth" (197).

Confabulatory History: *Laughing Wolf*

If, as Tsushima claimed, she experienced the fiction she wrote, then the ethical beliefs and aesthetic aims discussed in the essays referenced above did not so much guide her literary practices as emerge out of the act of writing itself. Her experience of devastating family losses and the personal struggles of single motherhood did not merely provide her with subject matter, but cultivated a vulnerability reflected in the grace and subtlety of her style, in her ability to create the illusion of complex subjectivities in her characters, and in the increasingly playful experiments of her later fiction.

One of the most formally daring of her mid-career works is *Laughing Wolf* (*Warai ookami*), a novel written and published at the turn of the millennium. The story is set in 1959 and is focused through the voices and perspectives of the two main characters. The first is Yukiko, a 12-year-old girl whose family background is the key autofictional element of the novel. Yukiko's father was an artist who abandoned his family for another woman when Yukiko was just an infant. The woman had been married, but her husband was presumed to have been captured and killed by the Soviet army in Siberia. When he was unexpectedly repatriated, the three of them decided to carry out a suicide pact. The shock and embarrassment Yukiko's mother feels at this betrayal and loss plays out in her distant, joyless relationship with her daughter. Their relationship is further complicated by the fact that Yukiko's older brother, Ton-chan, is mentally disabled. The mother, now a widow who makes her living as a teacher, is depicted as austere and strong-willed. Her long-term hope is to be able to look after Ton-chan by herself; thus she is strict with Yukiko, urging her daughter to study hard so that she will be able to live independently and free the mother to care for her disabled son. These plans come to naught when Ton-chan dies young, leaving Yukiko deeply estranged.

The second major character is 17-year-old Mitsuo (though that may not be his real name). During the last year of the Second World War, when he was still a toddler, his family's house was destroyed in an air raid. Only Mitsuo and his father survived, and they became part of the large homeless population in postwar Tokyo. They lived for a time in a small cemetery near Ikebukuro, but in the end the father, who was physically debilitated, died and Mitsuo was placed in an orphanage. He had only vague memories of his time in the cemetery, one of which was his discovery of the bodies of three people, two men and a woman, who had committed suicide there. When Mitsuo entered middle school, he began to search archived newspapers to find the cemetery and learn more details of what happened during that period. He wanted, above all, to confirm the *reality* of his memories, of his lived experiences.

Mitsuo eventually discovers that one of the suicides was Yukiko's father, and in 1954 he visits her house to share with her mother the memory that has been so meaningful to him. He feels an affinity with Yukiko and fantasizes that by telling his story he will be able to enter her world as a member of her family. But her mother rebuffs him, urging Mitsuo to forget the painful past and focus on the future. He returns to the orphanage and is allowed to remain there longer than most of the other wards because he is good at storytelling, which makes him useful to the staff in caring for the youngest children. After finally leaving the orphanage to take a job, his memories and longings drive him to reach out once more, and this time he decides to contact Yukiko directly.

Yukiko, who is bored and feeling oppressed by the strict atmosphere at her home and school, meets Mitsuo at the Yasukuni Shrine. It is late May, and Mitsuo, who has been given time off to replace the days he had to work during Golden Week, has decided to take a trip. He convinces her to go with him, and she agrees—a decision, she maintains, that she made freely. Mitsuo is aware that he cannot just leave with a young girl, so before they board a train at Ueno station, he has her trade her expensive school uniform and satchel for boys' clothing, and later cuts her hair short to disguise her. During the trip they privately assume different identities: first, as characters from Rudyard Kipling's *The Jungle Book*, with Mitsuo as Akela the wolfpack leader and Yukiko as the human man-child, Mowgli; later as characters from Hector Malot's *Nobody's Boy* (Fr. *Sans Famille*), with Mitsuo as the boy Remi and Yukiko as his loyal, intelligent dog, Capi.

Leaving Ueno, they head toward Japan's northeast. Mitsuo has a dream of going as far as Siberia, a place he heard about in connection with the repatriated soldier who committed suicide in the cemetery. On the way to Akita, they undergo the first of several time slips that jolt the narrative's temporal structure. They find themselves, without explanation, back in 1945 on a train crowded with people conscripted to work in mines in Hokkaido. Frightened by this mysterious experience and feeling sick, Yukiko abruptly gets off at a small station in Daigo. Rather than wait for the next train north they decide to head back toward the Kantō region. Over the next week they move from train to train, passing through various stations: Nikkō, Urawa, Hachiōji, Kurihama, Yokosuka, Numazu, Gifu, Osaka, Takarazuka, Maizuru, Naoetsu, and Tatsuno. This list may seem haphazard, but it is a crucial part of the narrative design: at each station on this random itinerary, they experience a time slip that takes them back to witness or participate in various catastrophes, crimes, or individual tragedies that occurred during the chaos of postwar Japan. They are finally stopped in Toyohashi, where Mitsuo is arrested and charged with kidnapping.

As this brief synopsis makes clear, the autofictional elements Tsushima employs help establish Yukiko and Mitsuo's backstories. As already noted, one of Tsushima's great strengths as a storyteller was her ability to transform her own experiences into credible, detailed, and moving representations of the inner lives of her characters. In the case of *Laughing Wolf*, this strength is amplified by the radical heteroglossia of the novel. The sheer number of voices involved in telling the story results in a complex temporal structure, deepens the illusion of subjectivity, and opens possibilities for ethical engagement.

The effect of multiple voices on the temporal order of the narrative is apparent from the very beginning, in the opening section that acts as a prelude to the novel. The reader is presented with a short history of human-wolf interactions, including the extinction of the Japanese and Ezo (Hokkaidō) wolves during the Meiji period (1868-1912). Most of the information for this history is taken from the work of the zoologist Hira'iwa Yonekichi and presented in a seemingly objective, academic tone. Unlike Europe, Japan was an agrarian society that did not rely heavily on livestock, and the wolf was seen as a helpful guardian of crops against deer and other pests and even worshipped as a *kami*, or divine spirit. It was only with the advent of modernization that the wolf came to be seen as a villainous creature. Modern culture effectively erased this manifestation of Japan's natural environment, a causal connection made clear in the coda to Tsushima's prelude:

> The Japanese wolf went extinct in 1905, the year the Russo-Japanese war ended. A little more than thirty years later, the Japanese islands were engulfed first in the war with China and then in the Pacific War, which ended in 1945 with Japan's unconditional surrender. The Japanese wolf was no longer around, but as things turned out, wild dogs who had lost their masters could be spotted running through the smoldering ruins of Japan's cities. (2011, 10)

Later in the novel, the playful choice by Mitsuo and Yukiko to assume the identities of Akela the wolf and Capi the dog pulls the reader back to this opening section—to moments outside of the temporal frame of the story proper. In so doing, the opening section no longer stands apart in terms of voice and subject matter but is integrated into the design and symbolic order of the novel. In echoes of the Meiji period extinction of the Japanese wolf and the wartime appearance of wild dogs, the violence of modern culture has a profound impact on Yukiko (Capi) and Mitsuo (Akela). Pushed to the margins of society, they decide to pursue a nomadic life, to emulate the freedom of movement of wild animals or the indigenous *emishi*.[5] Their efforts to escape the impositions of cultural norms, no matter what hardships they may face, require a leap of the imagination—a leap that sets up their experiences of time slips, which in turn allows them to experience and empathize with past traumas.

The narrative voices in chapter one are markedly different from the objective, academic tone of the prelude. The story begins to move between an omniscient narrator and two voices initially identified only as those of a young man and a girl: the former recounting memories of a father and child living in a cemetery following the end of the war; the latter expressing a young girl's fears that arise from hearing tales of abduction, sexual assault, and murder. Because the identities of the people relating these vignettes are not immediately specified, they feel disembodied, sharing the quality of timelessness found in folk tales or children's stories. The backstories of Mitsuo and Yukiko begin to come into focus for the reader only when the young man reveals to the girl his memory of the suicide of the girl's father and produces a newspaper article to verify his account.

The narrative voice abruptly shifts again in chapter two, with Yukiko now speaking directly to the reader to contextualize her connection with Mitsuo and explain how they came to set out on their trip. The tone is retrospective, but the moment of narration is clearly specified. It is 1999, and Yukiko is looking back at events of forty years ago. She insists at the outset that it was her choice to go on the trip, and there is no attempt on her part to conceal or foreshadow events. Instead, she tells the reader up front how things turned out:

> ...[I]t was all because of my carelessness that everything became such a big mess. Even now I'm not really sure if he realized at the time what might happen. I never heard anything more about him after it was all over. For a time, they called it a kidnapping, and it was written up in all the papers. I moved after that and changed schools. I didn't change my name, though, so if he had ever considered looking for me, he could have found me. But he didn't, and I never saw him again. Forty years have passed since then, and now we probably wouldn't recognize each other even if he passed me on the street. To tell the truth, that's why I find it hard myself to believe that the whole thing ever really happened. (23)

The note of uncertainty concerning the veracity of her account arises in part because of her suspicions about Mitsuo's reliability, which impinges so crucially on Yukiko's family history. Following this chapter, Yukiko's voice is not heard speaking directly to the reader again until the end of the novel. But by framing the story in this manner, the narrative cedes some authority to Yukiko to speak for herself despite doubts about her memories. Using Yukiko's voice as a framing device makes manifest the transformative possibilities of Tsushima's autofiction.

The narrative voice that dominates most of the novel (chapters three through ten) is third-person omniscient—a voice capable of relating actions, conversations, descriptions of place, and mental states that none of the characters would be able to do on their own. Nevertheless, a multiplicity of voices operates in all these chapters. Yukiko and Mitsuo continue to speak to the reader through reported accounts of their conversations, dreams, and flashbacks. The voices of Rudyard Kipling and Hector Malot come through in lines attributed to Akela and Mowgli, to Remi and Capi. The strict Catholic teachings that Yukiko's mother wants to instill in her daughter speak through references to Latin hymns, prayers, and liturgical services. Perhaps most striking of all are the voices of the reporters, police, politicians, and ordinary people who speak through the newspaper articles that first appear in chapter five and are included in each subsequent chapter of the novel.

These news articles act as a narrative supplement, providing historical context for the events enacted during the time slips. They tell of people smuggling black market food and contraband from the countryside to Tokyo; of murders, rapes, abductions, and robberies; of train accidents and shipwrecks; of cholera outbreaks; of wild dogs attacking people; of babies being abandoned to die and families committing suicide. In every case, Yukiko and Mitsuo either witness or relive these events. Near the end of the novel, in chapter ten, their identification with events recounted in the newspaper articles is so intense and absolute that their subjectivities effectively disappear as they merge with the various subjects from each news item: an infant boy and girl who are abandoned in a box and left to die; children who die with their desperate mother in a family suicide; a young boy and a girl who are murdered in a robbery; an older boy and girl who participate in a crime before fleeing the scene. No longer anchored by a single voice or perspective, the narrative is effectively free-floating, drawing the reader more closely to the plight of those who are most vulnerable and forcing us to confront the dire consequences of injustice and violence.

By refocusing the narrative through historical accounts, the newspaper articles serve to create confabulatory histories: that is, memories of events based on the accounts of other people rather than on personal experience. My use of the phrase "confabulatory histories" references the meaning of the word "confabulation" in the field of psychology. A confabulation is a memory error brought on by amnesia or by the implantation of memories (so-called false memories). In the case of amnesia, confabulations are quite often made-up stories used to cover the abyss of memory loss. In cases involving implanted memories, the confabulation may sometimes be grounded in verifiable events. The confabulatory quality of this autofictional narrative only becomes clear to the reader when the provenance of these newspaper accounts is more fully explained in the final chapter. After Mitsuo's arrest, Yukiko discovers that he left a folder in her backpack containing, in addition to the article about her father's death that he showed her the night they left Tokyo, twenty or so other articles from the years right after the war.

This revelation raises a key question: Were the time slips reenactments of stories Mitsuo told Yukiko based on those articles? Mitsuo is, on one level, a deeply sympathetic character who suffered great trauma, and who desperately wants to confirm his memories as something real and, through them, to forge familial connections he has never had. His desire for connection is made clear in the two personas he adopts: the wolf, Akela, who mentors Mowgli; and the boy Remi, who dutifully searches for his mother. Yet Mitsuo is also described as a talented fabulist, and in his interactions with Yukiko he comes across as a trickster, a Pied Piper-like figure. He is not depicted as a strong, threatening character. Indeed, Yukiko is convinced that she is the stronger of the two. Yet in the world a girl like Yukiko inhabits, stories of abuse abound, and her awareness of things society prefers not to talk about renders Mitsuo at best untrustworthy and at worst menacing. For all that, Yukiko defends him. His "stories" provide a way for them to escape the cold, indifferent constraints imposed by the human world—what Mitsuo, channeling Kipling, calls the "Cold Lairs." He and Yukiko struggle and their story ends unhappily, but the impulse to confabulate is liberating, producing a state of vulnerability that enables empathetic connection.

Conclusion

The newspaper accounts that contextualize the fantastical time slips in the *Laughing Wolf* narrative serve as more than just a means to affirm memories, whether autobiographical or experienced vicariously. They point to traumatic cultural events that have largely faded from memory or been repressed. For a Japanese reader in 2000, the year the novel was published, Heisei Japan must have seemed like a period of stasis compared to the long, turbulent history of the Shōwa era (1926-1989). The so-called "lost decade" of the 1990s was marked by efforts to rebrand Japan globally; to remake its image as cool, safe, and unthreatening; to move away from the past and escape the bonds of history itself. Yet Heisei Japan at that millennial moment was also a retrospective culture. *Laughing Wolf* effectively captures that moment with its presentation of a confabulatory history based on the memories of Yukiko and Mitsuo—memories that are, within Tsushima's complex autofictional world, at once real and fabricated. Such imaginatively reconstructed remembrances revive the voices of ordinary people otherwise lost to time.

It would be nice to think that *Laughing Wolf* might serve as a restorative tale, but the narrative itself is not so sanguine. Indeed, the story ends with one more time slip. When Yukiko and her mother return to Tokyo following her "rescue" in June 1959, they first go to a police station for interrogation, then to Yukiko's school to pay their respects, and finally to the mother's school to apologize. Once these tasks are completed, they get a taxi to go home. Caught in a traffic jam on the way the way to Shinjuku Station, they decide to get out and walk. In a reverse time slip, the child Yukiko suddenly finds herself in 1999, swallowed up in a chaotic, crowded scene with people dressed in all manner of outrageous fashions, speaking many languages, laughing, shouting, crying, singing, and trembling. The leaders of North and South Korea appear smiling on a huge television screen. At that moment all of Yukiko's memories and experiences with Mitsuo are overwhelmed by this hi-tech, globalized phantasmagoria:

> A wolf can be heard howling. The *Death Song* of a wolf, reverberating across the jungle. A python slithers away stealthily. The barking of the monkeys in the Cold Lairs swirls around. Gandhi, riding an elephant, and *The Swan*, frozen blue by grief, drift away slowly across the sky. The black shadows of a little naked boy and his father, both dragging blankets full of holes, steal behind the buildings and disappear.
>
> A red moon is floating in the brown, hazy sky of evening. The mouths of the trembling people are open. Their faces all seem to be laughing. Even the red moon is laughing. (237)[6]

Despite the rapid recapitulation of stories and memories Yukiko experienced with Mitsuo, the performative depredations of contemporary global culture produce a mad, atavistic ritual that pushes aside all traces of past trauma and profound loss.

This time slip is followed by three news articles that end the novel. They discuss the psychology of a girl, Kiyoko, who was abducted by, and then bonded with, a man named Higuchi. Her behavior is described as a form of Stockholm Syndrome, and all the articles note that because Higuchi shared hardships with Kiyoko and opened her up to new social roles, she found wonder and pleasure in their relationship. The account by Kiyoko's older brother is telling:

> It made me cry to think that even in the depths of her terrible ordeal, while she was growing stronger as a result of her harsh experience, she was also careful to protect her life and do her best to survive, even though she was a child. My father told me that she wrote a poem in her memos that says, "the moon that rises shines the same on everyone." (238)

One implication of this ending is that Yukiko has been manipulated by Mitsuo, who was perhaps inspired by stories of past abductions to create a family for himself. This realization may explain Yukiko's hesitancy concerning the veracity of her memories, but her predicament is a particular expression of a recurring theme in Tsushima's autofiction. If unhappiness may make a person stronger and thus make human sensibility possible, then the figure of Yukiko is emblematic of vulnerable imagination, which can turn unhappiness and suffering into art, into a liberating expression of beauty.

---

1 Tsushima recounts the impact of this prize in "Yuko Tsushima" (1989).

2 For an example of how Japanese authors have been read through the lens of Western feminist theory, see Hartley (2003).

3 Reiko Abe Auestad notes the importance of the concept of vulnerability for understanding Tsushima's fiction (2018).

4 The I-novel form also risks violating the privacy and agency of real-life individuals who may unwillingly have their affairs exposed. This is not a minor consideration, but for the purpose of this essay I am choosing to focus on what some Japanese critics have identified as the problem of creativity they see as inherent in the form. To be clear, I do not agree that the problem is inherent, but I am highlighting the critique here because it has been unequally applied to the work of woman authors.

5 For a discussion of the importance of the quality of "free/playful movement" (遊動性 [*yūdōsei*]) to Tsushima's worldview and literary practices, see Karatani Kōjin (2018). The word *yūdōsei* appears to be a neologism coined by Karatani.

6 "*Death Song*" is a reference to *The Jungle Book* and Akela's death. "*The Swan*" refers to the barge where Remi's mother lives as she searches for him.

References

Abe Auestad, Reiko. 2018. "Tsushima Yūko and the Ethics of Cohabitation." In *Memento libri: New Writings and Translations from the World of Tsushima Yūko (1947-2016)*, edited by Anne McKnight and Michael Bourdaghs. Special issue, *The Asia-Pacific Journal: Japan Focus* 16 (12), no. 4 (June 15, 2018). apjjf.org/2018/12/Auestad.html.

Hartley, Barbara. 2003. "Writing the Body of the Mother: Narrative Moments in Tsushima Yūko, Ariyoshi Sawako and Enchi Fumiko." *Japanese Studies* 23, no. 3 (December 2003): 293-305.

Hira'iwa Yonekichi. 1992. *Ookami: Sono seitai to rekishi* [*The Wolf: Its Ecology and History*]. Tokyo: Tsukiji shokan.

Karatani Kōjin. 2016. "Love and Empathy for the Oppressed: Remembering Yūko Tsushima." Translated by Geraldine Harcourt. *Asahi Shinbun*, February 23, 2016. http://www.kojinkaratani.com/en/.

———. 2018. "Tsushima to Ookami." In *Tsushima Yūko korekushon: Warai ookami*, 423-429. Kyoto: Jinbun shoin.

Tsushima Yūko. 1989. "Yuko Tsushima." Translated by Chieko Kuriki. *Chicago Tribune*, January 22, 1989. https://www.chicagotribune.com/news/ct-xpm-1989-01-22-8902270344-story.html.

———. 1994. "The Possibility of Imagination in These Islands." Translated by Geraldine Harcourt, introduction by Masao Miyoshi. *boundary 2* 21, no. 1 (Spring 1994): 191-197.

———. (1994) 2017. "Feminizumu to iu kotoba" ["The Word 'Feminism'"]. In *Ani no yume Watashi no inochi* [*My Older Brother's Dream, My Life*], 87-91. Tokyo: P + D Books, Shōgakukan. Originally published in *Subaru* (February 1994).

———. 2011. *Laughing Wolf.* Translated by Dennis Washburn. Ann Arbor: University of Michigan Center for Japanese Studies.

Usui Yoshimi. 1957. "The Young Woman Novelist of Today." *Japan Quarterly* 4, iss. 4 (October 1, 1957): 519-522.

Selected Works by Tsushima Yūko

Kusa no fushido. 1977. Tōkyō: Kōdansha.

Moeru kaze. 1980. Tōkyō: Chūō kōronsha.

Shanikusai. Shohan. 1981. Tōkyō: Kawade shobō shinsha.

Danmari'ichi. 1984. Tōkyō: Shinchōsha.

Yoru no hikari ni owarete. 1986. Tōkyō: Kōdansha.

Hi no yama: yamazaruki. 1998. Tōkyō: Kōdansha.

Ani no yume Watashi no inochi. 1999. Tōkyō: Kōdansha.

Ōgon no yume no uta. 2010. Tōkyō: Kōdansha.

Yamaneko dōmu. 2013. Tōkyō: Kōdansha.

Kari no jidai. 2016. Tōkyō-to, Chiyoda-ku: Bungei shunjū.

In English translation

Child of Fortune. 1991. Translated by Geraldine Harcourt. Tokyo: Kodansha International.

The Shooting Gallery and Other Stories. 1997. Translated by Geraldine Harcourt. New York: New Directions Pub. Co.

Laughing Wolf. 2011. Translated by Dennis Washburn. Ann Arbor: University of Michigan Center for Japanese Studies.

Of Dogs and Walls. 2018. Translated by Geraldine Harcourt. UK: Penguin Books.

Territory of Light. 2019. Translated by Geraldine Harcourt. First American edition. New York: Farrar, Straus and Giroux.

Woman Running in the Mountains. 2022. Translated by Geraldine Harcourt. New York: New York Review Books.

PART 2:

SPACES SEEN AND UNSEEN

I. Space

Kristina Iwata-Weickgenannt, Nagoya University

Beyond the Now and Then: Crafting Memory in Yū Miri's Literature

> Will people find it suspicious if I say it is all both 'true' and 'untrue?' Whether it is history, politics, or even someone's life story, I feel that it is true and untrue all at once, and I trust in that feeling. For me, the thicket, the chaos, of Akutagawa Ryūnosuke's famous story, *Yabu no naka* ["In a Grove"], *is* the truth. (Yū 1997, 220-221)[1]

In the afterword to her autobiography, *Mizube no yurikago* (*Cradle by the Sea*, 1997), Yū Miri formulated what was to become a core element of her literature: a profound concern with memory, both individual and collective. Her reference to Akutagawa's 1922 short story (2018)—famous worldwide thanks to Kurosawa's 1950 film adaptation, *Rashomon*—is highly illuminating, for "In a Grove" contains several equally plausible but contradictory eyewitness accounts of a murder. Three individuals, including the ghost of the victim, confess to the killing, leaving the reader confused and unsatisfied. Lacking both a narrative frame and a resolution, Akutagawa's story plays with readers' willingness to fill in the gaps with their imagination. Rather than insinuating that the truth remains hidden in the thicket, therefore, Akutagawa seems to suggest that truth is neither absolute nor universal, but hinges on the necessarily limited human ability to interpret perceived reality. If no two accounts of the same event are ever identical, truth must be spoken of in the plural. This opens endless possibilities for the tortured mind, another key trope in Yū's work; thus, her nod to Akutagawa is fitting in yet another way. Like much of Yū's own literature, "In a Grove" is a fragmented collection of voices retelling the unbearable violence they suffered.

As discussed below, the exploration—and narrative transformation—of pain is central to Yū's writing, which arguably takes quite a bit of inspiration from Akutagawa's irresolvable tale.

With few exceptions, most academic publications present a close reading of a single text. In this chapter, however, I endeavor to identify literary continuities over a period of more than thirty years in Yū's work. With the opening quote as a starting point, this chapter traces the complex ways in which Yū has, from the very beginning of her career, played with the unreliability and malleability of memory, exploring both its personal and political nature. The chapter follows a chronological approach to show how Yū's preoccupation with the intersections of memory, pain, and language has taken on a different character over the years. Specifically, I start with a discussion of *Mizube no yurikago* in which Yū describes her experiences growing up in a highly dysfunctional family. Her characterization of this text as a "way too early, autobiography-like essay" (1997, 217) is revealing in two senses. First, it indicates an acute awareness of "the autobiographical act as a creative rather than mimetic process" (Löschnigg 2006, 2). I argue that *Mizube no yurikago* must be read as an exploration—and conscious exploitation—of the ambiguous nature of autobiographical writing itself, of its oscillation between the factual and the fictional, and the importance of performative processes. Precisely for this reason, Yū's remark about premature timing must primarily be understood as a display of modesty. In fact, *Mizube no yurikago* lays the foundation for her identity as the *writer* Yū Miri.

The second focus of this chapter is on the shift from the introspection that characterized the early years of Yū's career to a broader concern with the political implications of an understanding of memory—individual and collective—as a product of the present. I discuss the two novels that best exemplify her turn to historical memory and historiography, *Hachigatsu no hate* (2004; translated in 2023 as *The End of August*) and *JR Ueno-eki kōen guchi* (2014; translated in 2020 as *Tokyo Ueno Station*)—which both received considerable public attention, if for very different reasons. I read these texts as postcolonial attempts to inscribe the experience of the weak and oppressed, and to undo the invisibilizing effects of power.

Finally, the chapter closes with a discussion of how, after the Fukushima meltdowns of 2011, Yū engaged in collecting memories with real-life local survivors. The experience of active listening—she recorded the disaster memories of more than six hundred people—allowed for a fusion of internal and external pain, which then found a transformative outlet in theater. I argue that the revival of the one-person theater production Yū founded before becoming a novelist implies both a return to and, at the same time, a significant departure from her literary origins. In the early years, her semi-autobiographical characters were highly isolated and unable to find a home outside literature, whereas the interaction with survivors results in a stronger emphasis on communal care.

A Brief Introduction to Yū Miri

Born in 1968 to first-generation immigrants from South Korea, Yū Miri is technically considered a foreigner in Japan. However, like the majority of so-called *Zainichi* Koreans—descendants of colonial era migrants (1910-45) who are commonly referred to as such—she is culturally and linguistically Japanese. She began her literary career as playwright, and with *Uo no matsuri* (*Fish Festival*), became the youngest ever recipient of the Kishida Kunio Theatre Prize, in 1993. In the mid-1990s she switched to writing novels, garnering an equal amount of critical attention. She received the prestigious Akutagawa Prize in 1997 for *Kazoku Cinema* (*Family Cinema*) and several other important prizes, including the Izumi Kyōka Prize and the Noma Newcomer Prize, for *Furu hausu* (*Full House*) in 1996.

In 2000, Yū became Japan's best-known single mother when she gave birth to a son out of wedlock, after separating from the child's father. In the four-part *Inochi* (*Life*) series (2000-2002), she chronicled the growing of a new life against the background of the rapidly deteriorating health of her long-time partner and mentor, Higashi Yutaka. Throughout much of the 1990s, she had deliberately avoided making her Korean heritage a central theme in her literature, fearing that it would pigeonhole her as Zainichi writer. However, the decision to give Japanese citizenship to her son prompted her to reflect on her own reasons for maintaining her South Korean citizenship despite being unable to speak Korean. Her exploration of colonial history and familial migration, a theme discussed below, is best exemplified in *The End of August*.

Following the 2011 tsunami and nuclear meltdowns, Yū became deeply involved in disaster relief efforts. In 2015, she relocated to Minamisōma, a small town located only twenty kilometers from the havocked nuclear power plant. In 2018, she opened a boutique bookshop in the area, with an attached café and theater space where cultural events are regularly hosted.

Yū's novels have been translated into various languages over the years, but it is only recently that translation into English and English-language scholarship has gained traction. In 2020 Yū received the US National Book Award for Translated Literature, which greatly elevated her prominence in English-speaking countries. Two years later, she was awarded the Berkeley Prize for Japanese Literature for bringing "critical attention to the challenges of socioeconomic inequality, ethnic discrimination, gender discrimination, and everyday precarities that continue to shape the life of the minoritized and traumatized" (UC Berkeley 2022). Thus, while substantial research on her literature can be found in Japanese and German, there is also now a growing interest being demonstrated in English-language academia.

Cradle on the Stage, or Writing "Yū Miri"

Published as an autobiography in 1997, *Mizube no yurikago* follows a narrative arc from Yū's birth in 1968 to the beginning of her writing career less than 20 years later. Told from the perspective of the first-person narrator, *watashi* (meaning the pronoun "I"), the book details a difficult childhood and adolescence in a marginalized family that was excluded from mainstream society in multiple ways: ethnically as Zainichi Koreans, but also economically and in terms of her parents' educational and occupational backgrounds. Domestic violence and ongoing bullying at school further contribute to the sense of an outcast existence, resulting in watashi's teenage suicide attempts. Yet, *Mizube no yurikago* also describes a gradual liberation from this past, which begins when watashi is expelled from high school and joins a well-known musical theater troupe. The troupe practices Method Acting, a technique that encourages actors to delve deep into their emotions and traumas to fully embody a character. Despite the emotionally challenging nature of this training, it gives watashi a fundamentally different perspective on her troubled past, which she comes to appreciate as an invaluable resource for creative work. After two years, she abandons her acting career, begins to write plays, and founds her own theater company, *Seishun gogatsu-tō* (Youthful May Party).

In the context of this chapter, *Mizube no yurikago*'s conceptualization of the theater as a space of self-realization is particularly relevant. A close reading of watashi's transition from the Japanese name she had been using as a child to her Korean name illustrates this point. To understand the significance of this transition, it is important to know that most Zainichi Koreans have two or more names that they often use simultaneously in different social contexts. Around the time *Mizube no yurikago* was published, more than ninety percent of Zainichi Koreans were using Japanese names—technically, pseudonyms—in everyday life (Harajiri 1998, 171). Reasons include a lack of identification with their Korean ethnicity, a desire to prevent discrimination, or a wish to avoid curious questions. According to Pierre Bourdieu, the act of naming establishes "a constant and permanent social identity that stands in for the identity of the biological individual in all the possible fields into which they enter as an *actor*, that is, in all their possible life histories" (1998, 78-79).

In premodern Japan, names were significantly less permanent (Plutschow 1995) than in the European Christian tradition Bourdieu refers to, but contemporary Japan generally shares the sense of stability of given names. An entry in Yū's *Shigo jiten* (*Private Dictionary*, 1996) illustrates just how extraordinary, if not outright suspicious, the multiplicity of Zainichi names is today: "NAME: People who have two names include writers, TV personalities (*tarento*), fraudsters, cult leaders, and so on. And Zainichi Koreans" (87). In Japan today, names are not only expected to be unchanging but come with assumptions about someone's ethnic and national identity. All of this explains the centrality of the name issue in Zainichi literature. *Mizube no yurikago*, too, begins with this topic:

> On June 22, 1968, I was born early in the morning on the summer solstice. It was my maternal *hanbae* [Korean for grandfather], Yang In-tŭk, who gave me the name Miri. I heard he was looking for a name whose characters could be read the same way in South Korea and Japan—a name like Miri. The character for my family name, Yū, is pronounced *Yanagi* in Japanese. I am convinced that the *hanbae* and my parents chose my name considering that I would be raised in Japanese society....The fact that, as a South Korean citizen, I was given a name that could pass as Japanese, has no doubt spared me from the various difficulties faced by Koreans in Japan. Had I been given a distinctly Korean name, such as Kim XYZ, it is likely that my consciousness would have developed quite differently. (Yū 1997, 11-12)

Watashi's parents enroll their daughter in educational institutions under the Japanese name, Yanagi Miri, in order to hide her ethnic background. The narrator recalls that, as a child, she perceived of her heritage as a "dark 'pit' which I must never ever tell anyone about" (50). But then, as a drama student she switches to her Korean name:

> Ah, I remember now—when I was cowering in the corner of the theater in my role as a blackout assistant, I used my real name (*honmyō*) *Yū Miri* for the first time. I reacted when someone called me *Yanagi* and jumped up just the same when I was addressed as *Yū*. Mr. Higashi eventually summoned me....
>
> 'It's not good to have two names. Choose one: is your name *Yanagi* or do you want to be called *Yū*?' he asked, sharply and unamused.
>
> I pressed my lips together, and after thinking for a few seconds, I answered, 'I'll go by *Yū*.'
>
> Since that day, I have called myself *Yū Miri* and still do so today. (183-184)

The transition from Yanagi to Yū is mentioned as if it were a minor, insignificant detail. This casual approach contrasts with the way previous Zainichi authors have described the adoption of a Korean name, which is often presented as the outcome of a long struggle and a positive embrace of one's ethnic heritage. Prominent examples include Yi Yangji's 1982 debut novel, *Nabi t'aryŏng* (1993); Sagisawa Megumu's *Hontō no natsu* (*A Real Summer*, 1992); and *Mesoddo* (*Method*, 1998), Kim Masumi's debut, which also describes a cathartic theater experience. In these novels, the emotional exertion surrounding names is closely tied to discourses of authenticity and ethnic identification.

In contrast, *Mizube no yurikago* can hardly be interpreted as describing the "awakening of an ethnic [Korean] consciousness" (Kawamura 1999, 286). Instead, I argue that the name change is based on a constructivist understanding of identity and reality. This is evident in watashi's response to the training in Method Acting, during which the director asks his students "almost like in a police interrogation" about their childhood experiences (Yū 1997, 174). He does not accept simple explanations or allow students to avoid painful memories, but rather insists that they thoroughly confront their personal histories, including the most difficult moments. At the end of the novel, the now 28-year-old watashi sits in a rusty baby stroller on a beach and, rocking quietly, gazes out to sea: "A cradle, all at once the word came to mind. I cannot remember ever having lain in a cradle. But that does not matter, *memory can be retouched at any time. It is all just fiction*" (218; emphasis added).

Similar to the nineteenth century writers whom Richard Terdiman discussed in his seminal study on time and memory, watashi too realizes that "*nothing* is natural about our memories, that the past—the practices, the habits, the dates and facts and places, the very furniture of our existences—is an artifice, and one susceptible to the most varied and sometimes the most culpable manipulations" (Terdiman 1993, 31). The realization that the past is not static or unchanging but rather a product of the present is by no means devastating for watashi. On the contrary, she confesses that "the idea that memories are no more than a fairy tale that anyone can shape as they please was very stimulating for me" (Yū 1997, 178).

For the drama student with writing ambitions, these insights open up entirely new avenues:

> Contrary to my belief, my own terrible memories might be nothing more than a fictional narrative born out of self-pity....I resisted the idea but at the same time felt as if I had been shown the possibility of rewriting my past. From that time on, I think I sensed that one day I would rewrite my life and turn it into a play. (Yū 1997, 178)

In this passage, theater, literature, and writing itself coagulate into a medium for redefining or even (re)creating one's identity. Terdiman sees literary writing, and in particular novels—the most organized "exercises in the process of memory" (1993, 25)—as playing a key role in the (re)invention of the past, the present, and the future. Similarly, autobiographical research has debunked the "presumed relationship between a narrating subject and lived experience, between a self, its patterns of internal growth and development, and external reality"; and now regards "the 'self' we observe remembering and recreating its past in a text [as] little more than a 'fictive structure.'" In this constructivist approach, autobiographic writing is seen as playing a key role in creating and sustaining "myths about the individual and self-formation" (Loftus 2004, 1-2).

With *Mizube no yurikago*, Yū takes these insights a step further. Not only does she encourage readers to interpret the book as either "autobiography," "novel," or "essay" at will (Yū 1997, 221), highlighting the fictionalizing effects of any autobiographical narrative, but she also incorporates a strong performative element in *Mizube no yurikago*. The heterotopic space of the theater is assigned a central role in identity construction. This is evident in the above-cited scene where the theater—a closed, dark realm where identities are playfully assumed, performed, and shed—is likened to a womb. After a long gestation period, the acting student and blackout assistant "Yanagi Miri" leaves behind the darkness of the theater hall, in the corner of which she had been cowering in a fetal position, and begins to write autofictional plays—and gives birth to "herself"— under the new name, "Yū Miri." Unlike Yanagi Miri, Yū Miri has no past: this identity (role) resembles a blank page that wants to be filled through writing. Therefore, Yū Miri can be seen as a *literary identity*, born from a creative milieu, which demonstrates not only the possibility, but the necessity, of being (re)invented and *performed* in public.

Accordingly, for about a decade from the early 1990s onward, Yū's writing can be described as trauma narratives, which involve the reiteration of largely the same semi-autobiographical plot with the addition of ever new twists. "I find it difficult to accept reality as it is, because I detest any reality that includes myself," Yū said in one of the interviews she gave during this period. "To be able to accept it, I have no choice but to rearrange reality with the help of my imagination. In other words, I rewrite reality until it becomes acceptable to me" (Enomoto 1999, 65). In addition to autofictional writing, Yū frequently spoke about her difficult upbringing in interviews and readily appeared in documentary films that depicted painful events. Together with her literature, these snippets functioned as "biography generators" (Hahn 2000, 100), helping Yū create and convincingly perform "Yū Miri." In other words, Yū initially proposed a strong concept of authorship that included not only her literary writings but also her authorial persona. "The author Yū Miri," she summarizes, "is a piece of art that I have created together with [my partner and mentor Higashi Yutaka]" (Fukuda and Yū 2002, 44). Through at least the first one or two decades of her career, if not beyond that, Yū attributed an existential meaning to writing. In the vein of classical *shishōsetsu*[2] writers such as Dazai Osamu, the most important literary influence of her teenage years, she often commented on the inextricable relationship between life and art, saying that "if one day I should no longer be able to play the *writer Yū Miri*, it will be time to die" (Kiridōshi 2000, 250, emphasis in the original).

Dead Voices and Un/Representation in Historical Memory

As described, Yū's exploration of the nexus of memories, writing, and the self had a strongly therapeutic vein in the early years of her career. Beginning in the 2000s, however, Yū gradually left the realm of individual memories and turned to interrogating collective memory. Two milestones of her literary career, *Hachigatsu no hate* and *JR Ueno-eki kōen guchi*, explore the tensions between personal and historical memory. Dealing with the question of whose voice does (not) get represented in textbook history and zooming in on the particularly sensitive issue of oral testimony, both novels can be read as an attempt to inscribe the memories of the marginalized and rewrite history from below.

Hachigatsu no hate is the more controversial—as well as much longer and far more complex—of the two novels. It marks a point of transition in Yū's writing in that it combines, or rather confronts, blank spaces in her family history with silenced aspects of Japan's national history, specifically colonial history. In *Mizube no yurikago*, the narrator quickly reaches a dead end when trying to sketch the family's origins. Her father volunteers no information at all, leaving watashi uncertain about fundamental things like his birthday, his true relationship to his much older sister, and even his family name. Her mother on the other hand seems to come up with a variety of contradictory versions of the past. Realizing that many first-generation Zainichi Koreans came to Japan under traumatizing circumstances, watashi presumes that "for the sake of sheer survival, they had to close off the entrance to the dark tunnel [they passed through] with a wall of silence" (Yū 1997, 18). But with *Hachigatsu no hate*, an extraordinarily well-researched historical account, Yū tore down that wall. Based on years of extensive fieldwork, the study of historical sources, and numerous interviews, this 800-page family saga is in many ways her most political novel. Despite its epic length, it is also the one text that most resembles "In a Grove," the very short Akutagawa story referenced at the beginning of this chapter.

Set in colonial Korea and early postwar Japan, *Hachigatsu no hate* too contains a multitude of voices. The most obvious polyphony is linguistic. More extensively than any other Zainichi writer before her, Yū resorts to a classical postcolonial writing strategy: the incorporation of "Korean" voices and Korean onomatopoeia.[3] In addition, she inserts children's rhymes, popular songs, and excerpts from imperial proclamations and other historical documents, all of which further enrich this novel's chaotic tapestry of sounds.

Corresponding to the rugged linguistic surface, the narrative structure is full of ruptures mirroring the violence of the plot. *Hachigatsu no hate* deals with colonial violence, guerilla resistance, collaboration, civil war, political persecution, flight, illegal immigration, and the experience of uprootedness. Multiple plotlines unfold simultaneously, some of them loosely interwoven and others simply happening unrelatedly in time and space. Moreover, Yū denies her readers the sense of integration a single narrator would provide. Instead, the narrative perspective keeps changing—from young to old, from men to women, from colonizers to colonized, from victims to perpetrators—at a rapid pace. All of this makes the novel very difficult to read.

Different from Akutagawa, however, Yū does provide a narrative frame to make sense of the chaos and see truth therein. As I have previously argued, what holds the polyphonic medley together are two shamanic rituals, described in the first and last chapters, held in the narrative present of early twenty-first century South Korea (Iwata-Weickgenannt 2020, 823). The restless ancestors of the narrative frame's protagonist, "Yū Miri," are summoned, listened to, and appeased at the end. In this reading, the unsteady narration and fragmented organization of the novel's core chapters appear as an effective way to represent the voices of the restless dead racing to possess the medium and be heard.

Despite her limited appearance in the novel, the character "Yū Miri" is crucial for understanding the theme of memory and generational trauma. As in *Mizube no yurikago*, the name her grandfather gave her plays a central role. During the first ritual, it is revealed that the name Miri, which means "beautiful village" and sounds somewhat like the name of her grandfather's ancestral village, has a strong historical connection to the region. The spirit of her grandfather obliges "Yū Miri" to listen to and write down the voices of her restless ancestors. Only by doing so, the spirit warns, will she be able to redeem their "sunken souls" (Yū 2004, 34) and become fully *herself.* It is therefore significant that, during the ritual, it is the fictional writer "Yū Miri," not the professional shaman, who is possessed and transforms into a medium. This reconfirms the significance of writing with the expressiveness of traumatic memory and the construction of identity as already observed in *Mizube no yurikago*.

The cacophony of voices in the core chapters—in my reading, the "possession" phase—has a confusing and yet illuminating effect on the reader.

Frequently, the same event is experienced and talked about very differently by multiple characters. It is unsurprising that Koreans and Japanese, guerilla fighters and collaborators, civilians and military personnel, "comfort women" and their "customers," would have different, often diametrically opposed perspectives. Yet, thanks to the shamanic narration in *Hachigatsu no hate*, readers may find that the "truth" Yū referred to lies precisely in the multitude of contradictory experiences we are encouraged to empathize with.

Yū does not give equal weight to all these voices. Arguing that the choice of narrative perspective was an "ethical question" (Fukuda 2004, 114), she proposes that it is a writer's responsibility to bear witness and expose acts of injustice that have gone unnoticed (Enomoto 1999). This stance strongly resonates with Ueno Chizuko's argument about the importance of power relations in the definition of "truth." Even in cases where historical accounts greatly diverge, Ueno holds,

> [T]his does not mean that one [experience] is correct and the other is mistaken. However, where power relations are asymmetrical the reality of the powerful becomes the dominant reality and this is forced on the minority party as a definition of the situation. In contrast to this, the act of bringing forth another reality that overturns the dominant reality is for the weak the battle itself…. (2004, 129)

By giving voice to the silenced, Yū creates empathic bonds and affords them humanity. It is this readiness to take sides—both in *Hachigatsu no hate* and *JR Ueno-eki kōen guchi*—that allows her to escape the pitfalls of historical relativism. The provocative nature of this approach is best illustrated by the scandal Yū's approach to the "comfort-women" issue in *Hachigatsu no hate* caused. When the daily installments in the newspaper serialization (*Asahi* 2002-2004) of the work shifted to the first-person narrative of a very young Korean girl who had been tricked into sexual slavery, the newspaper received a tsunami of complaints. Eventually, the publication was prematurely terminated, officially because the editors had lost confidence in the author's ability to complete the highly fragmented novel (Iwata-Weickgenannt 2020, 826-827). In the closing chapter, published soon after in a literary journal and set in the twenty-first century, the ghost of the abused girl is posthumously married to her childhood love—"Yū Miri's" great-uncle—who was tortured to death in the runup to the Korean War. Yū had likely planned this ending even before the newspaper publication was abruptly terminated. However, this intervention underscores the contemporary political relevance of the novel, as it recognizes the fates of two innocent youths whose lives were cut short in outrageous acts of politicized violence. The inclusion of the shunned former comfort woman in "Yū Miri's" family history specifically acknowledges an inconvenient truth—a historical injustice that has not been redressed—a perspective that was lacking from the public response to *Hachigatsu no hate* during the newspaper serialization.

If *Hachigatsu no hate* can be read as a meditation on the historical trauma of colonialism, *JR Ueno-eki kōen guchi* is a response to the destabilizing effects of the Great East Japan Earthquake of March 11, 2011 (commonly referred to as 3.11). The earthquake and the deadly tsunami it spawned were easily recognized as a national calamity. However, there was a political tendency to characterize the Fukushima nuclear meltdowns as a local disaster with only regional effects, which sparked a discussion about the Tōhoku region's status within the Japanese nation state. While academics had long regarded Japan's northeast as akin to an internal colony, exploited for rice, cheap labor, and energy (Oguma 2011), the discussion about the role of structural inequality between urban and rural areas in the wake of 3.11 now spilled over to the wider public. For a while, the hegemonic understanding of Japan's postwar recovery as an all-out success story—exemplified by the post-bubble, Shōwa-era nostalgia and the hopes to repeat the triumph of the 1964 Tokyo Olympics in 2020—appeared to lose its footing. Much of the cultural production that emerged in response to the calamity calls into question the Tokyo-centered narrative of progress by introducing counternarratives from the margin, implicitly calling for a reassessment of not only the past, but also the present and future. Although the actual disasters are not fully dramatized in *JR Ueno-eki kōen guchi*, Yū's novel is a prime example of the post-3.11 trend of re-examining Japan's recent history.

The story is told from the perspective of an unskilled migrant worker (*dekasegi*) from Fukushima. In the early 1960s, he helps build the Olympic facilities using only his bare hands. He spends his life toiling on various construction sites across the country to support a family whom he rarely gets to see, but still ends up homeless in Tokyo's Ueno Park, eventually taking his own life. The dead narrator provides a detailed account of his life of privation and yet, in his near-anonymity, he is also an archetype. In one of the few early reviews of the novel, the scholar Ishii Masato characterizes him as "the epitome of benignancy and diligence," who is "tread over and knocked down, turning into a collective symbol of those Fukushima men who collapsed and came down without even knowing the deeper reasons for their misfortune and hardship" (2014, 115). The protagonist's individual recollections are supplemented by historical episodes told by a another, significantly more intellectual homeless person whose accounts stress the experience of ordinary people that are often overlooked. Taken together, their narratives present a palimpsestic view of Japanese postwar history from below.

The timing of this novel's publication, three years after the disasters and shortly after Tokyo was selected to host the 2020 Olympics, adds another layer of meaning to *JR Ueno-eki kōen guchi*. Read against the state rhetoric of the "Recovery Olympics" (*fukkō gorin*)—later rebranded as the "Victory-Over-Covid Olympics" (*korona kokufuku gorin*)—the historical tableau of suffering that is so clearly askew with the hegemonic narrative of a glorious postwar recovery evokes an uncomfortable sense of déjà-vu in the reader. Just like the "economic miracle" of the 1960s and 1970s was built on the backs of migrant workers, Yū seems to suggest, the interests of (the) capital were once again about to be prioritized at the expense of Tōhoku.

As in *Hachigatsu no hate*, Yū draws on postcolonial ways of understanding history, memory, and trauma. Again, the narration is not linear but highly fragmented, jumping back and forth between past and present, life and death, and interrupted by casual voices. With no home to retreat to, the narrator is not just constantly exposed to the public gaze but also is vulnerable to outside sounds: snippets of conversations, radio broadcasts, news articles, and the various sounds of the nearby train station pierce his ears. This randomness, and the lack of control it implies, is reflected in an insight he shares on the first page:

> I used to think life was like a book: you turn the first page, and there's the next, and as you go on turning page after page, eventually you reach the last one. But life is nothing like a story in a book. There may be words, and the pages may be numbered, but there is no plot. There may be an ending, but there is no end. (Yu[4] 2020, 3)

It could be argued that by narrating his life history—by making use of the creative potential of autobiography—the protagonist manages to shape the chain of misfortunes that characterized his life into a coherent story. By giving voice to a ghost (which arguably enhances the narrator's already invisibilized existence as a homeless person), Yū provides meaning to silenced existences.

Yet, as I have previously argued (Iwata-Weickgenannt 2019), *JR Ueno-eki kōen guchi* is far more ambiguous about the empowerment of the subaltern than *Hachigatsu no hate*, largely due to the novel's structure and the way the Fukushima man's narrative is presented. While *Hachigatsu no hate* is framed by shamanic rituals—the dead are summoned, listened to, and pacified—in *JR Ueno-eki kōen guchi*, the dead migrant worker's narrative is framed by the sounds of the station. Since the passages are very short, they can be quoted in full length. The story begins with these lines:

> There's that sound again.
> That sound—
> I hear it.
> But I don't know if it's in my ears or in my mind.
> I don't know if it's inside me or outside.
> I don't know when it was, or who it was either.
> Is that important?
> Was it?
> Who was it? (Yu 2020, 3)

The other end of the story closes with these words:

> 'The train now approaching platform 2 is bound for Ikebukuro. Please stand behind the yellow line.' (168)

Even after death, the narrator is permeated by sounds from the outside. That is, rather than gaining a voice, he *becomes* sound; indeed, in the final scene, readers realize that those sounds echo the narrator's death from jumping in front of a train. Just as the Yamanote Line runs in circles around central Tokyo—and encompasses the Imperial Palace, the symbolic center of Japan—the narrator too is caught in endless cycles of repetition and is dying several times over. There is no exit, no shaman, no ritual, no resolution, no recognition.

While in *Hachigatsu no hate*, the battered former comfort woman is welcomed into Yū Miri's family, the Tōhoku victims and survivors remain trapped in Japan's structural inequality, which Takahashi Tetsuya poignantly called *gisei no shisutemu*, a "system of sacrifice" (2012). The lack of true empathy is perhaps mirrored in the scant critical response *JR Ueno-eki kōen guchi* initially received. Although overwhelmingly positive, the reaction was extremely limited in scope until the English translation was awarded the US National Book Award in 2020. Ennobled by the American prize, the novel was reviewed in countless Japanese media outlets—Yū compared the frenzy to that after her 1997 reception of the Akutagawa Prize (Yū and Kido 2021, 12)—and soared to the top of the bestseller lists. Moreover, the novel has since been translated into multiple other languages. Perhaps the *dekasegi*'s voice has finally been heard via the detour of the National Book Award.

Untangling the Knots, Reconnecting the Threads

Yū wrote *JR Ueno-eki kōen guchi* while commuting to Minamisōma, her protagonist's hometown. The coastal town was severely hit by the 2011 tsunami and, due to its location close to the Fukushima nuclear power plant, it was also strongly affected by the meltdowns. Roughly half of the municipal area was declared a no-entry zone in 2011 and remained cordoned off until 2016. Despite the lifting of all bans, only a fraction of the former residents had returned at the time of this writing, and those who remained tended to be older. Although Yū had no prior connection to Fukushima, her own diasporic condition sensitized her to the evacuees' agony over being torn from their ancestral lands. Hoping to salvage their memories and serve as a conduit for their grief, she volunteered as radio host for a weekly program, commuting to Minamisōma from her Kamakura home and talking to over 600 disaster survivors until the station closed six years later (Yū and Miyazawa 2020).

In her stated desire to become a "vessel of grief" (*kanashimi no utsuwa*) for the traumatized survivors (Yū and Kido 2021, 16), Yū curiously resembles the character of the shaman, Yū Miri, she herself created when writing *Hachi-gatsu no hate*. And just as Yū Miri in that novel had to open up to her ancestors' pain to fully become herself, the empirical author too registers a profound change in herself after listening to hundreds of stories. "I started to think that the 'Self' might be like a vehicle that the 'Other' could ride," she states, adding that while "previously, I had thought of the 'Self' as solid, I came to understand that it is actually made up of many different 'Others'...It's like a tangled ball of wool—if you carefully untangle it, the thread can be used again" (15-16). Again, instability—of memory, of one's understanding of self—is welcomed as liberating and opening up new opportunities, rather than being seen as threatening.

As is evident in *JR Ueno-eki kōen guchi*, perhaps due to this entanglement with the Fukushima survivors, Yū's work gradually shifted away from personal trauma to the pain of others. The focus on community healing intensified when she moved to Minamisōma in 2015. Against all economic odds, she opened a bookstore with an attached theater space in 2018, claiming that "when reality is excruciating, sad, and unbearable, books can become a 'soul's sanctuary'" (*Bungakkai* 2020, 203). In the same year she revived the theater she had founded in the late 1980s and staged two of her plays. Especially considering that she used local residents as actors in both plays—very young in the first, elderly in the second—it is possible to read them as a continuation of the therapeutic listening she practiced on the radio show. Drawing from her own experiences as a teenage playwright, Yū compares theater plays to funerals, where traumas can be laid to rest:

> I needed to give the unbearable agony I felt a form. I wanted to mourn, to lament....I believed that only by filling up the theater space with the waters of grief could I touch others, and they could touch me. For a miraculous instant, we would fuse into one. Those were my happiest moments. (Yū 2018a, 256-258)

Like many of the early cultural responses to the 3.11 disasters, Yū's first Minamisōma play, *Seibutsuga 2018* (*Still Life 2018*) is a palimpsest. Based on *Seibutsuga* (1991), Yū's first ever book publication of a play, the 2018 remake has a tangled timeline which links the past with the present, interweaving one's own and others' traumas to create "a beautiful pattern" (Yū and Kido 2021, 16). Both versions describe a group of high school students hovering between life and death, but the rewrite is suffused with the true-life experiences of the actors: teenage disaster survivors. The play was performed by students at a local high school, founded after the disasters to give the few remaining children a chance to study in the area rather than having to commute to Sendai. The students had been in elementary school when the disasters struck, and many had buried their traumatic memories deep within. During the rehearsals, Yū states, "I was able to witness countless moments when the voice that had formed inside them found its way out. By sounding their voices from inside their bodies—bodies that also form a boundary to the outside world—the students liberated themselves" (Yū 2018a, 255).

The porosity of boundaries between now and then, self and other, truth and untruth, is also central to Yū's second play, *Machi no katami* (*Memento of a Town*). Written from scratch in 2018, it propels Yū's recurring theme of the malleability of memory in (auto-)biographical narratives to a new dimension. The mutual contingency of the factual and the fictional is highlighted through the setting in a theater: *Machi no katami* is about the rehearsal of a play dealing with the memories of elderly Minamisōma residents.

Yū adds a further twist to memory-as-fiction by employing a mixed group of lay and professional actors. Several Minamisōma residents in their 70s whom Yū had met through her radio program play the part of the theater staff, appearing in the roles of producer, stage director, and blackout assistant. The script lists these lay actors under their real names, implying that *Machi no katami* can never be put on stage without their participation, while at the same time fictionalizing their identities. On the other hand, young professional actors from Tokyo are cast as actors in the play-within-a-play and receive instructions—including lessons in the local dialect—from the Minamisōma lay actors playing the theater staff. Established hierarchies of center and periphery, laity and professionalism, old and young are jumbled up and made visible in the process.

The confusion peaks when everyone on stage suddenly seems to forget about the rehearsal. The Minamisōma lay actors stop acting as theater staff and begin chatting about episodes of their childhood and youth, with the Tokyo actors asking all sorts of questions. Eventually, the conversation turns to the exceptional beauty of the area's spring flowers. At this point, the locals' recollections are overlapped by the voices of two of the Tokyo actors, who begin listing the English translations of technical terms that lay bare the invisible toxicity permeating the scene: "Evacuation Zone," "Difficult-to-Return Zone," "Evacuation Order Cancellation Preparation Zone" (Yū 2018b, 24-25). Finally, the Tokyo actors start narrating disaster-related reminiscences, which are clearly marked as "authentic memoirs" of the—silent/silenced—Minamisōma lay actors. In the final scene following these recitals, the lay actors step forward and shout out the addresses of their lost homes, which have been washed away by the tsunami.

By creating a highly confusing, inextricable knot of "truth" and "untruth," Yū renders *ad absurdum* the distinction between performance and testimony . In the same way, the temporal progression of past, present, and future is blurred in *Machi no katami*: on the same stage, events from different eras are recalled and memories are reenacted by actors belonging to different generations. At the end of the day, "past and future, both exist now, in the present alone" (Yū 2018a, 260)—and are therefore open to modification.

There can be no doubt that, with Yū's return to theater, her writing has come full circle, while at the same time clearly going beyond her literary beginnings through the involvement of others. *Machi no katami* is about a town that has been irrevocably changed, and about the process of mourning its loss and bonding with others. On a meta-level, if placed in the context of the post-disaster discourse about the structural marginalization of Tōhoku experiences that so prominently featured in *Tokyo Ueno Station*, not only *Machi no katami* and *Seibutsuga 2018* but theater in general can be seen as having an empowering effect. As Yū's observation about the high school actors demonstrates, collaborative memory work allows for the articulation of emotions and gives birth to voice—a voice whose existence is validated by the presence of an audience.

---

1 Translations from the Japanese are the author's own unless otherwise noted.

2 Although *shishōsetsu* is occasionally translated as "I-novel," texts categorized as such are not necessarily written in the first person. Shishōsetsu developed in the early 20th century from a curious interpretation of European naturalism, which called for objective and detached descriptions of social conditions but was understood as necessitating introspection and unsparing observation of one's innermost secrets. Therefore, shishōsetsu are not only deemed autobiographical, but are also characterized by a highly confessional tone. There is a debate about whether shishōsetsu represent a literary genre (Hijiya-Kirschnereit 1996 [1981], Fowler 1988) or should be understood as a reading and writing mode in which readers' "expectations concerning, and belief in, the single identity of the protagonist, the narrator, and the author of a given text ultimately make a text an I-novel" (Suzuki 1996, 6). Dazai Osamu (1909-1948) is widely regarded as a self-destructive shishōsetsu writer (*hametsugata shishōsetsuka*) who sought to eliminate the boundaries between precarious life and confessional art, merging them in a way that led to a vicious cycle of self-destruction, much like the early Yū Miri.

3 Rather than using the Korean script—which would create a visual barrier and only add silence—Yū relies on syllabic *katakana* transcriptions to create an approximation of the sounds of the Korean language. To gauge the meaning, readers need to rely on small-sized Japanese glosses placed right next to the normal-sized "Korean" conversations. This technique has been used by *Zainichi* writers since the 1970s to inscribe cultural difference.

4 "Yū" appears without the macron in instances where a quoted passage or citation is from the published English translation.

References

Akutagawa Ryūnosuke. 2018. "In a Grove." In *Rashomon, and Other Stories*, 25-40. Translated by Howard Hibbet. Hong Kong: Periplus Editions.

Bourdieu, Pierre. 1998. *Praktische Vernunft. Zur Theorie des Handelns.* Translated by Hella Beister. Frankfurt/M.: Edition Suhrkamp.

Bungakkai. 2020. "Intabyū: Shoten 'Furu Hausu' tenchō Yū Miri. Genjitsu ga tsurai toki, hon wa 'tamashii no hinanjo' ni naru" (January), 200-203.

Enomoto Masaki. 1999. "Yū Miri: Dokusen rongu intabyū." *Da Vinci* (November), 64-67.

Fowler, Edward. 1988. *The Rhetoric of Confession: Shishōsetsu in Early Twentieth-Century Japanese Fiction*. Berkeley: University of California Press.

Fukuda Kazuya. 2004. "Special Interview: Hachigatsu no hate tōsōki—Yū Miri." *en taxi* (July), 103-115.

Fukuda Kazuya and Yū Miri. 2002. *Hibiku mono to nagareru mono. Shōsetsu to hihyō no taiwa*. Tokyo: PHP.

Hahn, Alois. 2000. *Konstruktionen des Selbst, der Welt und der Geschichte*. Frankfurt/M.: Suhrkamp Taschenbuch Wissenschaft.

Harajiri Hideki. 1998. *"Zainichi" toshite no korian.* Tokyo: Kodansha gendai shinsho.

Hijiya-Kirschnereit, Irmela. 1996. *Rituals of Self-Revelation: Shishōsetsu as Literary Genre and Socio-Cultural Phenomenon*. Cambridge: Harvard University Press.

Ishii Masato. 2014. "Shisha no gen'ei: Yū Miri JR Ueno eki kōen guchi." *Minshu bungaku* (November), 114-117.

Iwata-Weickgenannt, Kristina. 2019. "The roads to disaster, or rewriting history from the margins—Yū Miri's *JR Ueno Station Park Exit*" *Contemporary Japan* 31, no. 2: 180-196.

———. 2020. "Broken Narratives, Multiple Truths: Writing 'History' in Yū Miri's *The End of August*." *positions asia critique* 28, no. 4: 815-840.

Kawamura Minato. 1999. *Umaretara soko ga furusato: zainichi chōsenjin bungakuron*. Tokyo: Heibonsha sensho.

Kiridōshi Risaku. 2000. "'Yū Miri' o enjirarenaku nattara, shinu shika nai. Yū Miri rongu intabyū." *Bungakkai* (September), 249-259.

Loftus, Ronald P. 2004. *Telling Lives: Women's Self-Writing in Modern Japan.* Honolulu: University of Hawai'i Press.

Löschnigg, Martin. 2006. "Narratological Perspectives on 'Fiction and Autobiography.'" In *Fiction and Autobiography: Modes and Models of Interaction*, edited by Sabine Coelsch-Foisner and Wolfgang Görtschacher, 1-11. Frankfurt/M.: Peter Lang.

Oguma Eiji. 2011. "The Hidden Face of Disaster: 3.11, the Historical Structure and Future of Japan's Northeast." *The Asia-Pacific Journal* 9 (31.6): 1-12. http://www.japanfocus.org/-Oguma-Eiji/3583.

Plutschow, Herbert. 1995. *Japan's Name Culture: The Significance of Names in a Religious, Political and Social Context*. Sandgate: Japan Library.

Suzuki, Tomi. 1996. *Narrating the Self: Fictions of Japanese Modernity*. Stanford: Stanford University Press.

Takahashi Tetsuya. 2012. *Okinawa, Fukushima: gisei no shisutemu*. Tokyo: Shūeisha shinsho.

Terdiman, Richard. 1993. *Present Past: Modernity and the Memory Crisis*. Ithaca: Cornell University Press.

UC Berkeley, Berkeley Institute of East Asian Studies. 2022. "Announcing 2022 Berkeley Japan Prize Recipient" (September 23). https://ieas.berkeley.edu/news/announcing-2022-berkeley-japan-prize-recipient.

Ueno Chizuko. 2004. *Nationalism and Gender*. Translated by Beverly Yamamoto. Melbourne: Trans Pacific.

Yū Miri. 1991. *Seibutsuga*. Tokyo: Jiritsu shobō.

———. 1996. *Shigo jiten*. Tokyo: Asahi shinbunsha.

———. 1997. *Mizube no yurikago*. Tokyo: Kadokawa shoten.

———. 2004. *Hachigatsu no hate*. Tokyo: Shinchōsha.

———. 2014. *JR Ueno eki kōen guchi*. Tokyo: Kawade shobō shinsha.

———. 2018a. "Kioku no sōshiki" In *Machi no katami*, 256-258. Tokyo: Kawade shobō shinsha.

———. 2018b. "Machi no katami." In *Machi no katami*, 7-89. Tokyo: Kawade shobō shinsha.

———. 2018c. "Seibutsuga 2018." In *Machi no katami*, 91-223. Tokyo: Kawade shobō shinsha.

———. 2020. *Tokyo Ueno Station*. Translated by Morgan Giles. London: Tilted Axis Press.

———. 2023. *The End of August*. Translated by Morgan Giles. London: Tilted Axis Press.

Yū Miri and Kido Shuri. 2021. "Watashi wa sudeni shi na no dewa naika (jō)." *Gendaishi techō* (April), 10-24.

Yū Miri and Miyazawa Akio. 2020. "Engeki no umareru basho." *Higeki kigeki* (January), 63-73.

Justyna Weronika Kasza, Seinan Gakuin University

The Space of Memory: Existential Quest in Shiraishi Kazufumi's Fiction

> Memory as a space, a building…the space in which a thing happens for the second time.…Memory as a room, as a body, as a skull that encloses the room in which a body sits. As in the image: a man sat alone in the room… (Paul Auster, *Portrait of an Invisible Man*)

> [W]e have nothing better than memory to signify that something has taken place, has occurred, has happened *before* we declare that we remember it. (Paul Ricoeur, *Memory, History, Forgetting*)

The aim of this chapter is to introduce to a wider audience the profile of Shiraishi Kazufumi (b. 1958). Originally from Fukuoka City, in Kyūshū, Shiraishi graduated from Waseda University with a degree in Political Sciences and Economics. His debut novel was *Isshun no hikari* (*A Ray of Light*, 2000). He is the recipient of a Naoki Prize for his 2009 novel, *Hokanaranu hito e* (*To an Incomparable Other*).

Shiraishi Kazufumi's major novels include *Boku no naka no kowarete'inai bubun* (*The Part of Me That Isn't Broken Inside,* 2002), a confessional narrative about the search for the meaning of life. This was followed by a series of stories often identified as *ren'ai shōsetsu* (love stories) that center around complicated emotions, unrequited love, and human efforts to reconcile broken relations. Among them are "Watashi to iu unmei ni tsuite" ("The Destiny Called Me," 2005), "Moshimo watashi ga anatadattara" ("If I Were You," 2006), "Donogurai no aijō" ("How Much Love," 2006), and "Eien no tonari" ("Next to Eternity," 2007). The novels *Kakō no futari* (*Lovers at the Crater*, 2012) and *Ichioku en no sayonara* (*A Hundred Million Yen Sayonara*, 2018) were both adapted into movies, in 2019 and 2020, respectively.

Shiraishi's 2018 novella, *Sutando'in konpanion* (*Stand-in Companion*), represents a shift in his work to speculative fiction, and deals with a topic frequently undertaken by contemporary Japanese writers: the impact of infertility on present-day Japanese society. The English translation appeared in 2019.[1] Likewise, the transition from realistic narrative to imaginative fiction, or even magical realism, is visible in his most recent publication, *Michi* (*Road*, 2022), which tells the story of a middle-aged man who crosses time and space using a single picture as a clue to regain something he has lost.

Despite his rich literary output—including over twenty novels and short stories, film adaptations, and major Japanese literary awards—Shiraishi remains on the fringes of established literary circles. This is reflected in the small number of foreign translations of his works; to date, only three novels have been translated into English. One of the major contributors in promoting Shiraishi's works is the website *Red Circle*, which introduces him as "A deeply thoughtful author who writes about love, life and the human condition and is unique in being the only Japanese author to follow in his father's footsteps by winning the same major Japanese literary prize."[2] This description perfectly captures the essence of Shiraishi's writing, which always centers around questions of the human condition, regardless of the plot. In simple storylines, Shiraishi draws exceptionally powerful and suggestive pictures of characters in the middle of an existential crisis—the origins and purposes of which remain ineffable—and who seem unable to properly address and elucidate the source of their suffering and pain. They find themselves lost and confused; they demonstrate a mistrust of life and question the reality of the people around them. They embark, metaphorically and literally, on an existential quest: a journey that, contrary to what one might expect, leads not toward understanding but only toward a seemingly better articulation of the ontological circumstances in which they find themselves. The quest does not provide answers, does not change one's predicament, and does not ameliorate the past.

My decision to contribute to this volume on Heisei literature with a chapter on Shiraishi Kazufumi was influenced by the fact that his works all have such a deeply philosophical dimension, which affects not only the plots of his novels but also their structure. Whether he is creating a simple love story, a domestic novel, or autofiction, his works often contain metaphysical elements, full of philosophical digressions and anecdotes that betray his strong affiliation with French existentialism, and especially the writings of Albert Camus. Here I apply the notion of "existentialism" as a generic term that references universal questions about the human condition, rather than elaborating on specific principles and theories within the existentialist movement. Nonetheless, Shiraishi's fiction echoes key existential ideas that frame entire narratives: puzzles of existence and freedom (Jean-Paul Sartre), the question of being (Martin Heidegger), absurdism and free will (Camus), and borderline situations (Karl Jaspers). I acknowledge that the term "philosophical novels" sounds vague and might require further elaboration and clarification, which, for obvious reasons, must remain beyond the scope of this chapter. Here I follow the definition proposed by Italo Calvino, who recognized that the purpose of the philosophical novel is "to confirm and to question what we already know, quite independently of the philosophy that inspired it" (1987, 43).

Some questions that constantly accompanied my thinking while working on this chapter were: To what extent can we treat Shiraishi's literature as being representative of the Heisei period? What is the best framework with which to analyze his writing against the background of Heisei literature? What aspects or features of his works should be taken into consideration to justify his inclusion in this volume? How valid it is to examine literature from the perspective of an historical framework? Is periodization an appropriate point of departure for the evaluation of literary texts; and is it a genre, a specific literary form, linguistic expression more broadly, or themes and motifs that align literature with a specific period? How do writers address or respond to the changes they witness? As such, this chapter testifies to the challenging task facing a researcher who wants to define the characteristics of Heisei literature.

Shiraishi's texts escape conventional genre classification or periodization. We are dealing with exceptionally realistic novels, mostly about domestic matters, depicting complicated relations between a man and a woman, who often attempt to reconnect after years of separation. Japanese critics term his works as *katei shōsetsu* (domestic novels) or *ren'ai shōsetsu* (love stories). However, I argue that beneath a modest storyline about family affairs lies a complex and multi-layered plot, full of references to the philosophy and critical thought of Heidegger, Camus, Jaspers, Emmanuel Levinas, and others. These references, to a certain degree, are additional voices that complete Shiraishi's narratives. They are the very personal comments from the author who, literally "in disguise," re-appears in the narrative. Mixing memories, personal accounts, and testimonies with creative writing has become the hallmark of his literature, leading us to question the "fictiousness" of literary creation. Self-reflexive fiction could be another way to characterize his writing.

Shiraishi himself describes his writing in the following way: "If I were to describe my novels in the simplest of terms, they could perhaps be said to be the products of adding Junpei Gomikawa's *Ningen no jōken* (*The Human Condition*, 1956-58)[3] to Albert Camus' *The Stranger* and then dividing by two" (2016, 124).

The focal point of my analysis is the function of memory—a recurring motif in his writing. Memory, portrayed in his narratives both as remembering and as forgetting, functions as a point of departure for the storyline. The plots of the stories discussed in this chapter might not follow a linear progression; rather, it is the memory—what is remembered, forgotten, blurred, or missed as a nostalgic feeling of bygone times—that imposes the dynamics of the story and determines the interpersonal relations between the characters.

I propose to read selected passages of Shiraishi's texts through the lens of "the space of memory": what is remembered, forgotten, erased (often deliberately), recreated, (re)imagined, or longed for. However, some linguistic nuances must first be clarified. "Memory" in Japanese is expressed by the word *kioku* 記憶, which contains two characters: *ki*, which can be read either as a noun (a register) or a verb (to register); and *oku*, meaning "to think" or "to remember." *Kioku* therefore signifies recollection, remembrance, a memory that is usually verifiable and truthful. Another word for "memory," also used by Shiraishi, is *omoide* 思い出, which refers to subjective memory, reminiscence, personal recollection, or even a sentimental or nostalgic feeling. I believe that the distinction between the two words is important in reflecting on the image of memory as depicted in Shiraishi's novels, and testifies to its ambiguity.

Memory can never be trusted as a source of knowledge; it only serves to reconfigure our perception of the past. Moreover, forgetfulness constitutes an immanent part of our memory. Accordingly, what Shiraishi attempts to challenge in his fiction is the notion of truth (*jijitsu*) and the (un)reliability of storytelling.

This complexity is an important feature in Shiraishi's view of the function of human memory; its doubtful reliability resonates in the words spoken by the narrator of William Faulkner's novel, *Absalom, Absalom!*: "That is the substance of remembering—sense, sight, smell: the muscles with which we see and hear and feel not mind, not thought: there is no such thing as memory: the brain recalls just what the muscles grope for: no more, no less; and its resultant sum is usually incorrect and false and worthy only of the name of dream" (1986, 178).

Indeed, Shiraishi's characters seem to rely on memories and recollections of the past, but memory is not necessarily an independent entity or an abstract concept. As the narrator of *Kioku no nagisa nite* (*The Sea of Memory*) states, "*Jibun ni wa kioku ga mieru. Soshite sono kioku koso ga genjitsu nanoda*"—"I can see the memory myself. And it is this very memory that becomes my reality" (2019a, 9).

We may question the accuracy of the past and truth retold in a narrative but, as in the case of most postmodern novels, it is the only accessible and available truth, however unreliable it may be. In this sense, what makes Shiraishi's fiction unique is the degree of realism and descriptive accuracy: in each of his major novels, he provides a painstaking description of the place, the train on which a character embarks, the surrounding area, the location of a bar in Asakusa that reminds the character of an encounter from the past. All of this impels my interest in examining the relation between space and memory in his work. On the one hand, space—the geographical location that constitutes a dimension in the narrative—determines the way memory behaves within the narrative. On the other hand, it is memory that makes the experience of space individual and singular.

The novels *Kono yo no zenbu o teki ni mawashite* (*Me Against the World*, 2008), *The Part of Me That Isn't Broken Inside*, *The Sea of Memory*, and *Koko wa watashitachi no inai basho* (*Here is the Place Without Us*, 2015) serve as a point of departure for this discussion. These novels not only center around the topic of memory but enable me to narrow the analysis to the interdependence between memory and space. While preparing this chapter, I was fortunate to address some questions directly to Mr. Shiraishi,[4] one of which concerned the author's view on Heisei literature and how it differs from Shōwa literature. According to Mr. Shiraishi,

> The difference between Shōwa literature and Heisei literature lies in the topic of 'death.' For me, Heisei does not show any concern for 'death.' There is

> another big difference between these two eras: this consists in 'thinking' and 'feeling.' Heisei literature does not put emphasis on human cognition, the way we think. In my opinion, human history is not a 'continuum of senses' but a 'continuum of thinking.' Heisei writers seem not too interested in history, but pay attention to 'individualism'—that's what characterizes the mood of the times.

I further asked Mr. Shiraishi if the writer should be aware of the historical period, to which he replied:

> I am not entirely conscious of historical time, but of course this could be essential for the artist. However, since writers work silently, often detached from the movements and currents of the world, they do not have much opportunity to directly experience the atmosphere of the times they live in. In that respect, it can be said that the very consciousness of the times is the domain of scholars, not the writers.
>
> Therefore, today's artists don't 'think' much about time or historical period. Instead, they are interested in how they 'feel' about it, so I don't think they're demonstrating 'age consciousness.'

With regard to personal experiences reflected in his text and the use of first-person pronouns, Mr. Shiraishi said:

> There is always a strong desire in me to use the first-person pronoun, like 'I' or 'myself.' And yes, each text reflects my experiences. I feel like I am writing novels because I want everyone to know what my life, my existence, is about. Maybe the biggest personal experience for me is that I've always felt that desire.

Another interesting aspect of Shiraishi's writing is his choice of a specific literary genre and the creative process. I was curious to find out why his novels mostly depict ordinary family affairs, and how, as a writer, he would define his style of writing. According to Mr. Shiraishi,

> Family affairs are always a very convenient topic for a writer. For most people, family is both the source of joy and pain—our lives revolve around family. It would be difficult to write novels without considering the problems affecting Japanese families.

Finally, with regard to the relationship between philosophy and literature, Mr. Shiraishi commented as follows:

> I think philosophy and literature are strongly related; they are almost like

> members of one family. I am not exactly sure if they are like brothers, parents, lovers, or married couples, but they are inseparable. We must not forget about religion. I think that even today, it is impossible to separate these three domains of our lives.

The Space of Memory

While Shiraishi's writing does not easily fall within the framework of Heisei literature by virtue of its narrative style and themes, it is difficult to prove his affiliation with postmodern literature either. Probably, the most accurate term would be that he is "writing in between," across time periods. At the same time, I am convinced that what connects Shiraishi with the postmodern is the recurring theme of memory as an inseparable condition of storytelling, thus affecting the way we perceive or formulate truth about ourselves. His flexible treatment of memory makes him an incredibly interesting case study, not only as a Japanese writer but also in comparison with other contemporary authors. Memory is an indispensable feature of human identity, but how reliable is our memory in reconstructing the moments of our life? Does memory condition narratives of our life? Does it have to reconstruct the past in a linear way?

The interdependence between memory and truth is one of the recurring themes addressed by several postmodern writers, including Paul Auster, Julian Barnes, Karl Ove Knausgaard, and Michael Chabon. These writers changed the paradigm of thinking about memory, truth, and fiction, and made memory and space recurring topics of their narratives. Paul Auster, in *The Invention of Solitude*, considers the meaning of both individual and collective memory and defines its function in the contemporaneity of the past and the present: "Memory, therefore, not simply as a resurrection of one's private past, but an immersion in the past of others, which is to say: history — which one both participates in and is a witness to, is a part of and apart from" (1988, 138). Michiko Kakutani in her book, *The Death of Truth*, speaks of "post-modern modes of bending the truth" and observes that

> [W]riters as disparate as Louise Erdrich, David Mitchell, Don DeLillo, Julian Barnes, Chuck Palahniuk, Gillian Flynn and Groff would play with devices (such as multiple points of view, unreliable narrators and intertwining storylines) pioneered decades ago by innovators such as William Faulkner, Virginia Woolf, Ford Maddox Ford and Vladimir Nabokov to try to capture

the new Rashomon-like reality in which subjectivity rules.... (2018, 9)

Karl Ove Knausgaard, in his bestselling novel, *My Struggle*, claims that the reliability of our memory and ability to reconstruct life depends on the perception of the future. Knausgaard addresses an important issue of understanding, envisioning the past in his novel:

> In recent years the feeling that the world was small and that I grasped everything in it had grown stronger and stronger in me, and despite my common sense telling me that actually the reverse was true: the world was boundless and unfathomable, the number of events infinite, the present time an open door, that stood flapping in the wind of history....Understanding must not be confused with knowledge for I know next to nothing. (2012, 196)

In the *Dictionary of Untranslatables*, Barbara Cassin devotes an entire section to memory, and traces back the origin of the concept in various languages. She differentiates four manifestations of memory, one of which is "memory-thought," and explains that "memory does not exist by itself, as a distinct intellectual faculty. The support it offers to man in his life is so central that it cannot be separated from the manifestations of thought; the making of the past; models of thought and forgetfulness of a condition of memory." She continues,

> [M]emory has double status in modern languages. It is either invoked or experienced. How this duality is translated in each language is essential since it results from the fact that the past, whether lived or imagined, personal or collective, is both always there and absent. It is forgotten, or on the contrary comes to meet us and imposes itself, which is why there is a constant crossover between invocation and visitation. The range of association relating to the ways one establishes a past or distant event, in one's mind or body, covers a broad spectrum beyond the specialized words. (2017, 645)

In her exploration of the topic, which takes the form of a philosophical and linguistic investigation, Cassin points to other key concepts, such as truth, time, consciousness and unconsciousness, history, present, and image. She also mentions forgetfulness, which she defines as "a power to tear one away from fullness of meaning, offer[ing] a means of perpetuating memory. Memory thinks but only manages to do so through forgetting if instead of signifying loss, flight, or abandonment, memory allows us on the contrary to reconstitute a reference. We choose what counts" (645).

The study I find particularly enlightening is Peter Middleton and Tim

Woods' *Literatures of Memory: History, Time, and Space in Postwar Writing.* They focus on the articulation of memory, the language of memory, its figurative meaning, and diverse manifestations in contemporary fiction, but they introduce the terms "physics of memory" (as a reference to Stephen Hawking's *A Brief History of Time*) and "spatialization of memory" (2000, 122 and 126). Both these terms are relevant to my reading of Shiraishi Kazufumi's texts.

The relationship between memory and space is also explored by Paul Ricoeur in his seminal study *Memory, History, Forgetting*, which constitutes the redefinition of Henri Bergson's *Matter and Memory* as well as Ricoeur's philosophical re-interpretation of Proust's *Remembrance of Things Past*. According to Ricoeur,

> This tie between memory and place results in a difficult problem that takes shape at the crossroads of memory and history, which is also geography. This is the problem of the degree of originality of the phenomenon of dating, in parallel with localization. Dating and localization constitute in this respect solidary phenomena, testifying to the inseparable tie between the problematics of time and space. The problem is the following: up to what point can a phenomenology of dating and localization be constituted without borrowing from the objective knowledge of geometrical…space and from the objective knowledge of chronological time, itself articulated in terms of physical movement? (2006, 40)

Memory as a literary motif of Shiraishi's fiction is often presented as a journey, a trip to a place remembered from the past, usually from childhood, hence a frequent image of the untranslatable notion of *furusato*, or characters' aimless wanderings around Tokyo. Still, Shiraishi is extremely meticulous: spaces in his narratives are easily locatable: they constitute geographical spots (Tokyo, Saitama Prefecture, Kyoto, Hakata); we can find them on a map; and, while reading the account of a character's journey through Tokyo or even as far as London, as in the novel *The Sea of Memory*, we are given an impression of truthfulness and consistency within the narratives.

> Both humans and animals leave traces of their existence. I term this sort of traces 'the smell of memory.' We are even unaware of this memory, when we smell it brings us back to the places it refers to. (2019a, 45)

The entire novel constitutes a multi-dimensional examination of human memory, from its biological function to its cognitive limitations. This thorough analysis is designed as a series of rhetoric questions that the narrator poses both to himself and to the reader:

> Why is that we do not remember the moment we come to this world for the first time? There is only one answer—that memory itself disappears completely from our head. Then, why is it that the memory of our birth disappears, yet we remember what we experience for the first time? (397)

In another part of the novel, the narrator affirms the unreliability of our memory—he has a vague recollection of the space he is supposed to be familiar with, but he remains passive, almost incapable of remembering or identifying the name of the place. This is yet another important aspect of Shiraishi's text: as much as the novel is set in a particular geographical location, at the moment the narrator reflects on his memory, it becomes just a place, a nameless spot on the map that only seems to exist in the narrator's imagination.

> That place must have been in my consciousness—I do not 'remember it,' but it is more accurate to say that I was 'brought towards this place.' As I was walking through the unknown place, I frequently felt that I knew this place. I realized that this was true.…That's why I felt so nostalgic about this place. I find it extremely difficult to put this feeling in words—the nostalgia was unusual. Maybe that was the universe I remembered from the time before I was born. (2019a, 408).

Memory serves to reconstruct the past, but by making forgetting an immanent part of human memory, Shiraishi challenges the notion of truth (*jijitsu*) and the reliability of what we can remember. In his two novels, *Me Against the World* and *The Part of Me That Isn't Broken Inside*, Shiraishi outlines the scope of human cognition: What are the limits of our knowledge? How much memory contributes to human cognition and understanding of our being in the world? What is the capacity of human memory?

The space triggers the memory, but it also reorganizes and restructures, changes the chronology of events. At the same time, memory rebuilds the space: as narratives progress, remembered, recalled, and experienced events expand the boundaries of the space inhabited by the characters, transitioning from the micro-space of *heya* (a room) toward *sekai* (world or universe). Yet Shiraishi does not allow his characters to live in parallel worlds but forces them to cover the route from one space to another. How does the space of memory manifest in his fiction? Let us consider three different forms with examples from selected texts.

The first form is remembered, visited, or experienced spaces, which within the narratives are referred to as *basho* (spot), *tokoro* (place), *sekai* (world), and also *furusato* (hometown). As mentioned before, Shiraishi provides a thorough topographical description: boarding the Keihin Tohoku train in Omiya Station, walking with a former lover around Biwa Lake, returning to their hometown of Kyushu. This is the most tangible form of space—these spaces seem as though they exist independently of the characters, but the concreteness of *basho*, *tokoro*, and *furusato* are reinvented by the memories of past events that affect the way the characters perceive the space they find themselves in present time. This form is most profoundly explored in the novel *Here is the Place Without Us,* which tells the story of an aging salaryman who is remembering his younger sister, who died as a toddler. The entire novel centers around her death, the family's breakdown, and other deaths that followed, but the most captivating scene in the story is the depiction of "shrinking spaces"—as soon as the main character remembers and recalls the moment of her death, the space of his existence changes from *sekai* to *jishitsu no beddo* (his own bed). The setting of the narrative is Tokyo, but the memory of his sister brings the main character to the place he refers to as *kodomo no inai sekai* (a world without children). This is the space that defines his own existence, as an unmarried man, when he realizes that "I came to understand that this world consists of two different worlds: it can be a world with children, and, in my case, a world without children. This is my situation, even as an adult" (2019b, 102-103).

The second form of space is "the space of books remembered"—a form that appears frequently in Shiraishi's texts. It is a space of intellectual experience, of encounters with the texts of Japanese and world literature. This form of space is particularly visible in the novel *The Part of Me That Isn't Broken Inside*, where the narrator tries to define the purpose of his life. The memory of his close friends and members of his family evokes the memory of books the narrator once read that mattered to him: passages from Leo Tolstoy, Eric Fromm, Yukio Mishima's *Runaway Horses*, and even Aleksandr Solzhenitsyn's *Cancer Ward* accompany the narrator through his journey to the past. He embarks on journey that takes him across Japan; throughout, the novels he reads and the authors he quotes intensify the memories, making them more believable and meaningful. They become the points of reference in his twofold journey: the one across Japan and the one into the past. As Raj Mahtani, who translated the novel, comments,

> *The Part of Me That Isn't Broken Inside*, as its straightforward unadorned title suggests, is certainly rooted in existentialism.…The novel is a portrayal of an unvarnished account of life as it is lived by someone who, without any rhyme or reason, happens to be in Tokyo, making a living as a publisher professional. The sense of abstraction, or this sense of life lived as a 'nowhere man'…heightened even more by the story's occasional, yet remarkable digressions into explorations of the meaning of 'place.' (2019b, 304-305)

The form of space of books remembered also appears in an earlier novel, *Here is the Place Without Us*. To understand the death of a younger sister, the narrator reaches for philosophical texts that, hopefully, will help him to reconcile with her death. The novel consists of extended quotations from Heidegger and references to Jasper's notion of "limit situations." These passages reveal the metaphysical dimension of Shiraishi's texts—yet another feature of his writing—where fiction overlaps and mingles with a series of philosophical and existential questions posed by the author.

Finally, "the space of death" is the most dramatic and vivid form of space used by Shiraishi. It is present in almost every novel, either as the starting point of a story or the point of destination; it is also expected and anticipated. The novel *Me Against the World* is written in the form of a manuscript that consists of loose and unconnected pieces penned by a writer who died, and after his death the manuscript is passed on to his friend, who serves as the reader in the text. Memory is not the main axis of the story anymore; it does not set the direction of the narrative, but it remains in the background, because, when thinking about death, one thinks about the past. The space of death might be real and physical—it is seen, experienced, and felt—but it is also the most intimate and indescribable example of space. To accentuate the tension between the seen and unseen, Shiraishi takes his character—the narrator of the mysterious manuscript, standing in as the author—across the most peculiar form of a journey: a dialogue with death, one that is filled with humility and understanding of its inevitability, but also one that registers human resistance to and disagreement with the approach of death.

> Where are we going? …Death, to us, is a clear and imminent possibility—one that could occur any time. The act of living is merely the act of extending as long as possible 'the condition of not being dead' while desperately trying to dodge the likelihood called the occurrence of death. Moment by moment, our lives are a fight against 'death' and an escape from 'death.'

(2016, 29)

Likewise, the space of death is presented dramatically in *Here is the Place Without Us*, in which the passing of a friend marks for the narrator the moment when the world (*sekai*), almost in a tangible way, is reshaped and drastically changed:

> Okuno's birthday was three months earlier than mine, so since I was born, I always lived in the *world* with Okuno. But just only five hours ago, this world turned into *a world in which I came to live in the absence of Okuno's image.* (2019b, 102, emphasis added)

During my correspondence with Mr. Shiraishi, I asked what "memory" means to him as a writer, to which he replied:

> We invented 'clocks' first to accurately remember things or events. And the invention of 'clocks' gave us time and divided our memories into segments that could be recorded and those that could not be recorded by time. We are so bound by time that we can't even distinguish what we remember from what has been recorded or registered. Consequently, we started to see my life from 'start and end,' and because of that, we became more and more isolated. We came to believe that consciousness of time exists only in the brain, and that memory also disappears with our death. What remains is only the record of our existence.

Further discussion on memory brought us to the question of truth: to what extent can we recreate what is remembered? I made reference to American authors of the 1980s and 1990s who expressed a relatively subjective truth while using memory as the theme of their stories. Since human memory is not entirely trustworthy, the truth of memory is not a universal truth but may be changed and adjusted. Thus, according to many contemporary writers, memory is unreliable, which is why their texts often deal with the topic of moral and ethical relativism. Mr. Shiraishi provided me with a rather unexpected yet intriguing response:

> I think that our inability to trust human memory is the result of our focus on the function of the brain. The human brain is an insufficient and ambiguous 'storage device'; the data accumulated in the brain cannot simply be used. What is our brain trying to do when it is so imperfect? I'm very interested in the communicative functions of the brain. They are called the sixth senses: inspiration, prediction, prophecy, telepathy, etc., and if we examine the functions of our brain thoroughly, maybe we could understand the source of its ambiguity.

I also asked about the semantics of memory in his writing—figurative expressions such as *kioku no nagisa* (the sea of memory), *kioku ga mieru* (memory could be seen), *kioku no nioi* (the smell of memory), and *mirai no kioku* (memory of the future)—that require decoding and remain untranslatable. Mr. Shiraishi explained their meaning as follows:

> 'Memory' is the foundation that supports all of our conscious activities such as self-awareness, the five senses, dreams, past and future. There are countless words that express memories.

In literary theory, memory is often connected to trauma and, in Shiraishi's work, the main characters are often returning to experiences of hardships, suffering, and traumas. According to the scholars Davis and Meretoja, once memory collides with trauma, it disturbs the narrative cohesion; the story we tell takes on a "fragmentary, non-linear style, by foregrounding reception, disrupted temporalities, absences, gaps and silences and indirectly point[ing] towards the unsayable.…This kind of aesthetics of trauma is often linked to poststructuralist philosophy of trauma that presents traumatic experience as beyond representation, fundamentally unknowable and incomprehensible" (2020, 26).

On the theme of trauma and the therapeutic power of literature, Mr. Shiraishi commented that,

> 'Memory' is a collection of personal experiences. Therefore, the word 'trauma' must be used with caution. If our brain has a communicative function, it is thought that there are memories other than our own. If that's the case, trauma is not limited to personal experiences. If we can investigate the source of 'trauma,' this can be a big literary theme, and I think it can play a therapeutic role. As long as you see only personal trauma, it's very hard to free that person from those traumatic experiences.

From Memory Into the World

In *The Invention of Solitude*, Paul Auster observes that, "To wander about the world is to wander about in ourselves. That is to say, the moment we step into the space of memory, we walk into the world" (1988, 166). These words are very relevant to the image of memory as a space in Shiraishi's fiction. What they mean by "world" (Auster) or "*sekai*" (Shiraishi)—a universe, a distant land, a hometown, a neighbourhood or the space of one's room—remains deliberately unspecified.

Memory in Shiraishi's texts is never static or fixed: it is all about movement, dislocation, covering and overcoming distance. This refers to geographical distance as well as moving backward in time, toward the past. I believe that topic can be approached from a different angle as well. What connects memory and space is, as we have seen, distance—in its temporal and geographical dimension. To whom does memory belong?

> Memory is never an individual possession. What I found out is that what we call memory is not something that resides inside myself but spreads like an ocean outside myself. That was the moment I jumped into the "the sea of memory." (2019a, 529-530)

In this chapter I have discussed memory in relation to space. I am aware that my approach only opens the possibility for further examination of memory as a literary theme in Japan, far beyond Heisei literature. For those interested in the literary representation of memory and truth, Shiraishi, in tracing autobiographical elements or in the process of fictionalization of the self, offers an interesting case study for comparative research with William Faulkner, Max Frisch, Philip Roth, Orham Pamuk, Paul Auster, or Nathalie Sarraute, to name just a few. This is all the more true since the scope and nature of Shiraishi's fiction has recently expanded; in experimenting with speculative fiction and crossing the limits of literary realism, he has proved to be a writer receptive to new and innovative narrative forms.

As I conclude this chapter, I would like to return to the issue I mentioned at the beginning: although the focal point of this discussion was narrowed to the interdependence between memory and space, it is a point of departure to demonstrate the philosophical dimension of Shiraishi's literature, in particular the influence of existential philosophy. As much as this statement may seem ambiguous and debatable, the manner in which Shiraishi outlines the axis of memory—human cognition; existence; world—can be interpreted with reference to not only Western traditions of thought but, interestingly, to the philosophy of Watsuji Tetsurō. For Watsuji, as opposed to Heidegger, human existence was conditioned not by its temporality but by its spatiality. In Shiraishi's description of the interdependence between memory and space it is possible to detect a continuation of space-oriented philosophy, or the topology of the self, as defined by Watsuji.

Watsuji's thinking reveals the applicability of his theory to the reading of Shiraishi's texts. First is the way this Japanese philosopher defined the human (*ningen*) as "being oriented towards a space of a symbolic life-world, or as he puts it a space that is structured by 'expressions'…human is ontologically situated in the space of life-world" (Liederbach 2012, 127). Here we touch upon possibly one of the most crucial aspects of Shiraishi's narration, which enables us to acknowledge the link between the fate of his characters and Watsuji's philosophy, in his argument that "spatiality is the conceptual framework for determining human's authentic existence" (130).

In a manner of philosophical meditation, Shiraishi continues to reflect on the authenticity and reliability of our memory—of what is stored, forgotten, misremembered, or confused, and how memory conditions and shapes our being in the world. Memory, in its vagueness and incoherence, leads his characters toward the world, however imprecise and unclear its boundaries may seem to us. In Shiraishi's words,

> I started to think deeply about the ambiguity of human memory and the ambiguity of our perception of the world we live in. We want to make sure that we spend our days reasonably, consciously, in a decisive way, we can't surely remember what we ate, who we met or what we did three days ago.…It is much more realistic to think of human beings as not accumulating memories, but of skipping memories and putting them 'to sleep again.' Memories are dormant. If so, is it true that we experience forgetting and memory as misremembering on a daily basis? Since we have forgotten, misunderstood, is our perception of the world accurate? Maybe, your world has moved in an unexpected direction? We have a habit of amending our memories as soon as we say, 'I forgot, I misunderstood,' but in fact, it is not that we have forgotten or misunderstood some fact, but that the world has changed into a different form, it took a completely different shape. To believe that only the reliability of our memory can be questioned, while the reliability of the world remains untouched is a misleading and false idea. (2019a, 246-248)

---

1 The story was specifically written for the *Red Circle* Mini series, and published first in English translation.

2 Quoted from the official *Red Circle* website: https://www.redcircleauthors.com/our-authors/kazufumi-shiraishi/.

3 Junpei Gomikawa's 1958 novel *Ningen no jōken* (*The Human Condition*), set against the background of World War II, is an account of Japan's involvement in war atrocities. Like Albert Camus's 1942 existential novel, *L'Étranger* (*The Stranger*), is a philosophical meditation on the absurdity and meaninglessness of human actions, and a revolt against the brutality of war.

4 This and subsequent quoted remarks are drawn from an email exchange between Mr. Shiraishi and me, which occurred between October and December 2021. I am extremely grateful to Mr. Shiraishi for his kindness and patience in responding to all my questions, and for granting me permission to use his words (in my English translation) in this chapter. I would like to also express my deepest gratitude to Mr. Richard Nathan and Mr. Kōji Chikatani from *Red Circle* for helping me to make initial contact with Mr. Shiraishi during my research activities in Japan in 2019.

References

Auster, Paul. 1988. *The Invention of Solitude*. London: Penguin Books.

Calvino, Italo. 1987. *The Uses of Literature: Essays*. Translated by Patrick Creagh. New York and London: Harcourt Brace Jovanovich, Publishers.

Cassin, Barbara. 2017. *Dictionary of Untranslatables: A Philosophical Lexicon.* Translated by Emily Apter. Princeton: Princeton University Press.

Davis, Colin and Meretoja, Hanna, eds. 2020. *The Routledge Companion to Literature and Trauma*. London: Routledge

Faulkner, William. 1986. *Absalom, Absalom!* New York: Random House.

Kakutani Michiko. 2018. *The Death of Truth.* London: Penguin.

Knausgaard, Karl Ove. 2012. *My Struggle*: 1. *A Death in the Family.* Translated by Don Bartlett. London: Vintage.

Liederbach, Hans Peter. 2012. "Watsuji Tetsurō on Spatiality: Existence Within the Context of Climate and History" (March). https://core.ac.uk/download/pdf/143632942.pdf.

Middleton, Peter, and Woods, Tim. 2000. *Literatures of Memory: History, Time, and Space in Postwar Writing.* Manchester and New York. Manchester University Press.

Ricoeur, Paul. 2006. *Memory, History, Forgetting*. Translated by Kathleen Blamey and David Pellauer. Chicago and London: The University of Chicago Press.

Shiraishi Kazufumi. 2016. *Me Against the World.* Translated by Raj Mahtani. Victoria, Texas: Darkey Archive Press

———. 2017. *The Part of Me That Isn't Broken Inside*. Translated by Raj Mahtani. Victoria, Texas: Darkey Archive Press.

———. 2019a. *Kioku no nagisa nite* [*The Sea of Memory*]. Tōkyō: Kadokawa bunkō.

———. 2019b. *Koko wa watashitachi no inai basho* [Here is The Place Without Us]. Tōkyō: Shinchōsha.

Valentina Giammaria, Sophia University

Tokyo's Hidden Spaces: Murakami Ryū and his Depiction of Kabukichō in *In the Miso Soup*

When Murakami Ryū (b. 1952) published his apocryphal novel *In za miso sūpu* in 1997 (subsequently translated as *In the Miso Soup*), he was responding in part to a Japanese society that had, in his words, "severely lost its confidence" (2006, 153). Set in Kabukichō, one of the seedier parts of Tokyo, the work follows an American serial killer named Frank, who moves through Kabukichō like a self-appointed angel of death, butchering anyone he deems unworthy to live. Kabukichō is presented to the reader as a space populated by troubled youngsters stereotyped as antisocial—and also, as the novel progresses, by a vengeful monster who sees his activities as a kind of purification rite. Frank's principal targets are teenage girls engaged in *enjokōsai* ("compensated dating," a euphemism for teenage prostitution) and the homeless.

This chapter will examine how Murakami depicts and critiques the isolated space of Kabukichō in ironic terms: he first presents the area in the familiar language of the Japanese collective imagination—dangerous, licentious, and full of people with whom "good Japanese" would never wish to associate—and yet, beneath this façade of critiquing the underworld qualities of Kabukichō and its inhabitants, Murakami directs his critical gaze back upon society as a whole. As I shall demonstrate, his purpose is really to expose the root cause of the "antisocial" behavior that goes on in Kabukichō: it stems from the fixation on high-end consumer goods that has persisted even following the bursting of the "bubble" economy. The result is a society at large whose values are superficial, empty, and meaningless. The overwhelming quality of Japanese society, Murakami suggests, is loneliness. His method in presenting this quality is to offer a hyper-realistic depiction of Kabukichō, giving the novel an air almost of documentary fiction.

A Spokesman for the Underworld

Murakami Ryū is a major media figure working as a novelist, magazine editor, filmmaker, and television personality. He was born in Sasebo, where he attended primary, middle, and senior high school. During his senior high school years, Murakami formed a rock band, for which he was the drummer, and developed an interest in hippie culture. During his third year in high school, Murakami and his fellow students barricaded the rooftop of their high school—probably to mimic the Japanese university protests of the late 1960s, which he was too young to take an active part in—an act that resulted in three months of house arrest. The impact of those high school years has remained powerful throughout Murakami's career; it was during these times that he was most influenced as a future writer and filmmaker. Murakami draws upon these personal experiences to portray characters who are often overwhelmed by despair and disappointment, echoing the young Japanese of the early 1970s who were victims of the political complacency that dominated the country.

As an author, Murakami Ryū's work explores that uncomfortable, hidden, underside of contemporary Japan through characters who struggle with drug abuse, disillusion, prostitution, and murder. As he explained in his essay entitled "Fiction as Documentary" ("Dokyumento to shite no shōsetsu," 2006), his novels are tools to address the issues of society, providing an in-depth analysis of those social phenomena as an alternative to the superficial and, in most cases, unproductive depictions by the media. Murakami, for example, frequently addresses problems such as child abuse, drug addiction, *hikikomori* (social isolation), and enjokōsai. Matthew Strecher argued that Murakami's fiction "has consciously laid the groundwork for new models of modernity and modern subjectivity (Strecher 2008, 343)" as Japanese individuals require the exploration and cultivation of a deeper sense of personal identity, separate from the collective society, but also for the rest of the world.

Among his best-known novels are *Almost Transparent Blue* (*Kagirinaku tōmei ni chikai burū*, 1976), *Coin Locker Babies* (*Koin rokkā beibīzu*, 1980), *Love & Pop: Topaz II* (*Rabu ando poppu: Topāzu II*, 1996), and *In the Miso Soup*, all dealing with acute problems facing contemporary youth.

Almost Transparent Blue, winner of the Akutagawa Prize, is Murakami's first work. It focuses on the life of Ryū, the narrator and main character, and his group of young friends living near an American military base, who are involved in a circle of drug abuse, sex, and violence in the mid-1970s. The novel is characterized by explicit and vivid images of self-destruction, capturing social issues that are often swept under the rug, a head-on approach in narrative that distinguishes itself from the more typical introspective postwar narrative.

This explicit way of portraying uncomfortable realities is what also characterizes *Coin Locker Babies*, a realistic text that includes surreal and horror-filled elements in addressing the theme of child abuse and abandonment. The plot revolves around two boys who were abandoned as infants inside two separate coin lockers in a station in Tokyo, and the hardships they experience during their lifetimes.

Love & Pop and *In the Miso Soup* came out just a year apart from each other. The first, for which a movie version was released in 1998 is centered on the issue of the enjokōsai. Murakami explains:

> I wrote *Love & Pop* after I finished filming the movie, *Kyoko.* For the first half of the 90's, I had traveled back and forth from Japan to Cuba to film *Kyoko*.…As I finished the movie, I turned my attention to Japan's reality, where high school girls were selling their bodies to buy luxury brand clothes and bags. If the high school girls were merely selling their bodies, I believe I would have not written a novel about it. I wrote that novel because I felt a sense of uneasiness about the circumstances revolving around those girls, especially about the media. (2006, 152)

The young girls at the center of *Love & Pop* are constantly in need of money—despite the fact that they do not come from humble families—just to satisfy their desire for brand goods. As a result, they practice enjokōsai. Hiromi, the protagonist, initiates herself into the practice for the sole reason of buying herself a ring. This behavior reflects what Murakami calls "the value system of the Japanese people," based on the insatiable, desperate appetite for luxury consumption that characterized the years of the bubble economy in the 1980s (152).

For Murakami, who likes to draw from actual places, social situations, events, and incidents for his fiction, the locale of Kabukichō in *In the Miso Soup* is a powerful setting through which to critique post-bubble Japanese society, a society that, according to him, "has fallen into a severe state of loss of confidence" (2006, 152). Kabukichō, in the Shinjuku section of Tokyo, is an area known for its seedy nightlife. It is an underworld right in the heart of the city, and sets the stage for the gruesome killings in Murakami's novel. Kabukichō is populated by people who are homeless, troubled youngsters, young girls engaging in enjokōsai, and prostitutes and their clients, all tainted by the stigma and stereotypes constructed upon them. As such, they become easy targets for crime and murder.

Murakami's novel paints a picture of Kabukichō that is faithful to the reputation it holds in the public mind: a dangerous place inhabited by *yakuza* (criminals) and degenerates, to be avoided at all cost by "good citizens." Kabukichō, situated right in the heart of Tokyo, is "reputed to be Asia's largest adult entertainment zone" (Schreibner 2020). It hosts a great number of nightlife related businesses, including host and hostess clubs, cabarets, lounges, snack bars, and boys' and girls' bars. These businesses offer *settai* (接 待), which refers to the practice of sitting next to a client to provide company by serving food and drinks, talking, and flirting, but without sexual services (Giammaria 2020). Kabukichō also offers nightlife entertainment that involves drinking, called *mizushōbai* (the "water" or "drinking" trade), and includes settai as well as sex-related businesses.

The novel *In the Miso Soup* is centered on the experience of Kenji, a twenty-year-old Tokyo nightlife guide, and his American client Frank, who asks for Kenji's services in Kabukichō during the last days of the year. Frank claims to want to enjoy the pleasures of the Tokyo red-light district, but he is in fact a homicidal sociopath, exhibiting distinct dissociated personalities, who kills people according to his own peculiar code of ethics. Although Kenji senses something wrong about Frank from the very beginning, he decides to accept the job because the money is good. The two spend three nights together and, on the second night, Frank shows his true colors in a gruesome murder scene at an *omiai* (match-making) pub, killing all the people there, including the staff, the hostesses, and their clients. He spares only Kenji, but threatens to kill Kenji's girlfriend if Kenji disobeys him.

Frank's victims have two commonalities: first, they are all killed in Kabukichō, and, second, they are all, according to Frank's standards, not worthy of being alive. They are the usual crowd for a place like Kabukichō, namely, nighttime workers and their clients, or girls engaging in enjokōsai. Yet within this killing rampage, Frank decides to spare Kenji and a Peruvian prostitute, even though they both work in Kabukichō, because he judges them as deserving to live: Kenji plans to quit his nightlife-related job to go back to school, and the Peruvian woman aims to return to her family to ensure a better life for them.

Behind this Dantesque Kabukichō underworld, where sinners are cruelly punished and the forgiven spared, lies Murakami's critique of Japanese society, a society that tends to create a space to systematically cordon off the promiscuous and unacceptable elements of the populace as a form of segregation and surveillance. Murakami uses Kabukichō, a place conceptually separated from ordinary Japanese society, as a mirror in which the Japanese can see themselves and see what they have created. As Murakami himself stated, "society's strange reaction to bizarre incidents and phenomena triggers my motivation to write a novel as a form of documentary" (2006, 153). His novels contain the elements of a documentary in that they portray aspects and issues of Japanese society through their characters and the space they inhabit. Behind the apparent critique of the "non-respectable types" in Kabukichō, Murakami is in fact pointing his finger at the superficiality and emptiness of a society where people have lost their humanity and values in the frenetic chase of wealth and material goods.

Murakami's work depicts a society where individuals are crushed by loneliness and reduced to survive in a dehumanized manner. In particular, the so-called "economic miracle" in the 1970s left a lasting legacy of consumerism: consumer culture has become the self-definition of Japanese youth, leaving no space for other forms of self-expression and self-discovery (Daliot-Bul 2014, 56). A major event that characterized the Heisei period was, undoubtedly, the collapse of the economic bubble in the early 1990s. According to Murakami:

> The collapse of the bubble made Japan fall into a severe state of loss of confidence, and all the fruits of the rapid growth have been almost forgotten. This is the contemporary era. Many grown-ups do not know how to live their lives. And the children who grew up looking up to these adults are even more confused. As a result, deplorable phenomena and incidents occur more frequently. (2006, 153)

Murakami's mission as a contemporary author lies in shedding light on Japan's social issues in the form of fiction, compelling readers to think about them. As a result, Murakami's fiction of the 1990s focuses on issues such as of the enjokōsai, a post-bubble phenomenon that was at the heart of Japan's social problems (152).

Murakami's Kabukichō

Natural disasters and the bombings of World War II destroyed a large part of old Tokyo, which was built of wood and other perishable materials (Seidensticker 2010). Tokyo also lacked preservation districts; thus, not many vestiges of the past remain. During the years following the end of the war, migrants flowed into Tokyo and the city was required to accommodate the newcomers. Starting in the 1960s, youth culture flourished and was reflected in fashion and lifestyle, and locations connected to youth culture play a central role in their self-definition (Daliot-Bul 2014, 48). The 1970s witnessed the so-called "economic miracle" of Japan, giving rise to a national identity of a "vast homogenous middle stratum, defined by the shared pattern of consumption and the aspiration for educational and material betterment of life, united in the endorsement of the 'post-war democracy' and its promise of peace, equality and prosperity" (54).

Rebuilding, relocating, re-mapping—the city continues to write its history in distinct chapters that can be taken as individual short stories. According to the urban scholar Jordan Sand, Tokyo was like a "growth machine," and its primary function was generating wealth and comfort according to the needs of the people (2013, 13). These ever-changing aspects of the city, always adapting to the most current circumstances, contribute to a phenomenon by which contemporary Tokyo appears divided into different cultural zones reflecting the identity of those populating each particular area. Tokyo was built around people, and contemporary Tokyo places in close physical proximity distinctly different cultural areas inhabited by different types of sub-communities.

The Shinjuku ward is a space that has tolerated all walks of life in the post-war years. There you can find "outcasts" such as prostitutes, the gay community, Japanese hippies, foreigners, outlaws, *yakuza* gangsters, *inakamono* (people from rural Japan), and so on (48). In the public's perception, Kabukichō is one of the most dangerous parts of Tokyo, populated by those who work in unsavory nighttime entertainment businesses such as *mizushōbai*, hostess and host clubs, cabarets, snack bars, girls' and boys' bars, soaplands (brothels specializing in exotic bathing experiences), and more. Kabukichō's importance in *In the Miso Soup* lies exactly in what this space means for the collective imaginary: it is an easily understandable mapping of the vices of the city. And one is in fact likely to find girls engaging in compensatory dating, swindlers, school drop-outs, and all sorts of "non-respectable" people in the streets and the bars and clubs of Kabukichō. Murakami draws a map of sin and singles out Kabukichō, highlighting it like a box right in the heart of the city, for the reader to see yet still keep it at a distance. What happens in Kabukichō is the problem of those who inhabit Kabukichō, while observers from the outside can remain detached. As Murakami puts it through Kenji's words,

> I won't say you'll only find depressive types working in Kabukichō, but everyone here has a past of some kind, not to mention a present that's less than ideal. (2014, 27)

In depicting the dark past that lurks in the shadows among Kabukichō's inhabitants, Murakami reveals the true nature of his critique: Japanese society, and in particular "the respectable types," has the tendency to ascribe the dark elements of society to this urban box instead of addressing them as larger social problems. Finding a culprit or scapegoat to blame for society ills is a tale as old as time. As a recent example, during the early stage of the Covid-19 pandemic, Kabukichō was depicted by the media as the hotbed of infections in the city, especially after the death of the famous Japanese comedian Ken Shimura, who had allegedly contracted the virus in one of the hostess clubs he used to frequent:

> The tendency of talk-shows, mass media, blogs, and social media platforms to point fingers mainly at *settai* businesses was most evident with Tokyo Governor Koike's press conference on March 30th, right after the death of the famous Japanese comedian Ken Shimura (age 70), known to be a frequenter of hostess clubs and bars. Shimura died on March 29th due to pneumonia caused by the new coronavirus and was the first Japanese celebrity known to have contracted the disease.…However, Shimura's death also resulted in more negative coverage of nightlife, as rumors about the comedian having contracted the virus from a hostess spread on the Internet and within Japanese news sources. According to some of these stories and rumors, Shimura might have contracted the virus in a hostess club during his own birthday celebration thrown by the club's *mama*, who had been in Spain a few weeks before where she allegedly contracted the virus. (Giammaria 2020, 4)

Scapegoating creates an even greater gap between those who are considered to be "respectable," that is, those whose lifestyles and choices reflect the mainstream national identity—for example, people who graduated from good schools, hold steady daytime jobs, and are married with children—and those who are considered "non-respectable," namely the outcasts, the nighttime workers, the homeless, and others who deviate from the established societal order. Kabukichō is home to the non-respectable, and thus is a perfect stage for Murakami's critique of the hypocrisy behind the scapegoating.

Enter Frank, the "Angel of Death"

Frank is the stereotypical American psychopath as portrayed in thrillers and horror movies and thus is the perfect villain for the Japanese common imaginary. He is cruel, pitiless, and bloodthirsty; even his voice sounds mechanical. Not only is he responsible for all the gruesome killings in *In the Miso Soup*, but he also embodies all the negative elements of the undesirable guest. As Kenji notes:

> I'd worked for nearly two hundred foreigners by now, most of them Americans, but I'd never seen a face quite like this one. It took me a while to pinpoint exactly what was so odd about it. The skin. It looked almost artificial, as if he'd been horribly burned and the doctors had resurfaced his face with this fairly realistic man-made material. For some reason these thoughts stirred up the unpleasant memory of that newspaper article, the murdered schoolgirl. (Murakami 2005, 12)

Kenji assumes that Frank is around 35 years old, but cannot ascertain his real age. He is chubby and unkempt, looking like an average American middle-aged man seeking pleasure in Tokyo's red-light district. However, Kenji feels from the very beginning that Frank is no ordinary customer, as he seems to hide an unhuman, dark side that surfaces whenever he feels offended or disturbed by other people's frivolous behavior. Frank makes a peculiar face, which Kenji calls "The Face," whenever his dark side is about to overtake him.

> Frank's expression underwent a disturbing change, though. The artificial-looking skin of his cheeks twitched and quivered, and his eyes lost any recognizable human quality, as if someone had turned out the light behind them.…Something ugly had reared its head for a second and then vanished again. (17)

Frank is also a compulsive liar. He lies about almost everything, even when "there is no conceivable need for him to lie" (35). His lies are inconsistent and incongruent, and he does not even try to defend himself when he is caught. Kenji is surprised when Frank tells him he comes from a family of only boys who loved playing baseball as children, just one day after telling him that he has one older sister. He also justifies his lies with other lies, making the reader wonder if he really has a past at all.

Frank defines himself a "sexual superman," but that is also a lie because he never actually has sex in Kabukichō (35). He claims that his primary goal as a visitor is to pursue sexual pleasure by experiencing whatever Kabukichō has to offer, and hires Kenji as his guide. Although Frank does not seem to be particularly rich, he sets no budget when it comes to sexual pleasure: "I want to try a lot of things, go to a lot of different places.…According to what I've read you can find it all here—Tokyo's like a department store of sex!" (15). He sounds obsessed about pursuing carnal pleasure, when in fact his agenda is to punish those who are not worthy of living, according to his judgment.

The criteria under which Frank chooses his victims are not random, even though his "acts of cleansing" do not seem to be driven by logic. He torches to death a homeless man, kills and chops into pieces a high-school girl, and massacres a whole omiai pub crowd. What his victims have in common is a lack of future goals and an inability to contribute to society in a useful way. The homeless man lives his life surviving in the streets; the high-school girl is engaging in enjokōsai; and the people in the omiai pub are too obsessed with material and ephemeral pleasures to go beyond their decadent lives. According to Frank, these people are eliminated not only because they are homeless or sex workers in Kabukichō but because they are not able to fight the ills of society. Frank's victims are society's victims; and eliminating them is his way of attacking society's toxic values.

Frank uses the metaphor of a "virus" for himself: as a virus, he infects all types of organisms, but he kills only those whose constitution is severely damaged or compromised to begin with. The fact that he spares Kenji and the Peruvian sex worker reveals the so-called logic in his murder scheme. Kenji and the Peruvian woman escape death from the virus because they both have goals—but more importantly, they treat Frank with humanity. Kenji is smart and loyal: even though he is a Kabukichō guide, he is not interested in materialism and does not try to take advantage of Frank by making him spend a fortune just for his own benefit. Kenji's values—friendship, loyalty, and honesty—and his hopes for the future are what save his life.

The Peruvian prostitute is spared for similar reasons. She sells her body to provide for her extremely poor family in Lima; her life choices are not motivated by materialism but, rather, she is working for a better future for herself and her loved ones. Coming from a very poor country, she turns to prostitution because she has no other means of making money. In addition, she has a long, deep conversation with Frank, sharing with him her thoughts about Japan, history, and spirituality, as well as about her family back in Peru. Frank believes she should be spared as she is not infected with poisonous values. In contrast, Maki, one of the girls in the omiai pub and Frank's victim, is obsessed with money and luxury goods, a typical product of Japanese consumerism. She sees Frank as a lonely *gaijin* (foreigner) and expects him to pay whatever she demands—and her superficiality and greed cost her her life.

In Murakami's portrayal, the Japanese seem to have lost any contact with the natural and spiritual worlds, as well as with themselves and each other. It is a country of loneliness, where a superficial lifestyle of wealth entices young girls to sacrifice their own bodies. His title, *In the Miso Soup*, suggests that all the different people in Kabukichō—the high school girl, the homeless man, the omiai bar crowd, the Peruvian prostitute, Kenji and his girlfriend Jun, as well as Frank, the foreigner, killer, and vigilante—are all bits and pieces of society, like the mixture of ingredients tossed into miso soup.

Conclusion

Kabukichō's importance in *In the Miso Soup* is based on what this location means in the collective imaginary. Murakami describes Kabukichō as a dangerous place, populated by sinners, prostitutes, enjokōsai, cheaters, thieves, liars, and a killer. To a great extent their lives define the space they occupy, and Murakami portrays Kabukichō as an easily readable map of the vices of Tokyo, where non-respectable types and delinquents find a home, while his readers can observe them from a distance. But what happens in Kabukichō is not only the problem of those who reside in Kabukichō—it is society's problem. There is no other locale that could function as a better stage for this story. The ills of society infect people and then confine them to a distinct urban space "quarantined" from the rest of society.

The people who Frank encounters in Kabukichō are all products of a society obsessed with materialism. In fact, apart from what they do for a living, the denizens of Kabukichō do not differ so much from people inhabiting other parts of the city, and their behaviors reflect the materialism endemic throughout Japanese society. They are all part of the miso soup that is Japanese consumerism.

Frank's "acts of cleansing" in Kabukichō are horrible and unjustifiable by any measure, but they force the reader to look at the ills of materialism and consumerism that distort the values of Japanese life and society. One wonders if it was Murakami's intention to convey that it takes a killer to wake us up to social problems, even though the killing is morally offensive and cannot be condoned. Kabukichō exists to cover the empty holes of Japanese society and provide illusory human company purchased with cash and luxury items. Through this awful story and its setting in Kabukichō, Murakami opens a Pandora's box and compels his readers to contemplate the dark issues of society hidden in a small area in the heart of the city, but which in fact spread far beyond.

References

Daliot-Bul, Michal. 2014. "The Formation of 'Youth' as a Social Category in Pre-1970s Japan: A Forgotten Chapter of Japanese Postwar Youth Countercultures." *Social Science Japan Journal* 17, no 1: 41-58.

Giammaria, Valentina. 2020. "Covid-19 in Japan: A Nighttime Disease." *The Asia Pacific Journal—Japan Focus* 18, no. 9: 1-10.

Murakami Ryū. 2005. *In the Miso Soup*. Translated by Ralph F. McCarthy. London: Bloomsbury Publishing PLC.

———. 2006. "Dokyumento to shite no shōsetsu" ["Fiction as documentary"]. In *Bungakuteki esseishū* [*An Anthology of Literary Essays*]. Tokyo: Shingurukatto shuppansha.

Sand, Jordan. 2013. *Tokyo Vernacular: Common Spaces, Local Histories, Found Objects*. Berkeley: University of California Press.

Schreibner, Mark. 2020. "Kabukicho Host Clubs under Fire for Spreading Coronavirus." *The Japan Times* (August 1). https://www.japantimes.co.jp/news/2020/08/01/national/media-national/kabukicho-host-clubs-coronavirus/.

Seidensticker, Edward. 2010. *A History of Tokyo 1867-1989, From Edo to Showa: The Emergence of the World's Greatest City*. Singapore: Tuttle Publishing.

Strecher, Matthew. 2008. "(R)evolution in the Land of the Lonely: Murakami Ryū and the Project to Overcome Modernity." *Japanese Studies* 28, no. 3: 329-344. DOI: 10.1080/10371390802446885.

Andre Haag, University of Hawai'i

Writing Back at Hate: Zainichi Fiction Between Korea-phobia, Korea-philia, and Anti-Racism

This chapter examines how new trends in contemporary Zainichi (literally, "in Japan") Korean fiction—or arguably *post*-Zainichi fiction—have navigated the diasporic dilemmas of a minority literature caught between old precarity and new prominence, virulent phobias and fevered fetishization. At the center of these trends is Fukazawa Ushio (b. 1966), an ethnic Korean novelist active since 2012, who writes under a Japanese penname and holds Japanese citizenship. Fukazawa works through the perennial Zainichi themes of anti-Korean discrimination and hate in unconventional, engaging ways, writing back against hate speech by providing unique glimpses into the "paradoxical dynamic" of being Korean in Japan in the early twenty-first century, buffeted by competing forces of Korea-phobia and Korea-philia.[1]

To briefly sketch the nature of the underlying paradox, by the late Heisei period (1989-2019), after decades of marginalization, invisibility, and "disrecognition,"[2] it appeared that Japan's postcolonial Zainichi Korean community was finally having its day in the sun, both domestically and internationally. This was particularly striking in the cultural sphere, where the increasing prominence of Zainichi Korean figures and representations across many domains signaled greater recognition and acceptance. Notably, Japanese consumers' early and eager reception of Korean wave (*Hallyu*; or, in Japanese, *Hanryū*) pop exports in the early twenty-first century not only boosted the image of the Republic of Korea but elevated the status of the resident Korean community in significant if complicated ways (Iwabuchi 2008, 244). Meanwhile, the place of Zainichi Korean literature was solidly established as an integral component of the field of contemporary literature in Japanese. For several decades, Zainichi Korean writers have attracted critical acclaim and mainstream attention, winning the literary establishment's highest awards and smashing sales records. One of the most commercially successful authors in Japan today is the second-generation Zainichi South Korean novelist Yū Miri, whose fiction seems to transcend the narrow confines of "Zainichi literature" and even represents the diversity of contemporary Japanese literature internationally.[3] The undeniable realities of Zainichi cultural integration have inspired movements to abandon "Zainichi" as a category of distinction and displacement, moving beyond into a "post-Zainichi" (*datsu-Zainichi*) sensibility (Hester 2008).

Other contemporaneous developments, however, raised concerns that the Zainichi Korean community—and the façade of a multicultural Japan—was imperiled like never before by a resurgence of racist hate. The same period brought the emergence of visible and vocal new movements organized around xenophobia, led by Sakurai Makoto's "Zaitokukai" (short for *Zainichi tokken o yurusanai shimin no kai*, or Association of Citizens Against the Special Privileges of the Zainichi), which held anti-Korean demonstrations in many Japanese cities. Although perhaps representing a right-wing fringe, movements self-avowedly driven by feelings of *kenkan* (嫌韓 , literally "Korea hating") demanded outsized attention because of the violent, eliminationist rhetoric they use to target Japan's Korean minority (Haag 2017). Juxtaposed against the possibility of post-Zainichi transcendence, the haters' rhetoric functions to remind resident Korean people of their continuing precarity in Japan, while deepening suspicions that the host country's avowed embrace of diversity and difference is merely "cosmetic multiculturalism" that goes no further than apolitical, surface celebrations of diversity or consumption of pop culture products (Morris-Suzuki 2002). Increasingly impossible to ignore, the problem of Japanese Korea-phobia has provoked a substantial social response, inspiring hate speech legislation, antiracist activism, and a great deal of critical commentary and research.[4]

In this chapter I focus on the distinctive reactions to new anti-Korean racism that arose from the edges of Zainichi literature in the late Heisei era. Focusing specifically on Fukazawa Ushio's *Green and Red* (*Midori to aka*, 2015b), I consider how, and to what ends, fiction has adopted shocking scenes of Korea-phobic hate speech as a major theme, motif, and plot device. While recognizing the outwardly didactic dimensions of the novel, I probe how Fukazawa mobilizes social concern about hate speech to bring into view a more fractured portrait of both contemporary Japanese cultural topographies and the position of Zainichi within them, neither of which can be understood solely in terms of Korea-phobia or hate speech.

Inscribing Hate as Zainichi Fiction in Late Heisei

In 2015, as social concern about anti-Korean movements surged, depictions of hate exploded onto the pages of new Zainichi fiction. The opening passages of Kinoshita Shigeru's novel *Moles and Kimchi* (*Mogura to kimuchi*, 2015) immediately confront readers with an anti-Korean demonstration taking place in Tokyo's Shin-Ōkubo Koreatown and a xenophobic diatribe that distills the Zaitokukai's rhetoric of paranoia and victimhood: "Zainichi are vermin, they're like moles, lurking unseen within Japanese society. If nothing is done, Japan's national territory will be left ravaged....If you hate Japan so much, get out! If they won't leave, kill them....Eradicate the vermin! Slaughter the moles!"[5] (5-6). Fukazawa Ushio's novel *Green and Red*, published only months later, also depicts a provocative hate rally in its first chapter. Screams of "Burn Seoul to the ground" and "Build a gas chamber in Shin-Ōkubo," echo throughout the novel, leaving one character fearing that Tokyo might be on the cusp of an explosion of racialized violence unseen since the 1923 Great Kantō Earthquake (17, 213).

In fact, a number of new Zainichi novels appearing around this moment, including Hwang Yonchi's *The Night Before* (*Zen'ya*, 2015), incorporated anti-Korean xenophobia—and the struggle against it—as central theme or plot device.[6] Even Che Sil's celebrated breakthrough *Jini's Puzzle* (*Jini no pazuru*, 2016), one of the decade's most talked about works of Zainichi fiction, prominently thematized how hate speech and hate crimes motivated by simmering (North) Korea-phobia force diasporic subjects to reexamine their ties to the ethnic homeland (81-86, 117-127; see also Yi 2022, 405). More recently, Yi Yongdŏk's novel *Before You Kill Me with Your Bamboo Spear* (*Anata ga watashi o takeyari de tsukikorosu mae ni*, 2022) conjures a dystopian near future in which the "xenophobes' dreams come true" under a rabidly anti-Korean administration that encourages ethnic violence against fortified Zainichi enclaves (12). Clearly, the problem of racial hatred has served as a powerful creative force for a new generation of writers whose work testifies to the enduring viability and relevance of Zainichi literary production in a supposedly post-Zainichi world.

That ethnic Korean novelists should seek to counter the resurgent xenophobia through their fiction is hardly surprising. Indeed, the act of representing—speaking for and depicting—Korean residents' struggles against discrimination and marginalization in Japanese society has long been seen as one of the core themes of Zainichi literature. Yet literary voices raised to counter anti-Korean hate resonated rather differently in the last years of the Heisei period, when national awareness of the problem of intolerance was higher than ever before. Notably, novels thematizing Korea-phobia emerged from new corners of the Korean diaspora in Japan and were packaged to target a broader audience, beyond those typically interested in Zainichi literature or even literature writ large, as evidenced by the stylized covers and engaging narratives of novels like *Moles and Kimchi* and *Green and Red*. These novels, furthermore, attracted popular interest and mainstream attention in the Japanese press.

In 2016, just as national hate speech legislation was working its way through the Diet, the *Mainichi* newspaper profiled Fukazawa Ushio and Kinoshita Shigeru as authors of popular fiction writing back against Korea-phobia. Kinoshita, known for the young adult fiction he published under his Japanese alias (*tsūmei*), had no connection to Zainichi literature prior to writing *Moles and Kimchi*. He lamented that most books critical of the resurgence of xenophobia in Japan were inaccessible academic texts, and his stated aim was to produce an anti-racist narrative "that even children would understand." Fukazawa Ushio, in turn, explained that she hoped *Green and Red* would drive home that "those who suffer from discrimination are real, living human beings. I wanted readers to know that hate speech inflicts profound damage on both bodies and minds" (2016). The *Mainichi* article framed these fictional works as effective vehicles of anti-racist education that could potentially reach a wider audience than other forms of activism.

That these novels were deemed worthy of showcasing in the national media reflects the extent to which anti-Korean racism had inspired concern and outrage on the national and international stage. In 2013, the loanword *heito supiichi* (hate speech) was even ranked as one of the top ten Japanese buzzwords of the year; the sudden salience of the term itself, Kim Wooja suggests, has engendered shared critical consciousness of the long-term problems of discrimination and violence against ethnic minorities in Japan (2016, 105). Thus, the new trends in Zainichi cultural production should be understood not only in the context of resurgent xenophobia, but also as a reflection of the robust political, social, and cultural resistance these racist movements elicited.

While discrimination against the Korean community in Japan is of course not new, the Heisei wave of Korea-hating, which originated in the 1990s just after the end of the Cold War, first festering within conservative magazines and on the internet and then exploding into street demonstrations, has strikingly novel features specific to its moment.[7] Sociologist Higuchi Naoto suggests that overtly xenophobic nationalist movements had rarely been seen in Japan before; traditional right-wing extremists were royalists and anti-communists, groups not as single-mindedly committed to the persecution of minority groups (2014a, 163-168). In contrast, the movements associated with this new breed of "Action Conservatives" openly broadcast anti-foreign agendas that fixate specifically on Zainichi Korean residents, demonizing them as parasites on the Japanese welfare system and "enemies within" working on behalf of hostile foreign interests (Higuchi 2014a,163-165; Itagaki 2015, 57). Unlike colonial-era "polite racism" (Fujitani 2011, 25-26), which was tempered by the official ideologies of imperial assimilation, or post-1945 currents of disrecognition that disdainfully ignored the legitimacy and very existence of the Korean presence within (Lie 2008, 80), contemporary Korean haters who take to the streets or lurk on the internet unabashedly use dehumanizing language, and frequently call for "undesirable aliens" to be expelled from Japanese territory or even murdered.

Public expressions of hateful xenophobia have been met with a largely negative social response in contemporary Japan because they are so at odds with the country's projected image as a society more tolerant of diversity. Not only do groups like the Zaitokukai appear to lack widespread support, but their rise has spurred the mobilization of anti-racist counter-movements whose activists crowd out the xenophobes at their own rallies. In this atmosphere, even conservative politicians have felt pressure to condemn hate speech and distance themselves from neo-racist groups (Shibuichi 2015, 736), allowing the passage of largely symbolic national hate speech legislation in 2016. It is far easier to denounce the public displays of hatred against the Korean minority than to address the entrenched structures of discrimination around citizenship, family registry (*koseki*), and immigration, or the rooted structures of feeling that attend them.

From this perspective, contemporary writers who take on anti-Korean racism in their fiction are not the marginalized voices from the wilderness of previous generations, but instead echo a broad consensus that hate speech is intolerable. Zainichi writers like Fukazawa Ushio might be suspected of leveraging social outrage about Korea-phobia as cultural capital to fuel fashionable, feel-good narratives of anti-racism, but it would be simplistic to regard them as offering little more than popular propaganda that condemns the most visible manifestations of anti-Korean sentiment. Fukazawa Ushio's *Green and Red* does appear to didactically textualize the effects of racist rhetoric "*on the bodies of others who become transformed into objects of hate*," to use Sara Ahmed's description of this phenomenon (2004, 60, emphasis in original). At the same time, the problem of hate provides an opportunity both to negotiate with the paradoxes of identity and cultural consumption in spaces where Korea-phobia coexists incongruously with Korea-philic fetishization of the Korean Wave as well as trendy anti-racist activism. Notably, Fukazawa's novel does not take for granted the existence of a stable Zainichi subject defined either by hate or in opposition to hate, instead centering the experiences of marginalized figures whose links to diasporic Korean identity are tenuous at best.

In sum, Fukazawa Ushio's confrontations with racial discrimination and conflicts over identity naturally draw from long-established legacies of resident Koreans writing in Japanese, but her approach to these topics is marked by a deep skepticism toward fixed borders and identities, which suggests affinities with more recent, post-Zainichi literary trends. While unequivocally calling out anti-Korean xenophobia, her novels question the impulse to either singularly fixate on racism's most blatant manifestations or to retreat into comforting fantasies of ethnonational community and identity, whether Korean or Japanese.

New Turns in an Old Zainichi Genealogy of Writing Back at Hate

On the surface, Fukazawa's *Green and Red* could easily fit within long-established genealogies of Zainichi writing. Using the Japanese language to write back against Japanese intolerance has been a perennial theme in Zainichi literature, as old as Japanophone cultural production itself. Literary scholar Kawamura Minato, for example, identified the act of "depicting from a political and ideological standpoint the resistance of Zainichi Korean people faced with oppression and discrimination" as one of four essential currents defining the genre. These core themes, he suggests, were first fully realized within the work of Kim Talsu (1919-1997), the writer canonically identified as the founding father of postwar Zainichi literature (1999, 16-18).

Kim Talsu's status as progenitor has been greatly emphasized in literary history, in part because he occupied the role of a mediating figure whose work made legible for Japanese readers the distinctive ethno-racial subjectivity and precarity of the Korean community in Japan. When founding his own Japanese-language journal, *Democratic Korea* (*Minshu Chōsen*, 1946-1950), Kim emphasized the pressing need to "rectify the erroneous understandings of Korea and Korean people among many Japanese people" (Sakasai, 268). To this end, he sought out venues across ethno-national lines, such as the Japanese literary journal *Shin Nihon Bungaku* (*New Japan Literature*), to which he contributed stories portraying the struggles of Korean subjects displaced in a hostile foreign land. His early postwar fictional portraits of Zainichi precarity, such as "After August 15" ("Hachi ten ichigo igo," 1947), evoked a community forged out of traumatic histories of colonial-era demonization and persecution emblematized by the 1923 Great Kantō Earthquake Korean massacres—an enduring moment in collective memory revisited by subsequent generations of Zainichi writers, including Fukazawa Ushio, who links that history of hate to its contemporary manifestations in Zaitokukai Korea-phobia.[8]

One key point of discontinuity between the progenitors of the genre and more recent popular fictions depicting anti-Korean racism and Zainichi precarity, however, is that Kim Talsu's critical exposés of Japanese intolerance were primarily targeted at a limited, sympathetic audience of progressive intellectuals. This was true of the Shōwa-era Zainichi literary luminaries who followed, such as Kim Sŏkpŏm (b. 1925) and Lee Hoesŏng (also known as Ri Kaisei, b. 1935), the first ethnic Korean novelist to win the prestigious Akutagawa Prize. Koichi Iwabuchi has observed that while some Zainichi Korean literary figures achieved critical recognition, their novels were "not for pleasurable mass consumption," and thus had limited impact and readership (2008, 254). At the same time, the representative figures of a postwar Zainichi literary canon were never truly reflective of the entirety of Zainichi experience or writing, and recent interventions in Zainichi literary historiography by Song Hyewon reveal that the canonization of a handful of male novelists beginning with Kim Talsu was premised on numerous exclusions, including the work of previous generations of Zainichi women writers (2014). Likewise, as John Lie has demonstrated, the category of Zainichi literature traditionally excluded an entire genealogy of more mainstream, popular writing in Japanese by ethnic Korean novelists, memoirists, and playwrights. Such writers, he suggests, were excluded not only for their failure to represent orthodox ethnic subjectivity and ideology, but perhaps because their novels enjoyed broader appeal among Japanese readers, fostering "the perception that they are light or popular writers, unbefitting of Zainichi literature" (2019b, 9-11).

The case of Fukazawa Ushio, however, hints at the peculiar potential for a fiction that calls out Japan's postcolonial xenophobia in narratives packaged for "pleasurable mass consumption." Making her literary debut at the age of 46 in 2012, Fukazawa's early efforts won not the lofty Akutagawa Prize, nor the Naoki Prize for mass literature, but instead Shinchō's "niche" Award for R-18 Literature by Women for Women (*Onna ni yoru onna no tame no R-18 bungakushō*). Although Fukazawa has been open about her own ethnic identity (as a naturalized Japanese citizen of Korean heritage), and often centers Zainichi characters and themes, it is likely that she would have been excluded from consideration within the circumscribed category of Zainichi minority literature a generation before. She not only writes under a Japanese penname for a more mainstream, presumably (but not exclusively) female readership, but took on Japanese citizenship of her own volition as an adult.

Nonetheless, Fukazawa's novels have been read, even embraced, within the expanding framework of Zainichi fiction, in part because of her commitment to exploring Zainichi topics of pressing relevance, most prominently hate speech. At the same time, her emergence reflects the extent to which the old exclusions and internal policing mechanisms that sustained Zainichi literature as a limited but coherent category have broken down in recent decades. The collapse of Cold War structures hastened the search for alternative modes of being Korean in Japan, such as the "Third Way" between assimilation and homeland-orientation, first articulated in the late 1970s, or more recently the "Fourth Choice," which includes the possibility of naturalization (Field 1993, 645-655; Chapman 2004). These shifts have brought greater recognition of the internal diversity of identification, ideology, and cultural expression among resident Koreans, but also might suggest the increasing fragmentation of Zainichi identity and Zainichi literature as coherent categories. As Cindi Textor recounts, the shifting generational, demographic, and cultural trends have prompted even Kim

Sŏkpŏm, a towering figure in the genre, to foresee the imminent "end of Zainichi literature," an apprehension that Textor juxtaposes against stirrings of so-called "post-Zainichi" frameworks that resemble problematic "post-racial" discourses elsewhere.[9] While the term "post-Zainichi" has been used to evoke the turn toward an embrace of "Japaneseness" and Japanese citizenship among ethnic Korean intellectuals and contemporary writers who reject the label Zainichi in favor of other labels like "Korean-Japanese," the framework remains rather unstable, and open to competing interpretations (Lie 2008, 127, 134).[10]

Although Fukazawa Ushio does not openly claim a post-Zainichi position, she has expressed discomfort with the restrictive category of Zainichi literature, which aligns her with a previous generation of female writers of Korean heritage, such as Yi Yangji (1955-1992), who similarly struggled against rigid expectations of representing ethnic themes and subjectivity in their fiction (Wender 2005, 126-128). In an essay titled "Can I Straddle the Line?" ("Sen o mataide ii ka"), for example, Fukazawa acknowledges that she is typically identified as a "Zainichi Korean writer" and that her novels "get lumped into the circle of Zainichi literature." But she repeatedly registers skepticism and frustration with the expectations, exclusions, and border-policing mechanisms that conventionally defined the genre. Alluding to the narrow classifications formulated by some critics and literary scholars, Fukazawa points out that not every novelist of Korean ethnicity published in Japanese gets counted as a "Zainichi Korean writer." To count as a practitioner of Zainichi Korean literature, she explains, one must not only have the correct identity (i.e., Korean heritage and nationality), but also capture in literary prose the essential quality of "Zainichi-ness" (*Zainichi-sei*). Pushing back against the imposition of borders that define the form, Fukazawa defiantly rejects the idea that classifications such as "Zainichi literature" or "Zainichi Korean writer" should define her fiction (2019, 4). Acutely conscious of the ways that her identity and writing fail to conform to the expected mold, Fukazawa questions what it would even mean for her to write more "like a Zainichi writer" (*Zainichi sakka rashii*):

> Conflicts over identity? A strong sense of ethnonational consciousness? Depictions of struggles against discrimination? All of these elements appear in my stories in abundance, of course. Perhaps in the end my expressions of resistance to being branded a Zainichi Korean writer, and lumped together in that circle of belonging, are my most Zainichi-like [*Zainichi-rashii*] feelings

of all. (5)

Consequently, Fukazawa Ushio's fiction has consistently resisted the pressure to exclusively portray Zainichi Korean characters, or to write about the inherited Zainichi themes she outlines above, according to amorphous notions of *Zainichi-sei* and *Zainichi-rashisa*. The result has been narratives that "straddle the line" between Zainichi literature and post-Zainichi fiction. If the prototypical postwar Zainichi novel adopted first-person narration that invited readers to collapse the distance between Zainichi narrator and Zainichi writer, Fukazawa Ushio favors a roving but limited third-person narration that shifts between multiple perspectives and fluidly crosses ethno-racial boundaries.

This unstable, borderline positioning has shaped Fukazawa's engagements with the perennial Zainichi themes of racial animus and discrimination. *To My Upstanding Father* (*Hitokado no chichi e*, 2015a), a novel published several months before *Green and Red*, was perhaps her first attempt to textualize the problem of Korea-phobia. But the novel avoids confronting the problem of hate from a stable Zainichi perspective, as a Zainichi problem, through its focus on a pair of seemingly Japanese women, mother and daughter, who must confront "the inescapable ties" that bind them to Korea (6). The central figure is the "Japanese" young woman, Tomomi, who is abruptly informed via sensationalized media reports that her long-lost father was allegedly a "North Korean operative." As Tomomi processes the revelation of her parentage, she is forced to face her own internal feelings of "rejection" and "loathing" for Korea, and the welling sense of anxiety at the possibility that "she might be the child of a Korean person" (36-37).

That revelatory twist, whereby a self-assuredly Japanese character, with unexamined Japanese prejudices, suddenly discovers their Zainichi Korean roots, has been a recurring, paranoid trope in fiction and internet discourse.[11] The fear or suspicion that one might have concealed Korean roots, which is the product of intertwined legacies of passing, disrecognition, and integration, gestures to the uncertain location of both resident Korean and ethnic Japanese identities today, several generations into the Zainichi sojourn. Deployed in Fukazawa's work, the trope of belated revelation serves to destabilize ethnic identities, binaries, and borders, including those separating the haters and the hated.

Motifs of Hate and Identity in Fukazawa Ushio's *Green and Red*

Although advertised on its cover as a "masterpiece" (*kessaku*) depicting youth, friendship, romance, and K-Pop cravings across borders, Fukazawa Ushio's *Green and Red* is likely the most prominent novel written in response to contemporary anti-Korean sentiment, all the more accessible because it is contained in an engaging and relatable narrative frame. Hate speech is undeniably the central theme and motif tying together its disparate stories and character sketches set in a familiar milieu of Tokyo's trendy cafes, creperies, and shopping districts, as well as social media platforms like LINE, Twitter, and Facebook. Through provocative depictions of xenophobic demonstrations and rhetoric, Fukazawa's novel probes the effects—rather than the causes—of racist hate that "inflicts profound damage on both bodies and minds" of victims, even where identification with the groups targeted for hate is weak or non-existent (2016).

While *Green and Red*'s roving narrator shifts between five different characters, the main arc follows the perilous, hate-induced ethnic awakening experienced by the novel's nominally Zainichi protagonist, Kaneda Chie (legally, Kim Jiyoung), a young woman whose sense of self is shaken, then shattered, by encounters with Korea-phobic hate speech. Chie is a fourth-generation Korean resident of Japan who was only informed of her nationality at age 16, when she was required by law to carry an Alien Registration Card. And she has assiduously avoided thinking about the matter of her ethnonational identity since then. To say that Chie does not strongly identify with "Korea" or "Zainichi" would be an understatement, yet her portrayal as a post-Zainichi *tabula rasa* paradoxically makes Chie an ideal surrogate for the reader to feel the effects of hate speech on its victims.

Through Chie, *Green and Red* evokes the sometimes arbitrary nature of group identities targeted by hate speech. The novel's title refers to the colors of passports issued by the Republic of Korea (Green) and Japan (Red). Indeed, the first chapter opens as Chie is handed her South Korean passport for the first time. While Chie has been casually concealing her roots from others to pass as Japanese, a summer holiday abroad with a college classmate (Azusa) has made the passport a necessity, forcing the character to confront proof of her national identity and raising the possibility that she will be outed by it. As documents of national belonging and keys to international mobility, passports have been centered in works of contemporary Zainichi fiction from Kaneshiro Kazuki's *GO* (2000) to Che's *Jini's Puzzle* (2016). As Christina Yi has observed, in such narratives the promise of an internationally accepted South Korean passport, as opposed to the stateless *Chōsen-seki* status often erroneously associated with North Korea, has allowed some Zainichi figures to regard nationality as "a pragmatic choice conditioned by the lures of global tourism and its attendant ideologies of capitalist consumption" (2022, 405-406). For *Green and Red*'s Chie, on the other hand, who is afforded no choice at all in the matter of nationality, the foreign passport is the inescapable material artifact of difference. The single green booklet makes her feel as if she "were being shrilly sentenced, 'You're not Japanese. You are Korean'" (9).

Similarly, it is awareness of the alien document that leaves the character psychically vulnerable to the forces of racial hatred. Following this prologue, an unsettled Chie, new passport in hand, wanders into the maelstrom of an anti-Korean demonstration sweeping Shin- Ōkubo. Just as she is trying to make sense of the charged atmosphere, unusually large crowds, battalions of riot police, and demonstrators with matching t-shirts, flags, and placards, the voice of a woman screaming through a loudspeaker reaches Chie's ears:

> She could clearly make out the words "Koreans" [*Chōsenjin*] and "South Koreans" [*Kankokujin*].
>
> "Kill them all."
>
> "Strangle them to death."
>
> "Burn Seoul to the ground."
>
> "Build a gas chamber in Shin-Ōkubo."
>
> Over and over, the voices shouted words that made her want to cover her ears. Chie felt a tightening pain in her chest....
>
> She made out the word "Zainichi" and reflexively turned toward the other side of the street.
>
> "Hang them!"
>
> "Drink poison!"
>
> "Go home, criminals!"
>
> "Drown yourselves in the sea!"
>
> Blatant hatred was flying right at her. (16-17)

This lightly fictionalized representation, introduced without elaborate commentary from the narrator, draws on actual rhetoric shouted or written on placards by anti-Korean marchers, often captured in video footage of their demonstrations. The passage captures the xenophobic essence of their message: the call for elimination of unsavory, parasitic foreign elements from Japan by any means necessary, whether death or (self-) deportation.[12] The emphasis in the narrative is on tracing the immediate and long-term effects of hate speech. The rhetoric of violence surrounding the keywords "Kankokujin" and "Zainichi" instantaneously triggers a psychosomatic feeling of pain in Chie, which echoes the noted effects of "vicious hate propaganda" on its victims.[13] However, Chie's initial reaction seems rather muted, as if she is refusing to process the implication of the words. Given the character's lack of strong identification as a Zainichi Korean person, she quickly tells herself that "It's got nothing to do with me" (17).

Despite such denials, the brush with hate has set in motion a shift in consciousness within this diasporic subject. With the shouts of the Korea-haters still echoing in her ears, Chie is suddenly moved to confess her origins to Japanese classmate Azusa for the first time. The ethnic "coming out" is another well-established trope in Zainichi literature and film, often depicted as a climactic moment of self-actualization.[14] In this case, however, it comes early and in a subtle form, as Chie simply passes her South Korean passport to Azusa in silence, as if awaiting her judgment. Yet, Azusa's reaction to this disclosure could hardly present a starker contrast with the scene of anti-Korean animus unfolding outside. Azusa immediately accepts Chie's newly revealed identity, if perhaps too enthusiastically. An ardent fan of South Korean popular music, Azusa elatedly discovers that Chie shares her Korean name, Jiyoung, with a member of the female K-Pop group KARA. Ultimately, Azusa's Korea-philic embrace of the ethnic confession—"I had wanted a Korean friend," Azusa chirps (22)—unsettles Chie nearly as much as the xenophobic rally. Here Chie's national identity arouses a Korean fetish that, not unlike the hateful demonstrators on the streets outside, makes Chie feel as if she is being reduced to the color of her passport.

The encounter with the hate speech rally, followed immediately by the scene of ethnic confession, initiates Chie's unsteady exploration of identity that asks what it means to be a South Korean resident of Japan in a time of Korea-phobia. This journey of self-discovery amidst subjection to racist hate is at the same time advanced by the Korea-philic prodding of Azusa, who insists that a holiday in Seoul will provide a necessary opportunity for Chie to learn to love her "own country" (24). During their trip to Seoul, Chie encounters Kaneda Ryūhei, a naturalized "Japanese of Korean descent" (*Kankoku-kei Nihonjin*), who will play dual roles as a love interest and a guide to navigating the diasporic dilemmas of ethnicity, nationality, and individual taste. Ryūhei, a graduate student at a university in Seoul, encourages Chie to learn more about her Zainichi roots. Could stronger ethnic consciousness and historical knowledge be the solution to the passing, assimilated Chie's sense of unmoored precarity? Ironically, the more conscious Chie becomes of her Zainichi identity, the more hate speech affects her, leading to a steep decline in the character's mental health. If at first relatively unfazed by the hate demonstration, Chie increasingly experiences "flashback" visions of the anti-Korean demonstrators, which are triggered by her new sensitivity to everyday racist interactions that accrete as microaggressions.[15] Borrowing library books about Zainichi Korean history to counter her feelings of anxiety with a greater knowledge of "who she is" only makes the situation worse. Chie learns the tragic history of displacement and poverty that seems to offer her nothing to be proud of, and uncovers stories about past discrimination against Korean residents that is eerily reminiscent of what she sees today.

The decisive blow is struck when Chie reads graphic descriptions of the 1923 Kantō Earthquake Korean massacres. Chie becomes so fixated on this violent episode from the past that she experiences a panic attack on the streets of present-day Shibuya, where she fears that "the people passing by might suddenly attack and slaughter her, just like at the time of the Great Kantō Earthquake" (213). This feeling is reinforced by yet another flashback of demonstrators in Shin-Ōkubo screaming, "Murder the damned Koreans!" Chie suffers a breakdown which leaves her socially withdrawn and contemplating suicide. The direct cause of her suffering is strongly implied to be hate speech, traced back to the character's initial subjection to Korea-phobia during the Shin-Ōkubo demonstration. At her lowest point, she wonders, "If only I had never encountered hate speech, would any of this have ever happened?" (230).

Chie's fears that the racist violence of the past could recur in present-day Japan might be dismissed as hyperbolic and paranoid—and the character herself seems to recognize this. At the same time, the novel musters substantial evidence that, for someone like Chie, contemporary Japan can be an intolerant place, where manifestations of anti-Korean hostility are inescapable: television specials about crime by Korean immigrants; Korean-hating books dominating the bestseller lists; racist comments on every internet site. Cumulatively, the idea that "the xenophobic atmosphere hanging over Japan now closely resembles the mood at the time of the Great Kantō Earthquake" is plausible not only to Chie, but contemporary media commentators (212).[16] Yet, there is more to Chie's ethnic subjection to hate than the direct connection between vicious speech and traumatic consequences. Fukazawa's narrative does not let highly visible xenophobia distract from the deeper structural forces beneath, which are glimpsed in the different colored passports and the notorious *gaijin* card —mechanisms of the discriminatory frameworks regulating contemporary citizenship and immigration—as well as in the specter of discrimination in housing and employment, and finally the everyday microaggressions that hit closer to home. *Green and Red* intimates that the explosions of violently racist rhetoric shouted by the Zaitokukai may only represent the most embarrassingly visible tip of a hateful iceberg of more subtle acts of hatred.

K-Pop Fandom, Trendy Anti-Racism, Intimate Cuts

A closer examination of the novel reveals that *Green and Red*'s positioning of Zainichi within the cultural milieu of Heisei is rather messier than a thumbnail sketch of Chie's tragic trajectory might suggest. While hate speech against Zainichi Koreans is ostensibly a central theme and motif, it is not the novel's sole focus. *Green and Red* essentially de-centers both hate speech and even the context of Zainichi to explore Korea-philic consumption patterns and fashionable anti-racism. In addition to the nominally Zainichi Chie, the narrative examines the positions of ethnic Japanese characters, including Azusa and an isolated middle-aged woman (Yoshimi), as well as a recently arrived South Korean exchange student (Jungmin), and a naturalized Japanese, "former Zainichi" Korean (Ryūhei). While multi-generational ethnic Korean residents of Japan may be the primary targets and victims of hate speech, in the novel they are not the only subjects affected by—or implicated in—the new tides of anti-Korean racism. Through this diverse cast of viewpoints, *Green and Red* also examines the countervailing forces opposing hate, as well as the K Wave (*Hanryū* or *Hallyu*) — associated Korea-philia that coexists with Korea-phobia.

Surprisingly, it is *Green and Red*'s non-Korean characters who are most outraged by encounters with anti-Korean hate, which is generally presented as a response derived from their consumption of Korean wave cultural exports. References to South Korean pop culture, particularly pop music, permeate the text. Both Azusa and Yoshimi are ardent followers of the K-Pop group CNBLUE;

they meet each other through a fan network and visit Shin-Ōkubo together. The pair are appalled to learn about the Korea-phobic demonstrations and join the anti-racist counter-protest movement. Chie's friend Azusa, for example, rallies against hate because she cannot stomach the sight of her beloved Shin-Ōkubo, "holy site of K-Pop," turned into a battlefield by racist demonstrators (75), though she is also aware that the xenophobes target Korea-philic women like herself, deriding them as "prostitutes" (54-55). Middle aged *Hanryū* stan Yoshimi is filled with righteous indignation when shown video footage of an "unforgiveable" anti-Korean demonstration targeting the homeland of her favorite K-Pop idol—"I simply could not bear to allow vile things to be said about Yong-hwa" (57)—and throws herself wholeheartedly into the counter-demonstrations.

Green and Red questions whether affection for South Korean pop culture can serve as a gateway to meaningful anti-racist activism, or whether it is just another iteration of consumerist, cosmetic multiculturalism, "divorced from politics" and uninterested in "major structural changes to existing institutions" (Morris-Suzuki 2002, 171). Links between transnational pop culture consumption and anti-racism have been observed elsewhere: in the U.S., for instance, K-Pop fans mobilized extensive online networks to contribute to the Black Lives Matter movement and other social justice causes (Kim Suk Young 2020). The impact in Japan, however, has been more complicated. In an early examination of the Korean wave's implications for the Zainichi Korean community, Iwabuchi suggested that "while the social recognition of resident Koreans has been much improved as the Korean Wave significantly betters the image of Korea," the phenomenon was marked by a tendency "to disregard the understanding of historically embedded experiences of resident Koreans" (2008, 244). These ambivalent effects are also registered in *Green and Red*, as Korea-philes Azusa and Yoshimi repeatedly subject Chie to insensitive microaggressions that reify or fetishize her Korean identity.

Nevertheless, the two K-Pop fans are genuinely outraged by the Korea-haters' rhetoric and commit themselves to anti-racist counter-protests organized online. Rather than painting anti-Korean xenophobia as the dominant force in contemporary society, many passages in the novel prominently acknowledge the robust opposition that hate movements have inspired. When another Shin-Ōkubo hate speech rally is depicted in the novel's second chapter (recounted by Azusa), the narration gives greater attention to the counter-demonstrators who shout

"Racists, go home" to drown out the racist calls of "Koreans, go home!" (74-75). Such passages capture the rise to prominence of anti-racist groups like the "Shibakitai" (short for *Reishisuto wo Shibakitai*, or Squad for Bashing Racists), a confrontational collective that since 2013 has repeatedly clashed with anti-Korean demonstrators.[17] The existence of robust counter-movements does not negate the problem of Korea-phobia, but it does provide another perspective.

Green and Red, however, registers ambivalence about the meaning and utility of popular anti-racist activism rooted in K-Pop fandom or self-satisfied condemnations of public hate speech. Specifically, the counter-protest movement is implied to be smug and self-righteous, and ineffectual to the extent that it turns off bystanders. The character Yoshimi, a stereotyped middle-aged K-Pop fan-turned anti-racist, presents a particularly problematic figure, as her newfound zeal for the cause can easily be read as an attempt to compensate for a sense of emptiness and aimlessness. The anti-racist declarations she posts to platforms like Twitter nauseate fellow K-Pop fan Hanae, who says of Yoshimi's activist social media:

> I don't know, but she's just so long-winded and tedious. All you can say is, yeah, yeah, whatever. It's like a principal's lecture, or a lesson from morals class. Just repeating over and over that discrimination is wrong. We get it. She's gotten herself all worked up with that sense of righteousness, like seriously. It turns me off. Isn't she just trying to show off how virtuous she is? Yikes. (67)

Far from an idealization of the forces mobilized against hate, the impression left by *Green and Red* is that characters like Yoshimi are futilely seeking a sense of purpose, community, and identity first in K-Pop, then in anti-racist movements. Furthermore, their involvement in activism turns out to be as faddish and short-lived as their attachment to Korean culture. Azusa quickly drifts away from counter-protests, and then from K-Pop altogether. Yoshimi, meanwhile, compulsively moves on to other social justice causes. Their examples do not inspire much hope that anti-discrimination movements will beat back the tide of contemporary xenophobia.

In contrast to the zealous anti-racists, other voices captured in *Green and Red* suggest that it might be best to avoid giving the lunatic fringe of racists more attention than they deserve. "It's only a few weirdos doing that, just ignore them," one character's mother remarks when shown video of a Zaitokukai rally (56). Newcomers from South Korea express some of the most measured perspectives on anti-Korean hate movements. Asked if he hates living in a Japan where anti-Korean bigotry is out in the open, Jungmin's coworker replies, "What is there to hate? I don't pay any attention to those demonstrations anymore. The ones demonstrating are just an extreme fringe. There are ladies who cannot get enough of me, but also guys who plainly show their loathing, and that is just Japan as it is" (88). The rhetoric of hate may be sickening, but *Green and Red* suggests that it would be myopic to allow the xenophobes to represent the totality of contemporary society.

Significantly, while the narration flits between disparate subject positions, one perspective it does not access is that of the anti-Korean activists. At numerous points, militant Korea-haters marching in the streets of Shin-Ōkubo are depicted at a distance, but *Green and Red* is not particularly interested in entering these minds to explore their motives and drives. Perhaps more insidious and disturbing are signs that less overt sentiments of Korea-phobia might be widely diffused in Japanese hearts and minds, rather than stably fixed within a minority of Korea haters. In unguarded conversations and remarks, characters casually divulge passing disdain or antipathy for Korea and Korean people. "I just hate them, South Korea and Koreans…" admits one character. "Almost all Japanese feel that way, aside from old ladies obsessed with the *Hanryū* and stupid little girls who love K-Pop" (160-161).

Ultimately, it is not the most toxic expressions of anti-Korean hate, but the intimate cuts closer to home, that inflict the most damage. K-Pop fan Azusa, who continually makes Chie feel that she is being "[forced to] wear the mask of a Korean, a Zainichi" (63), is by the last chapter flirting openly with the *kenkan* sentiment she had earlier protested against. She frankly admits to Chie that not only has she cooled on K-Pop, but now "hates everything about South Korea" (*tonikaku Kankoku no koto daikirai ni nachatta*, 202). While Azusa's passing experience of Korea-phobia is explained easily enough by her break-up with South Korean Jungmin, it is nonetheless an intimate betrayal to Chie: "Azusa's words cut into Chie's breast like a knife" (203). Subsequently, when Chie is haunted by visions of the Kantō Earthquake Korean massacres recurring in present-day Shibuya, it is not merely the mediated memory of historical persecution that torments her. Rather, the text suggests that it was Azusa's Korea-phobic turn that fuels Chie's suspicions that the Japanese people around her "might despise Korean people, and might loathe her personally. The face of the girl of about her age sitting right across from her transformed into the face of Azusa. Its demonic visage growled, 'I hate Koreans.' 'Die, Koreans, die.'" (213).

Compared to the more intimate fetishization and rejection from Azusa, the rhetoric screamed by faceless racist rioters on Japanese streets remains rather abstract and impersonal, as it is directed at the haters' phantasmal projections of "Korea" or "Zainichi." Ultimately, the novel suggests that Korea-phobia is not located within any fixed position, but ambiently circulates within contemporary society, infecting interpersonal relations because it is undergirded by discriminatory systems. Yet, with the tides of demographic change, cultural integration, and hybridity, the figure of Zainichi identity is shown to be just as diffused, fragmentary, and elusive, which may be precisely what provokes the Korean haters' impotent backlash. No individual in the novel can represent a stable Zainichi perspective or experience, and the essential qualities of "Zainichi-ness" are nowhere to be found. Paradoxically, the only force that gives meaning or coherence to Zainichi is the external threat of anti-Korean racism, which pushes Chie to fruitlessly seek solace in communal identity.

The novel presents an alternative model for inhabiting diasporic identity through the post-Zainichi figure of Kaneda Ryūhei, a naturalized Japanese citizen who acknowledges his Korean heritage and firmly opposes hate speech on the basis not of ethnonational consciousness but of a liberal, pluralistic individualism. It is Ryūhei who comforts Chie as she approaches her lowest point of ethnic subjection to hate: "There's no need to force yourself to feel like a Korean, and if you don't, that doesn't mean that you become Japanese. Nationality, it's just a condition. It doesn't have to define you...The idea of 'your own country,' that's an illusion" (204). In the face of xenophobia, Ryūhei extends an invitation to cross borders and renegotiate externally imposed collective identities, which resonates strongly with Fukazawa's literary endeavor to re-envision the boundaries of Zainichi, in pursuit not of a post-racial utopia, but of a society and culture where passports and bloodlines hold less power to determine one's place or precarity.

Conclusion

Fukazawa Ushio's *Green and Red* explores hate speech as a literary motif and strategy that can draw attention to more complex, contradictory formations of culture and affect that place Korea-phobia, Korea-philia, and Zainichi in a tense dialogue. In a sense, hate speech offers ethnic Korean writers, even those like Fukazawa who resist inherited molds and flirt with post-Zainichi positions, themes of substance that can energize their fiction, while allowing them to maintain ties to an established genre of minority writing and its core concerns. The old "dean of Resident [Korean] literature" Lee Hoesŏng once recalled that ethnic Japanese writers were envious of Zainichi Korean novelists because the latter have "themes to write about," while Japanese literature lacked themes of gravity because it had no "enemies" (Field 1993, 657, 669 note 25).[18] The implication is that Zainichi Korean literature does have enemies to oppose, and certainly discrimination and hate are forces lending weight to Zainichi creative production. Karatani Kōjin proposed that with the demise of national "modern literature" as a dominant institution of culture, "minority literature" often emerges as a site of new vitality, albeit one that by definition is unable to "move society as a whole" (2004, 7). Yet, in the late Heisei era, a confluence of phenomena elevated the problem of Korea-phobia to a matter of pressing national concern, allowing fictional engagements with hate by Fukazawa Ushio and other writers to speak to the concerns of an imagined national readership. Resurgent anti-Korean xenophobia, viewed from the perspective of the robust literary response it has inspired, seems to argue against the idea of a looming "end of Zainichi literature" or "rise of post-Zainichi fiction." Yet, the post-Zainichi creative potential of an anti-racist novel like Fukazawa's *Green and Red* might be identified not in any embrace of "Japaneseness," willful blindness to racial hatreds, or naïve belief that one can transcend identity categories entirely—avenues not open to Chie—but rather in an acceptance of inexorable mutual contamination and blurred boundaries between the unstable entities of "Korea" and "Japan" that neither Korea-phobia or Korea-philia can resolve or reverse.

1 On the "paradoxical dynamic" of (post-) Zainichi identity, see John Lie (2019a, 169).

2 Lie uses the term "disrecognition" to refer to the unacknowledged status of the resident Korean population in Japan, and the historical and social process that "made Zainichi objects of dislike, disenfranchisement, and degradation that were simultaneously unrecognized" (2008, 80).

3 For example, Yū Miri's 2014 *Tokyo Ueno Station*, a novel that does not feature Zainichi Korean characters, won the U.S. National Book Award for Translated Literature in 2020.

4 See, e.g., Higuchi (2014b), Yasuda (2015), Itagaki (2015), and Shibuichi (2015).

5 Unless noted otherwise, all translations in this chapter are the author's own.

6 On the thematization of hate in fiction by Hwang Yonchi and others from this time, see Hayashi (2019, 85-91).

7 See Haag (2017) and Sakamoto (2011) for a more extensive discussion.

8 For an overview of how the memory of the 1923 massacres became a touchstone of precarious identity in Zainichi literature, see Haag 2019.

9 Cited with permission; see chapter 7 of *Intersectional Incoherence: Zainichi Literature and the Ethics of Illegibility*, forthcoming (Textor, 2024).

10 Lie characterizes the post-Zainichi generation as "ethnic Koreans who are ready to embrace their Japaneseness, including Japanese citizenship," and associates its literary expression with the writers Gen Getsu and Kaneshiro Kazuki. For other perspectives on the post-Zainichi, see Hester (2008, 144-147).

11 This trope appeared in novels by Sagisawa Megumu and Iino Kenshi, writers who discovered their own mixed heritage as young adults; see Kawamura Minato (1995, 206-208). Similarly, Fukazawa recounted that her own teenage son, who had recently been influenced by anti-Korean books (*kenkanbon*), was shocked and distressed to learn of the family's Korean ancestry (2014).

12 For examples, see Itagaki (2015, 49-60).

13 For more on the somatic implications of racism, see Matsuda (1993, 24).

14 The confession is furthermore often a privilege of male Zainichi subjects, as discussed by Heneghan (2023).

15 On the experience of microaggressions specific to the invisible Zainichi Korean community, see Yamada and Yusa (2014) and Kim (2020).

16 Fukazawa draws this observation from Katō Naoki's *Kugatsu, Tokyo no rojō de* (Tokyo: Korocolor, 2014), which is included in the references for *Midori to aka*.

17 See, e.g., Shaw 2020.

18 As quoted from a 1988 conversation from the journal *Minto.*

References

Ahmed, Sara. 2004. *The Cultural Politics of Emotion*. Edinburgh: Edinburgh University Press.

Chapman, David. 2004. "The Third Way and Beyond: Zainichi Korean Identity and the Politics of Belonging." *Japanese Studies* 24, no. 1: 29–44. https://doi.org/10.1080/1037139041000l684697.

Che, Sil. 2016. *Jini no pazuru*. Tokyo: Kōdansha.

Field, Norma. 1993. "Beyond Envy, Boredom, and Suffering: Toward an Emancipatory Politics for Resident Koreans and Other Japanese." *positions: east asia cultures critique* 1, no. 3 (Winter): 640–670. https://doi.org/10.1215/10679847-1-3-640.

Fujitani Takashi. 2011. *Race for Empire: Koreans as Japanese and Japanese as Americans During World War II*. Berkeley: University of California Press.

Fukazawa Ushio. 2014. "Watashi no sōten: 'Zainichi' ari no mama ni hokori." *Mainichi Shinbun* (December 12).

———. 2015a. *Hitokado no chichi e.* Tokyo: Asahi shinbun.

———. 2015b. *Midori to aka.* Tokyo: Jitsugyō no Nihonsha.

———. 2016. "Heito supiichi taisaku ugoita, hitosuji no hikari Zainichi no sakka tachi." *Mainichi shinbun* (May 12).

———. 2019. "Sen o mataide ii ka." *Kokkyō (Border Crossings: The Journal of Japanese-Language Literature Studies*) 8, no. 1: 4-7.

Haag, Andre. 2017. "'Hating Korea' (*kenkan*) in Postcolonial Japan." In *Intercultural Communication in Japan: Theorizing Homogenizing Discourse*, edited by Satoshi Toyosaki and Shinsuke Eguchi, 114-128. New York: Routledge.

———. 2019. "The Passing Perils of Korean Hunting: Zainichi Literature Remembers the Kantō Earthquake Korean Massacres." *Azalea: Journal of Korean Literature & Culture* 12, no. 1: 257–299.

Hayashi Kōji. 2019. *Zainichi Chōsenjin bungaku: Han teiritsu bungaku o koete.* Tokyo: Shinkansha.

Heneghan, Nathaniel. 2023 (in press). "Beyond the Kokuhaku: Passing and the Tenacity of Confession in Zainichi Cultural Production." *Review of Japanese Culture and Society* 21.

Hester, Jeffry T. 2008. "Datsu Zainichi-Ron: An Emerging Discourse on Belonging among Ethnic Koreans in Japan." In *Multiculturalism in the New Japan: Crossing the Boundaries Within*, edited by Nelson Graburn, John Ertl, and R. Kenji Tierney, 138-150. New York: Berghahn Books.

Higuchi Naoto. 2014a. "Japan's Far Right in East Asian Geopolitics: The Anatomy of New Xenophobic Movements." *Social Science Research* 28 (December): 163-183.

———. 2014b. *Nihongata haigaishugi: Zaitokukai, gaikokujin sanseiken, Higashi Ajia chiseigaku*. Nagoya: Nagoya University Press.

Hwang Yonchi. 2015. *Zen'ya*. Tokyo: Kōrusakku.

Itagaki Ryuta. 2015. "The Anatomy of Korea-phobia in Japan." *Japanese Studies* 35, no. 1 (March): 49-66. https://doi.org/10.1080/10371397.2015.

Iwabuchi Koichi. 2008. "When the Korean Wave Meets Resident Koreans in Japan: Intersections of the Transnational, the Postcolonial and the Multicultural." In *East Asian Pop Culture: Analysing the Korean Wave*, edited by Beng Huat Chua and Koichi Iwabuchi, 243-264. Hong Kong: Hong Kong University Press.

Karatani Kōjin. 2004. "Kindai bungaku no owari." *Waseda bungaku* 29, no. 3 (May): 4-29.

Kawamura Minato. 1995. *Sengo bungaku o tō: Sono taiken to rinen*. Tokyo: Iwanami shinsho.

———. 1999. *Umaretara soko ga furusato: Zainichi Chōsenjin bungakuron*. Tokyo: Heibonsha.

Kim Suk-Young. 2020. "K-pop stans' anti-Trump, Black Lives Matter activism reveals their progressive evolution." *NBC* (June 27).

Kim Talsu. 1947. "Hachi ten ichigo igo." *Shin Nihon bungaku* 10 (October): 37-52.

Kim Wooja. 2016. "Maikuroaguresshon no gainen to shatei." *Ritsumeikan daigaku seizon kenkyū sentaa hōkoku* 24 (March): 105-123.

———. 2020. "Chaeil Chosŏnin yŏsŏnge taehan ilsangjŏgigo mimyohan ch'abyŏl." *Dong Bang Hak Chi* no. 191: 87-114.

Kinoshita Shigeru. 2015. *Mogura to kimuchi*. Fukuoka: Kobundo.

Lie, John. 2008. *Zainichi (Koreans in Japan): Diasporic Nationalism and Postcolonial Identity*. Berkeley: University of California Press.

———. 2019a. "The End of the Road? The Post-Zainichi Generation." In *Diaspora Without Homeland*, edited by Sonia Ryang, 168-180. Berkeley: University of California Press.

———. 2019b. "Introduction." In *Zainichi Literature: Japanese Writings by Ethnic Koreans,* edited by John Lie, 1-24. Transnational Korea 3. Berkeley: IEAS Publications.

Matsuda, Mari J. 1993. "Public Response to Racist Speech: Considering the Victim's Story." In *Words That Wound: Critical Race Theory, Assaultive Speech, and the First Amendment,* edited by Mari J. Matsuda, Charles R. Lawrence, Richard Delgado, and Kimberly Williams Crenshaw, 17-51. Boulder: Westview Press.

Morris-Suzuki, Tessa. 2002. "Immigration and Citizenship in Contemporary Japan." In *Japan: Continuity and Change*, edited by Javed Maswood, Jeffrey Graham, and Hideaki Miyajima, 163-78. London: Routledge Curzon.

Sakamoto Rumi. 2011. "'Koreans, go home!' Internet Nationalism in Contemporary Japan as a Digitally Mediated Subculture." *The Asia-Pacific Journal* 9, no. 10 (March). https://apjjf.org/2011/9/10/Rumi-SAKAMOTO/3497/article.html.

Sakasai Akito. 2018. *"Yakeato" no sengo kūkanron.* Tokyo: Seikyusha.

Shaw, Vivian. 2020. "Strategies of Ambivalence: Cultures of Liberal Antifa in Japan." *Radical History Review* 138: 145-170.

Shibuichi Daiki. 2015. "Zaitokukai and the Problem with Hate Groups in Japan." *Asian Survey* 55, no. 4 (August): 428–439. https://doi.org/10.1525/as.2015.55.4.715.

Song Hyewon. 2014. *"Zainichi Chōsenjin bungakushi" no tame ni: koe naki porifonii*. Tokyo: Iwanami.

Textor, Cindi. 2024 (forthcoming). *Intersectional Incoherence: Zainichi Literature and the Ethics of Illegibility.* Berkeley: University of California Press.

Wender, Melissa. 2005. *Lamentation as History: Narratives of Koreans in Japan*. Stanford: Stanford University Press.

Yamada Aki and Taiko Yusa. 2014. "Ethnic Microaggressions: The Experiences of Zainichi Korean Students in Japan." *Interactions* 10, no. 2. https://doi.org/10.5070/D4102017632.

Yasuda Kōichi. 2015. *Heito supīchi: "Aikokusha"-tachi no zōo to bōryoku*. Tokyo: Bungei Shunju.

Yi, Christina. 2022. "Intersecting Korean Diasporas." In *The Routledge Companion to Korean Literature*, edited by Heekyoung Cho, 399-411. New York: Routledge.

Yi Yongdŏk. 2022. *Anata ga watashi o takeyari de tsukikorosu mae ni*. Tokyo: Kawade.

Ⅱ. The Environment

Munia Hweidi, Sophia University

Through the Water Mirror of Amazoko in Ishimure Michiko's *Lake of Heaven*

"Somehow, tonight it seems the feeling has slipped away. It seems we can't make it back to Amazoko, no matter how much we look for the entrance."

"Even here at Utazaka?"

"Even at Utazaka. I wonder why."

"If we can't get there…why don't we call it up—call Amazoko to come to us?"

"Oh…"

Surprised, Ohina let out a sigh. Then she replied, "You're right. We need to summon it. Call it up from the bottom of the lake." (Ishimure 2008, 61)

Ishimure Michiko was born on the island of Amakusa off the coast of Kyushu in 1927. Her family moved to the village, now city, of Minamata when she was three months old. As an inhabitant of Minamata, she grew up within a close-knit community whose foundations were built upon traditional customs and a cultural heritage that emerged from living in a place of nature, beauty, and connection to the more-than-human[1] living world. She grew up in a realm of myths, modes of storytelling from dance to song, ceremonies, and festivals. However, Ishimure also grew up witnessing the devastating aftereffects of the Chisso Company's pollution of the Shiranui Sea, the locus of her village and its culture. This was the driving force behind her most well-known work, *Paradise in the Sea of Sorrow: Our Minamata Disease*, the first of her Minamata trilogy, in which she compiles reports and recollections, both fictional and real, reflecting the stories and aftermath of the industrial-based environmental poisoning experienced by the people of Minamata.

Likewise, Ishimure's 1997 novel, *Lake of Heaven*, contends with environmental themes. It tells the story of Amazoko, a village that has been flooded in the course of building a dam, and the human and the more-than-human living worlds it encompasses. Amazoko was inspired by the real-life village of Mizukami, which was sacrificed to the construction of the Ichifusa Dam along the Kuma River of Kumamoto prefecture. As the excerpt from *Lake of Heaven* that introduces this essay suggests, Amazoko is a place that is infused with memory, mystery, and reflection.

Ishimure's Amazoko

Even though she described herself as "just a housewife," Ishimure was a fierce activist and prolific writer. Her body of work is a collection of diverse writing and genres that focuses on the relationship between individuals and the more-than-human living world around them. She was extremely concerned about not only the preservation and protection of nature, but also the preservation of the traditions, stories, modes of storytelling, and cultural expressions that emerge from a natural world threatened and disrupted by the modern industrialized world. *Lake of Heaven* focuses on the recovery and forging of lost connections as well as the continuation of traditions despite massive losses and changes. It is a work about the connection between humans and the natural environment within which they live. Through a multi-layered journey of memory, myth, and self-discovery, Ishimure Michiko presents a resounding multiple-voiced narrative that attempts to reconcile the rift between what is traditional and modern, old and young, and imagined and real in the wake of the changes brought about by industrialization and modernization.

The locus of the narrative is Amazoko, a village that exists both in and out of time: now under the waters of the lake created by the dam, yet still above the waters in the memories of those who lived there thirty years prior to its submersion, who can only visit it in their dreams. The village also lives in the myths of the old and in the collective memory of the new, as members of the younger generation find their own stories intertwined with those who came before. Ishimure Michiko's evocative expression of the myths and traditions surrounding the village of Amazoko allows the narrative of the past to weave in and out of the present and become grafted onto that of the new generation. Through this forged connection, Amazoko is spiritually and metaphorically summoned from the bottom of the lake, and the younger generation becomes the new vessel of tradition in the modern world.

It is difficult to say if *Lake of Heaven* is the story of Masahiko, a man who brings the remains of his grandfather, Masahito, back to his village homeland; or if it is the story of Ohina, the elderly woman who preserves the legacies of the old village, and her daughter, Omomo, who becomes the next *miko* (shrine maiden). Or it could be the story of the gods and goddesses of water, sea, and earth who visit the villagers in their dreams. Or perhaps it is the story of the villagers' own lives. What is not difficult to say is that this is the story of Amazoko, the village named "Bottom of Heaven," a place that exists in both memory and reality.

Ishimure Michiko uses her works as a medium to conjure a connection between human beings, the environment, and the heavy shadow that modernization and industrialization have cast upon the natural world. But instead of lamenting what has been lost or calling for the replacement of one layer of reality, time, or space with another, Ishimure focuses on a rediscovery of what is already there, maintaining a connection between the planes of existence, as well as between the human and natural worlds. It is through this collective connection that individuals are able to find within themselves the lessons of the past and forge those of the future. This is a call that is not only felt in the remote villages of Japan, but a global call in the face of the rising awareness of the connection between human actions and environmental impact amidst rapid international industrialization.

Setting: Through the *Lake of Heaven* Mirror

Lake of Heaven tells the story of Amazoko's villagers as they grapple with displacement, a sense of loss, and the struggle to maintain their traditional culture in the face of a human-made environmental crisis—in this case, a dam that floods their home village, one of many consequences of the age of industrialization. It is also a story of reclamation, as the younger generation, in the form of Masahiko and Omomo, learns to connect with the past and weave it into the present. The story begins with Masahiko, a man from Tokyo who brings the ashes of his grandfather, Masahito, back to the village of Amazoko in Kyushu, where the grandfather grew up. Upon his arrival Masahiko encounters Ohina, a village elder, and her daughter Omomo, a recalcitrant woman who is disconnected from village life despite living on the banks of the lake overlooking the drowned village. As Masahiko learns the traditions of storytelling, music, dance, tradition, and myth from the village elders, both he and Omomo find themselves immersed in a space that exists in the present but also connects them with the past. This allows them to feel a sense of belonging and acceptance within the world, and gives the villagers a sense of hope that perhaps not all is lost, despite the skeletal remains of the village under the lake that haunts their dreams.

Ishimure's writing is heavily influenced by her appreciation and understanding of nature and her deep connectedness with place. She was witness to the devastating effects of environmental crises and industrialization on natural places and, in turn, saw how these often irrevocable changes negatively intersected with traditional society, the individual, and humanity's connection with nature. In *Lake of Heaven*, the characters feel a deep sense of loss and longing for the drowned village of Amazoko; however, this longing is not only for the physical place but also for the space it represents—the ghost of which can still eerily be seen submerged under the waters of the lake. The characters feel a need to reclaim a connection with nature and what Amazoko represents to them, and in this reclamation, they are able to gain a renewed sense of self and identity.

Lake of Heaven is Ishimure Michiko's answer for how to summon lost spaces and rebuild the connection with nature. Unlike *Paradise in the Sea of Sorrow: Our Minamata Disease*, which is a testimony of the devastation wrought upon the sea, *Lake of Heaven* calls for a reconciliation with nature and a new modernity that does not exclude tradition but embraces it. The very title brings an instant sense of place. There is a connection with nature in the form of the lake; at the same time, the reference to heaven is a reminder of the more-than-human living world, the world that encompasses individuals, nature, and the environment they share. The novel focuses on the interrelationship between these worlds, and how within these relationships there exist traditions, spirituality, and myths. It explores the devastation and sense of loss one experiences if relationships are severed or disrupted. This is a multidimensional space that encompasses nature and myth, and the people of Amazoko grieve for the erasure of this space in the wake of the modern encroachment of the dam.

Loss is embodied in the character of Masahiko, who has come to Utazaka Hill, adjacent to the lake that was once Amazoko, to scatter the ashes of his grandfather, who grew up in the village. Ishimure takes her readers on a journey through time, space, tradition, and memory toward a renewed discovery of self, beyond the self-centered and toward the self as centered within nature. The villagers recall to Masahiko the memory of a place he did not even know he belonged to: "The young man didn't quite know what to think, being asked if he had forgotten the road to the village" (2008, 14). His sense of confusion soon vanishes as he settles into his dual reality as a modern city person within this traditional space: "He couldn't help seeing his own self sinking beneath the mirror of the water. And it seemed there was yet one more of his selves, there on the bank of the stream" (278). In the process of guiding Masahiko through his journey of spirituality and awakening his reconciliation between the modern and the traditional, the villagers themselves are able to revisit the Amazoko of memory and dreams. "Masahiko felt he'd made his way into a world of the senses completely different from anything he had ever known before. This place, it seemed, was his point of entrance" (35).

Even though the storytelling in *Lake of Heaven* is centered on Amazoko, Tokyo features prominently in the non-linear narrative, often as a foil to the drowned village, the lake, and Utazaka Hill which overlooks it. The juxtaposition is a reminder of the need to engage with nature and tradition even in the face of the modern:

> If one compared these people who returned in their dreams to a sunken village with the people living in cities who, caught up in the march of civilization, have become so cut off from such things and no longer have a place of return, didn't it seem that the ones who returned in dreams were at least a little consoled, and perhaps better off? (282)

In this case, Amazoko and Tokyo are not only pivotal places where events and memories occur; they are also spaces of storytelling, history, tradition, and identity. As the narrative progresses, their layers become so enmeshed that it is sometimes difficult to untangle them. This is clear when Masahiko and Masahito, grandson and grandfather, are centered in Tokyo with no connection to Amazoko. They feel dissonant and disconnected from the world:

> Masahiko had reflected; all of us who consume these unnatural synthetic chemical things—like we're some sort of bacteria—can we survive in the midst of all this din and discord we've grown so accustomed to in the city? For that matter, the sound of sound itself has come close to becoming a lethal weapon. (36)

Masahito loses his grip on reality out of a desperate need to connect with his lost village, often searching for a "passageway" (184) to Amazoko via the gingko tree that stands near Nakano Station in Tokyo, which reminds him of the gingko guarding the entrance to the temple in the village. Masahiko recalls his grandfather spending many hours gazing at the Tokyo tree and sweeping the leaves as if this would open a passage back to the village and the living world he left behind in Kyushu. The fact that the grandfather is unable to find this passageway shows a disconnection with the place that had so deeply informed his identity. Masahito eventually dies after being taken away to a mental care facility without having found psychic relief or reconciling modernity and tradition. Masahiko only realizes the significance of his grandfather's actions in hindsight, as he observes the village elders and listens to their stories. He describes the elders' connection with the living world: "It seemed there was no border between their times of waking and those of dreaming. They could travel freely between both" (182). In contrast, the grandfather was no longer able to travel freely, having been uprooted and then firmly ensconced within the borders of the isolated and stark concrete of the metropolis of Tokyo.

Considering Ishimure's penchant for traditional modes of storytelling, the lost passageway here could be seen as a reference to Noh theatre. In Noh tradition, the act of crossing a bridge allows a story to move into the realm of the mystical. Masahito's inability to find the passage out of Tokyo is symbolic of his lost connection with the spiritual world that informs much of the villagers' daily lives. In an interesting reversal, Masahiko the grandson grew up in Tokyo yet never feels a sense of belonging in the city. He only truly finds his place in the world upon visiting the lake and, guided by the villagers, crossing over the metaphorical bridge into the space of tradition where he "felt himself harmonizing with everything around him" (252). Here, is he finally able to find his place, not only connecting to the living world but also traversing a generational connection through time. In this way he finally understands his grandfather's quest at Nakano Station and its significance to one's very existence.

Through the use of storytelling, memory, and a non-linear narrative, Ishimure presents three layers of the village of Amazoko. First is the Amazoko of the present: the submerged skeleton of a village whose outlines can still be seen underneath the surface of the lake. The mirrored sky of the entombed village is the bottom of the valley, a stark reminder of what has been lost. The villagers are often described by Ishimure as crossing narrow paths or bridges as they move through the valley, again evoking within the reader a sense reminiscent of Noh actors crossing the bridge into the spiritual realm. The villagers often speak of visiting the village in their dreams and memories, but this is something that the grandfather, Masahito, is unable to do once his connection with the village is severed by his move to the city of Tokyo. The loss of actual physical bridges due to flooding, as well as the loss of metaphorical bridges due to the weakened sense of belonging and connection to nature and the traditions born of those connections, brings a deep sense of tragedy, reflected in the skeleton of the submerged village. These losses make the villagers' final statements of wanting to build bridges in an attempt to reclaim the village and their connection to it all the more moving. The reader experiences this within the context of the image painted by Ishimure: the ghostly outlines of the village deep within the lake, preserved in a macabre snow globe.

The second layer is the Amazoko of the past—the Amazoko of dreams embedded in nature. The villagers are in a constant state of need when it comes to this Amazoko. They feel a need to visit it, remember it, and most importantly, they feel a need to conjure it and connect with it. The grandson, Masahiko, achieves what his grandfather, Masahito, had wished for, and is therefore able to reconcile his modern identity within the space of myth and tradition afforded by nature. He feels as if he has returned to Amazoko despite never having been there. Masahiko listens to the stories of the elders, accepts his place in the living world, and is able to finally feel in tune enough to hear the magical sounds of nature through the musical notes in the wind. He is able to find the connection to the village that his grandfather unsuccessfully sought through the gingko tree at Nakano Station. This layer highlights Ishimure's belief that we as humans are connected to a rich past through dreams and memory, and that it is through this connection that we are able to truly live and exist in the present. The sense of relief that Masahiko feels as he is able to reconcile his city self with this renewed self he finds in nature highlights the importance of these connections to the individual.

Finally, there is the timeless Amazoko. This is the Amazoko of myth and nature. This is the place where the gods and goddesses dwell, where songs and dances live, and where the entire soul of the world exists. The trees become gateways, allowing the characters to travel into this Amazoko and encounter the keepers of the lost memories, ready to be reclaimed. The cherry tree at the center of the drowned village, whose remains can still be seen underwater, at the bottom of the lake, is no longer simply a mark of a village that had been drowned, but a vessel of the dead and a giver of souls.

> No doubt even now that sacred old cherry tree still exists in the world of Amazoko Village, but it must have come on hard times since it was sunk to the bottom of the lake. Every year the villagers used to watch it blossom. But just now, I was the only one who saw it—alone, without a witness. It looks like the spirit of this cherry tree has come to depend on me, showing itself in the water like it's squeezing its body and spirit together and trying to say something. (7)

The gingko tree at Nakano Station in Tokyo, which reminds the grandfather of the gingko tree at the entrance of the temple in Kyushu, is no longer simply an entrance marker of the temple but a blocked passageway for a desperate grandfather trying to find a link to Amazoko from the confines of the city. Masahiko having followed his grandfather's voice to Amazoko, now considers Tokyo a "giant cancer cell" (77) as he escapes the confines of the cracked concrete and finds himself in the village. It is in this timeless Amazoko that the villagers discover nature, myths, gods, and goddesses. It is also in this Amazoko where Masahiko and Omomo find a self that belongs and learn to connect to the natural world, which in turn allows them to center themselves and find a more peaceful existence. At the beginning of his journey, Masahiko wonders how he, with his city upbringing, would be able to "pull together the scattered images of the village at the time it was flooded and had crumbled and been sealed off beneath the waters" (76). The answer becomes clearer as the story progresses in timeless Amazoko. Once Masahiko learns to listen and Omomo remembers the words of the village songs, they are both able to see Amazoko. They and all the villagers find hope in the knowledge that not everything has been completely lost and drowned in the waters.

In between the layers of Amazoko are stories of Tokyo. These episodes are grating and noisy in relation to the flow of the stories of Amazoko. "It seemed to [Masahiko] as if the roaring, screeching nightfall in Tokyo was all an illusion" (73). The separation of the worlds here is stark, and Masahiko's journey in trying to reconcile both into his own existence and identity is a lesson for the modern individual. It is in these stories of nature and humans that Ishimure illustrates that there is beauty in the world beyond the modern urban existence, and that to find this beauty one must not separate the past from the present nor the urban from the rural. She reminds the reader that beauty lies in the blending of these layers of existence, which must not exist in mutual exclusivity but must be part of a continuum, as if tracing a line in a mobius strip.

In addition to the multi-layered space, there is a sense of the otherworldly through the manipulation of time in *Lake of Heaven*. Ishimure reminds the reader that nature and history do not solely exist at the one point of intersection with the individual, but extend beyond the life span of any single person. In other words, the individual's life is a point within a larger narrative that extends through both time and space, encompassing the human and the broader living world. Ishimure creates this rich sense of history through the complex use of chronology in the novel. Time is both linear and circular. In the beginning of the story, the younger generation, represented by Masahiko and Omomo, is disconnected from the elders and the stories of Amazoko. During this part of the narrative, the distinct separation in the timelines between stories is clear, evident in the disjunction between Masahiko's memories of Tokyo and his present experiences at Utazaka Hill on the banks of the lake. However, as the younger generation becomes more receptive to the stories of the elders, imagination, dreams, and memories are assimilated into their modern selves. In this way, the multiple narratives and timelines loop into each other so that they are all the story of "life" rather than separate individual stories.

Cross-Dimensional and Cross-Generational Dialogue

The use of storytelling and the insertion of traditional genres of writing such as Noh and poetry are extremely impactful in Ishimure's work. As we see in *Lake of Heaven*, they become even more so as they illustrate the importance of using both modern and traditional modes of writing, melding them into a narrative of reconciliation between past and present, modern and traditional, and young and old. Ishimure is not presenting a tale of romantic nostalgia, nor is she calling for a return to the past. In this novel, she is invoking a recollection and reconciliation of past, present, and future in order for people to have a larger sense of belonging to the living world around them. This approach to storytelling is poignant when seen through the narratives of the generations.

Stories that fill the spaces between reality, myth, dreams, and history enable a conversation between the spirit of the dead grandfather and the city-dwelling grandson who, by looking through the mirror glass of the lake into the memory of the village, reclaims a sense of connection that spans generations. By taking the journey to bring his grandfather's ashes back to a place that no longer exists, Masahiko finds himself discovering that he already belongs to a place he does not know. His encounters with the people and creatures who inhabit this realm allow him to take a physical and poetic journey through time and space . Masahiko begins the narrative deaf to the world, unable to hear the sounds of the living world surrounding him. He is disturbed by the noisiness of Tokyo but is also disconcerted by his inability to hear the world of Utazaka Hill and Amazoko. As the narrative continues, trickles of sound start to come in. He begins to hear the sounds of nature, and then the stories of myth. By the end of the novel, Masahiko's ears can discern the sound of *biwa*[2] strings in the wind as he begins to compose his own songs. He feels almost as if he exists within both the foxes in the grass and the roots of the trees. The fact that the villagers keep mistakenly calling him by his grandfather's name no longer becomes an issue of physical resemblance, but rather a spiritual one. The elder Masahito had been unable to find the passageway in the gingko tree in Tokyo, but Masahiko is able to construct a bridge within himself. He listens to the songs of nature and then is able to translate them, composing songs for the *biwa* he inherited from his grandfather—an instrument made from the wood of the trees of the drowned village.

The old village woman Ohina is the keeper of traditions in this story; her predecessors are dead, and Sayuri, the shrine maiden, has drowned in the lake. Omomo, Ohina's daughter, begins as a cynical modern woman with only grudging ties to the traditional, but her story ends with a spiritual cleansing and bathing ritual in the lake, during which she becomes one with it and herself takes up the mantle of shrine maiden. There is an understanding between Omomo, Masahiko, and the natural world around them. They now sing and hear the stories of the past, present, and future in a timeless loop. Both experience their awakenings by the shores of the lake and the water shimmering above the drowned village, and gain a quiet understanding of what it means when the elders say they will rebuild the lost bridges.

It is poignant that Ishimure features these two characters and their awakening connection with nature. They are both children of an urbanized and industrialized world. Masahiko was raised in the city of Tokyo and had never been to Amazoko. Omomo grew up on the banks of the drowned village, yet she too had never been to Amazoko. Both the village girl and the city boy develop the capacity to conjure the shared memory of Amazoko through the songs and rituals of nature and the people whose identities are informed by their connection to nature. There is a sense of calm and a feeling of being centered that emerges from both characters as they reconcile the present with the past for a better future. Through these two characters, Ishimure is showing that there is a universal call for reconciliation, regardless of one's origins; to be alive is to be part of life, history, and myth.

Here Ishimure does not advocate for people to abandon the present and return to the past, nor does she judge one to be better than the other. She also does not convey that one must abandon the city permanently and go into nature in order to find one's identity or call for a life that emulates the past. In this narrative, Ishimure highlights the dualities: despite physical and temporal distances, all stories, both human and more-than-human, exist together and simultaneously. The villagers, when discussing the long-submerged village, realize that it is not truly lost: "It's strange, but if you look to the bottom the lost world seems to come back to life….Certainly there's a world that did exist" (136). They mention how the branches of the drowned trees seem to be reaching out to them, which make them feel they could still conjure and reclaim them in memory, if not in reality. It is the disruption and abandonment of the connections between these stories that leads to a sense of discontent in Omomo and Masahiko. Masahiko had to leave the city and go into nature and past memory to find himself; in contrast, Omomo had to interact with the man from the city in order to find her path, even though she lives right by the lake. In this way, Ishimure reminds the reader of a new modernity, one that enfolds the past into the present, and uses that connection to forge ahead into the future.

Ishimure's Spirit of Words

Through her storytelling and use of words, Ishimure depicts an image of a mythopoetic space that exists in the modern world through the bridge to the drowned village. Storytelling in all its forms is pivotal in this work. The human characters, the living creatures, the trees, the gods and goddesses of myth, are all vying for their place in this space. What would have been a mesh of confusing stories spanning realities, dreams, generations, and imaginations becomes a seamless mythopoetic work as they all settle and blend into the reality of Masahiko's existence and shared memory. They are embedded in the village women's songs, the ceremonial dances, the villagers' dreams, the *shamisen* and *biwa* players' music—and also in the ravings of an old man, Masahito, being taken to a mental hospital before he dies. It is up to individuals to find the version of the self that allows them to hear these stories, find reconciliation with nature, and tell their own stories in turn.

Ishimure never allows true silence to exist in this work. There is always a story and a sound that fills the spaces between words, worlds, narratives, people, and nature. Stories can be heard in the playfulness of a child, the call of a bird, or the ripples of the water. They jump from the realm of dreams to reality, casting doubt while also providing an odd comfort in the knowledge that it does not matter whether they are real or not, as long as they are part of nature and oneself. As Masahiko finally becomes at peace with the fact that he belongs to this place, the reflections of the people on the surface of the lake meld into the outlines of the drowned village; the images overlay, and he hears the sound of four notes in the wind, one from each of the four strings of the *biwa*. In the space between reality and dreams, nature and understanding unfurl at his awakening:

> He felt the sounds were drawing out and expelling the bad spirits that had been accumulating deep within himself.
>
> There's no way that I, by myself, can pluck those four strings strung from the moon over Amazoko. I'm nothing more than a tiny silkworm wrapped in a translucent cocoon, keeping my heart low and listening with my neck lifted up. (292)

Masahiko realizes the role each of the strings plays and the connectedness they create between the sky and the water and the human and the natural worlds. And from this realization they will build the Moon Shadow bridge, both the physical bridge that was lost to the dam and the metaphorical one to the space Amazoko represents. In the collective sensibility, this space not only warns of the losses that industrialization causes on both a spiritual and physical level, but also warns of the tragedy of losing connections to nature. However, it is also a space that brings comfort in the reminder that nature is never truly lost; the connection with this space can be rebuilt and rediscovered. In this spirit, the characters in *Lake of Heaven* tell stories about how they will reclaim their individual lost souls from the drowned cherry tree in the submerged village of Amazoko.

The scholar Ikezawa Natsuki discusses the significance of the names of places in Ishimure's writing. He explains that the place names in her works "embody the activities that people have engaged in for thousands of years. Her writings are always filled with such names" (2016, 33).[3] Several names are invoked in *Lake of Heaven*, carefully created by Ishimure to suggest a sense of the spirituality of the place and its connection to the people: Utazaka (Song Hill), Mimigawa (River of Ears), Amazoko (Bottom of Heaven), Oki no Miya (Palace by the Shore), Tsukikage (Moon Shadow). Even within the place names there are resonances. For example, upon hearing Omomo and Ohina sing the traditional songs, "Masahiko's entire body became an ear" (Ishimure 2008, 79) as he began to hear the sounds of nature, history, and myth, and the reader is listening with him. As the sounds of Tokyo fade, those of Amazoko become clearer to him. He slowly transforms into the "ear" when he hears the occasional string of the *biwa* in the wind. Finally, the four strings create a song that resonates both with him and the reader, and here, Amazoko itself is clearly heard. The slowly emerging harmony allows the reader to go through the journey with Masahiko, building the "spirit of words" (*kotodama*) into a melody of life that is dynamic and harmonious, instead of discordant and disturbing.

Lake of Heaven is written using Ishimure's signature style of mixed genres. She incorporates both modern and traditional modes of writing, melding them into a narrative that reveals her beliefs. She makes language choices accordingly. She does not believe that people are separate from the world but rather are part of the world, which is why she prefers not to use the word "humans" (*ningen* 人間). Instead, as noted in the documentary *Towards the Paradise of Flowers*, Ishimure refers to humans as "life" (*seimei* 生命). "Rather than saying 'humans,' let me use the word 'life'" (Allen and Masami 2016, 7).

Ishimure is not presenting a tale of loss and nostalgia. She is calling for the elimination of the division between humans and other living things so as to place humans in the more encompassing world of life. Her representation of space focuses on life. Even when recounting the deaths of insects and humans, life across time and space is at the fore, becoming part of the world of the "ten thousand beings."

> On a hill in the cemetery there was a stone pagoda with words written on it, *Memorial for the souls of the ten thousand beings*. And when it said it was for the souls of 'beings,' that didn't mean just the humans. That stone marker on the hill was dedicated to the souls of all beings—and not just the birds

and insects either; it was also for the souls of the things we can't see with our eyes. Our ancestors put it there out of thanks for all the creatures and beings that helped protect their village. (116)

The stories have always been there, and it is through conjuring these spaces and building bridges between them that life is rekindled. This bridging of the gap created by a sense of loss, as felt by the characters on the banks of the lake, is the function of *Lake of Heaven.* Many forms of loss are presented to the reader; we see the physical place that has been lost, and also its symbolic representation and its connection to the natural world that surrounds the villagers. The reader also experiences a sense of loss for a place that was known, as in the grandfather's story, but also for one that was not known, as in the sense of emptiness Masahiko experienced when he found Amazoko. Ultimately, this is not a story of searching for the invisible but a story of learning to listen and discovering what has always been there, with modes of storytelling connected through nature as the medium: Ohina re-enacts traditions and recalls the gods and goddesses, the shrine maiden dances, Omomo sings, the villagers dream, Masahiko composes music, Ishimure Michiko writes stories, and we, in turn, read and access what has been submerged in memory rediscovering our connection to the more-than-human space that surrounds us.

Conclusion

Three days after arriving at Amazoko, Masahiko remembers his life in Tokyo and the cacophony of the city. One memory is of his mother, who is ashamed of her father-in-law's traditional roots and hounds her husband about his embarrassing origins. Masahiko recalls that he had "to look for his father, but he didn't apologize to his mother. At times like this he felt himself shunning her, even though she was his own mother" (206). It is poignant that he is jolted out of his city memories by the cockcrow, a typical sound of rural life. In this moment he has a revelation about who he is, and experiences the jarring disconnect between his life in Tokyo and life in this place of myth and tradition. He thinks to himself:

Am I changing into a new person? Or, more than myself changing, is it that the world is entering into me and changing? Or, rather, is it that I've come to a place where the world my grandfather taught me about and this world are being mixed together?...But couldn't it also be that the world of the unconscious within me is sleeping along with the drifting people of that village?…[I]f you were really aware of all the life that's teeming about the earth, what might you see? And what might you hear? (207)

In their introduction to *Coming into Contact: Explorations in Ecocritical Theory and Practice*, a study on ecocriticism, the authors observe that "how *who* we are is related to *where* we are" and "how our ways of speaking and writing about the environment relate to our *actions* in it"; they conclude that "issues of identity and location are intimately related and cannot be teased apart" (Ingram, Marshall, Philippon, and Sweeting 2007, 3). Through Masahiko's awakening to and reconciliation with the natural world, Ishimure illustrates the importance of place and the connection to the space it represents. The identities of the characters are tied to their places, and any disconnection creates a sense of restless yearning that cannot be fulfilled unless a bridge is created between the human and living worlds. Ishimure depicts this rupture with the natural world through Masahiko's mother, who is completely tied to the concrete city of Tokyo and is an unpleasant presence in the narrative, and through his grandfather, Masahito, who has gone insane from being uprooted from the village to the city.

In conclusion, Ishimure takes advantage of a multidimensional narrative, one that loops around like a mobius strip, to create an image of modern everyday life within the context of the historical and the mythopoetic. The story of Masahiko is interspersed with recollections of myths and songs. There is a sense of an emerging song being channeled through Masahiko as he becomes "the ear,"' increasingly more open to and perceptive of the songs of nature. He allows nature to become a part of him, and in turn, the songs of nature become a part of the reader.

In *Towards a Paradise of Flowers*, Ishimure reflects on the current state of the world, which seems to be perpetually seeking a balance between destruction and hope, dissonance and resonance:

> It seems we may fall into an even more chaotic condition. But I don't think that such chaos would be all for naught. Someday, I think, we may find our way. It seems clear that our civilization is becoming something very different in nature. But now we are witnessing the very moment when destruction and creation are being born. The destruction and creation are now going on at the same time. Which of these has the stronger power now? But if things are to be annihilated, there should be something—what can I say—something pure, honest, likeable, and without malice. If this were to happen with

> a sense of consideration for others, and with our spirits linked, then our facing annihilation together might even be a good thing. Since the time for all things is limited, if we were linked together with—what should I call it—with a high, pure sense of morality—then it could be all right.
>
> Yes, this is a beautiful planet. With the sparkle of sunlight on the morning dew and the countless plants and flowers of unknown names, it has been such a beautiful planet. (2014)

In seeing Masahiko rediscover a world he did not know existed and Omomo embracing her role as the keeper of tradition, Ishimure offers contemporary readers hope that it is possible to live in harmony with nature, even in the context of increasing concern about environmental preservation and discourse. Through myth and memory, she brings forward an awareness of the responsibility the individual holds as a steward of nature and its many living things and traditions.

---

1 "The concept of more-than-human refers to the worlds of the different beings co-dwelling on Earth, including and surpassing human societies" (Souza 2021).

2 The *biwa* is a short-necked traditional Japanese lute often used as an accompaniment to narrative storytelling. The *shamisen* is another such instrument.

3 Ishimure's naming conventions when it comes to physical places are deliberate. She often uses real place names, such as the village of Minamata or the Shiranui Sea, to relate the true history of the place alongside the narrative message she wishes to convey about that place. In *Lake of Heaven*, while true events inspired the novel, Ishimure uses fictional place names to evoke an atmosphere of spirituality and human connectedness to natural spaces. This tells us that the focus of this narrative is not the mechanized and industrial process that has led to loss, but instead is on the efforts to recover and live in the aftermath of environmental destruction.

References

Allen, Bruce, and Yuki Masami, eds. 2016. *Ishimure Michiko's Writing in Ecocritical Perspective: Between Sea and Sky*. Lanham, Boulder, New York and London: Lexington Books.

Ikezawa Natsuki. 2016. "Antiquity and Modernity." Translated by Aihara Naomi. In *Ishimure Michiko's Writing in Ecocritical Perspective: Between Sea and Sky*, edited by Bruce Allen and Yuki Masami, 27-40. Lanham, Boulder, New York, and London: Lexington Books.

Ingram, Annie Merrill, Ian Marshall, Daniel J. Philippon, and Adam W. Sweeting, eds. 2007. *Coming into Contact: Explorations in Ecocritical Theory and Practice.* Athens and London: The University of Georgia Press.

Ishimure Michiko. 2008. *Lake of Heaven: An Original Translation of the Japanese Novel by Ishimure Michiko.* Translated by Bruce Allen. Lanham, Boulder, New York, Toronto, and Plymouth: Lexington Books.

———. 2014. *Towards the Paradise of Flowers* [*Hana no okudo e*]. Documentary film (DVD, 1 hour 42 minutes) directed by Kim Tai; English subtitle translations by Bruce Allen. Tokyo: Fujiwara shoten.

Souza, Carlos Roberto Bernardes. 2021. "More-than-human cultural geographies towards co-dwelling on Earth." *Mercator – Revista de Geografia da UFC* 20, no. 1. https://www.redalyc.org/articulo.oa? id=273665153007

Dan O'Neill, University of California, Berkeley

3.11 Animal Stories: The Possibilities of Entangled Lives

In this essay, my reading of Kawakami Hiromi's short story "Kamisama 2011" ("God Bless You, 2011") and Tawada Yōko's novella *Yuki no renshūsei* (*Memoirs of a Polar Bear*, 2010) is an attempt to come to an understanding of the range of affective responses to the 3.11 disasters.[1] I am interested in tracking how writers have responded to the disasters through their acts of rewriting and rereading. And I also want to explore how these responses may say something about our relationship to an ecological future that seems increasingly bleak. This is therefore not only a historical project but also a speculative one, another mode of inquiry organized around a sense of ecological precarity that has traveled more broadly across disciplinary and discursive boundaries under the name of the Anthropocene.[2] How might a certain moment of disaster give us the impetus to question our most basic narratives about the relationship between ourselves and nature, to rethink the ways we inhabit "the human" and our place with others in the wider world? How might the animal stories that emerged from 3.11 help us better understand and respond to an ecological horizon that is marked by escalating processes of biosocial destruction?

In the first part of the essay, I will discuss Kawakami's short story, "God bless you, 2011" (2012a), in order to develop a set of framing questions for our consideration: what is distinctive about these animal stories and what new lines of thought on creaturely relations (that is, relations between human and nonhuman animals) can be generated by them? Then I will discuss in detail Tawada's novella *Memoirs of a Polar Bear* (2016), first published in 2010.[3] My reading of the novella in a post-3.11 context is an attempt to install an alternate and biocentric perspective, if only as a means of extending the creaturely implications of 3.11

literature. Specifically, I will think through the animal as a figuration of the entangled life and consider how this entanglement may teach us to understand and to live with "precarity" as an ecological condition to which we are all exposed and share. By considering how the novella explores the entanglement between the human and the non-human, I hope to offer a rereading of that entanglement as a new affective space that pushes us to feel the possibilities of what could be in the aftermath of the 3.11 disasters.

Toward a Creaturely Poetics

Kawakami's "God Bless You, 2011" is a reworking of her earlier story "God Bless You," published in 1993. The first version of the story was about 10 pages, written on 400-character manuscript paper. The second version is not much longer, with details changed here and there. In essence, "God Bless You, 2011" is a slight modification of an existing story but with the setting relocated to a radiation-contaminated Fukushima.[4]

While the original storyline of a wilderness hike experienced between a human subject and a bear has been mostly preserved, Kawakami's rewrite incorporates the varying effects of a nuclear accident. Human characters are now covered with hazmat suits. The human subject of the story returns home from the hike, takes a bath, and takes radiation measurements from the body. The story concludes with a ritual that acknowledges both the presence of the body and the presence of the radiation that may already be attached to the body. It ends with a note of embodied vulnerability. As such, the rewriting of the story curates the uncanny ways in which life is implicated in a biological reality of radiation that it can neither escape nor fully inhabit.

To live with radiation constitutes a strange state of existence, partly because we do not know much about the long-term health effects of exposure to low levels of radiation; and as such, to live with radiation means we live chronically with a certain degree of uncertainty. Although we get the sense that we are living in an increasingly nuclear-powered world, we have also been living in ignorance of the nature of radiation, its durability as well as its instabilities. Even after the 3.11 disasters, scientists are still engaged in debate over what levels of exposure to radiation can be considered safe, and official discourse, in Japan and elsewhere, has consistently and effectively turned these gaps in knowledge about the health effects of radiation into assumptions of safety.[5] One of the most striking aspects of the literary works emerging out of the post-3.11 moment is precisely the ways in which they resist this easy conversion of uncertainty about radiation into assumptions of safety or security. And it is largely by thinking through the figure of the animal that we can begin to understand the necessity of lingering with precarity, an act that may allow us to understand, if only on the level of affect, the unpredictable movements of anthropogenic change.

In Kawakami's story, the bear's amiable character and his sociality are articulated with a clear sense of vulnerability. Although he appears to have a robust constitution, as may be expected of a bear, the creature reminds his human companion that he remains susceptible to the damaging effects of radiation. In the aftermath of the 3.11 disasters, the bear's social existence may be seen as an extension of the shared precarity in which life is confronted by radiation—a problem that no romanticization of nature can dissipate. Here, "nature" does not recover or return to an unspoiled original state; it is far from certain that the effects of radiation will dissipate in time. In both versions of the story, the old and the new, the bear remains a bear. The only change we encounter is the irradiated bodies and environments, both now buzzing with uncertainty.

Beyond animals serving as mere symbols, resources, or backgrounds for human lives, the figure of the bear provokes a generative tension between the social and the biological. In an interview, Kawakami offered some thoughts on the affective valence of the original story while reflecting on the bear metaphor itself as a device for making human meaning out of animal forms:

> [The story is] about a courteous bear who moves into the neighborhood one day, and he invites the main character to go down to the river. They go and eat lunch by the river and come back. That's practically about it. The bear also symbolizes a *minority*, so it does have that certain *sadness* to it, but still, it is a very peaceful story of everyday life. (2012b, emphasis added)

The "sadness" that is attached to the figure of the minority in Kawakami's original story reveals a certain allegorical drive for the bear to serve as a vehicle for the expression of a political view. The metaphor highlights the precarity of being a minority: those who live constantly with the threat of dispossession, those who need to be supported by an infrastructure of social services, and those who are denied access to proper economic conditions and prospects. What remains fascinating about Kawakami's rewrite, as we continue to linger with the sadness, is the invitation to think about what happens to the bear *as a metaphor* when we begin to understand precarity not only in terms of economic dispossession but also the destruction of biological life. What does it mean for us to relinquish the symbolic valence of the bear as a figure for human dispossession? What obtains if we think of the bear *as a bear*, or more precisely as a creaturely figure that ushers into the narrative fold a non-human-centric position? How would our understanding of precarity change by moving away from a human-centric reading to one that is bio-centric, from a story of precarity that is marked by social-economic dispossession to one that speaks to the escalating and mutually reinforcing processes of biosocial destruction?

In "God Bless You, 2011," the bear is no longer just a symbol that speaks to the intra-species failure of how humans treat other humans (or how the minority figure is treated in everyday life). The rewrite redirects our attention to the bear as an animal with a marked sense of biological vulnerability that an allegorical reading (that is, a reading of the story as a fable of human vulnerability) would otherwise disavow. Here, the bear becomes a part of the environment, a setting which is riddled with the forces of mutations, a figuration of creaturely precarity whose symbolic valence may hold a certain relation to the human world but is not reducible to it. This type of animality, forged by the entangled lives of the 3.11 disasters, does not deny relationality to the human, but rather serves to diffuse the anthropocentricism of our reading practices. Moreover, if the approach to animality in postwar Japanese literature has been framed to suggest, via the work of allegory, the corruption or the powerlessness of the modern human subject,[6] then in the context of the 3.11 disasters, questions about what the human and the nonhuman have in common are rearticulated to expose the extent to which the allegorical tendencies of our reading practices may obscure the experiential richness of animal bodies. We can find other notable examples of animal stories that emerged in the context of the 3.11 disasters: in writings by Furukawa Hideo and Kimura Yūsuke, the figure of the animal attains an astonishing range of variability to denote a particular intricacy of responsiveness to the conditions of embodiment and finitude.[7] From a bio-semiotic perspective that acknowledges non-human modes and experiences of existence as meaningful, these works constitute the first stepping-stones toward a literary genealogy of a creaturely poetics that acknowledges non-human creatures as a significant co-presence.[8]

The Songs of Creaturely Survival

Tawada Yōko's *Memoirs of a Polar Bear* offers another striking non-human perspective that unsettles the humanist vision of the bounded stable and autonomous subject. In the immediate aftermath of the 3.11 disasters, the Japanese media not only documented the loss of human lives but also followed the fate of animals that were abandoned by fleeing owners.[9] *Memoirs of a Polar Bear* marks an important departure from these media representations. It constitutes an especially compelling case in which we are invited, through the iconic figure of the polar bear, to reimagine a relational poetics that begins with the vulnerability of bodies, and not with the frenzied representations of the devastating consequences of disaster.

Tawada's novella, as suggested by its reception, can be regarded as a study of "blurred lines"; that is, the novella blurs the boundary between human and animal. In my reading, I would like to go further and think about what is gained by the blurring of the human/animal divide. In other words, I am interested in exploring the creaturely resonances generated by such a blurring.

In the novella, three generations of polar bears tell their stories. Part 1 is about the matriarch, who retires from the circus and is given a desk job. She goes to conferences. She writes an autobiography, which becomes a best seller. In Part 2, we meet Tosca, who is currently a circus performer. Her story is told by her trainer, Barbara—until it seems that Tosca may in fact be telling the story of Barbara telling the story of Tosca. This is an experiment of sorts in the possibility of a shared narrative perspective. Part 3 centers on the baby polar bear, Knut (Tosca's son), who finds love in his human caregiver, feeling more at home with his human companion than with the other animals at the zoo where he lives.[10] Knut's camera-ready cuteness transforms him into an international media star; his status as such is also a reflection on the capricious ways in which animals are turned into a proxy for an idealized notion of nature to which humans find themselves attached.

The events in *Memoirs of a Polar Bear* are given to us with precise details. Yet the details always seem to reveal more than what they indicate at first glance. While the bears are celebrated, they are not treated as such for their ability to navigate human society. That is not what is unusual about the stories. Indeed, the use of polar bears would seem at first to be somewhat of a cliché, given their iconic status in the discursive currency consolidating around environmental crisis. Yet the cliché is precisely what confronts the literary with the environmental; and, in the process, the cliché is transformed into something that does not fail to surprise us.

Animals abound in literature—and the representations of them have been seen first and foremost as metaphors for humans.[11] When such representations are brought into play, it is to reaffirm the distinctiveness of humankind, where animals are negated or subsumed into a deeper analysis of human relations.[12] The symbolic and anthropocentric representations of animals have most often yielded variations organized around a dualist ontology that assumes a divide between humans and animals and secures the superiority of the former. In these common evocations of the animal, what is obscured are the significant ways in which humans and animals are connected, how we are co-constituted and situated in entangled life-systems, even if the acts of co-constitution are always difficult and asymmetrical. Tawada's work is part of a larger literary assemblage that is relaying and absorbing the forces to which the entangled lives of both human and non-human animals find themselves exposed. If anything, the novella demonstrates how disaster can create strange new resonances for the literature that it infiltrates.

Memoirs of a Polar Bear is a rich novella, certainly one that deserves a fuller treatment than I can afford here, but I will mention a few salient properties that locate it at the affectively saturated meeting point of the literary and the environmental. First, the polar bears take on the role of narrators of their own lives. The matriarch, for example, writes an autobiography that becomes a best-seller among the human community. However, the task of writing the autobiography, we learn, is not an easy one. As the matriarch tries to give narrative shape to her own life, she finds her efforts frustrated time and again by her inability to remember her childhood:

> I kept painting over the same period of my childhood again and again, I couldn't seem to get beyond it. My memories came and went like waves at the beach. Each wave resembled the one before, but no two were identical. I had no choice but to portray the same scene several times, without being able to say which description was definitive. (Tawada 2016, 11)

Writing an autobiography involves conferring origins. But for the polar bear turned writer, this return to her origins, to the time before her socialization or domestication, is an impossibility. Though she tries, she seems unable to get to the starting point of her life, to her wildness before her domestication. She also struggles with giving her story a proper ending. Her life's account, in its inchoate state, seems to lack the concrete edges of a beginning and end that we have come to expect of the narrative form. Rather, her life story, like the other life stories in the novella, ends with a note of mystery, filled with details that are as captivating as they are unsettling.

Environmental factors, such as water and ice, seem to play an important role in blocking the matriarch's access to the memory of a wild primordial origin. Rather than the polished parameters of a life developed through linear time, she offers us instead a series of porous dreams:

> I gaze out at the wide field: not a house, not a tree, everything is covered in ice all the way to the horizon. With the first step I take, I realize that the ground is made of ice floes. My feet sink along with the floe I've just stepped onto, already I'm up to my knees in ice-cold water, then my belly is wet, then my shoulders. I have no fear of swimming, and the cool sensation of the icy water is rather pleasant, but I'm not a fish and can't stay in the water forever….After several disappointments I finally find an ice floe sturdy enough to bear my weight. I balance on top of it, staring straight ahead, feeling the ice melt away from second to second beneath the warm soles of my feet. This ice island is still as large as my desk, but eventually it will no longer be there. How much longer do I have? (73)

The politics of species (animals and humans) and textual relations both gain complexity through her failure to produce a coherent narrative form, dramatized in this passage as her inability to gain secure footing on something more permanent. On one level, her inability to create a life story with a proper beginning and ending is a failure of intellect. On another, we may reconsider the dream (in which she finds herself in the wild expanse of the artic, her original home, as it were) as an attempt to reframe this intellectual failure as an experience of vulnerability—here dramatized in the passage as a difficult balancing act on ice. The unresolved, anxious endnote to the matriarch's story suggests that the failure to write has been turned into a performance of precarity in which our attention is shifted from writing as a cognitive exercise to writing as an embodied experience.

These failures in securing narrative closure may be seen as productive in that we are left with an open-ended story. This weakness on the level of plot (i.e., the lack of a satisfying biographical closure) is also what allows the story to generate an affect that multiplies in quantities. It seems that the bear's narrative of life has no use for completeness. Rather, what is revealed is an exposure to the exigency of the outside world, an embrace of contingency that leaves us with a lingering incompleteness. The "un-tethered-ness" that characterizes her attempts to write an autobiography mirrors the un-tethered-ness of a melting ice floe that requires a constant effort at balancing. The story offers an opening that, by the end, is linked quite powerfully to a sense of uncertain precarity: "How much longer do I have?"

This image of impending death conjugates well with the extinction narratives that we hear now, almost on a daily basis, about climate change, with the doomsday storyline punctuated and concretized by photos of an emaciated polar bear who will eventually drown. Indeed, the image of the polar bear has been used more extensively than any other faunal or floral species as the figure through which to communicate human anxieties about global warming. Polar bears, like many other animals, are enlisted as fleshy metaphors, acting as charismatic receptacles to environmental distress. Polar bears may be disappearing in nature, but their effigies are certainly ubiquitous in our popular imaginary.

Though anxiety associated with reports of our impending environmental doom might function as a motivation for the representational abundance of the polar bear in popular media, this relationship does not bound the diversity of affective claims that Tawada's narrating polar bear holds. The important point here is that the matriarch finds herself unable to fully conjure the North Pole for her readers. Her story does not reproduce the trope of nature as a wild untainted frontier. And this brings me to the second point: her failure to conjure a reliable image of the North Pole allows us to forgo the fantasy of the wild as something we can authentically encounter, even as a construct in narration. The novella seems unwilling to give us a gratifying life story of wild origins.

Of course, literary animals, like Tawada's polar bears, are locked in representations authored by humans (and representations that justify their use by humans). Humans will continue to intervene in and interpret their lives. Though we cannot simply dismiss anthropocentricism by ignoring it, we can rearrange the coordinates of this orientation. In order to generate a space from which we can begin to understand the ambitions and limitations of the human perspective, I would like to suggest that Tawada's polar bears operate as an anthropomorphic trace, one that is tied to the human perspective but not entirely reducible to it, serving neither as a symbol for humans nor as a figure of pure otherness. This linkage to human is perhaps revealed most poignantly in Knut's story, based on the life of the first polar bear born in captivity at the Berlin Zoo to survive.[13]

Since the beginning, Knut's care has been entrusted to his human trainer Matthias, and Knut comes to feel more at home with this human companion than with the other zoo animals. Matthias acts as a surrogate mother to Knut. Through their close relationship, we see the wonder of a bear learning what it means to exist in the world first as a proxy for humans. As Knut is gradually exposed to the other animals, however, he gains an awareness of himself as a co-constituted being and takes over the narration by assuming a first-person perspective. He recalls a particular interaction with Matthias, who says:

> "You know what never fails to surprise me? When I was first hired as a bear keeper, I began to read books about North Pole expeditions. I wanted to know more about bears. One explorer wrote that he once looked a polar bear in the eye and almost fainted. He couldn't forget this moment of terror—not because of any concrete danger, but because of the emptiness he found in the bear's eyes. They didn't reflect anything at all…strangely, I felt the desire to experience this shocking gaze myself. But your eyes aren't empty mirrors—you reflect human beings. I hope this doesn't make you mortally unhappy."
>
> Matthias drew his eyebrows together and looked penetratingly into the depths of polar bear eyes.
>
> But Knut wanted to be a wrestler, not a mirror, and attacked this boring man who was trying to be a philosopher for a little while. (187)

For Matthias, the polar bear remains important as a reference point linked to the fantasy of a North Pole expedition where a man's experience of shock at encountering raw nature, an encounter that may lead him to confront his mortality, can be converted into a sublime adventure of self-recognition. Knut's symbolic significance inheres in the bear's ability to mirror human beings, to confirm the integrity of the human subject.

In an understated but nevertheless striking response, Knut abstains from participating in the visual exchange. He resists playing the role of a reflective surface, one that allows for human self-understanding: "Knut wanted to be a wrestler, not a mirror." His gentle refusal is at the same time an invitation to another kind of play. He wants to partake in a different game. This refusal to be a spectacle (an object of the gaze, a mirror, a reflection, knowledge produced through the ocular) becomes an invitation to hold, explore, and seek comfort from something wordless and precious, something involving the connecting of one body with another through touch (playful wrestling). Knut's redirection suspends the search for meaning and truth and allows the literary protagonists and reader alike to enjoy a respite from the philosophizing. Our cognition may separate us from animals (in that an animal cannot be a philosopher, as many have reassured us), but our bodies (as Knut's invitation to play suggests) tie us together in ways that our cognition cannot fully account for.[14]

Knut's refusal is an act that displaces the knowing Anthropos. His attempts to reconstitute the relationship between himself and his human partner offer an alternative model for inter-species interaction, one that does not result in the prioritization of the human nor in a sheer mindful pity to animal finitude. Throughout Tawada's novella, we hear from the narrating voice numerous limpid claims to not knowing (the three generations of polar bears seem always unsure of their positionality as they reassemble their lives into narrative form). Their perspectives are in a continual state of flux, dilating from the singular to the multiple, from third person to first person, composing with others a story that confronts us with the myriad ways in which we continue to not know the world.

These narratives do not grant us access to the inner world of the polar bears. Rather, they seem to articulate the epistemic limitations of our attempts to know this world. The training of animals (the training of Knut's mother Tosca as a circus dancer is staged repeatedly in Part 2) involves a form of communication between beings that are differently endowed with capacities for language, for hearing and scent discrimination, and for movement and kinesthetic sensation. We humans may have a capacity for language that animals do not exhibit (a stance commonly taken by philosophers). But animals are differently endowed: they have the capacity to make distinctions between sounds, scents, or movements in the air or water in ways that we cannot. What this means is that animals may also know us in ways that we cannot know, because they know us and the world through the acuity of multiple senses, not only through sight. Knut's desire to play shows us what would be missed, affectively and sensorially, if we engaged with the world only with cognitive knowledge.

These states of unknowing (or to be precise, knowing through other means) also highlight the environmental concerns that allow the novella to articulate a shared mode of embodiment. Through the mutability of the narrative voices, the novella contains the potential for a critique attuned to the corporeal materiality of interacting bodies and the sensorial knowledge generated by these interactions. As Stacy Alaimo argues, thinking across bodies and across species may catalyze the recognition that the environment, which is too often imagined as inert, empty space, is, in fact, a world of fleshy beings with their own claims and actions (2010). Certainly, Kawakami's insertion of an irradiated landscape into her existing story is an attempt to bring this world of fleshy beings with their own needs, claims, and actions to the fore. And animals, like Knut, are our guides in teaching us how to respond to this world.

Tawada's novella does not mine the figure of the animal for its hidden (anthropocentric) depths; it does generate a space for readers to become attuned to the animal's quiet tenacity, to our collective creaturely desires to breathe, to be present and to be. Toward the end of Knut's story, we are invited to a mise-en-scène in which the background noise of the natural world moves to the foreground. For Knut, the sounds of human animals become sounds that comingle with the sounds of other animals as he learns to recognize the language of his fellow creatures. Listening to these non-human animal voices, we might begin to hear other songs of creaturely survival.

The stories by Kawakami Hiromi and Tawada Yōko are a footnote to the untold number of animals that are living and dying anonymously under the Anthropocene. The mutability of these lives, the interwoven lifeways which are no less shaped by human activity and consciousness, indicates that there will be many more animal stories emerging to situate us in the humming indeterminacies of our ecological future.

---

1 On March 11, 2011, at 2:46 p.m., a 9.0-magnitude earthquake generated a record-high tsunami that flooded the Fukushima Daiichi Nuclear Power Plant in Tōhoku Japan. In the following weeks, the region saw the release of radioactive isotopes from the damaged nuclear power plant. What has come to be known as the "March 11 Triple Disasters" (earthquake, tsunami, and nuclear accident) will be glossed in this essay as "3.11."

2 A number of scholars have started to characterize our historical present as the "Anthropocene" — a period in which human activity is recognized to be the dominant influence on the climate and on the environment. The term Anthropocene measures the force of humanity's negative impact on the environment, a force registered on a geological scale that threatens to put all life on the planet

at risk of extinction. In short, the Anthropocene renders precarious all life on earth. For a critical reassessment that engages the term as an opportunity to crosshatch human and natural histories, see Chakrabarty (2009).

3 Tawada Yōko's *Yuki no renshūsei* was serialized in the magazine *Shinchō* at the end of 2010. The author then translated it into German as *Etüden im Schnee* in 2014. The 2016 English translation is based on the German edition.

4 Kawakami's original story, the new version, and an afterword in which she reflects on her decision to rewrite the story were published together in the literary magazine *Gunzō* in June 2011.

5 For a discussion of the range of issues related to the nuclear legacies of Chernobyl and Fukushima, see Monnet (2023, 3-38, 59-77, 78-93).

6 Postwar literature abounds in the use of animals as a means to stage the question of human violence. The works of Takeda Taijun, Kojima Nobuo, and Ōe Kenzaburō are but a few examples; see Takeda's *Shinpan* (1947), Kojima's *Uma* (1954), and Ōe's *Shiiku* (1957) and *Kojinteki na taiken* (1963).

7 See Furukawa Hideo's fictional reportage *Horses, Horses, in the End the Light Remains Pure* (*Umatachiyo, soredemo hikari wa muku de,* 2011; English translation, 2016) and Kimura Yūsuke's novella *Sacred Cesium Ground* (*Seichi Cs*, 2014; English translation, 2019).

8 For what that genealogy may look like in other literary traditions, see McHugh, McKay, and Miller's "Introduction" in *The Palgrave Handbook of Animals and Literature* (2021, 1-13).

9 According to The Animal Welfare Institute, well over half a million animals (pets and livestock) were left behind (https://awionline.org/awi-quarterly/2011-summer/animal-victims-tsunami-and-radiation-crisis). For a discussion of Japanese media's focus on animal corpses in the reporting of the disasters, see Wada-Marciano (2019, 35-45).

10 Both Tosca and Knut have counterparts in real life, while the matriarch bear is fictitious. Tosca, the real-life mother of real-life Knut, was part of a national circus for East Germany for many years (Peschel 2018).

11 Animal stories, in which humans seize upon the animal as a symbol into which to pour tales of anxiety and liberation, date back for thousands of years in Japan and elsewhere. For a wide-ranging account of the place of animal lives in Japanese culture see Gregory Pflugfelder and Brett Walkers (2005). For a sampling of animal stories in classical Japanese literature, see Kimbrough and Shirane (2018).

12 We can place this novella in the context of Tawada's other works, each of which seems to be working with the idea of displacement (in this case, displacement of the bear from her native context). This is not a story about diaspora, about longing for a homeland and alienation from home, but rather it is about how displacement continues to have an operative function in the relationship each bear forges with others within a human community.

13 This real-life Knut died of an encephalitic seizure at the age of four, the first known case of such a disease found in a non-human animal. Knut was an international celebrity.

14 Knut's rejection of the human gaze in Tawada's novella is but a gentle rebuke. It also recognizes the fact that our ways of talking about animals, our ways of knowing them, have always been tied to the specific anthropomorphic modes of envisioning and displaying them. A few years after Knut's death (in 2011), a full-sized sculpture covered in Knut's pelt went on display in Berlin's Museum fur Naturkunde (Museum of Natural History), and officials continue to implement a plethora of representational practices that work to bring the public visually closer to the bear.

References

Alaimo, Stacy. 2010. *Bodily Natures: Science, Environment, and the Material Self.* Bloomington: Indiana University Press.

Chakrabarty, Dipesh. 2009. "The Climate of History: Four Theses." *Critical Inquiry* 35 (Winter): 197-222.

Kawakami Hiromi. 2011. "Kamisama 2011." *Gunzō* (June 2011): 104-108.

———. 2012a. "God Bless You, 2011." In *March was Made of Yarn: Writers Respond to Japan's Earthquake and Tsunami,* edited by Elmer Luke and David Karashima, 37-48. New York: Vintage.

———. 2012b. "The Wavering World and Wavering Boundaries of Reality and Fantasy: Discussing the Novel *Kazahana* with Translators of Japanese Literature." Interview in *Wochi Kochi*. https://www.wochikochi.jp/english/topstory/2012/04/jbn2.php.

Kimbrough, Keller and Haruo Shirane, eds. 2018. *Monsters, Animals and Other Worlds*. New York: Columbia University Press.

Livia Monnet, ed. 2022. *Toxic Immanence: Decolonizing Nuclear Legacies and Futures.* Montreal: McGill-Queen's University Press.

McHugh, Susan, Robert McKay, and John Miller, eds. 2021. "Introduction: Towards an Animal-Centered Literary History." In *The Palgrave Handbook of Animals and Literature*, 1-13. Cham: Palgrave Macmillan.

Peschel, Sabine. 2018. "Yoko Tawada: 'Memoirs of a Polar Bear.'" In *Made for Minds* (October). https://www.dw.com/en/yoko-tawada-memoirs-of-a-polar-bear/a-45620835.

Pflugfelder, Gregory and Brett Walker, eds. 2005. *JAPANimals: History and Culture in Japan's Animal Life*. Ann Arbor: University of Michigan Center for Japanese Studies.

Tawada Yōko. 2011. *Yuki no renshūsei*. Tokyō: Shinchōsha.

———. 2016. *Memoirs of a Polar Bear.* New York: New Directions.

Wada-Marciano, Mitsuyo. 2019. "What Animals, Women, Children, and Foreigners Can Tell Us about Fukushima." *Journal of Japanese and Korean Cinema* 11, no. 1: 35-54.

Doug Slaymaker, University of Kentucky

After Postdisaster Theory

Kimura Saeko, in her important *Sono go no shinsaigo bungakuron* (*After Postdisaster Literary Theory*), offers a new critical apparatus for assessing the fiction, film, and other media that appeared in Japanese following the triple disasters—earthquake, tsunami, and nuclear meltdown—of March 11, 2011. The central contention of Kimura's book is that the disasters have forced upon us a new critical framework—"postdisaster literature"—with which to understand contemporary Japanese fiction, film, and other media.

Sono go no shinsaigo bungakuron was published in 2018. It was intended as a complement to, and an analysis building on, Kimura's 2013 work, *Shinsaigo bungakuron: Atarashii Nihonbungakuron no tame ni* (*Theories of Postdisaster Literature: Toward a New Theory of Japanese Literature*). As Kimura writes in the introduction to the latter volume, "'Theory' is [in the title of the 2013 book] in name only, since the book is primarily an introduction to the novels and films that deal with the Great Eastern Japan Triple Disasters of March 11, 2011" (2018, 7).[1] This analysis is unsparing but accurate; however, it also captures the value of the 2013 volume, which was one of the first books that assessed the artistic output, with a focus on fiction, following the disasters. Kimura seems to have read everything; that first volume is encyclopedic and tends to be more a compendium of synopses and summaries of works than analysis of those works. At the same time, she casts a net across a variety of media, including film and museum and other art exhibits. It will long stand as a valuable reference that captures the scope of immediate postdisaster writing.

In this chapter I take up Kimura's 2018 idea of postdisaster literature as a starting point of analysis. She describes it this way: "Postdisaster literature does not simply point to works that are written after the [2011] disasters, or about the disasters, but to the entire situation of literature since the disasters" (25). That is, the experience and trauma of the 2011 disasters were so profound that a new critical category has been opened up, a new position from which to analyze what has been offered, a new way of seeing the world which has been forced upon us. In this she draws from the large body of fiction and criticism associated with Japanese literature after the Asia-Pacific war to show the applicability of this approach: in the same way that "postwar" encompasses an entirely new expanse of creative and analytical activity, so does "postdisaster" after 2011. In part as an acknowledgement of how central the experience of the disasters has been in Japanese society—that March 11, 2011 marked the day when everything changed and life would never be the same—Kimura proposes that, in a certain sense, *all* literature since then has become postdisaster literature. The parallel here is to postwar literature: the immediacy of the Asia-Pacific war and its aftermath, and now the 2011 disasters, is so deeply engraved into society's consciousness that all works, even those not necessarily about the war or the disasters, can still be profitably analyzed as postwar and postdisaster, respectively. This is a sweeping contention that I will take up below.

I will also note here that, in the years since Kimura made this suggestion, I have continued to feel this seismic shift—both literal and metaphorical. The disasters forced many to question the limits of the imagination and the ability to transcribe an indescribable experience: Does imagination even help? Can anyone not there at the time of the water, waves, and radiation understand? Am I being presumptuous in trying to convey that experience? How will trauma affect and be portrayed by future generations? And radiation: similar to the postwar years, it cannot be sensed, so how might it be portrayed? More, ghosts, spirits, and phantoms are central to this imaginative exercise and seem to reflect the lived experience of many, marking a watershed.

Following this, I will discuss how "imagination" has become a key term for writers and artists processing the disasters. This point is less central to Kimura's analysis but I find it useful nonetheless in framing other of her points. One reason for the prominence of this theme might be that radiation presents a technical challenge for fiction, one that requires particular uses of imagination for description. Writers find themselves trying to describe what is literally unsensible to humans: we cannot see radiation, much less hear, feel, smell, or taste it. Dealing with the seeming impossibility of describing radiation, Japanese novelists refer to the imagination (*sōzōryoku*) in ways that I do not find replicated in the works of English language writers.

Another point of discussion will be that of memory and the passing down of traumatic memories. Fictional representation of disasters is often a method of interacting with disaster trauma; it also serves to pass on to future generations the memory of the disasters. It will be no great surprise, then, that many writing of the triple disasters draw from prior writings about Hiroshima and Nagasaki, Chernobyl, the Great Hanshin earthquake, and the Holocaust. How to remember and pass on traumatic memories? Kimura takes up this question in some detail, which I will expand on below.

Next, I will turn to hauntology and the uncanny. In her introduction to *Sono go no shinsaigo bungakuron*, Kimura invokes the "uncanny," which directs us to Freud (1919); whereas in the final chapter the term under consideration is "hauntology," which directs us to Derrida (Direk and Lawlor, 2014). These terms are brought to bear on explaining one of the characteristics of Japan's postdisaster literature: the many works that feature characters who are dead, or that feature dead characters who narrate their own stories. Kimura argues that it is repressed anxiety and traumatic memories of the disasters which are highlighted in the appearance of ghosts and wandering spirits. Hauntology and hauntings will be analyzed in the final section of this chapter.

The Triple Disasters

First, I want to clarify what I am referring to here as "disaster" and "postdisaster." "Disaster" refers here to the events of March 11, 2011, the day that an earthquake of historical proportions off the northeast coast of Japan launched a massive tsunami that flooded the Fukushima Daiichi Nuclear Power Plant and led to a nuclear meltdown on par with the catastrophe at Chernobyl in 1986. This event, as with Chernobyl, has no conceivable end in sight; the once-in-a-century disaster looks to be a centuries-long mess. Also, again like Chernobyl, it is not confined to borders—consider the debris washing up on the west coast of the United States—or to neat categories—radiation is unequally distributed. Further "3.11," as it is often called, marks a date on the calendar while "Fukushima" points to a place—unfortunately, as with Hiroshima and Chernobyl, the names of cities have been conflated with the massive radiation disasters that occurred there. In other words, the shorthand naming of "3.11" or "Fukushima," while perhaps convenient, does not begin to capture the breadth of scope or the duration of these disasters.

"Triple disasters" is the term I rely on most heavily because it encompasses the devastating constellation of earthquake, tsunami, and radiation. The 3.11 Great East Japan Earthquake off the northeast coast of Tōhoku, at a magnitude of 9.0, registered as the most powerful earthquake recorded in Japan and the fourth most powerful in the world since 1900, when such records began to be kept. It shifted Japan seventy-three centimeters to the east; it shifted the earth on its axis by as much as twenty-five centimeters. The tsunami it caused brought waves topping thirty meters in some places, wiping huge swaths of the landscape clean and, literally, washing cities and towns off the face of the earth. In the wake of the earthquake and tsunami, 18,500 people were dead or missing, the single greatest loss of life to Japan since the atomic bombings of 1945. (We will see multiple resonances between these events.) Moreover, the waves inundated the Fukushima Daiichi Nuclear Power Plant and triggered the meltdown of three nuclear reactors. Two hundred thousand people were evacuated during the triple disasters; because of radiation, huge areas of the region are uninhabitable and are sure to remain so for many years.

It is important to note the uneven distribution of these events. Not every person, community, or place had the same disaster experience. For some, the experience was of all three disasters—earthquake, tsunami, radiation; some areas were most concerned with radiation; other regions recall the water; still others, the shaking. Christophe Thouny and Mitsuhiro Yoshimoto have suggested the necessity of a "new cartography" in considering post-3.11 work, arguing that we need a more robust mapping that can account both for the "punctual event" of March 11 and the "ongoing everyday eventfulness" of postdisaster life (2017, 21). We have trouble accounting for both the moment and the duration. Part of that is the very strong impetus in many quarters to wish it to be "over."

The trauma of disaster carries forward, at some future point becoming "postdisaster." Radiation pollution is unlikely to ever be over. Nor is it likely that the trauma and the desire to present and represent it, to explore it imaginatively, will wane any time soon. In the context of Japanese atomic-bomb literature, where we find many parallels, John Whittier Treat explicates how, in the representation of disaster, one must draw from vocabulary, "some of which limits its meaning and some of which defers it." The words matter and the words are complicated.

He then references Maurice Blanchot's aphorism: "I call disaster that which does not have the ultimate for a limit: it bears the ultimate away in the disaster." Treat continues: "[Blanchot] was attempting to fix that word [i.e., disaster] as something ultimately unfixable, a synecdoche of the open-endedness many writers of atrocity have wanted to establish in their works" (1995, 32). Disaster, and radiation in particular, is in fact always ongoing and open-ended stretching across generations, even if the news, the politicians, and overwhelmed and traumatized individuals would wish differently.

Postdisaster Theory and the Role of Imagination

The days and years following Thouny's "punctual event" now bring us to Kimura's theorizing of postdisaster:

> It is not just that works of film and fiction are produced taking the East Japan disasters as material, but that the existence of this postdisaster literature shakes up the convenient structures of reading and pushes for a transformation of the methods of criticism. Postdisaster literature does not simply point to works that are written after the disasters, or about the disasters, but to the entire situation of literature since the disasters. For example, if we include the many war novels set in the Second World War that flourished after the disasters, then works that urge us to reconsider past history might be the situation of literature after the disasters. If one takes up war novels written before the disasters and reads them after, as a sort of postdisaster novel layered atop the disasters, one finds that the conditions of reading have also changed. Memories of the disasters, not forgotten, become part of the reading. (2018, 25-26)

I will come back to the issues of memory and of haunting below because this idea of postdisaster forces us, productively I think, to consider how, and to what degree, the repressed trauma of war or other disaster permeates every corner of culture and daily life. In making her argument, Kimura writes, "Furthermore, on this issue of how to read postdisaster literature, we cannot limit ourselves to literature written after the disasters. It might be a mistake to insist on reading an event still-future at the time of writing into novels written before the disasters, nonetheless, it is incontrovertible that after the disasters our readings changed" (34). And further, anticipating the question of how something written before the cataclysmic event can be said to bear the analysis of the "post," after the event:

> Just as one can use a gender-based analysis on works that predate even the invention of the word "gender," or, similarly, bring queer analyses to works from a time period when the word "gay" or "lesbian" did not yet exist, then, surely, we can employ the viewpoint of postdisaster literature as a method for explicating works. When ways of reading change then our methods of criticism must change as well. Thus, whether or not there is any meaning in continuing to assign value with an ossified literary eye becomes something that will be taken up by future research into postdisaster literature. (33)

Another way Kimura frames the argument for postdisaster reading is through the example of photographs. Photographs taken of the afflicted seashore areas used to be just brilliant photos of beautiful places along the seacoasts of northern Japan; now that those places no longer exist, we "read" the photos differently. What we see in them has changed radically. Which gets to her point that literature written before the disasters can still be read as postdisaster in the same way that photos taken before March 11 suddenly become postdisaster when viewed following these events. Things look different; we are forced to read them differently even though the text itself has not changed. Likewise, in Kimura's argument, prewar and wartime fiction can be said to display a different nexus of themes once we have lived through the experience of war.

Kimura brings her experience as a scholar of gender in the literature of the Heian period (794-1185) to bear on the argument being made here. Her intimacy with Japan's early traditions also informs her analysis of ghosts and spirits in the contemporary, postdisaster media landscape. Kimura is not explicit on this point, but it seems to me that these questions and manifestations (i.e., configurations of memory and appearance of spirits) continue a lineage of associations long familiar within Japanese culture and media. This is not an essentialist argument—Japanese literature looks like *this* because Japanese culture is like *that*—but rather one that recognizes the historic traditions out of which these artists have been working since the disasters. That is, a noticeable number of postdisaster works draw explicitly from early traditions within Japanese art and literature, particularly the long and rich imaginative history of thinking about the dead—Kimura compellingly shows how the ghosts that appear and narrate their own stories in fifteenth century Noh drama are part of a lineage leading to the characters narrating their own stories following the disasters. The Japanese tradition also has a very rich vocabulary for the dead and spirits, including *bōrei* (ghosts), *yūrei* (specters), and *yōkai* (apparitions, demons, or monsters), among others, as we will see in the final section.

Likewise, we find that much of this postdisaster writing draws from traditions often associated with the Tōhoku region. Furukawa Hideo is one of the best examples of this. Although Furukawa was born in Fukushima prefecture, it would be wrong to pigeon-hole him as a "Fukushima writer." Still, his emotional ties to that region are apparent in many of his works, particularly those he wrote immediately after the disasters. I am thinking, in particular, of *Umatachiyo, soredemo hikari wa muku de* (*Horses, Horses, in the End the Light Remains Pure: A Tale That Begins with Fukushima*, 2016), one of the first creative works to appear after 3.11. Furukawa's work is shot through with a sensibility of the area, of the history of the region, and local speech patterns. This is some of what I mean by referring to traditions often associated with Tōhoku.

We also see it in the ways Furukawa explicitly leans on another Tōhoku writer, Miyazawa Kenji, as he works through how to present and describe these disastrous events. Furukawa has rewritten many Miyazawa stories, updating them to reflect the postdisaster moment and expanding them to encompass current issues. There are many points of resonance: there was a major earthquake and tsunami in the year of Miyazawa's birth (1896) and another in the year of his death (1933), for example. We also know of Miyazawa's long association and identification with the Tōhoku region and its history; Furukawa shares these preoccupations and builds on them. Just as Miyazawa made extensive use of regionalisms and dialectic language, his style of multivocal storytelling also is reflected in Furukawa's fiction.[2]

The challenge remains: How to portray this disaster? In particular, how to portray radiation? The echoes and usefulness of the works of atomic bomb literature growing out of Hiroshima and Nagasaki, and the long, rich history of analyzing the issues those works bring to the fore, is of great relevance here. Kimura draws heavily from this legacy. Among those issues is one of the thorniest: the fictional representation of someone else's trauma. In postdisaster Tōhoku, as in Hiroshima and Nagasaki, there is appropriate tension between those who lived through the experience and those who did not when attempting to describe it. The pointed question being: "You weren't there—what gives you the right to try and describe it?" Kimura also brings the vast body of literature and theory from the Holocaust to bear when analyzing how memories of trauma are passed down, presented, represented, and imagined. John Treat phrased it this way: "In fact, the role of imagination in Japanese atomic-bomb literature, as in Holocaust literature, has been both to facilitate figural representation and to obstruct it" (1995, 37). One of the things this points to is that humans seem compelled to try and express, to put into words, these seemingly "inexpressible" events and experiences. They have no limit in experience, a la Blanchot, so they must also exceed the limits of comprehensibility and representation.

The process of taking on the task to describe an event and make it intelligible, however much it can expand and enrich our understanding, also runs the risk of cheapening that very event. There is danger in making an incomprehensible occurrence somehow comprehensible because it limits the limitless. There is arrogance and hubris in trying to convey what cannot be conveyed, trying to express what cannot be expressed. One thinks of Adorno's famous statement, later amended, that "to write poetry after Auschwitz is barbaric" which, Kimura writes, "has been bandied about [in Japan following the disasters], but this in contexts where silence would have been best" (75). She pulls from a conversation (*taidan*) between Asada Akira and Azuma Hiroki to further the point that we might have done well with less noise and less talk:

> There is, oddly, no need to be in an agitated rush, it seems to me. That's the reason that I felt such a strong, consistent, sense of unease when all at once these artists and intellectuals (*bunkajin*) began talking about the disasters. My knowledge is not very broad, but I thought that the best response came from the Deleuzian philosopher Higaki Tatsuya who said, since philosophers are of no use in times like these, "We should just go take a nap."[3] Now, he said this, but he also went and wrote an essay which makes him inconsistent in the end. Be that as it may, I did in fact take a nap, and nothing more.... Nonetheless, Mallarmé's "I am completely dead" launched modern poetry; then Adorno told us that "to write poetry after Auschwitz is barbaric"; after which people like Celan, in order to somehow or another keep poetry alive, produced contemporary poetry....This is an extreme example, but all those people, novelists and other literary types blithely going on about how the novels that had been impossible to continue writing were now writeable following the disasters...all started making pronouncements right away. I was, frankly, aghast. I have long wondered why they cannot even manage to keep their mouths shut, even for a little bit. (Asada and Azuma 2014, 421)

I include this long quote for a number of reasons. For one, that sense of overwhelming noise is part of the experience—the flush of too many words and too much experience to make sense of. As in atomic bomb and Holocaust writings, what seems inexpressible in the moment of inundation and death nonetheless drives us, seemingly of its own volition, to attempt articulation. Impossible though it may be to fully convey what we experienced, the event demands to be narrated, often over and over again, a phenomenon observed by Freud.[4] For another reason, while Kimura's analysis shows how many writers interacting directly with the Tōhoku disasters do so by drawing from the wellspring of Japanese narratives, motifs, and symbols, these artists also feel completely at home within the traditions of Europe. Hiroshima and Nagasaki are on their minds to be sure, but so are Auschwitz and Chernobyl. The *taidan* quoted from above introduces some of the philosophical lineages brought to bear on the responses to the disaster.

To return to the "how" of the description, there is much written on the role of the imagination in Japanese responses. Randy Taguchi,[5] who has long worked on nuclear issues, with extensive writing and experience in Chernobyl, raises important questions in relation to imagination and fiction. For example, how does one represent the physical effects of a terrifying phenomenon that is totally beyond the sensory capabilities, at least of humans? Here she is raising the topic of radiation and our inability to sense it, and how that fact has exponentially increased the horror of living in a post-3.11 (post-Chernobyl? post-Hiroshima and Nagasaki?) world. By way of example, Taguchi points out that the number "70" on a Geiger counter signifies dangerous levels of radiation, but we must rely on the sounds of a machine to know its presence. We have learned that the number represents something deadly, even if the experience of exposure cannot be sensed. So now, when she sees the number "70" on a Geiger counter, she becomes nauseous and feels she will throw up. To paraphrase her point, the mechanism that gets us from the number 70 to a reality of physical revulsion is not, of course, the work of the senses, nor is it simply the result of brain activity. Rather, she suggests, it is the work of the imagination. And that sort of imagination makes literature possible:

> Even though we know the [fictional] world is one woven out of words, we can empathize with the work's characters, and we feel and experience it as an actual experience. [That is, what we experience within a fictional world

> is no less real and "actual" than what we experience in our physical world.] It is while within the world of the story that we feel excitement, that we cry tears. This is an intellectual activity available only to humans. We have the ability to feel, as real, things that do not exist in actuality.
>
> And therefore, by means of that ability, numbers alone can cause me to feel like I am going to throw up. Radiation, precisely because it is invisible to the eye and cannot be sensed, stimulates the human imagination. (Taguchi 2012, 22)

I look again to Furukawa Hideo here. In conversation with Shigematsu Kiyoshi, Furukawa said, "What I felt at the time of the disasters was that my imagination, as a novelist, was ineffectual. It accomplished nothing; it saved no one" (2012, 178). Contained here are questions about "What can art do?" "Can art really change anything at all?" Furukawa goes on to state that he realized that one of the things imagination could do was to bring an element of hope and possibility to those who had been affected by the disasters. If we can imagine better, things might seem, or perhaps be made, better.

Itō Seikō put the word "imagination" in the title of his celebrated 2013 novel, *Sōzō rajio* (*Imagination Radio*), which opens with:

> Good evening to you!
> Perhaps "good morning,"
> Maybe "good day."
> This is Imagination Radio.
>
> Starting off with this sort of vague greeting, this radio program is "On Air" without concern for noon or night but solely within your powers of imagination.... (2015, 9)

Novelist Ikezawa Natsuki has also articulated the "empathy" side of the work of imagination in this situation. One of the ways he has been answering the question of "Why write at all in the aftermath of this disaster?" has to do with literature (*bungaku*) as a conduit for empathy, sympathy, and assuagement, which he phrases as "*issho ni modaeru...dōjō de ari, kyōkan desu*" and also as "*shinpashii de ari, konpasshon desu*" (sympathy, compassion) (2017, 5). Ikezawa borrows from Sartre's challenge that "a novel does not feed a starving child." Of course, a novel cannot prevent a child from starving but, he writes, "Literature can preserve the dignity of dying and starving children, it has that sort of power. A single child grows close to death and how are we going to make sense of it?

It is via literature that we can think about it, explicate it, represent it; there are any number of things it can do. That's the work of literature, as I see it" (7). That is, fiction and art can raise and deepen our empathy, understanding, and respect for the plight of those who are starving, or otherwise suffering under a disaster. Imagination is the conduit.

Literature for Ikezawa is, then, literature as support and encouragement. It also helps explain the irony and absurdity of a collection such as *Sōtō no fune* (*A Two-Prowed Boat*, 2013).[6] His response to the criticisms of its overly optimistic ending, of its frivolity in the face of disaster, is to say "No, it is precisely because the reality is just too miserable that we need this sort of irony" (2017, 7). What motivates such writing, he goes on, is that we need fiction—i.e., imagination—for the work of thinking about what happens to those who have died, who have gone over to the other side. There is something eulogizing about this, a sending off of the dead.

Traumatic Memory

Within these imaginative works we are confronted with the ways that memories of traumatic experiences are passed down across generations. Kimura draws heavily from the creative works and analyses of atomic-bomb literature coming from Hiroshima and Nagasaki in her writing. Further, she also considers the memories of Chernobyl and memories from the Holocaust.

From my experience of the period immediately after the triple disasters, the strongest, first lineages of memory among the Japanese public were not that of radiation but of evacuation centers. The centers set up in schools and other concrete-block municipal buildings were reminiscent of the wartime evacuations necessitated by intensive bombing during the Asia-Pacific War. Given the demographic of the Tōhoku area and the large numbers of octogenarians, many 3.11 evacuees had also been evacuated during the 1940s. To experience it again was powerfully evocative. The imagery/memory of food dispersal, the cardboard used to fashion rudimentary living spaces in gymnasiums, the dearth of useful and reliable information, and the anger at the national government in Tokyo for misleading and being responsible for their current condition were all too familiar. Memories of wartime experience were among the first sentiments to be articulated in the evacuation centers. It was only later, perhaps filtered through reports from outside Japan, that the association of radiation with atomic bombs came to the fore. In contrast, it was my experience that in the US and Europe, the first associations were to radiation, with the line drawn immediately from nuclear plant meltdowns to atomic bombs.

The fact that Kimura discusses radiation and connects the events and experiences of being irradiated at Fukushima Daiichi to the experience of the nuclear fallout at Hiroshima and Nagasaki may reflect her attention to Euro-American perceptions. It may also reflect the long view of radiation in the disasters, since so much writing now returns to this point. Thinking about the seventieth anniversary of the end of the Second World War, in 2015, Kimura writes:

> Literature of the Asia-Pacific War—"that war"—a war that had been for a time relegated to a place of complete oblivion, began to appear again in a steady stream as though some sluice gate had swung open in 2015 on the occasion of the seventieth anniversary of the war's end. New questions were asked in 2015. There was a sense of urgency not seen on the fiftieth or sixtieth anniversaries. One reason is surely that the Great Eastern Japan Earthquake Disaster caused us to think again about that war, because imagery of that war's destructive crisis was used to describe the triple disasters; but even more because the nuclear accident, which once again irradiated land and people, prompted us to examine once again the path we have trod in the years since the war. (139)

Given the attention that Kimura pays to postwar fictional representations, drawing from both the evacuation and radiation memory lineages would have been natural and fruitful.

This is to suggest that perhaps the trauma and resurrected wartime memories of the Tōhoku disasters—whether of radioactivity or evacuation—is one explanation for the noticeable number of works that link the two events. But memory and trauma are remembered and experienced by later generations too. Kimura points out that the writers active in the last decade were mostly removed from the war by three generations. Writing tales of the war from the perspective of those who heard about it but did not actually live through it leads to questions as to how memory works in these cases. It also reiterates the questions of what right or responsibility, danger or taboo, is involved in narrating events of which one does not have first-hand experience. Another technical challenge arises here as fiction writers struggle with how to narrate traumatic events that they themselves have not experienced.

Kimura suggests that this conspicuous increase in tales of the war might have been prompted—or the memory dislodged—by the trauma of the triple disasters because of the resonances with the war being commemorated in that year. For example:

> Descriptions appearing seventy years after the war, be they those that portray "Hiroshima" and "Nagasaki" or those that rethink the 3.11 disasters, for example, have become ways to reread earlier depictions of war and disaster. Likewise, the point of view that immediately likened the disasters to war, again, needs rereading and reevaluation. This does not mean that "Fukushima" was a wartime situation. Rather, since "Fukushima" we read the postwar period in a different way; we discover "Fukushima" within the postwar. At the time that "Fukushima" occurred more than a few people felt that "we *already knew* this would happen." Memories buried in the abyss of forgetting are now being called forth a second time. (135)

This phenomenon of memory, whether or not related to direct experience would seem to be the impetus that leads Kimura to propose a "postdisaster" reading of disaster literature.

The Hauntology of Disaster

I have mentioned above Kimura's analysis of the uncanny, of hauntings, of ghosts and spirits in these works. One way to place it is within the Japanese traditions of Noh drama and other creative arts. She also looks to Derrida and follows his lead to the English literary tradition:

> Derrida, in his *Specters of Marx*, touches on the appearance of a ghost (*bōrei*) in the first scene of Shakespeare's *Hamlet* to point out that "this haunting thing, this obsession [Fr. *hantise*] is historical, to be sure, but it is not *dated*, it is never docilely given a date in the chain of presents, day after day, according to the instituted order of a calendar."[7] Further, when considering Derrida's quite careful analysis of the line "Time is out of joint," together with Sekiguchi Ryōko's[8] line that the ghosts "stir up the tenses," we find an overlap of a "hauntological" manner of being. (Kimura, 172)

In considering Derrida's focus on Marx's "specter" that resides in and haunts our lives, Kimura is picking up on the ways that Derrida's sense of "hauntings" is useful in analyzing this literature.[9] Likewise, spirits and specters reside in the memories of trauma and haunt our consciousness. This seems especially manifest in the context of postdisaster literature. Which leads Kimura to ask:

> Why is it that we must make the dead speak following the disasters? One reason is that since those lives were cut off so suddenly and unexpectedly due to the tsunami, and those of us who remain feel as a community that, surely, there were many things left unsaid. Therefore, the dead—as we saw with the taxi drivers in Ishinomaki—make appearances to people they may or may not have any connection to.
>
> Death without a corpse and the difficulty of accepting that death is also an issue associated with the many soldiers who have died on overseas battlefields. (190)

Which is another way to articulate the tendencies and obsessions that postdisaster fiction has proven to share with postwar writings. She writes further:

> We have seen how ghosts and spirits (*yūrei*) appear in postdisaster fiction in a manner that resonates with the narration of war; in the same way, I want to stress here, postdisaster fiction also calls forth memories of war in the midst of disaster. To now go back and once again revisit war, or perhaps the history of war is, metaphorically speaking, to hear again the voices of people who lived in the past; it is to turn our ears to the voices of the dead. The concept of hauntology is necessary at just such a time because it not only provides a critique against too-easy self-serving interpretations, it also provides a critique against the "introjection" resulting from interpretations that are advantageous to those still living, and a means to square off against the tendency to relegate anything foreign to the past. (193-194)

In other words, the return of the ghosts of the dead is the result of unfinished business, and that situation being described in literature written after the triple disasters is similar to the unfinished business of soldiers killed in Asia-Pacific battlefields. Ghosts return as manifestations of repressed anxieties following the disasters just as they did as repressed anxieties following the war.

Kimura goes on to discuss the temporal (present versus past tense) nature of hauntology:

> …hauntology and haunting are metaphors for the ghosts of a past that haunt the present. As far as thinking about hauntology as it occurs in postdisaster fiction, here I want to bring back and free them from metaphor so that I can take up hauntology as a method to consider the issue of the hauntings

and ghosts (*bōrei*) that appear in postdisaster fiction and to consider it as an issue of grammatical tenses. (168)

Kimura discusses Sekiguchi Ryōko's work as a striking example of hauntology as a characteristic of fiction in the years after the disasters, observing that wandering spirits and ghosts populate Sekiguchi's postdisaster writing as contemporary beings. In "La voix sombre [The Dark Voice]" (2015; subsequently translated into Japanese as "Koe wa arawareru," 2017),[10] Sekiguchi expresses the desire to preserve a loved one in the present and to not force them into the past. Kimura writes that, in the aftermath of the disasters, Sekiguchi contemplates that while individuals may be dead, their voices unexpectedly materialize in the present tense as real and living to the still-alive. Even after their physical bodies and vibrating vocal cords have departed this world, their voices, when played back via a recording or a forgotten phone message, for example, leave the hearer feeling that they are being addressed in the very moment of listening. What the dead have to say is occurring in the "present" of the listener (Sekiguchi 2017, 196-197; Kimura 2018, 170-172).

The voice that continues to exist—or, more precisely, the voice which inhabited the body which produced the voice that continues to exist—comes to us through *fantômes,* writes Sekiguchi. "Phantoms come and go. In the space between two tenses [temporalities] not knowing themselves if they are in the present or past." In this way they "stir up the tenses." She closes "Koe wa arawareru" with the following:

> Voices exist and continue in the present, they do not know death,
> At least as long as the voices exist.
> They are gone, the living are no longer here, the appearance is partial, relentless
> Still, their lives have ended yet the air continues to reverberate. (Sekiguchi, 198)

In Japanese postdisaster fiction, communication with the dead is not established in order to recall the past but to construct links to the present. In the literature of an earlier age, ghosts often appear in order to complete unfinished business—the warriors in Noh drama who want us to know the story of their deaths, for example—whereas in postdisaster fiction we are more likely to encounter ghosts returning to bid a final farewell to those who are still living. Kimura phrases it this way, in the context of Doris Dörrie's film *Fukushima Mon*

Amour (*Grüße aus Fukushima*, 2016), "An important aspect of this film lies in the fact that the ghosts are not visible to people who remain in this world and that those who remain feel guilty about unfinished business with those who have now passed, as tradition might lead us to expect, but rather, these ghosts are of people for whom traces of the past continue to exist in this world" (Kimura, 172). Sekiguchi's *fantômes* are a version of these hauntings, as are the *bōrei* and *yūrei* that Kimura points us to. Similarly, these sorts of connections—those now-dead reaching out to say goodbye to those still-living—drive the plot of Itō's *Sōzō rajio* (in chapter four, for example, the character S, who went to Tōhoku as a volunteer, uses writing as a means to communicate with a lover from an illicit affair who died before the disasters).

Kimura has suggested that the triple disasters mark a significant a moment in the historical flow of Japanese fiction and the arts, just as was the case after the war. This provocative suggestion opens up multiple readings of Japanese fiction. The appearance and representation of ghosts in various forms following the disasters also reminds us of the rich tradition in Japanese literature of beings that live in realms different than this one. This break—"postdisaster"—may not prove as long-lived as the rupture after war and defeat, but it does challenge us to look more critically at what has been produced earlier.

---

1 Unless otherwise noted, all translations in this chapter are by the author.

2 Furukawa, Hideo, private conversation with the author, December 10, 2017, Tokyo. See also the *taidan* (conversation) between Furukawa and Suga Keijirō, in which Furukawa recalls that in live readings near the time of the disaster, he only felt like reading Miyazawa Kenji poems. (Kawade, 2013, 33). Further, it is worth noting the numerous contemporary retellings of Miyazawa stories that Furukawa has done for the *Monkey Business* project, including "The bears of Nametoko" (see https://monkeymagazine.org/).

3 See Higaki's essay in Ataru, et al. (2011).

4 See, for example, Freud (1917). This phenomenon may also explain why some of our most compelling narrators (whether or not they are writing in response to a disaster) frequently work and rework variations of the same events throughout their oeuvre.

5 Randy Taguchi (b.1959) is a prolific writer across genres. Her 2000 bestseller, *Outlet* (*Konsento*), brought her wide fame. She has long engaged with issues of radiation (see, e.g., *Hiroshima, Nagasaki, Fukushima: genshiryoku o ukeireta Nihon*).

6 This is the story of a ship, reminiscent of Noah's Ark, that sails through the disaster zone, picking up stranded animals and humans as it goes, absurdly growing in size to accommodate them all.

7 Kimura is quoting from Derrida (1994, 4); translation by Slaymaker to reflect the Japanese.

8 Sekiguchi Ryōko's work is discussed in detail later in this chapter.

9 To be precise, Marx was writing of economic systems, but the metaphor of haunting holds.

10 Sekiguchi resides in Paris and writes in French, primarily for a French audience. To my mind she is a French intellectual, with much of her writing appearing only later in Japanese.

References

Asada Akira and Azuma Hiroki. 2014. "'Fukushima' wa shisōteki kadai ni nariuru ka." *Shinchō* 111 no. 6 (June): 417-447.

Derrida, Jacques. 1994. *Specters of Marx: The State of the Debt, the Work of Mourning and the New International.* Translated by Peggy Kamuf. New York: Routledge.

Direk, Zeynep and Leonard Lawlor, eds. 2014. *A Companion to Derrida.* Chichester West Sussex, UK: John Wiley & Sons.

Freud, Sigmund. 1917. *Trauer Und Melancholie* [*Mourning and Melancholia*]. Merck, Sharp & Dohme, 1972.

———. 1919. *The Uncanny.* Translated by David McLintock, introduction by Hugh Haughton. New York: Penguin Books, 2003.

Furukawa Hideo. 2016. *Horses, Horses, in the End the Light Remains Pure: A Tale That Begins with Fukushima.* Translated by Doug Slaymaker with Akiko Takenaka. New York: Columbia University Press.

Ikezawa Natsuki. 2013. *Sōtō no fune.* Tokyo: Shinchōsha.

———. 2017. "Shinsaigo no bungaku wa kanōka." *Shakai bungaku* 44 (2016): 2-17.

Itō Seikō. 2015. *Sōzō rajio.* Tokyo: Kawade bunko.

Kawade Mukku. 2013. *Miyazawa Kenji: Shura to Kyūsai: Botsugo Hachijūnen.* Tokyo: Kawade shobo.

Kimura Saeko. 2013. *Shinsaigo bungakuron: Atarashii Nihonbungakuron no tame ni.* Tokyo: Seidosha

———. 2018. *Sono go no shinsai go bungakuron.* Tokyo: Seidosha. Translated by Doug Slaymaker and Rachel DiNitto as *Theorizing Post-disaster Literature in Japan.* Lanham MD: Lexington Books, 2022.

Sasaki Ataru, Shunsuke Tsurumi, Takaaki Yoshimoto, Hisao Nakai, Gen Kida, Tetsuo Yamaori, Norihiro Kato, Masaki Tajima, Ichiro Mori, Shinya Tateiwa, Yoshiyuki Koizumi, Tatsuya Higaki, Yuichi Ikeda, Tsutomu Tomotsune, Takao Egawa, Iwasaburo Koso, and Jun Hirose. 2011. *Shiso toshiteno 3.11* [*3.11 as Philosophy*]. Tokyo: Kawade shobo.

Sekiguchi Ryōko. 2017. "Koe wa arawareru." *Bungakukai* 71, no. 3 (March): 140-197.

Shigematsu Kiyoshi and Furukawa Hideo. 2012. "Ushi no yōni, Uma no yōni." In *Shinsai to fikushon no "kyori"* [*Ruptured Fiction(s) of the Earthquake*], 175-199. Tokyo: Waseda bungakukai.

Taguchi, Randy. 2003. *Outlet.* Translated by Glynne Walley. New York: Vertical.

———. 2011. *Hiroshima, Nagasaki, Fukushima: genshiryoku o ukeireta Nihon*. Tokyo: Chikuma purima shinsho.

———. 2012. "Bungaku no riaritii." *Nihon Bungaku* 61, no 4 (April): 20-30.

Treat, John Whittier. 1995. *Writing Ground Zero: Japanese Literature and the Atomic Bomb*. Chicago: University of Chicago Press.

PART 3:

FAMILY, IDENTITY, GENDER, BODY

Barbara E. Thornbury, Temple University

Gender, Aging, and Family in Kore'eda Hirokazu's Kiki Kirin Films

A leading figure in world cinema, Kore'eda Hirokazu (b. 1962) is particularly well known for his fine-grained portrayals of families. Actress Kiki Kirin (1943-2018) played significant roles in six of his family-focused films, beginning with *Still Walking* (*Aruite mo aruite mo*, 2008) and ending ten years later with *Shoplifters* (*Manbiki kazoku*, 2018). In between, Kiki appeared in *I Wish* (*Kiseki*, 2011); *Like Father, Like Son* (*Soshite chichi ni naru*, 2013); *Our Little Sister* (*Umimachi Diary*, 2015); and *After the Storm* (*Umi yori mo mada fukaku*, 2016).[1] Five of these six films were directed, edited, and entirely written by Kore'eda himself—the single exception being *Our Little Sister*, for which he wrote the screenplay based on the *Umimachi Diary* manga series by Yoshida Akimi.

Tapping into widespread anxieties in Japan that stem from the declining birthrate and the rapidly aging population, Kore'eda's Kiki Kirin films powerfully question the continued viability of the family unit and, by extension, the ongoing strength and stability of society overall. On the surface, the women and men of Kiki's generation looked strong: generally speaking, they married and stayed married, raised well-educated children, and helped build the Japanese economy so that, by the late 1960s, it was the second largest (since 2010, the third largest) in the world. In Kore'eda's depictions, however, the ideologically sanctioned, twentieth-century nuclear family was deeply flawed and unsustainable.

The focus of this chapter is on how those flaws and that unsustainability are expressed in Kore'eda's Kiki Kirin films. We see this in the aging matriarch's fears of loneliness and abandonment and her perplexity in the face of rapid social change. Above all, we see it in her anger and resentment—sometimes overt, sometimes implicit—at the cards dealt her in life even as she is made to witness her adult children's unease and helplessness as they try to make their way in the twenty-first-century world. What is also interesting is the variety of ways that Kiki's characters attempt to cope with the situations in which they find themselves in the latter years of their lives.

It is Kiki's role as the aging matriarch of families weighed down by psychological and, in several instances, financial stress that so evocatively and unmistakably links together all six films and brings them into dialogue with each other. (Although Kore'eda cast several actors—Lily Franky, Abe Hiroshi, Maki Yōko, Harada Yoshio, and Maeda Ōshiro—in more than one of these films, none links them to the extent Kiki does.) Moreover, viewers cannot help but be acutely aware of the temporal framework of the films as they witness the passage of ten years of Kiki's life, from age 65 in *Still Walking* to age 75 in *Shoplifters*.

Kiki's presence in Kore'eda's films underscores Mariko Asano Tamanoi's point that "we must listen to what women have to say about their experiences, emotions, and thoughts," given that "[t]heir voices…may lead to different views of Japanese culture and history" (1990, 17). Kiki opened for Kore'eda a broad range of storytelling possibilities that bring to the fore issues of gender, aging, and family. The complex richness of Kiki's roles places Kore'eda among those relatively few directors who can be credited with having passed the Bechdel-Wallace test (also known as the Bechdel test), an informal, though widely cited, "method of evaluating the way women are depicted in a film" (Nichols 2021). To pass the test—named for feminist cartoonist Alison Bechdel, who "introduced the idea as a winking criticism of male-dominated movies"—a work "must 1) have at least two women in it, who 2) talk to each other, about 3) something other than a man" (Garber 2015). *Shoplifters*, just to cite one example, stands out in this regard.

Kore'eda, Kiki, and Issues of Gender, Aging, and Family

Since the early 1990s, when Kore'eda began his career as a director, screenwriter, editor, and producer, he has made some twenty films and has won many prestigious international awards—including the Cannes Film Festival's highest accolade, the Palme d'Or, for *Shoplifters*. Prior to the release of *Still Walking*, Kore'eda had already won national and international renown for *Maboroshi* (1995), *After Life* (*Wandafuru raifu*, 1998), and *Nobody Knows* (*Dare mo shiranai*, 2004). When Kiki started working with Kore'eda, she, too, was well established in the film industry, with acting roles in almost one hundred feature films to her credit. Although best known internationally for her work with Kore'eda, Kiki is also widely acclaimed for roles she played in films such as *Tokyo Tower: Mom and Me and Sometimes Dad* (*Tōkyō tawā: Okan to boku to tokidoki oton*, 2007), directed by Matsuoka Jōji, and *Sweet Bean* (*An*, 2015), directed by Kawase Naomi.

It is possible to trace a direct line from *Nobody Knows*, with its focus on four abandoned children epitomizing the failure of the nuclear family, to the films Kore'eda began making with Kiki four years later. As with *Nobody Knows*, the storylines in each of Kore'eda's Kiki Kirin films are entwined with an array of demographic, sociocultural, and socioeconomic issues that became of central concern in Japan starting in the late twentieth century. Most of those issues directly or at least indirectly find expression in the characters Kiki plays.

When Kiki's characters came of age during the postwar era of rapid economic growth, the "good life," Anne Allison has written, was "closely linked to a heteronormative and increasingly nuclearized family." It was "defined in large part by familial roles. This meant, for a man, providing for family; for a woman, raising children and running the home; and for a child, excelling academically and acquiring a job and family of one's own as an adult" (2015, 38). In short, becoming an adult, as Kiki's characters did in the 1960s, was synonymous with getting married and having children. "Throughout Japan's postwar period," notes Allison Alexy, "heterosexual marriage has been a powerfully normative social force, marking married people [as] responsible social adults (*shakaijin*, literally 'social person'). The vast majority of people got married, and being in a heterosexual marriage demonstrated a person's 'normalcy.'" In time, though, there was a shift in people's—especially women's—outlooks: "In the early twenty-first century," Alexy adds, "both the centrality of heterosexual marriages and the particular forms those relationships should take are being implicitly and explicitly called into question" (2020, 4). With a lifetime of experience behind them, the characters Kiki plays in Kore'eda's films are among those who call into question the degree to which women are able to find satisfaction in the roles of wife and mother.

Each of Kiki's Kore'eda characters, too, exemplifies Japan as the world's first super-aging society and the issues that entails for individuals. "Today," writes Sawako Shirahase, "Japan is undergoing a major demographic transformation marked by both a decline in fertility and a rapidly aging population" (2015, 11). Japan's notable rates of longevity are coupled with fewer women choosing to get married and have children (see Thornbury 2020, 59-61). At the same time, the three-generation households that were once commonplace (see Shirahase 2015, 20) have given way to much more atomized arrangements, with a sizable percentage of the population living on their own. Three of the characters Kiki plays in Kore'eda's films reside by themselves.

The result of this atomization in society is a well-documented epidemic of loneliness, especially among older people—for which even marriage and children do not necessarily provide an antidote. The word *kodoku-shi* (lonely death)—a reference to isolated people tragically dying on their own, the body sometimes not discovered for days—began appearing in the Japanese media in the 1970s and 1980s (Dahl 2020, 86-87). Two of the most eye-opening pieces of writing on the topic in English are the section titled "Missing Elderly" in Anne Allison's book *Precarious Japan* (2013), and the *New York Times* article "A Generation in Japan Faces a Lonely Death" by Norimitsu Onishi (2017). The characters Kiki plays in Kore'eda's films put a human face on these social issues.

Still Walking (2008): A Wife and Mother's Disappointment and Grief

Kore'eda brings Kiki onto his cinematic stage in the role of Yokoyama Toshiko who, as a young mother carrying a baby on her back, witnessed her physician husband Kyōhei (played by Harada Yoshio) spending time in the company of another woman. Despite his infidelity, she did what was expected of her generation: she stayed married to the man and raised their children. Kore'eda drives home to viewers Toshiko's enduring emotional pain by employing as the title of the film words from Ishida Ayumi's 1968 hit song, "Blue Light Yokohama,"[2] the sound of which Toshiko heard drifting out of the room where her husband was meeting his lover. At one point during the family reunion that takes place in the film, Toshiko brings out a vinyl record containing that very song that she secretly bought those many decades ago, and makes everyone listen to it. "Blue Light Yokohama" symbolizes her pain and her determination never to forget or forgive what happened back then—and, as Kore'eda suggests in scenes showing the almost too friendly interaction between Kyōhei and the aging yet attractive woman next door (played by Katō Haruko), may in fact have continued to happen. Although long retired from practicing medicine, Kyōhei dotes on the woman next door. He addresses her in the gentlest of tones when they happen to pass each other in the street and she confides to him that she has been feeling unwell. In marked contrast, he has little to say to Toshiko when they are together at home. When he does speak to her, his tone of voice is gruff and irritable.

Toshiko's greatest reward for her suffering endurance as a wife would have been the success and devotion of her two sons—particularly her firstborn, Junpei. But he died as a youth while saving a child from drowning at a beach near the Yokoyamas' seaside home. It is to commemorate the anniversary of his death that the family reunion of the film takes place. Toshiko's second son, Ryōta (played by Abe Hiroshi), cannot take Junpei's place in his mother's affections any more than her daughter, Chinami (played by Yū), can. Toshiko does not defend Ryōta, an underemployed art restorer, from the scorn of her husband, who had wanted a son to take over his medical practice. She does not even seem very interested in him. At the very least, Ryōta lacks the financial wherewithal that may have raised him in Toshiko's estimation. He gives her a small gift of money just to show that he understands how an adult son should behave toward his aging mother, but she regards it as the trifle it literally is. She wants a son with a car to take her shopping, she says. At this point in his life, Ryōta does not even have a driver's license.

More than not having the material trappings of success, Ryōta has married a widow with a child—so the boy is not Toshiko's biological grandson. She derisively refers to Ryōta's stepson, Atsushi (played by Tanaka Shōhei), who is a quiet and well-behaved child, as "the prince" (*ōji*). In a scene with Atsushi's mother, Yukari (played by Natsukawa Yui), Toshiko seems affectionate enough as she offers her daughter-in-law gifts of the kimonos she has acquired over the years—items that she knows her own daughter does not want anyway. But, when Yukari responds to Toshiko's abrupt question about her plans to have more children by saying that she and Ryōta are taking their time to think about it, Toshiko's comeback is that maybe it is better for them not to. While seemingly concerned that Atsushi might have a hard time accepting a half-sibling, Toshiko comes across as a grandmother who does not necessarily want her second son's children—biological or not—as her grandchildren.

For Toshiko, life has certain rules. A son from a "good" family does not marry a woman who was already married (and has a child, no less)—despite

Ryōta's assertion that society has changed. Although Yukari was widowed, Ryōta's comment no doubt refers to the fact that, as Allison Alexy has written, "early in the twenty-first century divorce in Japan rapidly became a newly visible and viable option in ways it had never been before" (2020, 2). More divorces means that there are more women with children getting remarried. It can also be assumed that in Toshiko's mind an adult son (the elder or eldest, if there is more than one son) is supposed to take care of his parents, as was traditionally the case when three-generation family households were the norm. That certainly would have been the expectation had Ryōta taken over his father's medical practice after Junpei died. Toshiko says that she does not want to be bothered by noisy grandchildren when Chinami expresses her willingness to move with her husband and two children into her parents' house so she can be on hand for them should they need help. The real issue is that Toshiko wants a son (specifically, her deceased elder son) to be there for her, not a daughter.

Toshiko's disconnection from Ryōta is vividly encapsulated near the end of the film as he, Yukari, and Atsushi wait for the bus to start their journey home. By way of saying goodbye, Toshiko startles her departing visitors by first shaking Atsushi's hand, then Yukari's. When she gets to Ryōta, he adamantly refuses this unambiguously "foreign" gesture, which his mother perhaps picked up from television shows or movies. He knows that by extending her hand she is in reality pushing them away. Shaking hands, after all, is basically what strangers do. Toshiko may have spared no effort or even expense in lavishly feeding her visiting son and daughter and their families. Indeed, it can be said that the very act of cooking and feeding others is her principal coping mechanism insofar as the kitchen is a place where she has a modicum of control. However, her disappointment at how life turned out prevents her from viewing those who were gathered around her (and ate her food) as the family she wants or thought she should have had. Toshiko's handshaking gesture of family disconnection is well matched when Ryōta and Yukari are headed away on the bus and agree that there is no need to make another visit in the near future—and can even bypass stopping by at New Year's. Toshiko would agree that New Year's, that most sacred of family holidays in Japan, has lost its meaning for the Yokoyama family.

I Wish (2011): Matriarch of an Incomplete Three-Generation Household

Ōsako Hideko, Kiki's character in *I Wish*, appears to find an escape from her disappointments in the flower-bedecked, idealized world of hula dancing. The return of the Ōsakos' recently divorced daughter Nozomi (played Ōtsuka Nene) to her parents' home in Kagoshima, along with her elder son Kōichi (played by Maeda Kōki), puts a strain on the extended family's finances. There is also the emotional strain of living with a grandchild who sorely misses the company of his younger brother Ryūnosuke (played by Maeda Ōshiro), who is living with his father Kenji (played by Odagiri Jō) in Fukuoka, and of living with a grown daughter who finds herself adrift in her old hometown.

Hideko, it can be imagined, once worked with her husband, Shūkichi (played by Hashizume Isao), in his home-based specialty cake (*karukan*) shop. However, the labor-intensive business run by an aging couple could not survive competition from the likes of the much bigger operation shown in the film that can afford a high-rent location and the cost of hiring employees to do the work. In addition to whatever savings and pension income they may have, the Ōsakos now get by with Shūkichi's income as a part-time bike parking lot attendant. Shūkichi, with whom Hideko barely exchanges a word in the course of the film, exudes an air of melancholy. The world has changed and left the aging man behind. Whereas Hideko continually stays on her feet practicing hula dance patterns in defiance of the passage of time, Shūkichi spends a good part of the day sitting, smoking, and apparently brooding.

Like Toshiko in *Still Walking*, Hideko is a woman whose long marriage has not necessarily brought happiness or even contentment. Hideko's disappointment in marriage and men in general (including her rock musician ex-son-in-law) can be inferred from her disgust at the wet toilet seat her husband's friends leave behind when they visit and have had a bit too much to drink. Moreover, although she is now part of an extended family household, the circumstances that brought it about are not happy ones—and, at any rate, especially without Ryūnosuke, it is incomplete. But, just as the film ends with Kōichi coming to terms with the dissolution of his parents' marriage and his new life in the volcano-ash-dusted city of Kagoshima, Hideko—along with a group of like-minded women that comes to include Nozomi—have found in hula dancing a way to cope with what life has thrown at them. However old they become, the identities of men like Kyōhei in *Still Walking* and Shūkichi in *I Wish* remain tied to the careers they pursued during their working years. For them, the loss of those careers results in a loss of identity. The women view life differently: just as Toshiko still proudly reigns over her kitchen, Hideko too refuses to sit down.

Like Father, Like Son (2013): Conveying Lessons from History to a Younger Generation

Kiki's character, Ishizeki Riko, in *Like Father, Like Son* enters the world of her six-year-old grandson Keita (played by Ninomiya Keita) by playing Wii videogames with him—and brings him into her world by teaching him how to honor the family's ancestors at the home altar.[3] The most significant scene in which Riko appears in this film takes place when she joins her daughter, Nozomi (played by Ono Machiko), and son-in-law, Ryōta (played by Fukuyama Masaharu), in celebrating little Keita's first day of elementary school. It is a bittersweet moment for the parents because, although Keita won admission to a highly competitive private school, they are wrestling with the knowledge that just after the child was born he was switched with another baby in the hospital and is not their biological son.

The climax of the scene occurs when Riko, finding herself alone for a few moments with Ryōta, tells him that after the war ended in 1945 many orphaned children in Japan became the adoptees and foster children of non-biologically related adults. When Riko states simply and unequivocally that what matters is who raises the child, it is as if Kore'eda himself is speaking directly to the film audience. That said, Riko's words represent the postwar situation in a far more positive way than the actual circumstances warranted overall. Philip Brasor has written that large numbers of the orphans to whom Riko refers "had nowhere to go and ended up sleeping in train stations, begging for food or resorting to criminal activity to stay alive. These children were not pitied—they were vilified. The police called them '*furōji*' [literally, vagrant children], an extremely derogatory word that was subsequently adopted by the public." Some were placed "in the homes of relatives, no matter how distant. However, many of these families didn't want them and often forced them out." Large numbers died on the streets. "Even as conditions improved for society in general," Brasor notes, "the situation for many war orphans did not. Average people viewed them as a public menace and there was no incentive to help them" (2018). Despite Riko's seemingly encouraging lessons from history, it is a fact that in the postwar period large numbers of orphaned children did not find homes and some of the homes in which they were placed were not secure or loving. To this day, Japan lags behind other nations with respect to families' willingness to foster non-biologically related children (see Thornbury 2017, 143). Nevertheless, her point reflects the sincere feelings of a woman who loves the boy she has always known as her grandson. Her attitude stands in contrast to Kiki's Toshiko in *Still Walking*, who had trouble accepting her son's marriage to a widow with a son.[4]

Riko's good intentions are met with a figurative slap in the face by Ryōta, a reaction that is emblematic of the obtuse arrogance that defines the character for most of the film. Laying bare the dismissive attitude of younger generations towards society's elders, he essentially tells her that the situation in which he and Nozomi find themselves regarding Keita is none of her business. They will make their own decision about what to do going forward. Riko's response is a deep, contrite bow accompanied by words of apology. Although Ryōta makes amends of a sort by saying that he does value Riko's opinion, her bow and words of apology powerfully convey the woman's hurt and anger. In the end, Ryōta actually comes around to his mother-in-law's way of thinking insofar as he winds up embracing Keita as his son. However, this well-meaning matriarch, as she herself is well aware, is in her son-in-law's eyes just a foolish old woman. For Kiki's Riko, coping means keeping a smile on her face and simply internalizing her hurt feelings.

Our Little Sister (2015): A Woman of Strong Character with Strong Opinions

Kiki's Kikuchi Fumiyo, the great-aunt of the Kōda sisters in *Our Little Sister*, is a woman who does not hesitate to express strong opinions about family life and marriage. As in *Still Walking*, the interpersonal dynamics of a family that briefly reunites to memorialize the deceased are explored in *Our Little Sister*. Although viewers do not learn if Fumiyo was married or had children of her own, she is now the senior member of the clan and its matriarch. The memorial is for her sister, the Kōda sisters' grandmother—and the woman who raised them after their parents' marriage ended a decade and a half earlier, with both parents going their separate ways, leaving their children behind.

Fumiyo speaks out in defense of a world in which couples stay married and children are taken care of by their biological parents. After the sisters have brought their middle-school-aged half-sister, Suzu (played by Hirose Suzu), to live with them, Fumiyo warns that they may be making a mistake. It is a lot of work to bring up a child, she says, and besides, she adds, Suzu is the daughter of the woman who "broke up" their parents' marriage. But the sisters—who are as outspokenly assertive as Fumiyo herself—see things differently. It was their father who broke up the marriage. And, anyway, no matter who was at fault, Suzu is their father's daughter—and, therefore, she is their sister. The sisters may live in the old family house and carry on the tradition of making plum wine (*umeshu*) from fruit that grows on an ancient tree in their backyard, but as matriarchs-in-the-making they have a more flexible understanding of family and society than Fumiyo does.

What makes Fumiyo especially compelling is the strength of character that, to a greater or lesser degree, comes through in all of the roles Kiki plays in Kore'eda's films. In their own way, the Kōda sisters, Suzu included, display the same strength of character as their great aunt. When Fumiyo assertively asks Suzu if she did not get along with her stepmother, Suzu steadfastly refuses to bad-mouth the woman, even though in fact they did not get along. And when Fumiyo goes on to ask Suzu about her life with the Kōdas, Suzu again holds her own. The household is like a girls' dorm, Suzu replies, an answer that Fumiyo appreciates for its diplomatic cleverness.

It is noteworthy that when the Kōda sisters' mother, Miyako (played by Ōtake Shinobu), returns for her mother's memorial service, she stays with Fumiyo—not with her own daughters. Miyako has an especially fraught relationship with her oldest daughter, Sachi (played by Ayase Haruka), who views her mother as a hypocrite for having left her children behind those many years ago. On her side, Fumiyo just wants family harmony. Although she had earlier declared that Suzu's mother broke up the marriage, she now angrily tells Miyako that its dissolution is partially her fault. Following this line of reasoning—which holds that both Miyako and the other woman caused the marriage to fail—it is only the man who walked out on his wife and family who bears no responsibility whatsoever.

Fumiyo is not simply looking for someone to blame. Her way of dealing with the situation before her (in other words, her way of coping) is to cling ever tighter to her generation's view that, even in the face of a husband's transgressions, it is the woman's duty to keep the family together—or, at least, not to allow it to fall apart. For the Kōda sisters, women are indeed the ones who keep the family together insofar as it was Fumiyo's sister who picked up where her daughter and son-in-law left off when they left their children behind. Then it was Sachi who, in caring for her two younger sisters, picked up where her grandmother left off when she passed away. Now, in caring for Suzu, Sachi has picked up where Suzu's father (who, of course, was also her own father) left off when he passed away. Fumiyo is rightfully concerned that Sachi may be sacrificing her own future by taking on these caretaking responsibilities—a theme that Kore'eda touches on in *After the Storm*. Thus, in the end, Fumiyo's viewpoint prevails, just not in the way she might have imagined.

After the Storm (2016): A Mother Trying to Keep Her Children Close

Kore'eda uses Kiki's characters Shinoda Yoshiko in *After the Storm* and Shibata Hatsue in *Shoplifters* to foreground a new thematic focus on loneliness and abandonment in old age, a topic that in recent years has been receiving a great deal of attention in the media and, increasingly, in the scholarly press (see, for example, Allison 2013, Dahl 2020, and Onishi 2017). Kore'eda makes this new focus clear from the outset of *After the Storm*, when Yoshiko's son, Ryōta (played by Abe Hiroshi), runs into one of his former school classmates on his way to visit his mother. The down-at-the-heels *danchi* public housing complex where Yoshiko lives once bustled with growing families, but is now mostly home to older people—a number of whom are leading solitary lives.[5] Ryōta's former classmate tells him that she has moved back in with her parents after she heard that the deceased body of one of the aging residents in the housing complex was not discovered for days. The person died alone, uncared for, unnoticed, and unmourned—a prime example of *kodoku-shi* (lonely death). The woman tells Ryōta that she does not want that to happen to her parents, so she has given up the life she was leading to be with and take care of them. Here, as elsewhere, Kore'eda makes clear that family life often comes with sacrifice.

Yoshiko, whose gambling-prone husband recently died, does not have the comforts—especially housing that is more convenient and better equipped—that would make life easier for her in her senior years. Moreover, maintaining an ongoing relationship with her two adult children means that she has no choice but to accept the fact that both of them—Ryōta and his sister Chinatsu (played by

Kobayashi Satomi)—are needy in their own way and even look for a chance to get their hands on the limited money she has. While Ryōta and Chinatsu visit Yoshiko on occasion, neither intends to move in with her or have her move in with them. Ryōta, a divorced man with a predilection for gambling like his father, is way behind on his child-support payments; Chinatsu is a mother who cannot afford on her own the extras (such as figure-skating lessons) she would like her children to have.

To some extent, the world at large tries to lend a helping hand to this aging woman who is struggling physically. The neighborhood grocery store offers home-delivery service to seniors who, like Yoshiko, live in walk-up apartments above a certain floor. And when her arthritic hands prevent her from writing the customary acknowledgment cards following her husband's funeral, her daughter and even her ex-daughter-in-law step in to help with the task.

Perhaps the most poignant moment in all of Kore'eda's Kiki Kirin films occurs in *After the Storm* in a late-night conversation between Yoshiko and Ryōta. Echoing words from the 1990 Teresa Teng song "Wakare no yokan" (A premonition of parting), she reflects out loud that she never had the experience of loving someone deeper than the ocean (*umi yori mo mada fukaku*)—which is the title of *After the Storm* in Japanese.[6] Yoshiko's marriage was not happy, her aging body is making daily life increasingly difficult, and her son's various problems include the fact that he is divorced, leaving her to worry that she will lose contact with her beloved grandson. Kiki's Toshiko in *Still Walking* may have spurned her daughter's offer to move in so she can be on hand to help out her parents, but at least Toshiko knows that assistance is available should she need it. Kiki's Yoshiko in *After the Storm* does not have such assurance from either of her children, and her way of coping with an uncertain future is to forthrightly tell her son that she wants him to be there for her. This stark portrayal of elderly people in need is carried over into Kiki's Hatsue in *Shoplifters*.

Shoplifters (2018): An Aging Woman's Insurance Plan

The role of Shibata Hatsue in *Shoplifters* serves as a profoundly moving finale to Kiki's work with Kore'eda. It is thanks to Hatsue that the extended family—four biologically and legally unrelated adults and two children—portrayed in the film has a place of refuge from the prying eyes of the outside world. She has somehow managed to hold onto the functional, although rundown and cramped, house she has long inhabited, which sits on property that real estate developers very much want to get their hands on. (New apartment buildings are filling in the area of the Tokyo Metropolis where Hatsue's house is located. The skyline-altering Sky Tree communications tower, which is clearly visible from the neighborhood, is emblematic of the continuously changing cityscape.) Moreover, Hatsue has somehow managed to gain access to her deceased ex-husband's pension, which provides a measure of financial stability to the household.

If the real estate man who comes calling—one of those agents and developers who have their greedy eyes on Hatsue's property—is to be believed, Hatsue has a son living in Hakata, which is a considerable distance from Tokyo. More to the point, there is no evidence that she has any contact with him. What she needs is family here and now. To that end she has created what she calls an "insurance plan" as protection against a lonely death—meaning the people she has gathered around her, all of them individuals with their own problems. It appears that Osamu (played by Lily Franky) and Nobuyo (played by Andō Sakura) killed Nobuyo's ex-husband in self-defense and illegally disposed of the body. Until, during the course of the film, Osamu is injured on the job, he made money as an unskilled laborer. (Skills aside, his criminal record for illegal burial, apparently the only crime for which he was charged, makes him ineligible for more lucrative employment.) Although Nobuyo might have been able to keep her job at a commercial laundry in the face of a workforce retrenchment, she loses out to a fellow worker who blackmails her. The basis for the blackmail is that Nobuyo has been seen in the company of the child Yuri (played by Sasaki Miyu), a member of the Shibata household who was belatedly reported missing by her birth parents and who the authorities believe was kidnapped. Aki (played by Matsuoka Mayu) is the estranged daughter of Hatsue's ex-husband's son—and earns money by doing sex work, although (thanks to Hatsue's intervention) she is not made to contribute to the household's finances. A large portion of the family's food and other daily necessities is obtained by means of the shoplifting forays Osamu goes on with Shōta (played by Jō Kairi), the young boy he views as his son. Osamu and Shōta are joined in this pursuit by little Yuri when she enters the Shibata household.

There is an earthiness about Hatsue. She trims her toenails even while everyone is gathered around near her and eating. She lacks teeth. At the same time, she is a tender woman whose pain is palpable when she notices the scars on the arm of Yuri, who had been abused at home. Showing Yuri what true familial love and caring mean, Hatsue gently feeds the hungry and troubled little girl and even comes up with a comforting way to help her stop wetting the bed at night. Hatsue is also particularly kind to Aki, who in turn is most expressive of her love for "grandmother." Hatsue has a soft heart for Nobuyo as well. When Nobuyo muses on whether Yuri has chosen to join the Shibata family, Hatsue states forthrightly that she has made the same choice about having Nobuyo with her.

Kiki's Toshiko in *Still Walking*, Hideko in *I Wish*, and Yoshiko in *After the Storm* exemplify women whose marriages, for better or worse, were permanent. In contrast, Hatsue's husband left her for another woman. Refusing to be easily dismissed, Hatsue regularly makes visits to the home of her deceased ex-husband's son, claiming that she does so in order to honor her former spouse's memory at the family altar. But it is a kind of psychological revenge, not to mention a clever bit of extortion—knowing as she does that the son feels compelled to make a show of regret for what happened in the past and will make tangible that expression of regret with a modest gift of money. Viewers of the film may well cringe at the way this episode graphically mocks idealized notions of family unity and affection—particularly when they realize that Aki, the young woman in the Shibata household whose earnings come from sex work and who literally clings to Hatsue for emotional support, is actually the estranged daughter of the man who hands Hatsue an envelope with 30,000 yen following her most recent visit to his house.[7]

The Shibatas' joyous seaside outing in the latter part of the film is a chance to see the pleasure that Hatsue takes knowing that she is not alone as she approaches the end of her life. Sitting on the beach, she laments her aging body. But, with the camera focused closely on her face as she looks out at Osamu, Nobuyo, Aki, Shōta, and Yuri frolicking in the surf, she quietly articulates her gratitude. Inasmuch as they are not hers in a legal or biological sense, Hatsue is metaphorically a shoplifter extraordinaire—having acquired in a most unconventional way a family that cares about her and that she cares about.

Conclusion

No matter how many or how few lines she spoke, or how much or how little screen time she had, Kiki Kirin played a significant role in each of the six Kore'eda films in which she appeared. Together, these roles produce a noteworthy cumulative impact. In Kore'eda's career as a filmmaker, the six films directly followed one after the other—with only two exceptions: *Air Doll* (*Kūki ningyō*, 2009) came out between *Still Walking* and *I Wish*, and *The Third Murder* (*Sandome no satsujin*, 2017) came out between *After the Storm* and *Shoplifters*.

Kore'eda's Kiki Kirin films form a critical mass of work both temporally and in terms of the ways that their stories incorporate and, to a large degree, coalesce around the characters that Kiki plays. Over the ten-year period that she worked with Kore'eda, Kiki offered the director the opportunity to examine the family unit from a multi-generational perspective. It is Kiki's persona as the aging matriarch of families under stress that evocatively links *Still Walking*; *I Wish*; *Like Father, Like Son*; *Our Little Sister*; *After the Storm*; and *Shoplifters* and brings them into dialogue with each other. Together, the films form a rich and powerful body of work that encourages viewers to consider the question of how families and society itself will—and even should—look like in the future.

---

1 The English-language titles given here are those used by Kore'eda's distribution partners for the purpose of overseas sales. While "Still Walking" adequately conveys the meaning of *Aruite mo aruite mo*, more literal translations of the original Japanese film titles include: "A Miracle" for *Kiseki*, "Finally I Become a Father" for *Soshite chichi ni naru*, "Diary of a Seaside Town" for *Umimachi Diary*, "Even Deeper Than the Sea" for *Umi yori mo mada fukaku*, and "A Shoplifing Family" for *Manbiki kazoku*.

2 http://www.natsumelo.com/2011/10/ayumi-ishida-blue-light-yokohama-1968/

3 At one point when Keita spends time with the Saikis (his actual biological parents), he tells them that his grandmother taught him how to honor ancestors at the family altar—the point being that such old-fashioned practices do not have a place in the Nonomiyas' household.

4 In *Still Walking*, Toshiko's daughter-in-law Yukari had to swallow her anger and disappointment at the fact that Toshiko went out of her way to buy fresh pajamas for her son Ryōta, as a mother might for a son staying overnight, but does not do the same for her grandson Atsushi—in effect treating the boy as if he is a stranger rather than a member of the family.

5 There is a particular poignancy to the setting. As Linda Ehrlich notes, "[m]ost of *After the Storm* takes place in the Asahigaoka apartment complex in the Kiyose section of Tokyo where Kore'eda himself had lived" (2019, 71).

6 https://www.youtube.com/watch?v=wDWGAfOmJjA. The singer says that the love she feels for the person who may soon be leaving her is even deeper than the ocean and bluer than the sky.

7 It is not clear whether Hatsue's ex-husband's son and his wife know that their daughter Aki is not studying abroad as they claim she is, but is actually living with Hatsue.

References

Alexy, Allison. 2020. *Intimate Disconnections: Divorce and the Romance of Independence in Contemporary Japan*. Chicago: University of Chicago Press.

Allison, Anne. 2013. *Precarious Japan*. Durham: Duke University Press.

———. 2015. "Precarity and Hope: Social Connectedness in Postcapitalist Japan." In *Japan: The Precarious Future*, edited by Frank Baldwin and Anne Allison, 36-57. New York: New York University Press.

Brasor, Philip. 2018. "Japanese Media Begins to Break War Orphan Taboo." *Japan Times*, August 25, 2018.

Dahl, Nils. 2020. "Governing Through *Kodokushi*: Japan's Lonely Deaths and Their Impact on Community Self-Government." *Contemporary Japan* 32 (1): 83-102.

Ehrlich, Linda C. 2019. *The Films of Kore'eda Hirokazu: An Elemental Cinema*. New York: Palgrave Macmillan.

Garber, Megan. 2015. "Call it the 'Bechdel-Wallace Test.'" *The Atlantic,* August 25, 2015. https://www.theatlantic.com/entertainment/archive/2015/08/call-it-the-bechdel-wallace-test/402259/.

Nichols, Lynn. 2021. "The Bechdel-Wallace Test in 2021." *The Vindicator: Cleveland State University's Art and Culture Magazine*. https://www.thevindi.com/post/the-bechdel-wallace-test-in-2021.

Onishi, Norimitsu. 2017. "A Generation in Japan Faces a Lonely Death." *New York Times*, November 30, 2017.

Shirahase, Sawako. 2015. "Demography as Destiny: Falling Birthrates and the Allure of a Blended Society." In *Japan: The Precarious Future*, edited by Frank Baldwin and Anne Allison, 11-35. New York: New York University Press.

Tamanoi, Mariko Asano. 1990. "Women's Voices: Their Critique of the Anthropology of Japan." *Annual Review of Anthropology* 19: 17-37.

Thornbury, Barbara E. 2017. "Cultural References in the Novels of Fuminori Nakamura: A Case Study in Current Japanese-to-English Literary Translation Practices and Challenges." *Asia Pacific Translation and Intercultural Studies* 4 (2): 132-46.

———. 2020. "The Thirty-Something 'Tokyo Daughters' of Kawakami Hiromi's *Strange Weather in Tokyo*, Shibasaki Tomoka's *Spring Garden*, and Murata Sayaka's *Convenience Store Woman*." *U.S.-Japan Women's Journal* 57: 57-77.

Angela Yiu, Sophia University

Awakening the Wild Things in Oyamada Hiroko's Stories of Women

> His eyes have got so weary of the bars
> going by, they can't grasp anything else.
> He feels like there's a thousand bars,
> a thousand bars and no world beyond.
>
> The soft tread of his strong, supple stride
> turns him in ever tighter circles,
> like the dance of force about a centre
> in which a great will stands, stunned.
> Rainer Maria Rilke, *The Panther* (1902)[1]

I begin this essay with a tribute in my title to Maurice Sendak's famous and beloved children's story *Where the Wild Things Are* together with an excerpt from Rilke's poem about a caged panther in the Jardin de Plantes in Paris, because both serve as underlying metaphors for the bizarre and fantastic life forms—insects, reptiles, birds, beasts—that emerge in Oyamada Hiroko's strange and haunting stories of women in Japan. The lives of ordinary women and the roles they conventionally play—part-time or full-time non-permanent employees,[2] daughters, wives, mothers—are often dominated by prescribed social scripts that value conformity, docility, domesticity, and uniformity over anything that is individual, strange, outlandish, peculiar, or wild. Oyamada senses the caged wildness inside the hearts and minds of women within the confining gender strictures of Japanese society, and transforms that wild energy into untamed and unruly life forms that disrupt and question the women's otherwise under-stimulated and mundane lives. These moments of rupture are Oyamada's signature of resistance to the limitations that women face daily in patriarchal Japanese society.

This essay will start with a brief introduction of the author, and examines three selected stories that feature strange experiences happening to women who are leading otherwise commonplace lives. "Kōjō" ("The Factory," 2010) features a single woman in her late twenties who is hired as a temp worker in an enormous factory, where she becomes aware of the existence of some fantastical and grotesque birds, beasts, and reptiles. "Ikobore no mushi" ("The Outcast Bug," 2011) is about a married woman in her early thirties whose awkward personality and lackluster performance in the office lead colleagues to shun and avoid her, while strange larvae, pupae, and insects begin to appear in the office and everywhere she goes. "Ana" ("The Hole," 2014) depicts another married woman, similar in age, who quits her non-permanent job to move to the suburbs following her husband's transfer. Not only does she have to deal with overbearing in-laws and strange neighbors, but she also falls into a hole in pursuit of a fantastical big black beast and begins to see other phantom characters that others do not see. I will discuss these stories of women under four themes: the working woman (this section includes information about the social context as well), family, encountering the wild things, and transformation. In doing so, I hope to trace, on the one hand, the small window of liberation and hope acquired through a fertile imagination in an otherwise barren and alienating work and home environment, and, on the other, the bleak reality of endless resistance to limitations in a society that refuses to recognize the potential and desperation of the "wild things" in women, and instead insists on caging them within the so-called traditional values of domesticity and docility.

About Oyamada Hiroko

Born in 1983 in the city of Hiroshima, Oyamada graduated with a degree in Japanese literature from the Faculty of Humanities at Hiroshima University. During the next five years she changed jobs three times, first working on a local magazine in an editorial firm, then as a salesperson in an eyeglasses shop, and finally as a contract employee sent by a temp agency to a subsidiary factory under a major automobile maker. None of these were full-time positions, which means that she did not receive full employment benefits and job security, a fate that many female workers share. About her work experience at the editorial firm, Oyamada said in an interview, "It appeared that my writing was strangely self-assertive, and I was told later, after I quit the job, that it was more suited for fiction" (Ishii 2013). She liked her job selling eyeglasses but was troubled by having to decide what outfit to wear each day, and ended up quitting after seven months. The third job, at the factory, was the most alienating:

> In the previous job, I experienced the simple gratification that selling a pair of glasses translates directly into profit for the company. But in the factory, I was assigned duties that were just a tiny part of subdivided work, and I couldn't figure out what I was really doing. For example, it seems to me that chores such as making a clean copy on the computer or sending a fax have nothing to do with the world, and I was overwhelmed with anxiety and fear. I probably wouldn't feel the same way now, but at that time I couldn't help but feel that I was wrongly paid. (Ishii 2013)

Oyamada married a senior colleague she met at the editorial firm and eventually started writing fiction. Even though none of those early jobs were long-lasting or fulfilling, the experiences find their way into her fiction in a creative mode of social critique and self-reflection. Many of her stories feature women in their thirties who share her experiences as a poorly paid temp office worker, a wife dealing with her spouse and in-laws, a woman anticipating but also fearing pregnancy, and a mother with a young child. Her work and life experiences are also reflected in her story settings: drab office spaces (especially kitchenettes and restrooms where female workers chat and gossip), gigantic and dehumanizing factory floors, claustrophobic urban apartments, and isolated suburban housing where relationships with neighbors and in-laws form a suffocating web.

The physical environment of Oyamada's childhood contributed to her love of plants, insects, and animals, the "wild things" in her stories. She grew up in what she called a "plain countryside house" with an unkempt yard and a small pond filled with carp (*Book Shorts* 2018). Many of her stories feature the in-between or heterotopic space—a garden, a zoo—that is neither entirely wild nor fully cultivated but, rather, concurrently natural and artificial, and her writing flourishes at the blurred boundary between the two. This is where eerie and amazing transformations take place—from daily life to fantasy, from human to other life forms (botanical, aquatic, animal)—a process that is often irreversible, leading to escape and liberation from a dull and frustrating existence but also to a frightening surrender to an unknown dimension. Many stories collected under the titles of *Niwa* (*The Garden*, 2018) and *Kojima* (*A Small Island*, 2021) fall under this category. Indeed, the titles of her anthologies show a singular obsession with various kinds of spaces—natural, constructed, liminal, utopic, dystopic, heterotopic; this is the playground where her imagination roams to capture the real and conjure the unreal and surreal, enabling her to mix realistic depictions of a woman's workplace with flights of fantasy to an alternative reality of dark and hidden realms.

Similarly, instead of using an omniscient narrative voice typical of the orthodox novel in the Western tradition, she favors the first-person, introspective, or confessional mode of narration common in Japanese fiction, and many of her stories have multiple first-person narrative voices that shift from one to another, creating a sophisticated and challenging multi-angle, multi-layer, polyphonic narrative with Rashomon-like complexity. Her endings are often ambiguous, open-ended gestures, again typical of Japanese fiction that lacks solutions and closures, denying the reader a clear conclusion to life's ongoing complexity.

Oyamada has been the recipient of multiple literary prizes, including the 42nd Shinchō New Writer's Prize (2010), the Oda Sakunosuke Prize (2013), the 150th Akutagawa Prize (2014), and the 30th Hiroshima Cultural Prize (2014), and she was nominated for the Mishima Yukio Prize (2013). These honors have enabled her to establish a footing in the competitive publishing world in Japan, and her works have earned steady and quiet attention at home and abroad.

The Working Woman

Oyamada's representative works often feature women in their early to mid-thirties in contract or part-time positions in an office setting. As we prepare to enter her depictions of working women, a brief introduction to Japanese laws about gender equality and a description of contemporary employment conditions for Japanese women are in order.

Article 14 of the Constitution of Japan (effective from 1947) stipulates that "All of the people are equal under the law and there shall be no discrimination in political, economic or social relations because of race, creed, sex, social status or family origin."[3] Article 2 of the Civil Code specifies that "This Code must be construed in accordance with honoring the dignity of individuals and the essential equality of both sexes."[4] The law for "Equal Opportunities for Male and

Female Employment"[5] was established in 1985, the law for "A Society of Gender Equality"[6] in 1999, and the law for the "Promotion of Female Active Participation (in Professional Occupations)"[7] (the name itself sounds condescending) in 2015.

However, the reality for women in the workplace in Japan's predominantly patriarchal society belies the legal standards. According to the *Economist*'s 2022 "glass-ceiling index," which measures "the role and influence of women in the workforce" across 29 rich and advanced countries in the OECD (Organisation for Economic Co-operation and Development) Club, Japan ranked 28th, just one place above South Korea at the rock bottom (2022a).[8] This is no surprise since Japan remains a society where women for the most part must choose between family and career; married couples are not allowed to keep separate family names and must legally choose either the husband's or the wife's surname although, in reality, most women end up giving up their own name (as of 2019, only 5% of married men adopted the wife's family name);[9] women's income is significantly lower than that of men; and women occupy only slightly over 10% of administrative positions in the workforce (Miyazato 2016, 14). In the World Economic Forum's 2022 *Global Gender Gap Report*, which also factors in political representation, Japan ranked the lowest among developed countries—at 116th out of 146 countries, below Tajikistan (114th) in Central Asia and Burkina Faso (115th) in West Africa (2022, 10). Again, this is hardly surprising considering that women comprised only 9.7% of national Diet members in 2022,[10] and nearly 40% of Japan's 1,788 local and municipal legislative councils have either zero or one female legislator in 2023.[11]

A huge gender-based economic gap between male and female workers remains the norm in Japan. First, women earn much less than men. Even without factoring in the wages of non-permanent workers, the income ratio for males to females is 100 to 72.2. Second, only 11.3% of women are employed in administrative and managerial positions, an extremely low percentage among economically advanced nations. Third, the female Economic Activity Rate exhibits an "M curve"[12] in that many women are forced to quit work for childrearing; over 60% of women leave their jobs when they have their first child. Fourth, 56.7% of all female workers are non-permanent workers. The income ratio for male full-time permanent workers to female non-permanent workers is 100 to 50.4 (Miyazato, 14). Finally, there is the notorious "1.3 million-yen barrier" stipulating that women who earn above 1.3 million yen (under 10,000 U.S. dollars by the current exchange rate) can no longer be included in their spouse's social insurance plan and must pay for their own health insurance and pension, a reality that forces most part-time working women to remain within the economic corral of dependency. Patriarchal Japanese society clearly wavers between wanting to tap into the under-utilized female work force and keeping women controlled and financially dependent in the name of tradition and protection.

Such dismal data about the long-standing gender gap in one of the world's supposedly most advanced nations inspires ridicule, despair, and resignation—but, as we will see, Oyamada responds with poker-faced humor and persistence in giving the women in her stories a voice, a growing awareness, and a powerful imagination to question the bars that curb their aspirations. The first-person narrator Asa in "Ana" is an Oyamada signature character: a woman in her early thirties who quits her non-permanent job when her husband is transferred to a suburban branch of his office. The story begins with the commiseration between two women in the same work situation:

> We were both putting in overtime, even though it wasn't in our contracts. We were even handling tasks outside of our job descriptions—receiving orders, interacting with clients—but our base pay remained the same. The only appreciation our employers ever showed us came when the permanent employees got their winter bonuses. Instead of bonuses, we got envelopes with A SMALL TOKEN OF OUR GRATITUDE printed on the front in a cursive script. It really wasn't much. From what I'd heard, the permanent employee bonus was three months' pay—at a minimum—but I only got 30,000 yen, in cash. I did the math. Permanent employees likely got somewhere between 600,000 and 700,000. My envelope had maybe a twentieth of that. (Oyamada 2020, 9-10)

In "Ikobore no mushi," the main character Nara Yurie is one of the rare species of permanent employees among Oyamada's female office workers, but she is socially awkward, lacks confidence, and keeps to herself most of the time. She wears no makeup and serviceable, plain outfits. As a result, she becomes a kind of pariah in the office and is assigned only simple tasks such as filing, stuffing envelopes, or running errands. Her family name Nara also becomes the butt of jokes and disparagement. Alluding to the famous statue of the Great Buddha (Nara Daibutsu) in the historic city of Nara, she is called "Būtsu" behind her back, a nasty and unpleasant sounding nickname that she overhears. After making multiple errors and losing track of time in running an office errand, she is made to believe that she is suffering from depression and finally quits her job.

Ushiyama in the story "Kōjō" finds herself hired as a contract worker in an enormous factory and is assigned to the "shredder squad," feeding unwanted documents into gigantic shredders, five days a week, seven and a half hours per day. This is how she describes the job:

> Flipping on the main power to the shredders, I pull paper from yesterday's load and set up a ten-gallon trash bag. The bags fill twice in the morning and three times in the afternoon. We mostly shred standard A4-size documents and feed them in lengthwise. For a seamless feed, you grab the next stack with your left hand while loading the paper with your right. The machine tugs on the paper, drawing your hand toward it, almost like a handshake. (Oyamada 2019, 56)

Given the alienation and lack of fulfillment at work, what does the other major component in a Japanese woman's life—family—have in store for the Oyamada women? Let us turn our attention to the depiction of family in her stories.

Family

Even though the Japanese government has for years touted the slogan of "A society in which women shine," Japanese women continue to live in the shadow of men and their families. While the Meiji ethos of "good wife, wise mother" may sound old-fashioned, women in 21st century Japan are still expected to fulfill the traditional female roles of homemaking, childrearing, supporting the spouse, and nursing the elderly, in addition to bringing in subsidiary income as part-time non-permanent workers. Japanese labor law includes a provision for men to take childcare leave, but the percentage of men utilizing that right remained under 14% in 2021,[13] and men spent on an average one hour per day on housework compared to 7.4 hours for women.[14] Most women still find themselves the sole caregiver for small children at home, and the neologism *wan-ope* (one-person operation) has become a standard descriptor of this circumstance. For many women, the anticipation of pregnancy, sometimes out of family and social pressure, and the dread of an isolated struggle with childrearing, come hand-in-hand.

This dilemma translates into a disturbing first scene in "Ikobore no mushi."

At the dinner table, sitting with her husband, a man of few words, Nara Yurie bites into something small and hard mixed in with her food:

> There was something small and hard in my mouth. I bit on it unwittingly. Was it a piece of grit mixed with the rice? It was a disgusting feeling in the mouth, and a thin layer of sweat broke all over me. My husband stared at me. In the mouthful of food I spit out on a piece of tissue paper, I could see a black and red glob of chewed up *mapo tofu* mixed with some turnip green and rice. (Oyamada 2014b,153)[15]

Later, in wrapping up the leftover turnip greens to store in the refrigerator, Nara discovers a thick covering of pale-yellow round insect eggs stuck to the hairy bottom of the leaves, and realizes that is what she has eaten. She imagines a moth or a butterfly, weaving unsteadily with a swollen belly of eggs, laying them on the underside of the leaves with a quiver. After this scene, Nara shows signs of malaise that can be taken as morning sickness: poor appetite, nausea, and a pale demeanor. Since the story strongly suggests an asexual relationship between the couple, the reader is compelled to imagine that something alien and abject is growing inside Nara, something that she detests and fears. Her husband notices that, in her sleep, she scratches and scrapes herself in the neck, the crook of her elbow, and her chest, and then sucks on the grime under her fingernails as though she unconsciously wants to rid herself of some bodily contamination (180).

The imaginary pregnancy caused by ingesting an insect egg becomes a powerful and grotesque metaphor to capture the alienation and isolation of pregnancy and motherhood in Japanese society, a state that often forces women to quit their jobs, put their aspirations on hold, abandon their individuality, and devote themselves to an other-oriented existence as the sole caregiver of the family. The conventional image of a family may appear cheerful and rewarding, but the reality can resemble an invisible cage that confines women to years of domesticity and subservience. Some may argue that women choose to sacrifice themselves for the family out of love and affection, and that may be true for some; it is also certainly true that many women who resent or regret the sacrifices that motherhood entails still love their children dearly. But it is preposterous to force a woman to choose between loving her family and pursuing her individual dreams, aspirations, and career.[16] The term *aijō no sakushu* (exploitation of affection), made well-known by a popular television drama in 2016, exposes the societal malaise of forcing women to comply with self-sacrifice for the family by making them feel guilty or unworthy should they expect compensation or question the value of sacrifice made in the name of affection.[17] There is little doubt that the incompatibility of career aspirations and family, as well as the sacrifice of individual identity and freedom required of women, have played an important part in the declining birth rate in Japan.[18]

In "Ana," after Asa falls into the titular "hole," she gains new insights about her husband and the bizarre world of real and imaginary in-laws. Asa's husband, like many millennials, is always glued to his smart phone, talking, swiping, texting, and netsurfing when they are together. It is taken for granted that Asa will quit her job when he relocates to a branch office in the suburbs, and they move into a rent-free house which is next door to and owned by his parents. This allows her mother-in-law, Tomiko, a seemingly capable working woman in her sixties, to keep a close watch and tight leash on the young couple, especially her son. The father-in-law leads a shadowy existence, and the grandfather-in-law appears to be senile and is preoccupied with silently watering the garden a few times a day, even on rainy days.

Without a job and deprived of a convenient mode of transportation (the bus runs only once an hour, and it takes forty minutes to get to the nearest station), Asa walks to do her marketing and errands. Taking advantage of Asa's "idleness," Tomiko sends her on an errand to pay bills at the convenience store but fails to provide enough money to cover the cost, forcing Asa to silently cover the difference with her own meager savings. Oyamada frequently writes about the uncomfortable relationship and power dynamics between mothers- and daughters-in-law. In the story "Higanbana" ("The Equinox Flower," 2014), the grandmother-in-law tells the first-person narrator, a young wife by the name of Yuki, that when she was a lactating young mother, her own mother-in-law asked her to drip droplets of breast milk directly into her father-in-law's eye when he had chalazion (a cyst in the eyelid), believing that breast milk is a cure-all (Oyamada 2018). That obviously implies that the father-in-law would be staring with open eyes at the nipple and breast of the daughter-in-law, and the mother-in-law and her son (the husband of the lactating young wife) would be glaring on the side. In an interview, Oyamada mused that the relationship between mother- and daughter-in-law is an unnatural one. "A woman chooses or is chosen by the husband, but it's not a matter of choice when it comes to in-laws....Something warped is bound to arise from such relationships" (*Book Shorts* 2018). In "Ana," the metaphorical hole into which Asa falls awakens her awareness of the strange and distorted relationship between in-laws.

Ushiyama in "Kōjō" is a single woman who makes no mention of her family; she is like one of the fully-grown black birds in the story that appear in the flock without going through the stages of being a hatchling or fledgling. She apparently has no communication with her brother, and she is surprised when she overhears a conversation between him and his girlfriend in a coffee shop and finds out that her brother, after losing his computer-related job, has been sent by his girlfriend's temp agency to work at the same factory where she herself works. The brother's job as a dispatched/temp worker involves mind-numbing editing of product manuals that resemble gibberish. The two siblings never interact in the story even though they are aware of each other's presence. The brother appears embarrassed to face his sister, considering himself to be even below her in the pecking order of menial labor. He bemoans his situation to the unsympathetic girlfriend: "I don't know how to tell my sister. I mean, contract work is better that temp work, right?" (Oyamada 2019, 79). Ushiyama's connection with her brother is only as fellow down-trodden workers in an inhuman system, and she feels angry and jealous of his girlfriend, who holds a permanent position. "What the hell is wrong with the world? To think that a first-rate idiot like that can be gainfully employed, while me and my brother, good and humble citizens, are disenfranchised, unable to find permanent work" (80). Perhaps to emphasize their dehumanized and isolated state, the two siblings never come together to provide solace or sympathy for each other.

Encountering the Wild Things

Nara, Asa, and Ushiyama are all trapped in the drab reality of work and family until they begin to encounter the wild things that disturb the order of ordinary life, forcing them to question reality as they have never done before. In "Ana," Asa begins to encounter unusual human and non-human creatures in the heat of the summer, around the time of the Obon Festival, when traditionally the living commemorate the dead. Her first encounter is with a big black beast:

> It had to be as large as a retriever, maybe bigger. It had wide shoulders, slender and muscular thighs, but from the knees down, its legs were as thin as sticks. The animal was covered in black fur and had a long tail and rounded ears. Its ribs were showing, but its back was bulky, maybe with muscle or

with fat. (Oyamada 2020, 30)

Asa follows the beast and falls into a narrow hole that seems to be made for her size, with just her eyes visible above the ground. After some futile attempts to lift herself out of the hole, Asa receives help from a woman wearing a long white skirt and sunglasses—a neighbor by the name of Sera—who appears from nowhere to pull her out. They exchange a few words, and Asa proceeds to the convenience store to pay the bills for her mother-in-law. There she encounters a horde of children blocking the aisle and paying no heed to her request to make way. Rowdy or bratty children are often called "gaki" (餓鬼), a colloquial term derived from a Buddhist reference to starving ghosts, the dead who are made to suffer from acute hunger in hell because of their bad deeds in life. The only person who commands their attention is a middle-aged man they called "Sensei" (teacher), and even though the children continue to squeal and laugh in the convenience store, the store clerk remains expressionless, as if she has not noticed anything, suggesting that Asa is the only one who sees and hears them.

When Asa encounters the big black beast again on another day, she follows it to the edge of her mother-in-law's house. There, instead of the beast, she sees a middle-aged man who introduces himself as her brother-in-law, that is, the older brother of Asa's husband. Asa has always believed that her husband is an only child, and had never heard of the existence of an older brother. The man explains that he is a "hikikomori"—a shut-in—who for the past twenty years has lived in a shed at the back of the house. When Asa mentions the black beast, he claims that it is in a "round hole in the ground covered with a metal grill" (58). When Asa asks why other people fail to notice it, the man simply says, "It seems like most folks don't see what they don't want to see" (67). At the end of the story, Asa realizes that the shed is in fact covered with cobwebs and has been in disuse for years, suggesting that the man she saw is a ghost and the beast is a precursory or alternative form that the man takes. Indeed, the "rejects" of society—the homeless, the mentally ill, the hikikomori—are "invisible" to most people and exist as ghosts even when alive.

Oyamada borrows generously from literary and folkloric sources to open the passageway to the other world that only Asa can see and hear. The hole is a homage to the rabbit hole in *Alice in Wonderland*,[19] but instead of leading Asa to the magical world of the Cheshire Cat and Queen of Hearts, she tumbles into the liminal space between the living and the dead in the season of the Obon, guided by the black beast. The beast alludes to the black dog associated with death and the underworld in European myths, folklore, and literature, such as the multi-headed hound of Hades, Cerberus (now of *Harry Potter* fame) and the diabolical black hound made famous in Conan Doyle's *The Hound of the Baskervilles*. Asa's monotonous life as a housewife is now filled with the sights and sounds of phantoms who lead an otherwise invisible existence.

Three types of fantastical biological life forms inhabit the enormous grounds of the factory in "Kōjō": a huge flock of low-flying black birds resembling enlarged river cormorants, called factory "shags," that live on fish and factory food waste where the river meets the sea (Oyamada 2019, 76); hordes of "Grayback Coypus," oversized semiaquatic rodents also known as nutrias that live on discarded factory food and whose dead bodies clog up drainage pipes (72); and small "washer lizards" whose entire life cycle is tied to the washing machines in the factory cleaning facilities, where they feed on lint and leftover food scraps, lay eggs and hatch them in nests made of lint, then die in huge numbers under the washing machines (75). Each of these life forms are dehumanized reflections of the hordes of workers whose lives depend on subdivision work in the factory and whose existence is made into a series of dull, irrelevant repetitions of alienated labor.[20]

Ushiyama is obsessed with the birds, even though she cares nothing about birdwatching. Standing on the bridge where she has a view of the factory and the birds, she contemplates the futility of her daily engagement with estranged work for mere survival:

> I want to work, and I'm lucky enough to be able to. Of course I'm grateful for that. How could I not be? Except, well, I don't want to work. I really don't. Life has nothing to do with work and work has no real bearing on life. (84)

The existence of the birds and the other life forms that survive on factory by-products or waste awakens a painful awareness in Ushiyama, whose internal monologue is a plaintive wail to question the connection between work and life, so vital to a meaningful existence.

In "Ikobore no mushi," after ingesting the insect egg, Nara begins to see larvae and pupae everywhere. Out on an office errand, she notices red, black, and yellow hairy caterpillars all over the weeds by the roadside and imagines the egg she swallowed hatching in her belly (Oyamada 2014b,167). In the office, finishing her lunchbox by herself at her desk, she hears her female colleagues laughing and chatting as they return from lunch, and she feels a host of colorful and hairy caterpillars nibbling on her stomach wall as they wriggle their small heads (178). Visiting her husband's relatives, Nara is treated to snacks of stewed pupae (a gift from Korea) that she must force down whole (184-185). Hanging laundry on the verandah, she notices countless tiny mosquito larvae bending and stretching their tiny bodies in a little pool of dirty water that has accumulated in the unused base of a flowerpot (195). On her desk at work, she sees a green caterpillar inching across and picks it up with tissue paper to flush it down the toilet, only to notice unflushed excrement inside, a scene that compounds grotesquery with disgust. Bugs in various life stages begin to infest the vision of people around her. Doing dishes, her husband notices a swarm of several dozen brown-headed, pale-yellow larvae, the size of the tip of a fingernail, covered with water and detergent and clinging to the sink (181). At work, a young female colleague screams when she sees an armyworm crawling on her arm (233), and it is discovered that the cheap potted plant a male section chief brought into the office is infested with eggs that hatch into the pestilent worms (237). A squashed armyworm leaves a brown stain the size of a segment of a tangerine on the carpet, and this turns into another haunting visual preoccupation for Nara (237, 239).

In this story, the larvae in different forms and shapes invite sentiments of fear, disgust, scorn, and loathing—and also generate an overwhelming desire and group mentality to squash or exterminate them, even though the tiny life forms are not particularly aggressive, harmful, or territorial. Nara, having inadvertently swallowed the insect egg, becomes the embodiment of an alien life form that in turn defines her own existence: a small, inconspicuous presence to be avoided, shunned, and ostracized. She becomes the titular "outcast bug" by being the odd one out in an office and a society that stress uniformity and conformity.

Transformation

Each of the three women in these Oyamada stories goes through a metaphorical transformation at the end of an ambiguous closure. In "Kōjō," Ushiyama's identification with the factory shags culminates in her transformation into one of them. She is aware that factory personnel capture the birds and return them to the water after some time, often emaciated, as though the birds have survived some cruel extraction or extreme exertion like the unskilled and low-paid workers in the factory. Some of the exhausted birds blend into the flock and survive while others perish. One day, Ushiyama notices a pudgy woman grabbing a black bird by the wing and walking up the stairs with it into the factory. The bird is alive but not struggling against whatever fate awaits it.

> I turned back toward the morning container, grabbed a handful of pages and fed them into the shredder. I wasn't thinking about anything at all, just feeding paper into the machine. Then, as soon as the shredder swallowed the last pages, I became a black bird. (Oyamada 2019, 101)

The temp female worker, whose alienated work drains her of meaning and humanity, finally crosses over metaphorically to join the factory shags as disposable life forms used up for whatever purpose they may serve.

In "Ikobore no mushi," given the sustained insect metaphor, it is tempting to call Nara's evolution a metamorphosis, but the changes she experiences do not follow the natural stages of growth in an insect's life, so transformation is a more appropriate interpretation than metamorphosis. Toward the end of the story, when the section chief insinuates that she is suffering from depression, she begins to see pupae rather than squirming or crawling larvae, since the immobile, non-consuming, silent pupa is an even closer reflection of Nara's isolated existence. "I noticed a small reddish-brown thing on the white wall of the restroom, and when I looked closely, it had a dull shine with horizontal stripes. A pupa? Why?" (Oyamada 2014b, 239). She decides to quit, and on her way out of the office after the pro forma farewells she hears a tiny sound in the elevator. "Something small had dropped from the ceiling of the elevator, but I didn't feel like opening my eyes to check" (240). Days later, sitting in the waiting room in the hospital waiting for her turn to see the doctor for indigestion, she asks the child sitting next to her what she is reading.

> "*An Illustrated Book of Insects*."
>
> "*An Illustrated Book of Insects*?" I gazed at the round eyes, wings, and comb-like feelers of the enlarged moth on the page that the child pointed to, and for some unknown reason I suddenly felt ravenously hungry. (245)

Despite the ambiguous ending to the story, Oyamada completes the process that begins with Nara ingesting the egg and then identifying with the larva, pupa, and moth in stages of metaphorical embodiment. Nara, who has been suffering from a loss of appetite, has suddenly regained her desire for sustenance, which biologically translates into a desire to live. But it is too simplistic to see this as a positive or optimistic transformation. If it had been an enlarged and gorgeous butterfly Nara had seen in *An Illustrated Book of Insects*, it would be reasonable and comforting to imagine Nara metaphorically breaking out of her shell into a new, colorful life form to flutter among the flowers. The image of a moth that hovers around pale-white light at night, with powdery wings, a swollen belly, bulging eyes, and bushy feelers only invites antipathy and disgust, so Nara's outcast state may become worse with maturity. Oyamada leaves that open to interpretation.

Asa's transformation in "Ana" is brief and subtle. After slipping into the hole and gaining the ability to see and communicate with phantoms of the underworld, toward the end of the story she realizes her access is blocked, when the Obon festival in August gives way to a rainy September. The ghost of the hikikomori brother-in-law is nowhere to be seen, and the shed he used to occupy is empty.

> The shed was dark. Same as before. I tried the door. After a moment's resistance, it opened. The smell hit me right away. Dust and mildew. It was dark inside, but I could see all kinds of shapes, stacked up, against the walls, on the floor. It looked like no one had been there in a very long time. (Oyamada 2020, 88)

In addition to losing the ability to see the hidden and the invisible, the story ends with Asa—as would be typical for a housewife—acquiring a part-time job as a cashier in the 7-Eleven where she first encountered the gaki and the Sensei. It is the season of the Autumn equinox when spider lilies begin to bloom, the time of the year in Japan when traditionally the spirits of the dead are put to rest. "I saw no animals, no holes, no children. When I got home and put on my uniform in front of the mirror, I couldn't help but see Tomiko staring back at me" (92).

This is how the story ends, with Asa seeing a growing resemblance with her mother-in-law despite the absence of biological links. Again, Oyamada leaves it open-ended and invites interpretation. Asa and the reader have no information about the reason for the brother's hikikomori status or the relationship between the eldest son and the mother or the rest of the family. One can only make guesses about the situation: a teenage boy who refuses to leave the house and remains a shut-in for twenty years would be such a mental, physical, and emotional drain on the family that his mother lets him hole up in the shed, provides food and other necessities, and pretends that he is invisible so that the rest of the family can lead a "normal" life. The hikikomori would be such a family shame and social pariah that everyone—mother, father, younger brother—would pretend and convince themselves that he does not exist, and eventually erase his existence from their lives. Any family with a hikikomori member would likely tell a story in which there is no right and wrong, but simply that something has gone irretrievably wrong over time to create a tragic situation. Asa gains access and momentary insight into a hidden past and an invisible world, but that fact that she begins to resemble Tomiko suggests that she follows her mother-in-law's lead in covering the hole to prevent the big black beast, along with its buried memory and pain, from emerging and roaming free to haunt the living. Once the hole is covered metaphorically, life resumes normality, and it is up to Asa and the reader to decide whether the short-lived awakening of the beast brings about any lasting change in her life.

Conclusion

In these stories of women Oyamada meshes ordinary life and mundane reality with fantasy and phantasmagoria, and thereby awakens our awareness to family, work, and social issues in multiple dimensions, where the past grapples with the present, internal psychological and emotional needs wrestle with the external physical realities of daily life, and the dead speak with the living. Each story is a complex configuration of space in which the real meets the unreal and the visible collides with the invisible. Yet to one so obsessed with the natural world and various life forms as is Oyamada, these dichotomies and opposites are neither mutually exclusive nor different, but are part of each other. Place a flake of your own skin or a drop of your own saliva in a petri dish under the microscope, and an unknown world will appear. We do not usually see ourselves as embodiments of an unknown and alien world because, to quote the hikikomori brother-in-law in "Ana," "most folks don't see what they don't want to see" (67). Oyamada's stories of women open our eyes to the questions associated with non-permanent, low-paying labor, the lack of a sense of belonging at home and at work, and the search for meaning and identity in various stages of existence. In that sense, her stories surface extremely realistic and practical concerns, but her modes of expression go beyond realism to draw out the hidden and unknown wild things—the individuality, intuition, dreams, desires, ambitions, frustrations, anger, fears, passions—in every woman, no matter how unassuming in demeanor and regardless of her station in life.

Oyamada's stories remain open-ended and unresolved because awakening is an opening, a beginning, not the end. The saying "ignorance is bliss," though a cliché, may explain why growing awareness brings with it pain and anxiety rather than solutions. Awakening to external and internal limitations or a vision of a world that curbs one's potential and aspiration—which is the reality for many Japanese women—can result in great sadness and loneliness. The last verse of Rilke's poem reads:

But now and then, the curtains over his eyes
quietly lift…and an image enters,
goes through his tense and silent limbs…
And dies out in his heart.

Despite the sense of loss and frustration, none of the women in these stories regrets or resents encountering the wild things, and awakening to their own wild existence in their personal sense of self and body has an impact on their lives. None of the women's circumstances change substantially for the better, an honest reflection of the problems of gender inequality in Japan, but Oyamada suggests that to be awake and to be able to hear the sound of the wild things inside and out is better than a somnambulant existence.

---

1 As translated by Paul Archer. n.d. Accessed February 14, 2023. http://www.paularcher.net/translations/rainer_maria_rilke/der_panther.html.

2 Non-permanent workers can be divided into two main categories: part-time workers and dispatched workers (*haken rōdōsha* 派遣労働者). Part-time workers, according to Japanese labor law, are those who work fewer hours per week than the number of hours specified for regular workers at the same workplace. They are also called part-timers, *arubaito* (after the German word *arbeit*, for work), contract/temp workers (this includes *shokutaku shain* 嘱託社員 and *keiyaku shain* 契約社員), short-term workers (*rinji shain* 臨時社員), junior employees (*jun shain* 準社員), etc. (Miyazato et al. 2016, 115). Dispatched workers are employed within a triangular structure: there is a worker-dispatching contract between the dispatch agency (sometimes called the temp or recruitment agency) and the employer, and a labor contract between the dispatch agency and the worker, but there is no contract between the employer and the dispatched worker, even though the dispatched worker takes orders from the employer. The dispatch agency gets a commission for matching the employer with the dispatched worker (138-139).

3 *Nihon kenpō* 日本憲法. https://japan.kantei.go.jp/constitution_and_government_of_japan/constitution_e.html.

4 *Minpō* 民法. https://elaws.egov.go.jp/document?lawid=129AC0000000089.

5 *Danjo koyōkikai kintōhō* 男女雇用機会均等法 .
https://elaws.e-gov.go.jp/document?lawid=347AC0000000113.

6 *Danjo kyōdōsankaku kihonhō* 男女共同参画基本法 .
https://www.gender.go.jp/about_danjo/law/kihon/9906kihonhou.html#anc_top.

7 *Josei katsuyaku suishinhō* 女性活躍推進法 .
https://elaws.e-gov.go.jp/document?lawid=427AC0000000064.

8 See also "What to Read (and Watch) to Understand Women in Japan: Six Books (and One Film) on Life in One of the Rich World's Most Sexist Countries" (*The Economist* 2022b).

9 Gender Equality Bureau Cabinet Office. Accessed Feb 15, 2023.
https://www.gender.go.jp/research/fufusei/index.html

10 Gender Equality Bureau Cabinet Office. Accessed February 15, 2023.
https://www.gender.go.jp/about_danjo/whitepaper/r04/zentai/html/zuhyo/zuhyo01-03.html.

11 Of the 1,788 local and municipal legislative councils, 256 (14.3%) have no female legislators, and 436 (24.4%) have only one. Of the total 31,722 municipal legislators, only 4,940 (15.6%) are women. *Asahi Shimbun*, February 18, 2023.

12 A reference to the shape of the letter M: the number of female workers before marriage and childbirth is high, then dips during the childrearing years, then rises steadily once women reach their late forties or fifties.

13 In 2020, the percentage of eligible male employees taking childcare leave was 12.65%, compared to 81.6% for women. Ministry of Health, Labor, and Welfare (MHLW), "R2 Business Survey" (*reiwa ninen jigyōsho chōsa* 令和 2 年事業所調査) (18).
https://www.mhlw.go.jp/toukei/list/dl/71-r02/03.pdf.
In 2021, the percentages were 13.97% for men and 85.1% for women.
MHLW, "R3 Business Survey" (19). https://www.mhlw.go.jp/toukei/list/dl/71-r03/03.pdf.

14 In 2021, for families with children under six years of age, women on average spent 7:28 hours on housework (including 3:54 for childcare) and men spent 1:54 hours (1:05 for childcare). In 2011, during the time frame closer to the Oyamada stories, the corresponding figures were 7:45 hours on housework (including 3:22 on childcare) for women and 1:07 hours on housework (0:39 on childcare) for men. Ministry of Internal Affairs and Communications, "R3 Survey on Social Activities" (*Reiwa sannen shakai seikatsu kihon chōsa* 令和 3 年社会生活基本調査) (2).
https://www.stat.go.jp/data/shakai/2021/pdf/youyakua.pdf.

15 Excerpts from "Ikobore no mushi" are translated by Angela Yiu.

16 For a stimulating discussion of the taboo subject of women who regret having children, see Donath 2017.

17 The TV drama series *Nigeru wa haji da ga yaku ni tatsu* (*We Married as a Job*) features a former dispatched female employee, Mikuri, who decides to work for a single man, Hiramasa, as his domestic helper, and the two settle on a business agreement of a "contract marriage" in which Hiramasa pays her to do housework. In Episode 10, after they develop feelings for each other, Hiramasa wants to reduce expenditures after being restructured out of his job, and he proposes marriage to Mikuri, thinking that he will not have to pay a real wife to do housework. Even though Mikuri loves Hiramasa, she declares that "I, Moriyama Mikuri, firmly reject exploitation of affection!" See https://www.tbs.co.jp/NIGEHAJI_tbs/.

18 According to MHLW, the birth rate in Japan was 1.37 in 2021 and 1.26 in 2022. While the government previously predicted that the number of births per year would fall below the "dangerous" line of 800,000 in 2030, the decline has been more rapid, already falling to 770,728 in 2022. MHLW, "A Future Strategy for Children" (*Kodomo mirai senryaku hōshin* こども未来戦略方針) (1).
https://www.mhlw.go.jp/content/12601000/001112705.pdf.

19 The hikikomori brother-in-law references Alice in a conversation he has with Asa (Oyamada 2020, 62-63).

20 For a full discussion of the concept of Marxist alienated or estranged labor in connection to this story, see Yiu (2020).

References

Book Shorts. 2018. "Oyamada Hiroko-san intabyū" ["An interview with Oyamada Hiroko"]. Accessed February 14, 2023. https://bookshorts.jp/oyamadahiroko

Donath, Orna. 2017. *Regretting Motherhood: A Study*. Berkeley: North Atlantic Books.

The Economist. 2022a. "The Economist's Glass Ceiling Index," March 7, 2022. https://www.economist.com/graphic-detail/glass-ceiling-index.

The Economist. 2022b. "What to Read (and Watch) to Understand Women in Japan: Six Books (and One Film) on Life in One of the Rich World's Most Sexist Countries," December 9, 2022. https://www.economist.com/the-economist-reads/2022/12/09/what-to-read-and-watch-to-understand-women-in-japan.

Ishii Chiko. 2013. "Kōjō: Oyamada Hiroko intabyū" ["*Kōjō*: An interview with Oyamada Hiroko"]. *All About*. Accessed February 14, 2023. https://allabout.co.jp/gm/gc/426424/.

Miyazato Kunio, Furuta Noirko, and Shino Masako. 2016. *Rōdōhō jitsumu kaisetu 6: josei rōdō, paato rōdō, haken rōdō* [*Commentary on Labor Law Practice 6: Female Labor, Part-Time Labor, Dispatched Labor*]. Tokyo: Junposha.

Oyamada Hiroko. 2014a. *Ana*. Tokyo: Shichōsha.

———. 2014b. "Ikobore no mushi." In *Kōjō*. Tokyo: Shinchōsha.

———. 2018. "Higanbana." In *Niwa*, 25-46. Tokyo: Shinchōsha.

———. 2019. *The Factory* [*Kōjō*]. Translated by David Boyd. New York: New Direction Books.

———. 2020. *The Hole* [*Ana*]. Translated by David Boyd. New York: New Direction Books.

———. 2021. *Kojima*. Tokyo: Shinchōsha.

World Economic Forum. 2022. *Global Gender Gap Report 2022: Insight Report*, July 2022. https://www3.weforum.org/docs/WEF_GGGR_2022.pdf.

Yiu, Angela. 2020. "The Strange Birds and Beasts in Oyamada Hiroko's 'The Factory' (*Kōjō*)." In *Differences in the City: Postmetropolitan Heterotopias as Liberal Utopian Dreams*, edited by Jorge Leon Casero and Julia Urabayen, 275-287. Hauppauge: Nova Science Publishers.

Daryl Maude, Duke University

Learning Queerness: Pedagogy and Normativity in Tagame Gengorō's *Otōto no otto*

Tagame Gengorō (b. 1964) is a manga artist, writer, and editor. Most of his published work has been gay erotica and pornographic manga, with strong sadomasochistic themes and a butch, masculine aesthetic to his characters. He has been involved in the publication of gay magazines such as *G-Men*, and edited and provided critical introductions to three volumes of *Gay Erotic Art in Japan*. In 2014, he published his first manga for general audiences, *Otōto no otto* (*My Brother's Husband*), which he continued until 2017. It was serialized in *Monthly Action* and published by Futabasha in four volumes. The manga was very successful: an English version, translated by Anne Ishii, was published in two collected volumes by Pantheon Books; and in 2015, the Japanese Agency for Cultural Affairs awarded *Otōto no otto* the Japan Media Arts Festival Prize for Excellence in the manga division. In 2018 it was adapted for television as a three-part live action drama—starring Satō Ryūta as Yaichi and retired Estonian sumo wrestler Baruto Kaito as Mike—and shown by the national broadcaster, NHK. Tagame followed *Otōto no otto* by creating *Bokura no shikisai* (*Our Colors*), a manga about a high school student coming out as gay, published from 2018 to 2020 in three volumes.

The protagonist of *Otōto no otto* is Yaichi, a single father of an elementary school-age daughter, Kana. Yaichi has been estranged from his twin brother, Ryōji, a gay man living in Canada, who has recently died when the story begins. Yaichi and Kana are visited by Mike, Ryōji's widower, who comes to Japan for three weeks to see where his late husband grew up (figure 1).[1] Yaichi is uncom-

Figure 1: The characters of Mike, Kana, and Yaichi. *Otōto no otto*, vol. 1, front cover.

fortable with the openly gay Mike, and with having to explain Ryōji and Mike's relationship to Kana. But Yaichi confronts his own homophobia throughout the narrative and eventually comes to like Mike over the course of the three weeks he stays with Yaichi and Kana. Subplots include Kazuya, the junior high school-age brother of one of Kana's friends, coming out to Mike, who is the first openly gay person he has met; a family trip to a hot spring (*onsen*) with Natsuki, Kana's mother and Yaichi's ex-wife, with whom he is on good terms; and Mike's meeting with Katō, a Japanese friend of Ryōji's, who is gay but still in the closet to his straight friends and family.

In this chapter, I read *Otōto no otto* as a pedagogical work that tries to instruct straight readers on the importance of tolerance for gay people and the ultimately unthreatening nature of homosexuality. In the context of debates over same-sex marriage and official recognition of same-sex partnership in Japan in the Heisei Era and into the Reiwa Era, *Otōto no otto* is a call for the dignity and normality of gay people, and points out the misguided nature of homophobia. The pedagogy of this work, I argue, relies on demolishing homophobic myths as portrayed in the thoughts of the protagonist, and on opening up the possibilities for different meanings of family. It portrays Yaichi's movement toward acceptance and openness, which the straight reader is also expected to follow. This pedagogical mode is augmented by the fact that Mike's foreignness is linked to his gayness, and the manga shows the reader many structural similarities between interacting with people with different cultural backgrounds and people with different sexualities. Just as one should treat people from different countries as normal, the manga shows that one should treat people of different sexualities as normal.

Being "normal," however, has its own problems, and in this chapter I also want to think critically about the way the manga seems to be aiming toward normality. Many queer critics have questioned the value of being normal, seeing assimilation into a majority straight, cisgender society as not being a desirable goal. Michael Warner's 1999 work, *The Trouble with Normal: Sex, Politics, and the Ethics of Queer Life*, for example, argues against normalcy being a goal for queer political movements, and notes that the dignity and respect afforded gay people is often proportionate to the ways in which they present themselves as desexualized.[2] This radical rejection of normality is connected to the idea that society is not constantly progressing forward, and that things are not always getting better. However, at the same time, it is undeniable that wider acceptance of gay relationships and alternate families does make people's lives better. Heather Love, in talking about the importance of not forgetting the more difficult parts of queer history as ideas around sexuality and gender become more open, encapsulates this idea neatly: "Although many queer critics take exception to the idea of a linear, triumphalist view of history, we are in practice deeply committed to the notion of progress; despite our reservations, we just cannot stop dreaming of a better life for queer people" (2007, 3).

In thinking critically about the use of "normativity" in *Otōto no otto* in this chapter, I do not wish to suggest that I am opposed to the right for gay people to marry, or the promotion of different forms of families in media. Both are important, and I think Tagame's work is valuable in its portrayal of these realities to a straight audience. Rather, I want to tease out the textures of normativity and think about how it is at work in the manga, while being aware of the limits of the normal.

Queerness and What's Normal

"Queer" is a reclaimed slur. Originally meaning "strange" or "odd" in English, it is used to denigrate people with non-normative sexual or gender identities, such as gay people and trans people. The term was reclaimed in the 1980s in English-language contexts, and formed part of a rejection of the idea of heteronormativity: that gay and trans people have to (or want to) look and behave in "normal" (i.e. straight and cisgender) ways, forming nuclear families, maintaining monogamous relationships, and having their differences from straight people minimalized. Being queer or organizing under the banner of queerness meant being different from straight and cis people, embracing the fact that one was different, strange, or odd—rather than trying to blend in and mimic straight people or straight culture—and questioning normativity itself.

Queer as a term was taken up by academics, and queer theory has emphasized the unfixed nature of sexuality and identity, as well as the political potential of queer identity. The historically contingent nature of homosexuality as category is famously noted by theorist Michel Foucault in the *History of Sexuality*, where he states that homosexuals become "a species" at a certain moment in time: before this people engaged in homosexual acts but their sexuality did not bear upon their identity in the same way, for either themselves or for others (1990, 43). In contrast to a more established term like "gay," which fixes sexuality in a minoritarian framework, Judith Butler states that the term queer itself is "never fully owned, but always and only redeployed, twisted, queered from a prior usage and in the direction of urgent and expanding political purposes, and perhaps also yielded in favor of terms that do that political work more effectively" (1993, 19). Queer in this understanding is not the name of a species, but rather a rejection of classificatory logic itself.

At the same time, queer is also sometimes used as a catch-all term for people with non-normative sexual or gender identities: lesbian, gay, bisexual, transgender, questioning, intersex, asexual, two-spirit, and others. This list of identities and its various iterations in acronyms such as LGBTQ can be unwieldy, and specific identities and groups are often left out, so the word queer can be a useful and inclusive shorthand that registers a distance from or uneasy relationship with norms of gender and sexuality. Queer can provide a means of identification and solidarity for people who are not cisgender or heterosexual: a loose and provisional but nevertheless politically important term.

Questions over what it is to be gay or queer are happening in multiple languages, and we should not assume that there is a universal notion of sexual identity that transcends geography, just as there is not one that transcends history. Thinking about the unfixed nature of queerness, therefore, means thinking about the ways in which terms for sexuality travel, are translated, and are taken up in different languages. This will be elaborated on later in this chapter.

To address some of these questions, I turn to *Otōto no otto*, thinking about its possibilities and limitations as queer literature to help me tease out the questions of normativity in the manga and queerness in Japanese literary production in the Heisei Era. It is true that during this period there are various literary texts that deal with gay characters or queer relationships, by writers who are out as LGBT, such as Fujino Chiya (b. 1962), Fushimi Noriaki (b. 1963), Chiba Masaya (b. 1978), Osano Dan (b. 1983), and Li Kotomi (b. 1986), who won the Akutagawa Prize in 2021. There are also out gay literary figures who have been active for a long time, such as Takahashi Mutsuo (b. 1937). Nevertheless, in this chapter, I look at a manga rather than a more straightforwardly literary text such as a novel for two reasons in particular. Firstly, in thinking about the relationship between sexuality, gay identities, and literature in the Heisei period, *Otōto no otto* explicitly tackles a number of pressing issues being discussed in mainstream and gay media: gay marriage, gay identity, and coming out.[3] Secondly, manga as a form makes sense for thinking about these questions, as it is both a popular genre with a wide reach and one that is frequently used by Japanese gay creators: Japanese queer culture has placed a lot of importance on magazines, manga, and other forms of media that exist next to "pure" literature.[4]

Pedagogy in *My Brother's Husband*

Homophobia

Otōto no otto is Tagame Gengorō's first manga for general audiences, rather than being a work of erotica or pornography. Its setting, with a straight protagonist whose homophobic imagination is frequently illustrated in thought bubbles, but who gradually learns to love his brother's widower and accept him, has a primarily pedagogical aim: to instruct a straight audience on the importance of accepting gay people and the misguided nature of homophobia. Yaichi's status as a straight protagonist provides a simple pedagogical tool; Tagame himself says that "The setting with a straight protagonist was there from the start…I thought it would be easier to understand and more interesting for straight readers" (2017a, 29). Although the author is gay and the character of Mike fulfils the role of guiding both Yaichi and the reader into a more accepting attitude, Yaichi is the main character. His homophobic discomfort with Mike, and his gradual overcoming of this discomfort and his standing up for Mike against the homophobic attitudes of other people, model a pattern of growth for straight readers of the work.

Yaichi's discomfort toward Mike arises most immediately from perceiving him as a threat. This is illustrated by frequent thought bubbles: at their initial meeting, when Yaichi answers the door and Mike immediately hugs him, Yaichi imagines a scenario in which he shouts at Mike, "What the fuck? Get off me, faggot!" ("*Teme...kono yaro...nan da! Hanase homo!*"[5]) but does not in reality. Instead, he says "Hey, sorry, but…" ("*Oi, chotto waruin da ga...*"), at which Mike apologizes and lets him go (2015, 17). Here, social pressure prevents Yaichi from saying what he wants to, but his restraint is not evident at first. Yaichi's imagined scenario is illustrated in the same visual idiom as is what happens in the reality of the narrative, only marked as imaginary by the wavy bottom border of the second panel and the bubbles that link it to Yaichi's head in the "real" third panel. Initially, on reading the first panel of the page, readers are led to believe that Yaichi really did say this; only when their eyes move down to see the bottom of the second panel do they realize that this is not happening in the reality of the story. The manga thus takes Yaichi's homophobic imagination seriously and dramatizes it, bringing it into the realm of the possible and expressing it as just as likely a scenario as what Yaichi politely ends up doing.

Yaichi's perception of Mike as a threat is made explicit in the next section of the manga. Mike, Kana, and Yaichi eat dinner, and then each takes a bath. Having gotten out of the bath, Yaichi examines himself in the mirror, wearing only his underwear. Drawn as a muscled, attractive man in the style of many of Tagame's characters, he looks at himself and says, "I can't go out in just my underwear," before euphemistically adding, "Mike being…*that* way" ("*Maiku wa sono...are nan dashi,*"). Here Yaichi illustrates the typical fear of predatory gay men preying on straight men: a feeling that has been tartly summarized as the fear that gay men will treat straight men how straight men treat women. In this scene, however, Yaichi's mirror self talks back to him: "You idiot, what're you saying? They said it on TV a while back, right? Seeing a gay guy (*homo*) and thinking he'll assault you is the same as a woman who thinks that every man is interested in her (*kanchigai onna*)." "That's true," his real self counters, "but he was married to my twin brother…and when we met, he hugged me without thinking. Ryōji and I look so much alike." "You're overthinking it! You're too self-conscious!" his mirror self tells him (47-48). Yaichi concludes, finally, that he should at least be polite to Mike, diverting his line of thought from an enquiry into his own perception of gayness to social propriety. Even his "better self" dismisses the problem as one not of homophobia but of self-consciousness (*jiishiki kajō*): a minor failing of character that can be logically addressed, rather than participation in a structural form of oppression. Yaichi knows that he *should* be polite to Mike and that his homophobia is unfounded, but in the realm of his *feelings* he is still homophobic.

Yaichi's discomfort again comes into play in the next scene. We see a frame of Yaichi coming out of the bathroom and standing in a doorway while he hears Kana shouting "Can I touch it?! Can I touch it?!" from outside of the frame. In the next frame, we see from Yaichi's viewpoint the scene of Mike facing Kana, holding his shirt up over his hairy chest, with Kana touching it. "Dad!" she exclaims, "Mike's covered in hair!" Yaichi, curtly, tells Mike to put his shirt back on (51). This scene dramatizes another homophobic fear about gay people: that they are pedophiles. Yaichi comes into a room to find a virtual stranger in a state of undress with his daughter. Kana's excited request, "Can I touch it?! Can I touch it?!" is decontextualized and sounds obscene: what is "it?" But the scene, when read as a child's interest in physical difference and an adult's willingness to indulge the curiosity in an unembarrassed way, is innocent and deeply sweet. Later, ruminating on his attitude toward Mike, Yaichi realizes that he has been too hasty, and that his discomfort was motivated by the homophobic attitude that links gay people to pedophilia.

In conveying this pedagogical message, the manga uses formal techniques that are specific to the medium of comics. The panels in which Yaichi's imagination is illustrated are depicted in the same way as—just as real as—what actually happens within the story. They are presented as possibilities for bad events that are overcome by Yaichi's constant striving to correct himself and work through his discomfort. Furthermore, in a sequential art form such as manga, the depiction of timing is particularly important.[6] The timing of the sequence described above is carefully planned to set up assumptions that are then dispelled. There is the set-up of Yaichi's perception of Mike as a potential threat, followed by his diffusion of his tension through his self-talk with his own image in the mirror; and then the further set-up of Kana's "Can I touch it?!" with the diffusion of tension when it is revealed that "it" is Mike's hairy chest rather than something more sinister. He later fully diffuses the tension through reflecting about his own prejudices. In this depiction of temporality, *Otōto no otto* models a sequence of acceptance, understanding, and growth in Yaichi, and by extension in a straight reader.

Sex (or Lack Thereof)

Important to the acceptability of the pedagogical elements of the manga is the fact that, in contrast to Tagame's previous work, *Otōto no otto* lacks any sex scenes, and romance between living characters is not dealt with. Mike has been widowed and Yaichi and Natsuki are divorced. Mike, the titular *Otōto no otto* is, in many ways, an ideal homosexual for a straight audience: he is consistently portrayed as being unthreatening, kind, and caring, having an easy manner with the people he meets. As noted above, Michael Warner argues that the perceived dignity of homosexuals, and therefore the palatability of gay liberation movements, is directly connected to the ways in which they are seen as non-sexual. Mike's lack of overt sexuality, therefore, is important for his acceptability in the manga, and Yaichi spends a lot of time, especially in the first volume, trying to understand—and the story spends a lot of time demonstrating—Mike's innocence in this regard.

At the same time, even in Tagame's manga for general audiences, his illustrations of the bodies of Mike and Yaichi are done in the same style—often called "*bara*" outside of Japan[7]—as many of his pornographic works: they are portrayed as muscled, and Mike is hairy. The manga has multiple scenes of Mike or Yaichi undressing or bathing, either alone at home or together when they go to the local gym or take a trip to the hot spring. The sexuality in these depictions is not explicit. On the one hand it is presented as a kind of "fan service."[8] Gay or queer readers familiar with Tagame's artistic conventions and the way he draws male bodies will understand this depiction, and it offers some additional enjoyment without the normal pornographic components. On the other hand, reading *Otōto no otto* in the idiom of Tagame's pornographic manga can be instructive to think about the way it plays with these tropes. One night, coming home drunk from a bar, Mike is being helped to his futon by Yaichi. There is a close-up of Mike's face, and then of Yaichi's as he realizes Mike is looking at him differently. Then Mike pushes himself on Yaichi, crying "Ryōji! Ryōji!" They fall to the floor and Yaichi protests, telling Mike to stop and get off him. This scene reads initially as an attempted seduction or sexual encounter, but a close up of Yaichi's eyes shows his wide-eyed realization, before the next panel shows Mike's head on Yaichi's chest, with Yaichi's undershirt wet from Mike's tears. "Ryōji!" he says in English, with translations provided in notes to the side of the panel. "Why… why did you have to die. You promised me… And after I finally made it to Japan… Why can't you be here with me!" (148-149, punctuation as in the original). Yaichi understands, yet again, that Mike is not a threat, but rather is dealing with his grief over the loss of his husband. Tagame's visual idiom here is being used to set up, again, a pattern of expectation and diffusion.

Family and Identity

The *obi*[9] of the first volume of *Otōto no otto* calls the work "A warm and sometimes sad family story" (*Attakakutte toki ni wa setsunai famirii sutōrii*), and the narrative arc for Yaichi is not only of overcoming his homophobia, but also of accepting Mike as a member of his family. Yaichi's family is already a little out of the ordinary, as he is a single father, and in the first chapter we are introduced to his morning routine: getting Kana up for school, putting on an apron, making her breakfast, brushing her hair and putting it in pigtails, worrying that she will be late. After she leaves the house, he vacuums. It is revealed that Yaichi gets money from the apartments that his parents left to him. "I'm not proud of it," he says, "being this old and still living off my parents' inheritance. It doesn't feel like much of a job." Mike counters, "But Yaichi-san, you're Kana-chan's dad, and you make food for her every day. You clean and you do the laundry—that's a fine job (*rippa na oshigoto*), don't you think?" (70). The scenes of Yaichi's domestic work already do not meet the gendered expectations of labor in a two-parent household, but Mike's validation of the domestic labor as *work* is important, demonstrating as it does both the feminist ethos of the manga and the reimagination of a viable, happy family structure that it offers.

Otōto no otto shows its readers several different possible family structures, with no one being presented as better than the other. In addition to Yaichi and Kana, Kana's mother Natsuki also takes an active part in her daughter's upbringing and is on good terms with Yaichi. Mike and Ryōji were a family, and scenes of Mike's parents at his and Ryōji's wedding demonstrate their acceptance. Mike also shows Kana a photograph of his friends: a lesbian couple and their son. The question of what a family is, or could be, is made explicit when Yaichi, Kana, and Natsuki take Mike to a hot spring for an overnight trip before he leaves the country. Yaichi comments to Natsuki that the staff of the inn where they are staying probably assume them to be a "normal" family: a straight couple with a daughter, and a foreign guest. Instead, Yaichi comments, he and Natsuki are no longer married, and Mike is not just a foreign guest. He comments that it's "weird" (*fushigi*) and wonders what to call their various relationships. Natsuki responds that "it's fine that it's weird," and that they should call it a "family." Despite their separation, she and he are still bound by the relation (*en*) of being parents to Kana; Mike's connection to Yaichi is due the relation they both have to Ryōji. "So, 'family' is a good thing to call it," Natsuki states. (2016b, 49-50) Natsuki's statement shows that even as *Otōto no otto* works to normalize homosexuality, its view of family is expansive and at home with the non-normative. Natsuki does not deny the weirdness of the situation: it *is* weird, but that's fine.

Mike's being out as gay, and Ryōji's having come out, is contrasted in *Otōto no otto* with Ryōji and Yaichi's friend, Katō, also known as Katoyan. Katoyan was Ryōji's one gay friend in high school, and when he and Mike meet, Katoyan is still closeted. Talking to Mike over dinner at a fancy restaurant in Shinjuku, Katoyan states that, unlike Ryōji, he does not feel the need to come out, arguing that his sexuality is not something he needs to tell other people, even Yaichi, from whom he asks Mike to keep their meeting secret. He apologizes for asking Mike to meet him somewhere far from home, but states that it would be awkward for him to be seen with Mike. In contrast to the warmth of the experience of Yaichi and Kana's house, this dinner is shown to be awkward and sad. In one frame, Mike is shown at the table with Katoyan (figure 2). He is facing forward and to the right of the frame; Katoyan is facing Mike on the opposite side of the table, so that his back is shown. Looking down at the dinner table with a sad expression on his face, Mike's thoughts are shown in squares at the top of the frame: "I understand your feelings, Katoyan, but I kept the fact that we're having dinner together a secret from Yaichi-san. Hiding things means you just have to hide more things (*kakushigoto ga kakushigoto o umu koto*). I didn't like that, which is why I came out" (2016b, 138).

Figure 2: Katoyan and Mike in the closet. *Otōto no otto,* vol. 3, p. 138.

The two figures are surrounded by blackness, but behind Mike two slatted doors are open and show white beyond. The light of the whiteness illuminates both figures. Mike and Katoyan are in the closet, hidden. Mike feels unhappy at being back in the closet, whereas Katoyan is apparently willing to stay in the closet. The image of the closet serves as a way of highlighting the problems of this way of life, showing the complex secrecy that it requires: creating the necessity that certain details of one's life (or other people's lives) are hidden from some people at the same time as they are revealed to others; as well as the discomfort that such secrecy generates. The manga, through this episode—and in contrast to the figure of Kazuya, the junior high school student who comes out to Mike and later to Yaichi—portrays leaving the closet as something necessary and important.

Foreignness

A final important aspect of the manga's pedagogy is the way that *Otōto no otto* makes much of Mike being a foreigner, and draws parallels between Mike's different cultural context as a Canadian and as a gay man, analogizing the status of foreigners and sexual minorities in Japan. He is portrayed as the "bringer" of gay culture to Yaichi. The volumes of the manga contain "Mike's Gay Culture Lectures": sections interspersed between the chapters in which Mike directly addresses the reader to teach important aspects of gay culture. As in a language textbook in which, along with grammar and vocabulary, students learn cultural things about a foreign country through asides and columns—such as the gift-giving culture in Japan, or secularism in France— the readers of *Otōto no otto* are presented with eight different lectures on the following subjects:

1. Gay Marriage
2. The Pink Triangle
3. The Rainbow Flag
4. Other Pride Flags
5. Coming Out
6. Pride Parades
7. Gay Pride
8. Outing

Here, the topics are of gay public culture, including gay symbols and the history of homophobic discrimination. In this way, *Otōto no otto* presents gay difference as something cultural. Homophobia in the manga is linked with misunderstandings and an insufficient understanding of homosexual culture. Gay difference is presented as something not unknowable or unintelligible, but rather understandable through study. These lectures emphasize the pedagogical aim of the manga. Notably, English translations of *Otōto no otto* leave the lectures out, perhaps because the editors assumed that readers would be more familiar with these aspects of gay culture.

While Mike's foreignness makes sense as a vehicle to emphasize the pedagogical aims of the manga and the strangeness and otherness of queerness in a heteronormative life, it risks portraying him as a colonial "white savior" figure, who comes to intervene in the lives of people of color with a moral authority that is portrayed as inherent. This is especially apparent in the scene with Mike and Katoyan, where Mike's and Katoyan's ways of being gay are portrayed as radically different, with Katoyan's requiring secrecy and omission and Mike's being open and honest. The manga leaves us in no doubt as to which way is a "better" way to live. Certainly, Ryōji was out and honest, and Kazuya comes out in the course of the manga, but, even so, Ryōji's living a gay life meant his leaving for another country in order to be openly gay, and Kazuya's coming out is helped by Mike. While *Otōto no otto* does have a humanizing message about gay people and the importance of tolerance, its portrayal of Mike's whiteness and the way that this works in tandem with his gayness flattens the complicated racial dynamics at play in such situations, and risks implying that to be happy and gay in Japan one must also have a certain relationship to foreignness and being "out," neither of which is necessarily true.

The interplay of foreignness and homosexuality in Japan is evident from the outset in *Otōto no otto*. The first chapter of the first volume of the manga is entitled "Kurofune ga yatte kita!" ("The Black Ships Have Arrived!") in reference to Commodore Perry's forced opening of Japan in the 1850s. The title page features an illustration of the three main characters on a ship, with Mike in an American naval uniform like Perry's, Kana in a Victorian dress with her hair in ribbons, and Yaichi in Japanese garb—hakama and kimono—looking on skeptically (figure 3). This illustration primes us to understand Mike as a foreign invader, bringing a different set of cultural norms to the skeptical Yaichi. While it is undeniably *playful*, with the characters being put in cosplay to emphasize their personalities, the figure of Mike as an invading (even threatening) force to Yaichi's homeland sets up an analogue between gayness and foreignness: an otherness or alienness that is not welcome, is going to cause turmoil, and ultimately will result in a huge shift in understanding.

As scholars such as Saeko Kimura and Gregory Plugfelder have observed, ways of understanding gender and sexuality in Japan are historically quite different from the ways in which they have been understood in Europe and America (Kimura 2010; Plugfelder 1999). In particular, there is a long history of male-male sexual activity in Japan, which Hiratsuka Ryōsen notes was called dozens of different things throughout history in Buddhist temples, samurai traditions, kabuki theatres, and tea houses that served as locations for sex work, but is generally referred to as "*nanshoku*" (1987, 11-12). Indeed, Tagame's more explicit work often draws on these historical traditions, particualrly nanshoku among samurai, as settings for his erotica. Because of widespread stigmatization of homosexu-

Figure 3: "Kurofune ga yatte kita," "The Black Ships Have Come." *Otōto no otto,* vol. 1, chapter 1 title page.

ality in Europe and America, Japanese advocates of modernization in the Meiji Restoration (1868) that followed Commodore Perry's arrival regarded nanshoku customs as backward, and legal penalties for anal intercourse were introduced in 1873 (Reichert 2006, 13-14).[10] There is, therefore, an irony to the idea of the gay Mike being a foreign invader, given that Japanese male-male sexual traditions were stigmatized in the name of Westernization and modernization. We should be careful when reading the manga that we do not take the ahistorical view that homosexuality is something foreign to Japan.

Thinking about queerness or gayness in modern Japan means we have to consider the complicated process of how sexuality has come to be understood in dialogue with Western ideas. It also means we have to avoid the assumption that Western ideas about sexuality are universally applicable, or are better than Japanese ideas about sexuality; or that Western ideas exist discretely, apart from Japanese ideas of sexuality. At the same time, Japan is not isolated, and ways of understanding sexuality in Japan have been in dialogue with the West since the Meiji Restoration.[11] As Katsuhiko Suganuma shows, contact between Western and Japanese queer cultures resulted in "translational processes" rather than straightforward copies (2012, 25). The goal of thinking about sexuality in Japan and historicizing it should not be to go back to some originary state before Japan's contact with the West: such a shift is not possible, and that pre-modern state is not necessarily better. Rather, we should aim to be aware of the unequal field of relations, terms, and ideas, and to remember that identities such as gay or queer are historically contingent. Furthermore, as Akiko Shimizu notes, it is crucial to aim for solidarity among queer and feminist groups in different countries while still also maintaining an awareness of our differences. She argues for the importance of asking:

> [H]ow do we best navigate the incessant and increasingly rapid flow of transnational feminist, queer, and also anti-gender movements and discourses so that we can learn from and work with each other, without losing sight of our respective local, distinctive, and messy amalgam of translational politics between the imported and the indigenous, the transnational and the local? (2020, 104)

Otōto no otto, in bringing our attention to this "messy amalgam," is helpful in that it encourages us to ask the question of how we should navigate the issues of sexuality and foreignness as they bear on identity and family in Japan, thinking both about transnational solidarity and also local specificity.

Conclusion

The climax of *Otōto no otto*, in the fourth volume, shows Yaichi standing up for Mike in a conversation with Kana's homeroom teacher. The teacher has called in Yaichi to talk to him, and states that he is worried about Kana saying that gay couples can get married in Canada. The teacher's homophobia shows, as it emerges that he is uncomfortable with Kana even talking about Mike. Yaichi states that Mike is his brother's spouse, and Kana's uncle, and that it is natural for her to want to talk about him (2017b, 61). The pedagogical journey is complete, and Yaichi walks out of the office into the sunshine, looking happy with himself. He has overcome his embarrassment and become a straight person who is willing to name gayness by telling other people who Mike is (unlike previous encounters, when he has hesitated) and has stood up for him in the face of the everyday homophobia of the world. This scene of the manga is the public culmination of the pedagogical aim of the work.

The manga's goal of normalizing homosexuality is noble. But we should bear in mind that this normalization is being conducted within certain constraints. For gay people or trans people, indeed for all minorities, becoming "normal" often means adapting themselves to the values of mainstream society. As we have already seen, Warner has argued that, for gay people, this can involve downplaying the sexual component of their lives to make themselves more palatable to straight people. Mike's portrayal as a largely desexualized character is an example of this. His foreignness helps to emphasize the ways in which homosexuality may not be seen as radically other to what is normal, and should be learnt about and understood; and it reminds us of the ways in which queerness can travel and be translated into different contexts.

Nevertheless, Mike's portrayal as a character to learn from and whose model of identity and sexuality is advocated, together with his whiteness, risk making him into a white savior whose moral authority is coeval with his race. How then, in this context, should we think about the solidarity that Shimizu calls for? It is important to imagine alternative ways for queer lives and families to form without reproducing notions of sex and gender that either validate an essentializing model in which the West is seen as more advanced than Japan, or a culturalist model in which Japanese ways of doing things are unique and somehow always better suited to Japanese queer people. Moments in the narrative of the manga, such as when Natsuki comments to Yaichi that their grouping is weird but is still a family, suggest a critical position toward what is normal. Likewise does the story's refusal of an overly sentimental "happy ending," when Yaichi reflects on the relationship that he and Mike built and the fact that Ryōji and Mike were happy together in Canada. Yaichi concentrates on the value in *that*, and in doing so the manga contextualizes the encounter as something that is deeply meaningful, but not reducible to more normative narratives of the certainty of seeing Mike again or the security of a knowable future. Ultimately, *Otōto no otto*, in its entanglement of discourses over normativity and queerness, serves as a useful object through which to think about these discourses in Japan in the Heisei Era.

1 The editor would like to thank Futabasha for the permission to print three images from *Otōto no otto* in this chapter.

2 See, in particular, chapters 1 and 2.

3 Nagata Kabi's *Sabishisugite rezu fūzoku ni ikimashita repo* (2016, translated by Jocelyn Allen in 2017 as *My Lesbian Experience with Loneliness*) is also an excellent example of dealing with gay identity and sexuality in modern Japan. In this autobiographical work, the author describes her depression and struggles in the precarious environment of neoliberal Japan. Her feelings of wanting intimacy from women, including her mother, culminate in her employing a sex worker from a lesbian escort agency. Unlike in *Otōto no otto*, Nagata's homosexual desire is not expressed in a straightforward way that translates neatly to identity; rather it emerges in tandem with her struggles with mental illness and her sense of self-confidence.

4 Especially before the widespread availability and use of the internet for community-making, gay magazines were particularly important for the creation of gay communities in Japan. The magazine *Barazoku* (*Rose Tribe*), for example, was published from 1971 to 2008, and was highly influential and widely read. See Mackintosh (2006); see also Suganuma (2012), particularly chapter 2, "Hybridized Whiteness in 'Rose': The Displacement of Racialized/Gendered Discourses."

5 The Japanese slang term, "*homo*," derived from the English "homosexual," is used in different ways to refer to gay men, by gay men themselves and by straight people. I translate it here as a slur, but subsequently as "gay guy" to reflect the homophobia in the first instance and the attempt to overcome it in the second.

6 As Will Eisner notes in *Comics and Sequential Art*, "Critical to the success of the visual narrative is the ability to convey time" (1985, 26). He notes the role of the artist in capturing the movement of time in the narrative and conveying this to the reader through the use of frames which allow the reader to "fill in" the gaps of what is happening: "The act of framing separates the scenes and acts as a punctuator. Once established and set in sequence the box or panel becomes the criterion by which to judge the illusion of time" (28).

7 This terminology is not the same in Japan, however. As Tagame himself notes, the term "*bara* manga" emerged overseas due to the popularity of gay Japanese comics on the internet (2018, 15).

8 Patrick Galbraith defines "fan service" as the "convention of including titillating content for fans" and notes that it is a common practice in manga and anime (2019, 117).

9 *Obi* is short for *obigami*, a paper band for a blurb on a book jacket.

10 Reichert notes that these legal punishments were rescinded in 1882.

11 They have also been in dialogue with other ideas in Japan, as Stephen Dodd notes on writing about same sex desire in Natsume Sōseki's 1914 novel, *Kokoro*:

> [J]ust as pressure from the West forced Japan to reevaluate its political and social systems, so also earlier forms of erotic desire became problematized and had to be reimagined in ways responsive to new social formations. It should be kept in mind, however, that the tensions reflected in Sōseki's texts did not result solely from external forces exerted by the West. They also were the product of pressures for change arising from within Japanese culture itself. (1998, 474).

References

Butler, Judith. 1993. "Critically Queer." *GLQ: A Journal of Lesbian and Gay Studies* 1 no. 1: 17–32.

Dodd, Stephen. 1998. "The Significance of Bodies in Sōseki's *Kokoro.*" *Monumenta Nipponica* 53 no. 4: 473-498.

Eisner, Will. 1985. *Comics and Sequential Art*. Tamarac: Poorhouse Press.

Foucault, Michel. 1990. *The History of Sexuality: Volume I: An Introduction*. Translated by Robert Hurley. New York: Vintage Books.

Galbraith, Patrick. 2019. *Otaku and the Struggle for Imagination in Japan.* Durham: Duke University Press.

Hiratsuka Ryōsen. 1987. *Nihon ni okeru nanshoku no kenkyū* [*Research on* nanshoku *in Japan*]. Tokyo: Ningen no kagakusha.

Kimura Saeko. 2010. *A Brief History of Sexuality in Premodern Japan.* Tallinn: TLU Press.

Love, Heather. 2007. *Feeling Backwards: Loss and the Politics of Queer History*. Cambridge: Harvard University Press.

Mackintosh, Jonathan D. 2006. "Itō Bungaku and the Solidarity of the Rose Tribes [*Barazoku*]: Stirrings of Homo Solidarity in Early 1970s Japan." *Intersections: Gender, History and Culture in the Asian Context*, no. 12. http://intersections.anu.edu.au/issue12/aoki.html.

Nagata Kabi. 2016. *Sabishisugite rezu fūzoku ni ikimashita repo*. Tokyo: East Press.

Plugfelder, Gregory. 1999. *Cartographies of Desire: Male-Male Sexuality in Japanese Discourse, 1600-1950.* Berkeley: University of California Press.

Reichert, Jim. 2006. *In the Company of Men: Representations of Male-Male Sexuality in Meiji Literature*. Stanford: Stanford University Press.

Shimizu Akiko. 2020. "'Imported' Feminism and 'Indigenous' Queerness: From Backlash to Transphobic Feminism in Transnational Japanese Context." *Jendā kenkyū: Ochanomizu joshi daigaku jendā kenkyūjo nenpō*, no. 23: 89-104.

Suganuma Katsuhiko. 2012. *Contact Moments: The Politics of Intercultural Desire in Japanese Male-Queer Cultures*. Hong Kong: Hong Kong University Press.

Tagame Gengorō. 2015. *Otōto no otto.* Vol. 1. Tokyo: Futabasha.

———. 2016a. *Otōto no otto.* Vol. 2. Tokyo: Futabasha.

———. 2016b. *Otōto no otto.* Vol. 3. Tokyo: Futabasha.

———. 2017a. *Gei kuruchā no mirai e* [*To the Future of Gay Culture*]. Tokyo: Ele-King Books.

———. 2017b. *Otōto no otto.* Vol. 4. Tokyo: Futabasha.

———. 2018. *Nihon no gei erottiku āto* [*Gay Erotic Art in Japan*]. Vol. 3, *Gei zasshi no hatten to taiyōka suru sakkatachi* [*Growth of Gay Magazines and the Diversification of their Artists*]. Tokyo: Potto shuppan.

Warner, Michael. 1999. *The Trouble with Normal: Sex, Politics, and the Ethics of Queer Life.* Cambridge: Harvard University Press.

Maria Roemer, University of Leeds

Queering Heisei Patriarchy: Homosocial Narrative in Abe Kazushige's "Massacre"

This chapter investigates male homosocial narrative in Heisei literature through an analysis of Abe Kazushige's (b. 1968) short story, "Minagoroshi" ("Massacre," 1998). Keith Vincent, in his scholarship on Japanese fiction written between the 1920s and 1960s, discusses the prominence of "homosocial narrative"—i.e., literature that depict intense relationships between men while retaining a degree of ambiguity about the presence of homoerotic elements. Vincent argues that homosocial narratives are "not "gay" texts; rather, they subvert the heteronormative exclusion of male same-sex relationships devoid of homoerotic implications (2012, page 4). As such, homosocial narrative fulfills the transgressive function of a literary counter-discourse against cultural narratives of heteronormativity.[1]

I suggest that in the 1990s we see a resurgence of homosocial narrative in Japanese contemporary literature. Multiple novels and short stories by emerging male Heisei writers, identified as heterosexual, destabilize hegemonic masculinity through their use of queer images. R.W. Connell calls hegemonic masculinity the dominant heterosexual masculinity type of a patriarchy (1995, 77). The literary works of this decade that destabilize hegemonic masculinity include but are not limited to Machida Kō's *Kussun daikoku* (*Damn God of Fortune*, 1996), Medoruma Shun's "Suiteki" ("Droplets," 1997), Hoshino Tomoyuki's *Naburiai* (*Torturous Love*, 1999), and Suzuki Seigo's *Rokkunrōru mashin* (*Rock 'n Roll Sewing Machine*, 1998). Abe Kazushige is at the forefront of this movement with multiple early novels and short stories, such as *Amerika no yoru* (*Day by Night*, 1994), *Indibijuaru purojekushon* (*Private Screening*, 1997), "Toraiangurusu"

("Triangles," 1997), "Mujō no sekai" ("Pitiless World," 1999), and "Massacre," all depicting male same-sex relationships of rivalry, friendship, and mentorship connoting homoerotic preoccupations.

"Massacre" depicts a day in the life of a part-time worker and small-time criminal, Ōta Tatsuyuki, who waits in a Denny's restaurant for his married lover, Hitomi, to return his call. While he is waiting he encounters a salaryman, who is spying on his adulterous wife through a portable computer. A long conversation unfolds between the two lonely men, in which the husband confesses his unhappy marriage to Ōta, who himself is reminded of his own unhappy affair. An intimacy develops, with Ōta feeling self-conscious about the possible homoerotic implications of their connection. However, their closeness quickly transforms into competitiveness as they begin to see their respective love rivals in the persona of each other: Ōta sees Hitomi's husband in the salaryman, while the salaryman sees his wife's student lover in Ōta. Ultimately, Ōta provokes the salaryman into the titular "massacre" by humiliating him and calling him a loser. The salaryman hands his portable computer over to Ōta so that Ōta can watch as he restores his male honor by running home and killing his wife and her lover on camera, then returning to the restaurant to kill the customers there. Ōta manages to escape, and is finally granted Hitomi's attention when she comes to see him to receive payment on a debt he owes her. Ōta's behavior, however, makes Hitomi run away from him, and in the end he is left alone.

Against this background, I will analyze "Massacre" as a homosocial narrative in three respects: first, the absence of heterosexual relationships and the trope of the male gaze; second, the question of to what extent we can read Hitomi, the only notable female character in "Massacre," as an empowered woman despite her flat characterization; and third, the homosocial mediation of desire in the projected erotic triangle filtered through computer technology. I argue that the men's competitiveness shows a libidinal investment in each other, which renders everything else secondary and drives the plot to the final massacre; the massacre is less the salaryman's act of revenge on his wife than his proof of masculinity to Ōta. Referring to how Eve Kosofsky-Sedgwick analyzes male homosocial desire in heterosexual erotic triangles (1985, page 1-2), I suggest that the salaryman's wife, who also represents Ōta's projection of Hitomi in the scene, becomes but a medium through which the desire of the salaryman and Ōta is channeled toward each other.

No Real Heterosexual Relationships: Absent Women, Watching Men

Abe's fiction is "quintessential" homosocial narrative in the sense that "none of the characters get what they want and men and women remain walled off from each other in utterly separate narrative worlds" (Vincent 2012, 42). In "Massacre," these separate narrative worlds are divided by and mediated through technology. Technology has always been a major theme in Abe Kazushige's writing: he has repeatedly voiced his concern about the reliance on digital technologies and the internet, and his works, from *Private Screening* to *Ōga(ni)zumu* (*Orga(ni)sm*, 2019), may be read as a critique of digital media in the Heisei era (see Abe 2018, 9-10; Naitō 2005, 35-40). Indeed, a major paradigm shift in Heisei literature may be the way writers have responded to the emergence of the internet and the resulting new challenges by reflecting on virtual reality and digital technologies. In "Massacre," technology is utilized to problematize the gendered power asymmetry of the gaze.

Stalking is a recurrent theme in Abe's fiction and oftentimes is used to invoke male homosociality: the male characters in Abe's novels and short stories are usually lonely and unable to form successful heterosexual relationships, engaging instead in the pathological behaviors of pursuing and watching women, as portrayed, for example, in "Triangles" and *Shinsemia* (*Sinsemilla*, 2003). Stalking isolates the stalker from the prey and encapsulates the stalker in his own lonely world. "Massacre" queers this form of male surveillance (and thus destabilizes the male gaze) in that the husband who stalks his wife through a portable computer while he sits in a restaurant is disconnected from his wife and, instead, forms an intimate homosocial bond with protagonist Ōta. This homosocial bonding turns into the most important relationship in the plot.

Media and technology mediate between two otherwise entirely separate male and female worlds in "Massacre." Male preoccupation with female targets remains unrequited and heterosexual relationships do not actually exist for the main characters; instead, we exclusively see a homosocial relationship between two men who are abandoned by the women they long to be with. Female characters in the short story are physically absent until Hitomi, Ōta's lover, makes her brief appearance in the end. Technology characterizes female "presence" throughout "Massacre." Hitomi is mediated through Ōta's cell phone; the wife of the man in the restaurant is mediated through his personal computer and its surveillance camera. The only relationship the husband has with his wife is through spying on her; the control of marital fidelity through surveillance serves as a pretext for a husband who wishes to establish some form of access to a wife who has no interest in him.

In fact, all the men in "Massacre" fit this pattern of behavior. Ōta's boss Uno, described as a "classic perverted old man" (*inkō oyaji*), likes high school girls (*joshikōsei*) and no longer has a sexual relationship with his wife, instead watching pornographic videos as a diversion and a substitute for sex (1999, 121-122). Here, again, "Massacre" reveals a one-sided heterosexual relationship in which a man seeks access to a woman via technology. With his wife unavailable to Uno, he resorts to watching other women who exist only in virtual reality. Even the anonymous man in the park at the end of Abe's narrative fits into the general scheme of the narrative: he visits online sites through which he can spy on women in their bedrooms (205-206). As such, he represents the typical male in "Massacre": although affluent, he is lonely, and his only access to women is mediated through technology, in this case, the internet. His desire is for women who are absent or not interested in him.

Is Ōta Superior to Other Woman-Watching Male Characters?

How does Ōta, the protagonist, fit into this pattern? Ōta is an antihero typical of Abe's fiction: the narrative describes him as a "male loser" (*dameotoko*). Notably, Ōta exists outside the overall masculine proclivity of watching women. In the opening passages, we find him waking up beside a naked woman (it is not clear whether she is sleeping or dead) and watching a clay anime on television (Abe 1999, page 111). This scene suggests that Ōta does occasionally have direct contact with the opposite sex through sexual intercourse and that he does not watch women mediated by technology as do all the other male characters in "Massacre." While the latter men's actions are characterized by their sense of vision (woman-watching via technology), Ōta's actions are characterized by his sense of hearing—he accesses Hitomi on the phone. The fact that Ōta does not engage in woman-watching lends him a somewhat superior moral tone vis-à-vis the other male characters; in fact, we may take Ōta's lack of understanding of the salaryman's surveillance of his wife as an indirect critique of male stalking.

However, what remains the same is that Ōta's relationship with Hitomi is also virtual in "Massacre," in his case mediated through the technology of the cellphone. Indeed, the overall structure of the short story is sustained by Ōta's perpetual waiting for Hitomi's call, which does not occur until toward the end, with a negative result. When Hitomi finally comes to meet Ōta in person as he wishes, their confrontation quickly becomes an argument which prompts her to run away and vow to never see him again (1999, 201). As a result, Hitomi is never actually present throughout the story and does not engage in a relationship with Ōta over the phone.

Ōta waiting for Hitomi's phone call "feminizes" him by virtue of the fact that "waiting" as a trope is often gendered as a female characteristic. Roland Barthes, in somewhat dated rhetoric, argues that men waiting for women is a feminization of men:

> Historically, the discourse of absence is carried on by the Woman: Woman is sedentary, Man hunts, journeys; Woman is faithful (she waits), man is fickle (he sails away, he cruises)....It follows that in any man who utters the other's absence *something feminine* is declared: this man who waits and who suffers from his waiting is miraculously feminized. (2010, 13-14)

In Japanese literature, men waiting for women is an inversion of the trope of "feminine patience" seen in classical poetry and prose (Strong 1991, 178). Ōta, as the only man not engaged in woman-watching, seems to critique the narrative of male surveillance, but in the end he is reduced to a man who waits. Male characters are subject to criticism and irony in "Massacre," and Ōta's case is no exception.

Queering the Woman: Hitomi Reverses the Male Gaze

The lexical choices of the characters' names in "Massacre" underscores the fundamental gender divide that distinguishes the narrative. While all men are signified in *katakana* (オータ , タケダ , ウノ), Hitomi's name is written in a single kanji: 瞳 , meaning "pupil" or "eye"—a logographic cue to her ability to revert the male gaze. As the only woman given an appearance unmediated by technology, Hitomi is alive, awake, and speaks through her own voice.

In accordance with the one-dimensionality of female characters in traditional homosocial narrative (Kosofsky-Sedgwick 2002,163), Hitomi is not granted her own subjectivity in "Massacre." Still, "Massacre" allows for a feminist understanding of Hitomi. While Ōta, with straightforward misogyny, keeps feminizing Hitomi by relegating her to the traditional female image of a housewife within patriarchy, the narrative itself positions Hitomi as the leading role in their heterosexual relationship. She is the empowered party in that she makes Ōta wait. Moreover, while Ōta claims that "Hitomi loves melodrama" (*merodorama zuki na Hitomi*) (Abe 1999, 144), the narrative points out that "it was exclusively Ōta who got emotional about things" in their relationship (117). Moreover, Hitomi is depicted as being smarter than Ōta. While she is described as someone who only looks at the pictures in magazines and does not read the text, the narrative points out her capacity for "self-analysis" (*jiko bunseki*), a self-awareness which Ōta lacks (116-117). Hitomi's most significant upper hand with regard to Ōta is her financial superiority, thanks to her rich husband. While Ōta may be successful with women, he is not so financially: indeed, he borrows money from Hitomi and is dependent on her (129). His financial reliance on Hitomi may also explain why he clings to their relationship despite her absence.

Overall, Ōta appears to be weak compared to a seemingly stronger, absent Hitomi. If we are to follow the theory posited by scholar Lauren Berlant, who suggests that love implies non-sovereignty by "entering into relationality" at one own's risk, "without guarantees, without knowing what the other side of it is" (Berlant and Hardt 2011, page 9), then it is only Ōta who is non-sovereign: he becomes relational, while Hitomi keeps to herself and remains independent. Ōta acts as if he is in love; Hitomi does not.

Hitomi as the strong female character among all the struggling male characters in "Massacre" calls into question the patriarchal logic of Heisei Japanese society. The narrative clearly makes her stand out through the choice of kanji for her name and its suggestion of vision. Judith Butler argues that the feminine gaze is a reversal of what traditionally is a male gaze: "For that masculine subject of desire, trouble became a scandal with the sudden intrusion, the unanticipated agency, of a female 'object' who inexplicably returns the glance, reverses the gaze, and contests the place and authority of the masculine position" (1999, vii-viii). This is exactly Hitomi's agency in "Massacre": among all the male subjects of desire, Hitomi is the empowered female object who looks back, as signified by her name and its meaning of "eye." In doing so, Hitomi reverses the gaze of the male subject who objectifies her and in turn objectifies Ōta. The impact of her reversed gaze and its relevance for destabilizing patriarchal norms becomes all the more compelling as we observe the men in "Massacre": while not able to have actual contact with women, they still *look* at women, even though it remains ambiguous whether the men engaged in woman-watching experience it as pleasurable or not. In the case of the salaryman in the restaurant, monitoring his wife turns into self-inflicted torture, as he is forced to witness her adultery while remaining powerless to do anything about it.

According to Laura Mulvey, the male gaze renders the male active and the female—the gazed-upon object—passive: "In a world ordered by sexual imbalance, pleasure in looking has been split between active/male and passive/female. The determining male gaze projects its phantasy on to the female figure which is styled accordingly" (1999, 837). In reversing the gaze, Hitomi also reverses traditional patriarchal power dynamics by turning men into the gazed-upon objects. In other words, Hitomi's name becomes a metaphor for her empowerment in a narrative where heterosexual gender relations are structured through the eyes only; other interactions do not take place. Abe Kazushige makes effective use of the metaphoric qualities of the Japanese logographic script as a formalist technique to indicate agency in a female character within the context of a homosocial narrative where female characters typically remain one-dimensional or insignificant.

Queer Intimacies: The Male Complaint

"Massacre" characterizes itself as homosocial narrative through the specific trope of the love triangle, in which two men compete over a single woman. As Keith Vincent explains: "Homosocial narratives like this are so common that virtually the entire edifice of modern literature in Japan could be said to rest on a foundation in the shape of the homosocial triangle comprising two male rivals and a woman.…[T]he list of texts featuring such triangles is effectively synonymous with the modern Japanese canon" (2012, 7). In "Massacre," the narrative's complicated heterosexual relationships set the tone for its main scene, the long conversation between Ōta and the unnamed salaryman husband, who spies on his wife through a portable computer. The conversation between Ōta and the husband oscillates between companionship and competition. For all its ambivalence, it is the only real human connection in the narrative.

Lauren Berlant defines intimacy as communication; intimacy is contingent on verbal or gestural exchanges between two parties, who thereby create an attachment with each other:

To intimate is to communicate with the sparest signs and gestures, and at its

> roots intimacy has the quality of eloquence and brevity. But intimacy also involves an aspiration for a narrative about something shared, a story about oneself and others that will turn out in a particular way. (1998, 281)

Intimacy in "Massacre" unfolds through communication: a narrative about something shared, a personal story. Ironically, the something shared here is the men's respective obsessions about the salaryman's wife and Ōta's lover Hitomi. Their shared emotion makes their mutual projections possible and gives rise to jealousy and, ultimately, the massacre at the end, when the husband sets out to kill his wife and her lover after being provoked into action by Ōta's humiliating comments.

According to the narrative of "Massacre," adultery is a common phenomenon in Japan at this time, a social pattern, and as such is part of a shared cultural memory. This is how Ōta's and Hitomi's adulterous relationship is described:

> His partner was a woman named Hitomi. Radically speaking, they were in an adulterous relationship. While Ōta Tatsuyuki had no wife, Hitomi had a husband. Hitomi, who is said to have married right after college, still had a lot of exploring to catch up with and thus had met Ōta on some night out. Hitomi had met him in a discotheque while her husband was on a business trip, and they had done it once that time and ended up doing it again a couple of times after that. Recently such examples appeared quite often, and various media are saying they are typically the contemporary image of coupledom. (1999, 116)[2]

The salaryman husband shares his own story with Ōta, and this confession emasculates the man because complaints are typically gendered as being female. According to Lauren Berlant, "Everyone knows what the female complaint is: women live for love, and love is the gift that keeps on taking" (2008, 1). Accordingly, the "female complaint" is homosocial speech among women that fosters an attachment; complaining is a bonding experience. Interestingly, in "Massacre" we have the case of a *male* complaint: the husband complains about his wife to Ōta, which "feminizes" him in the conventional social script. To reject the female role, and reclaim his masculinity, he turns to the radical masculine acts of violence and killing. His complaint fosters an attachment to Ota, which constitutes a form of homosocial intimacy.

Abe's narrative describes their homosocial bond by first invoking the creation of mutual intimacy, which makes the man sufficiently comfortable to confess his private complaints to Ōta. They are described as sharing a common liking: an exoticist interest in America as the "other" (1999, 152). In fact, this may be the only time Ōta connects to another human being, since the woman at the beginning of the story is not awake and Hitomi rarely answers her phone. This initial connection, in which both men seem to have found a sense of belonging, quickly turns to ambivalence as they project their respective conflicts onto each other. In other words, Ōta and the man meet their respective opposites here: the story of the salaryman husband is Ōta's story told in inversion. Here is a husband whose wife cheats on him with a lover, while Ōta is Hitomi's lover with whom she cheats on her husband. Ōta's and the salaryman's homosocial bond is a mirroring of their respective heterosexual relationships.

Initial Homosocial Bonding

In this section, I will analyze Ōta's and the salaryman's conversation for its dialectic of bonding and rivalry. While an intimate relationship emerges between Ōta and the man in the public environment of a restaurant, their intimacy is ambivalent. On the one hand, both men find comfort in each other. On the other hand, their closeness leads to a projection of their internal conflicts onto each other, which ultimately leads to a fatal unravelling of their bond.

In the beginning, we are exposed to Ōta's homosexual panic, in the sense that he wonders about the implications of his interest in talking to the other man; he is afraid of his own possible homosexual attraction (Abe 1999, page 150). According to Eve Kosofsky-Sedgwick:

> So-called "homosexual panic" is the most private, psychologized form in which many twentieth-century Western men experience their vulnerability to the social pressure of homophobic blackmail; even for them, however, that is only one part of control, complementary to public sanctions through the institutions described by Foucault and others as defining and regulating the amorphous territory of "the sexual." (1985, 89)

The salaryman suddenly stops watching the screen of his computer and turns his gaze onto Ōta, to which Ōta gruffly replies, "What?" The salaryman responds by saying, "Do you have time right now?" Ōta reacts by being afraid that the man intends to pick him up (*nanpa suru*). He articulates this thought manifestly as if joking, but the moment betrays his homosexual panic. This is underscored by the fact that Ōta's latent anxiety is followed immediately by self-reassurance that the salaryman cannot possibly be interested in him: "However, from his perspective, I might appear puzzling as well. In any case, I am restless, I look terribly unhealthy, and my clothes are dirty from sweat and vomit." Thus, Ōta assures himself that the man cannot be interested in him. Ōta replies, "Well, I'm waiting for someone" (1999, 150).

Ōta decides to let the salaryman join him, since sitting alone makes him uncomfortable. Again, the narrative alludes to a homosocial attraction, this time through the notion of the Japanese word *aiseki* (相 席), which means "sitting at the same table." However, the kanji suggests an ambivalent reading: *ai* (相) alone means "mutual" or "together" and is included in compounds such as *aikata* 相 方 ("partner"). In telling himself that he does not know if and when Hitomi will show up, Ōta justifies his action of sharing a table. Initially, out of the fear of his own homoerotic attraction, Ōta has reservations about letting the man enter his space and come physically close to him. But ultimately he allows the proximity to happen and the two men approach each other. In doing so, they enter their projected erotic triangle, in which Ōta becomes a stand-in for the lover of the salaryman's wife and the salaryman a stand-in for Hitomi's husband. The two women filtered through technology fuse into one point of existence in that erotic triangle.

Competing through Masculinity: Calling Hegemonic Masculinity into Question

By entering the triangle, Ōta and the salaryman quickly start seeing their respective male opponent in each other. As a result, both men's initial bonding quickly turns into a competition for masculine superiority. They attack each other in their insecurities: Ōta is insecure about being a low-skilled worker with a part-time job, whose lack of adequate income, he believes, makes him unattractive to the other sex. The salaryman is insecure about his sexual prowess since, despite his breadwinning ability, his wife seeks sexual satisfaction with a younger man. In its portrayal of their conflict, "Massacre" challenges the idea of hegemonic masculinity in 1990s Japan, which was premised on the image of the salaryman as breadwinner, a point that I will elaborate below.

Once they share each other's space, Ōta fully projects his own struggle with his personal situation onto the salaryman. The narrative first indicates this projection by describing Ōta's studied composure in smoking a cigarette. While smoking, he becomes incredibly relaxed and even begins to feel superior, which slowly changes into an open disdain for the salaryman (1999, 160). Ōta projects his own inferiority complex vis à vis Hitomi's husband onto the salaryman—which supports the hypothesis that Ōta's motivation is not so much to win over Hitomi herself, but to out-rival a competitor who is financially superior. Their rivalry exemplifies the social difference between male part-time workers and male white-collar-workers; indeed, both men consciously bring up these categories themselves, indicating that they perceive their respective male identities through the labels of these sociotypes. Ōta finds the man in the restaurant to be "white-collar-like" (*sararīman-fū*, 178), and the latter is identified as a salaryman by virtue of wearing a suit (*sūtsu sugata*), the typical attire of white-collar workers (185). In a further expression of social strata, the salaryman contemptuously calls his wife's lover a "student or a *freeter*" (*gakusei ka furīta ka*) (166). He apparently generalizes that *freeters*—men who are not tied down by regular employment and are usually younger—are more attractive to women.

This is an inversion of the conventional understanding of hegemonic masculinity in post-bubble Japan, according to which male white-collar workers are the group of men who are most successful with the opposite sex due to their capacity as breadwinners in a heterosexual family unit, while male *freeters* struggle unsuccessfully to marry due to their precarious income (Cook 2013, 30-31). According to Romit Dasgupta:

> Over much of the post-World War II period Japanese masculinity had come to be signified by the figure of the be-suited urban, white-collar "salaryman" loyally working for the organization he was employed by, in return for benefits such as secure lifetime employment and almost automatic promotions and salary-increments linked to length of service.…In this regard the discourse of salaryman masculinity, premised on the notion of the male as breadwinner and provider for a dependent family, could be considered the hegemonic discourse of masculinity in Japan for these decades. (2009, 82-83)

"Massacre," by contrast, evokes a societal pattern of adultery in which salaryman husbands are cheated on by their wives. The narrative does not thematize the possibility of wives being cheated on by their husbands, despite the high rate of male marital infidelity in Japan. What "Massacre" dramatizes instead is a husband who literally clings to a relationship with his absent wife by carrying her image with him in the form of a computer through which he observes her in secret. In comparing the steadily employed salaryman husband to the good-for-nothing Ōta, "Massacre" seems to ask which of them is the empowered man. It also questions the way hegemonic masculinity in post-bubble Japan is challenged when financial stability competes with *erotic* capital, measured by their cumulative sexual performance—traditionally a male "currency" (Illouz 2011, 39-114).

As their rivalry gradually escalates, Ōta defends his superior attitude and openly humiliates the salaryman. The salaryman ultimately responds to these humiliations with an extreme outburst of anger and physical violence to guard his honor. Honor is an emotion that is conventionally gendered as male—with its inversion being shame. Both men use their antagonistic encounter as a mutual defense of dwindling male honor. By continuously humiliating the salaryman, Ōta dishonors and emasculates him. In turn, the salaryman reclaims his honor in the end through the drastic act of a massacre, which both men agree is a genuine masculine reaction to a wife's adultery.

Conclusion: Homosocial Narrative in Heisei Literature

"Massacre" addresses a common theme of Abe's early fiction by looking into the homosocial world of men. Homosocial narrative is not explicit gay literature and is not necessarily written by gay authors, but rather is a revelation of underlying currents of male same-sex eroticism sometimes derived from male rivalry over a woman. It also reveals unfulfilled desire in heterosexual relationships that ends up being projected onto other male characters. Furthermore, it typically depicts flat, one-dimensional female characters deprived of subjectivity in a narrative dominated by male narrators or characters.

Keith Vincent suggests that literature as a form of artistic expression has a particular potential to depict homosociality's capacity to embody ambivalence and explore "the multiplicity and malleability of the trope of men loving men" (2012, 5). Homosocial narrative is not about straightforward "gayness" but rather reveals an eroticism in male same-sex relationships that is too nuanced to be labelled. This is, essentially, the subversive potential of homosocial narrative: it takes gayness out of the stigmatized niche to which it has been relegated in heteronormative society and instead suggests that same-sex erotic preoccupations are everywhere. At the same time, homosocial narrative being written within the context of heteronormative society uses literary techniques of ambiguation to blur the constructed boundary between "hetero" and "homo"—making it adequately suggestive to be subversive, but so explicit to be censored or labelled. We can also argue that the ambivalence is performative: homosocial narrative shows that same sex erotic preoccupations can take multiple shapes and are not reduced to one explicit expression.

As we have seen, homosocial narrative creates a literary counter-discourse to cultural heteronormativity. How can we understand the counter-discourse of homosocial narrative in 1990s Japanese literature? What does it subvert through queer images? In Abe's case, homosocial narrative serves to destabilize hegemonic masculinity in Heisei patriarchy. It undermines the postwar hegemonic masculinity associated with the persona of the salaryman and highlights social issues in post-bubble Japan, such as the pathology of stalking as a form of male transgression. "Massacre" serves to queer the monopoly of power men hold in a patriarchal system. It does so by showing us a white-collar husband who is disempowered and compensates for his lack of agency by resorting to physical violence, killing his wife and her lover. At the same time, it thematizes the conflict between hegemonic and subordinate masculinities through a confrontation between the sociotypes of a salaryman and a part-time *freeter* in the guise of Ōta.

Finally, "Massacre" questions the power of the male gaze over women by depicting the watching men as powerless to control the women. Male stalking through a surveillance camera emphasizes the loneliness of watching men who can only have access to the opposite sex through the mediation of technology, resulting in a contact that remains virtual and unrequited. At the same time, the female characters, while not given an opportunity to -express themselves, appear to gain an upper hand in their relationships with their respective male partners—the salaryman's wife is cheating on him, leaving him powerless, and Hitomi does not respond to Ōta's desire. Indeed, the narrative indicates Hitomi's power to revert the objectifying male gaze through her name, "eye," thus suggesting a means to endow female characters in Japanese homosocial narratives with agency. In doing so, Abe Kazushige opens new frontiers in homosocial narrative by probing the malaise of human relationships mediated largely by technology.

1 According to Michel Foucault, literature as a "counter-discourse" has the potential to oppose dominant cultural narratives by being a fictional forum in which transgression can be expressed, be it openly or implied (2002, 48; 1979, 91).

2 The translation is by the author of this chapter.

References

Abe Kazushige. 1999. "Minagoroshi." In *Mujō no sekai*. Tōkyō: Kōdansha.

———. 2018. "The Meaning of Massacre in Dawn of the Dead." Translated by Maria Roemer. *SOAS Occasional Translations in Japanese Studies* No. 8 (August). https://www.soas.ac.uk/jrc/translations/file134064.pdf.

Barthes, Roland. 2010. *A Lover's Discourse: Fragments*. Translated by Richard Howard. New York: Hill and Wang.

Berlant, Lauren. 1998. "Intimacy: A Special Issue." *Critical Inquiry* 24, no. 2 (Winter): 281-288.

———. 2008. *The Female Complaint: The Unfinished Business of Sentimentality in American Culture*. Durham: Duke University Press.

Berlant, Lauren and Hardt, Michael. 2011. "On the Risk of a New Relationality: An Interview with Lauren Berlant and Michael Hardt." *Reviews in Cultural Theory* 2.3: 7-27. http://reviewsinculture.com/wp-content/uploads/2015/10/RCT-SP-On-the-Commons.pdf.

Butler, Judith. 1999. *Gender Trouble: Feminism and the Subversion of Identity*. Milton Park: Taylor and Francis.

Connell, R.W. 1995. *Masculinities*. Cambridge and Oxford: Polity Press.

Cook, Emma E. 2013. "Expectations of Failure: Maturity and Masculinity for Freeters in Contemporary Japan." *Social Science Japan Journal* 16, no. 1: 29-43.

Dasgupta, Romit. 2009. "The Lost Decade of the 1990s and Shifting Masculinities in Japan." *Culture, Society and Masculinities* 1, no. 1: 79-95.

Foucault, Michel. 1979. "The Life of Infamous Men." In *Power, Truth, Strategy*, edited by Meaghan Morris and Paul Patton, 76-91. Sydney: Feral Publications.

———. 2002. *The Order of Things: An Archaeology of the Human Sciences*. Oxford and New York: Routledge.

Illouz, Eva. 2011. *Warum Liebe wehtut*. Frankfurt a. M.: Suhrkamp.

Kosofsky-Sedgwick, Eve. 1985. *Between Men: English Literature and Male Homosocial Desire*. New York: Columbia University Press.

———. 2002. "The Beast in the Closet: James and the Writing of Homosexual Panic." In *The Masculinity Studies Reader*, edited by Rachel Adams and David Savran, 157-174. Oxford: Blackwell.

Mulvey, Laura. 1999. "Visual Pleasure and Narrative Cinema." In *Film Theory and Criticism: Introductory Readings*, edited by Leo Braudy and Marshall Cohen, 833-844. New York: Oxford University Press.

Naitō Chizuko, 2005. "Settō tōsatsu: Abe Kazushige, Shinsemia." In *Bunka no naka no tekusuto: Karuchuraru sutadīzu e no izanai*, edited by Ichiyanagi Hirotaka, Kume Yoriko, Naitō Chizuko, and Yoshida, Morio, 35-40. Tokyo: Taiyōsha.

Strong, Sarah M. 1991. "Aspects of Feminine Poetic Heritage in Yosano Akiko's Midaregami and Tawara Machi's Sarada Kinenbi." *The Journal of the Association of Teachers of Japanese* 25, no. 2 (November): 177-194.

Vincent, J. Keith. 2012. *Two-Timing Modernity: Homosocial Narrative in Modern Japanese Fiction*. Cambridge and London: Harvard University Press.

Index

List of Contributors

GIAMMARIA, Valentina holds a PhD in Japanese Studies from Sophia University in Tokyo. Her primary research focus centers on the depictions of pleasure spaces in Japanese literary works, from pre-modern to contemporary, with particular attention to the analysis of the literary space. Among her recent publications is "COVID-19 in Japan: A Nighttime Disease" (*The Asia-Pacific Journal: Japan Focus*, 2020).

HAAG, Andre R. is an assistant professor of Japanese literature and culture at the University of Hawai'i at Mānoa. He received his PhD in Japanese literature and cultural history from Stanford University. Haag's research explores how the insecurities and terrors of colonialism attendant to the annexation of Korea were inscribed within the literature, culture, and vocabularies that circulated in the Japanese imperial metropole. Other research interests include Zainichi Korean literature in Japanese, postcolonial legacies, and xenophobic hate speech in contemporary Japan. Recent publications include *Passing, Posing, Persuasion: Cultural Production and Coloniality in Japan's East Asian Empire* (University of Hawai'i Press, 2023).

HWEIDI, Munia is a postdoctoral research fellow in the Faculty of Global Studies at Sophia University. She received her PhD in Japanese Studies from Sophia University. Her dissertation explored literature and the environment in Japanese and Arabic literature. Her research interests include modern literature, world literature, and literature with a focus on the environment. Recent publications include "Voices of the Desert and the Sea: Literature and the Environment in Abdel Rahman Munif's *Cities of Salt* (1984) and Ishimure Michiko's *Paradise in the Sea of Sorrow* (1969)" (*Incubation: The Osaka Journal of Global Japanese Studies*, 2023) and "Space, *Makan, Kūkan*: Phenomenology of Space through Etymology" (*Critic|all*, 2023).

IWATA-WEICKGENANNT, Kristina is a professor of Japanese modern literature at Nagoya University, Japan, whose work has focused on geographies of marginality and marginalization in contemporary Japanese literature. Her research is informed by a framework of gender studies, post-colonial literature studies, and eco-critical and posthuman approaches to literature. She received her PhD from Trier University (Germany) with focus on performative identity construction in Yū Miri's work and has written extensively on Yū's literature in German, Japanese, and English. Recent publications include "Writing back to the Capitalocene: Radioactive Foodscapes in Japan's post-3/11 Literature" (*Contemporary Japan*, 2023, co-authored with Aidana Bolatbekkyzy).

KASZA, Justyna Weronika is an associate professor at Seinan Gakuin University in Fukuoka, Japan. She received her PhD from the University of Leeds. She teaches courses in foreign language acquisition, world literature, and translation. Her research interests include the works of Endō Shūsaku, life-writing narratives in Japan, and translation theories. She is the author of two monographs: *Hermeneutics of Evil in the Works of Endō Shūsaku: Between Reading and Writing* (2016) and *The "I" in the Making: Rethinking the Japanese Shishōsetsu in a Global Age* (2021), both published by Peter Lang.

KONO, Shion is a professor of literature in the Faculty of Liberal Arts, Sophia University. He received his PhD in comparative literature from Princeton University. He is the author of *Sekai no dokusha ni tsutaeru to iu koto* ("Delivering Texts to the World Reader," Kōdansha gendai shinsho, 2014) and a co-editor of *Nihon bungaku no hon'yaku to ryūtsū* ("Translation and Circulation of Japanese Literature," Bensei shuppan, 2018). He also co-translated Hiroki Azuma's *Otaku: Japan's Database Animals* (University of Minnesota Press, 2009). His current areas of interest include plurilingualism in modern and contemporary Japanese literature and contemporary Japanese criticism.

KURITA, Kyoko is a professor of Japanese in the Department of Asian Languages and Literatures at Pomona College (California). She received her PhD from Yale University with a dissertation on Kōda Rohan. Her research interests lie mostly in literary developments during the Meiji Period and in the concept of the future in modern Japan. The articles that represent this focus best are: "Meiji Japan's Y23 Crisis and the Discovery of the Future: Suehiro Tetchō's Nijūsan-nen mirai- ki" (*Harvard Journal of Asiatic Studies*, 2000) and "Kōda Rohan to mirai" ("Kōda Rohan and the Future," *Bungaku*, 2005).

MAUDE, Daryl is a postdoctoral associate in the Department of Asian and Middle Eastern Studies at Duke University. He completed his PhD in Japanese literature and critical theory from the University of California, Berkeley, in 2023. He researches futurity and intimacy in contemporary Okinawan and mainland Japanese literature, drawing from queer and feminist theory. Recent publications include "Queer Nations and Trans-lations: A Review of Akiko Shimizu, "'Imported' Feminism and 'Indigenous' Queerness: From Backlash to Transphobic Feminism in Transnational Japanese Context" (*Postmodern Culture*, 2020) and a translation of Shinjō Ikuo's essay, "Male Sexuality in the Colony: On Toyokawa Zen'ichi's 'Searchlight'" (Hong Kong, 2019).

O'NEILL, Dan is an associate professor at University of California, Berkeley, where he teaches courses in modern Japanese literature, cinema, and cultural history. He received his PhD from Yale University. His research interests include nonfiction and experimental media, the intersections of media theory and eco-criticism, the locations of disability in critical sexuality studies, and the history of science and technology. Recent publications include "Rewilding Futures" (*Journal of Japanese and Korean Cinema*, 2019) and "Ecomedia in the Wild" (*Critical Inquiry*, 2023).

ROEMER, Maria is a Japanese translator based in Newcastle upon Tyne, England. She is a research associate at Heidelberg University (Germany) and is currently a visiting fellow at the University of Leeds. Her research focuses on how Japanese male writers reflect masculinity in contemporary literature. She received her PhD in Japanese literature from Heidelberg University and has taught at the universities of Heidelberg, Newcastle, Leeds, and Birkbeck. She is the author of "Precarious Attraction: Abe Kazushige's Individual Projection Post-Aum" in *Visions of Precarity in Japanese Popular Culture* (Routledge, 2015).

SLAYMAKER, Doug is a professor of Japanese at the University of Kentucky (USA). He received his PhD from the University of Washington. His research focuses on literature and art of the twentieth century, with particular interests in the literature of post-3.11 Japan literature about animals and the environment, and Japanese writers and artists traveling to France. He is the translator of Kimura Yūsuke's *Sacred Cesium Ground* and *Isa's Deluge* (Columbia University Press,

2019) and co-translator of Furukawa Hideo's *Horses, Horses, in the End the Light Remains Pure* (Columbia University Press, 2016) and Kimura Saeko's *Theorizing Post-Disaster Literature in Japan: Revisiting the Literary and Cultural Landscape after the Triple Disasters* (Lexington Books, 2022).

STRECHER, Matthew C. is a professor of Japanese literature at Sophia University. He received his PhD from the University of Washington. He is the author of *Dances With Sheep: The Quest for Identity in the Fiction of Murakami Haruki* (University of Michigan Press, 2002), *Haruki Murakami's* The Wind-Up Bird Chronicle*: A Reader's Guide* (Continuum, 2002), *The Forbidden Worlds of Haruki Murakami* (University of Minnesota Press, 2014), and numerous essays on Murakami; and co-editor of *Haruki Murakami: Challenging Authors* (Sense Publishers, 2016). He has also published articles on Kawakami Hiromi, Kanagaki Robun, Kaikō Takeshi, and Murakami Ryū. His research interests include literary history, genre studies, global literature, literary journalism, mythology, and psychology.

THOMPSON, Mathew W. is an associate professor of Japanese literature in the Faculty of Liberal Arts at Sophia University. He received his PhD from Columbia University. Current research interests include the study of warrior themes in medieval and early modern Japanese literature and theater, designing game-based pedagogies for teaching literature and history in the classroom, and trying his hand at translation. He is the author of "A Medieval Warrior in Early Modern Japan: A Translation of the Otogizoshi Hogan Miyako Banashi" (*Monumenta Nipponica*, 2014)

THORNBURY, Barbara is a professor of Japanese in the Department of Asian and Middle Eastern Languages and Studies at Temple University (Philadelphia). She holds a PhD from the University of British Columbia. Her current research focuses on place and gender in contemporary Japanese literature and film. Recent publications include *Mapping Tokyo in Fiction and Film* (Palgrave, 2020) and "Murakami Haruki's Tokyo: Spatial Transformation and Sociocultural Displacement, Disconnection, and Disorientation" (Routledge, 2021).

WASHBURN, Dennis is Burlington Northern Foundation Professor in Asian Studies at Dartmouth College (New Hampshire). He holds a PhD from Yale University. He is the author of *Translating Mount Fuji: Modern Japanese Fiction and the Ethics of Identity* and *The Dilemma of the Modern in Japanese Fiction* (both by Columbia University Press, 2006). He has translated several works of modern fiction and is the most recent translator of *The Tale of Genji* (W.W. Norton, 2015), which is now included in the Norton Critical Editions series (2021). He is currently working on a study of the sublime in Japanese aesthetics. He received his PhD from Yale University.

YIU, Angela is a professor of modern Japanese literature in the Faculty of Liberal Arts at Sophia University. She holds a PhD from Yale University. She studies modernism, cross-border literature, Sino-Japanese literary studies, postwar literature, utopian studies, and contemporary literature. Publications include *Chaos and Order in the Works of Natsume Sōseki* (1998) and *Three-Dimensional Reading: Stories of Time and Space in Japanese Modernist Fiction, 1911–1932* (2013) (University of Hawai'i Press); *Sekai kara yomu Sōseki* Kokoro ("Reading Soseki's *Kokoro* from a World Perspective," Bensei shuppan, 2016); and "Literature in Japanese (*Nihongo bungaku*): An Examination of the New Literary Topography by Plurilingual Writers from the 1990s" (*Japanese Language and Literature*, 2020).

Literature in Heisei Japan, 1989-2019
平成文学における様々な声

2024 年 1 月 30 日　第 1 版第 1 刷発行

編　者：Angela Yiu

発行者：アガスティン　サリ

発　行：Sophia University Press
上智大学出版
〒 102-8554　東京都千代田区紀尾井町 7-1
URL：https://www.sophia.ac.jp/

制作・発売　㈱ぎょうせい
〒 136-8575　東京都江東区新木場 1-18-11
URL：https://gyosei.jp
フリーコール　0120-953-431
〈検印省略〉

印刷・製本　ぎょうせいデジタル㈱
ISBN978-4-324-11374-5
(5300339-00-000)
［略号：(上智) 平成文学］

Sophia University Press

上智大学は、その基本理念の一つとして、

「本学は、その特色を活かして、キリスト教とその文化を研究する機会を提供する。これと同時に、思想の多様性を認め、各種の思想の学問的研究を奨励する」と謳っている。

大学は、この学問的成果を学術書として発表する「独自の場」を保有することが望まれる。どのような学問的成果を世に発信しうるかは、その大学の学問的水準・評価と深く関わりを持つ。

上智大学は、(1) 高度な水準にある学術書、(2) キリスト教ヒューマニズムに関連する優れた作品、(3) 啓蒙的問題提起の書、(4) 学問研究への導入となる特色ある教科書等、個人の研究のみならず、共同の研究成果を刊行することによって、文化の創造に寄与し、大学の発展とその歴史に貢献する。